Prai

"*Last Night Was Fun* is a delightful spin on *You've Got Mail* and is filled with heart, wit, and steam galore. Holly Michelle has written a love letter to jock nerds everywhere—perfect for fans of banter and baseball."

—Laura Hankin, author of *One-Star Romance*

"Equal parts tender and steamy, *Last Night Was Fun* serves up a perfect game of a romance. Holly Michelle is such a talent!"

—Grace Reilly, *USA Today* bestselling author of *Wicked Serve*

"Crackling banter and page-turning prose make *Last Night Was Fun* truly enjoyable from start to finish. Holly Michelle hits a homer with this delightfully charming and tropey novel."

—Suzanne Park, author of *One Last Word*

"*Last Night Was Fun* is a delightfully swoony read that I couldn't resist inhaling in one very fun night! Full of delicious chemistry, playfulness, and sizzling vacation vibes, it features an engaging duo of baseball-loving co-workers who realize that they don't know as much about each other as they think. It's a charming story that celebrates the terrifying, exhilarating process of making yourself vulnerable to another person. I adored it!"

—Jamie Harrow, author of *One on One*

"A fake-numbered situation turns into HEA in this fun, swoony, and sporty rom-com reminiscent of *You've Got Mail*!"

—Jennifer Snow, *USA Today* bestselling author

"Brains, banter, and baseball—Holly Michelle's *Last Night Was Fun* is one for the baseball girlies who crave that rivals-to-lovers magic on and off the field!"

—Jennifer Hennessy, author of *Degrees of Engagement* and *For the Ring*

LAST
NIGHT
WAS
FUN

LAST NIGHT WAS FUN

A Novel

HOLLY MICHELLE

AVON

An Imprint of HarperCollinsPublishers

LAST NIGHT WAS FUN. Copyright © 2025 by Holly Rus. All rights reserved. Printed in the United States of America. No part of this book may be used or reproduced in any manner whatsoever without written permission except in the case of brief quotations embodied in critical articles and reviews. For information, address HarperCollins Publishers, 195 Broadway, New York, NY 10007.

HarperCollins books may be purchased for educational, business, or sales promotional use. For information, please email the Special Markets Department at SPsales@harpercollins.com.

Avon, Avon & logo, and Avon Books & logo are registered trademarks of HarperCollins Publishers in the United States of America and other countries.

FIRST EDITION

Designed by Chloe Foster
Title page art by Chaiyaphon from Adobe Stock

Library of Congress Cataloging-in-Publication Data
has been applied for.

ISBN 978-0-06-342036-6

25 26 27 28 29 LBC 5 4 3 2 1

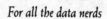

For all the data nerds

Author's Note

This book centers on characters who work for a fictional professional baseball team. As a lifelong baseball fan, I shot for accuracy in describing everything on the field, but fair warning that I took creative liberties with depiction of the operational business side of the sport where our characters work. I did this, dear readers, largely for what we in the genre refer to as *romance reasons*. Please enjoy with that spirit in mind.

Also, while this is a romantic comedy, the story does contain references to some heavier topics. If you feel that content warnings are spoilers and you don't need them, skip this next part. This book contains depictions of gender bias in the workplace, grief, and addiction, and references to the past death of a sibling. Please visit my website for further content guidance: hollyjamesbooks.com.

LAST
NIGHT
WAS
FUN

Chapter 1

Emmy Jameson once heard a statistic that someone, somewhere gave out a fake phone number every twenty minutes. At the time she'd heard it, she'd found it both sad and a useful addition to her list of reasons for not dating because surely and statistically, she would end up on the receiving or giving end of one of those fake numbers eventually. And that was simply too tragic to aspire to. But as she sat tangled in a blanket on her couch spooning cereal one Saturday morning, she received a text that made her wonder if her time had finally come despite abstaining from the dating race.

> Hey. Last night was fun 😊

She squinted at the message from an unknown number. Her first instinct was it was her upstairs neighbor Tom messing with her given the local area code and the fact they'd had a brief and *unfun* interaction the night before. How he would have gotten her number, she didn't know. Nor did she know why she was fated to live below a crotchety old man with a mean cat that had a habit of parkouring down onto her balcony just to lick its butt when every single woman her age in a book or movie by law shared buildings with brooding, interesting men who looked good leaning in doorjambs. Alas, the only brooding person in her Little Italy complex was the teenaged daughter in apartment 108 Emmy sometimes passed in the lobby, who she feared might melt her with all the angst shooting from her coal-rimmed eyes like lasers.

The chance Tom had texted her was slim, but so too was the chance he'd ever call maintenance and get his leaking sink fixed and stop her ceiling from dripping—the very thing they'd argued about the night before—so she figured responding to the text with a reminder in the event it was him wouldn't hurt.

> Listen, Tom. I don't know what passes for fun up there on the third floor, but those of us on 2 don't consider skating around the kitchen with bath towels for shoes a great way to spend a Friday night. PLEASE call maintenance about the sink.

She hit send and dropped her phone on the cushion beside her. If Tom had the nerve to respond at all, he'd write back a treatise on all her shortcomings as a neighbor. As such, she had time to wait for a response and returned her attention to the *Bake Off* marathon she was watching in light of her terrible cramps.

Her uterus was a real cranky bitch sometimes, and Emmy didn't feel the behavior should be rewarded with a morning at the farmers' market tasting cheeses and picking out flowers. She wasn't even feeling up for getting ahead on work as she was wont to do on Saturday mornings. So instead, she was on the couch under a pile of blankets watching mild-mannered contestants do their best with soufflé.

Her phone pinged from beside her, and she saw another message from the same number.

> Umm . . . Who's Tom?

Emmy frowned and lifted it to tap out a response with one thumb. She had to hit delete several times and watch the blinking cursor eat her errors before she revised and hit send.

> Is this not Tom from 304?

> No.

A pause long enough to pique her curiosity passed before the typing dots reappeared.

> This is the guy from the bar last night.

With a hot flash of embarrassment for them both, but mostly for him, she saw the situation for what it was. She had not been at a bar last night; she'd been where she was now, working late on her laptop with one eye on a *Real Housewives* marathon—that was, until she'd had to mop up the mess in the kitchen from Tom's sink. This guy obviously had the wrong girl. She didn't have any enemies who'd give out her number instead of their own just to spite her—except maybe Gabe Olson, her archnemesis at work, the bane of her professional existence, and the *last* person she would *ever* willingly give her number to, so there was no chance he had it and could stage a prank—so she had to assume the man texting her was the victim of being given a fake number that just so happened to be hers.

What were the odds?

She reconsidered his original message, the innocent greeting and the perky smiley face when he could have sent a dick pic (she'd heard horror stories from her single friends on the front lines), and decided to go easy on him. If he was texting his hookup smiley faces at 9 a.m. on a Saturday, he was probably a decent guy. Maybe a young San Diego professional like her given the crowd that went out on Friday nights and woke before noon on Saturdays.

> I think someone gave you the wrong number last night.

The dots disappeared for long enough that Emmy assumed he'd left the chat to hurl his phone into the ocean in humiliation. Until there was another ping.

> Well, this is embarrassing. Are you sure?

Emmy couldn't help the quiet laugh that escaped her mouth. She wasn't sure if it was pity or some inexplicable charm pulling it from her, but it came out, nonetheless.

> What did she look like? Your girl from the bar.

If he came back and said anything about her boobs or body shape or what she'd been wearing, Emmy was going to lose her faith in men completely. Not that she had much to begin with.

> Umm, about 5'8", brunette, green eyes. Said her name was Lacey, which I'm guessing wasn't true either.

Emmy tucked a rebellious blond curl back into place and looked down at her sweatpants as if to check if she'd grown two inches while sitting on her couch.

> Yeah, definitely not Lacey. Sorry.

> Well I am mortified.

> Don't be. Happens every twenty minutes, so I've heard.

> What does?

Getting fake numbered.

Is that a verb?

. . . asks the man in the throes of the consequences of said action right now.

Good point.

She found herself smiling at their exchange and oddly wanting to continue it. She swung her legs up onto the couch and leaned back on a squishy pillow the color of a peacock.

Tell me about the date. Where did it go wrong?

Who says it went wrong?

The fact you're texting with a stranger who happens to own the fake number someone made up to avoid you speaks pretty clearly to the date's quality.

Fair.

He went silent again. Long enough for Emmy to watch a *Bake Off* soufflé collapse to a restrained round of softly clucked tongues and disappointed sighs.

It wasn't even a date, actually. We met at a bar and hung out.

Wait, you MET last night and you're already texting this morning? What about the three-day rule?

(Emmy had only heard of this rule's existence. She knew nothing about its application in the wild.)

Well, I thought things went pretty great, so I assumed it would be fine to text sooner.

(Aha! It did exist.)

You assumed wrong, buddy.

Clearly.

Did you kiss her?

That's an incredibly personal question.

Hey, I'm just trying to diagnose your date's cause of death here. I can take my services elsewhere.

What makes you such an authority on all-cause date mortality? Get fake numbered a lot?

One would have to actually date to get fake numbered.

Wait. Who am I talking to here? You're not, like, a kid, are you?

> No, perv. And how are you just now asking me that?

> Honestly, it didn't cross my mind until you mentioned your lack of love life.

His comment speared her like a cocktail umbrella through a wedge of pineapple. Her love life was certainly lacking—by choice, thank you very much—and she hadn't minded one bit until this strange encounter had put something that felt like tiny fluttering wings in her belly, a symptom she would surely need to see a doctor about.

> If you must know, I'm a 67-year-old grandmother in North Park with three chihuahuas and a parrot that knows all the words to Call Me Maybe.

He responded with a crying eyes laughing emoji and then,

> Wait. Are you serious?

> I'll have Cawly Rae Jepsen record you a voicemail to prove it.

> That's the best bird-band pun you could come up with?

> List me three better ones. I'll wait.

> Beak-182, Bird Eye Blind, Cheep Trick.

She glared at her phone but couldn't help smiling, not wanting to admit how impressed she was he'd come up with a response so quickly.

Okay fine. Good work.

Thank you. You're kind of strange, Bird Girl.

I take that as a compliment.

I meant it as one 😉

Well thank you. And if I'm going to be Bird Girl, then I'm saving you as Axe Murderer in my contacts. That way, the cops can trace back to you when they find my body.

Solid plan.

Thank you, I agree.

Bird Girl?

Yeah?

I'm not going to murder you.

You certainly have a way with words. Is that what you said to Lacey last night before she fake numbered you?

She thought she could feel him cringing through her screen, and it made her bite at the smile pulling her lips.

> Okay, well, I think that's enough humiliation for one day. Thanks for the chat. If you hear news later of a man feeding himself to the sharks because he killed two dates in under twelve hours, it was me.

Emmy laughed out loud, feeling bad for him.

> I didn't know this qualified as a date, unless you mean you are currently in someone else's presence and ruining their experience by spending the whole time texting me.

> Indeed, I am not. I am alone at home enjoying this fortunate consequence of being fake numbered.

Heat splashed Emmy's cheeks at the thought he was enjoying the fallout too. It was all very strange, and she had no idea who she was really talking to—a hipster in Pacific Beach, a tech bro in Carlsbad, a pharma exec in his downtown high-rise—but she would have been lying if she didn't admit the whole incident had brightened her morning. She could hardly feel her cramps anymore.

> Well, fwiw, and even though this doesn't count as a date, you didn't kill anything here.

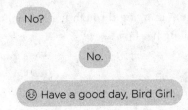

Emmy grinned, and despite herself, she really did save his number in her phone under Axe Murderer. With a little smiley face next to it.

Chapter 2

On Sunday morning, Emmy found herself in a circle of hell reserved especially for single women of a certain age: in a bridal shop watching her younger sister try on her wedding dress.

Piper looked like a certified cake topper in the beaded ball gown that was, in Emmy's opinion, more fitting for a black-tie ceremony than a destination wedding in Mexico. But hey, what did she know? Her only knowledge of weddings came from casual glances at the bridal magazines Piper had carted around like survival manuals for the past year and a half. Ever since her fiancé, Ben, had popped the question and sentenced them all to months of minutiae like color palettes, invitation fonts, floral designs, *freaking frosting flavors*. Until recently, Emmy had no idea one could even weigh in on the color of foil lining an envelope. But Piper's obsession dated back further than her engagement. Emmy could trace its origins to her childhood bedroom where Piper pinned up cutouts of brides and officiated wedding ceremonies for her dolls. The train had left the station decades ago. The only thing missing was the person who'd stand with Piper at the altar someday. And she'd found herself a prince.

Emmy wished Ben was there in the bridal shop with them to diffuse the imminent tempest she could see brewing in her sister's face because her dress's hemline wasn't hitting her feet right, but of course Ben couldn't see his future bride in her gown before the big day. So it was only Emmy, Bridezilla, their mother, and Natasha, a sprite of a woman fluttering around fluffing Piper's skirt and plying them all with champagne.

"I don't know, is it hitting right?" Piper said, and swished the billowing skirt once more. The tiered layers of tumbling white fabric elegantly rippled around her toes.

"The hem was cut to the exact specifications," Natasha assured her with a nod as she grabbed a handful of skirt and fluffed it once more.

"Well, sure. But it's not like I've grown since I was here last. It should skim my toes but not show my feet. I can see my feet." Piper stuck out her foot from under the cumulus cloud of skirt and wiggled her painted toes. A delicate gold chain with a heart pendant glinted from her ankle.

"Pipes, who cares if anyone can see your feet? We'll be on the beach. Everyone will see everyone's feet," Emmy said, and sipped another mouthful of beautiful, glorious bubbles.

Piper gasped as if she were scandalized. "I certainly *hope* people aren't going to show up barefoot *to my wedding*!"

Emmy frowned at her. "Barefoot to your wedding . . . on a beach in Mexico?"

Piper clucked her tongue and swiveled to face the other corner of the small suite where their mother sat. The room looked like her princess brain had exploded inside it with antique velvet furniture, beaded chandeliers, gilded mirrors. "Mom, Emmy is being mean!"

Emmy clucked back. "I'm not being mean! I'm only pointing out the obvious. I mean, beach wedding; barefoot. Kind of seems apparent?"

"Girls, relax," their mother said. Vera Jameson looked more like her eldest daughter than her youngest. Curvy with blond hair, hazel eyes, and creamy smooth skin, she was a picture of middle-aged but understated radiance. Emmy only hoped she was as well-preserved as her mother in later life. She probably needed to spend less time in the sun at baseball games if she wanted to achieve such standards. Piper shared their curves but was brunette and, rudely as a younger sibling, a few inches taller than Emmy. "Everyone at the wedding will have shoes. And, Piper, the hem looks great," Vera said.

Piper grumbled and pivoted back to the mirror. "I just don't know . . ." Her face twisted into the annoyed pinch Emmy knew well. The one that said a tantrum loomed on the horizon. Everyone in the room felt it crackling like electricity. Natasha chewed her lip in worry. Vera spun her champagne flute stem between her fingers.

"At least your boobs look amazing," Emmy said to diffuse the situation. She was fluent in Piper tantrums, knew the signs like symptoms of a head cold. She knew what words to say to spare everyone another meltdown.

Piper's face split into an enormous grin. She grabbed her chest and squished her breasts together in glee. "They do, don't they."

In fairness, the tailor had done an impeccable job with the bodice. The sweetheart cut (another term Emmy had picked up over the past year) hugged Piper's body like an elegantly beaded glove. The silhouette showed what Piper had termed a *princess amount of cleavage*, which Emmy translated to understand meant contoured enough to show she had curves but nothing indulgent or lascivious. A hint and nothing more.

"Yes! The detail here is *amazing*," Natasha groveled, relieved to have avoided stepping on another land mine.

Vera caught Emmy's eye and winked from across the room, silently thanking her for deftly diffusing the situation.

Piper preened in front of the mirror some more, still holding her chest, before she dropped her hands into the fluff at her waist. "Okay, let's try it with the veil now."

"Of course!" Natasha chirped, and skipped over to the waterfall of gauzy white mesh hanging from the wall on one of those puffy, silk-bound hangers that only seemed to exist in lingerie shops or bridal salons.

While she fussed with it, Vera stood from her chair to help. "Emmy, sweetheart, what's the latest on your promotion?" she asked.

Emmy thought for a moment the booze was getting to her head. Her mother hardly ever asked about her job. Not because she didn't care about her daughter's successes in life, but because her chosen profession was a bit of a sore spot for their family.

More like a gaping wound that would never fully heal, and Emmy's choice to spend day in and day out in the industry that had torn their family apart was baffling to most everyone, to say the least.

"Um, it's still on the table. I find out tomorrow who the pool has been narrowed to."

Vera took the veil from Natasha and wedged the comb into Piper's hair. She jammed it into Piper's bun hard enough that her head jerked around with the force.

"Ow, Mom," Piper whispered, and reached up to intervene.

"Sorry," Vera said, and Emmy couldn't help wondering if the tiny burst of aggression was due to her. "Well, that's excellent. Are you in the top choices still?"

"Yes. As far as I know."

Piper felt for the veil hanging behind her and pulled it forward like a cape. It hung nearly to the bottom of her dress. "You better get it. And if they give it to that d-bag Gabe, I will burn the stadium down."

Piper may have had her faults as a bride, but she was fiercely, undyingly loyal as a sister. She knew all about Emmy's workplace nemesis and had partaken in many a Gabe Olson bashing at Emmy's insistence. They'd even thrown darts at his name on a piece of paper one drunken night at a dive bar in Pacific Beach after he'd been chosen over her to join a players' luncheon.

Emmy felt her blood begin to boil at the mention of his name. No one could send her into a fit of fury faster than Gabe Olson. The cocky pretty boy obsessed with winning—who often unfairly *did* win at everything because he had a penis and used to play baseball. And sure, he was good at his job, whatever. But so was Emmy! Arguably, she was *better* at their job, but she was constantly climbing an uphill battle as a woman in the world of men's professional sports. Every single time—seriously, she could count them all!—something came down to a choice between her or Gabe—even when they were *iden-*

tically qualified on paper—he got it. The unjustness of it made her want to peel her skin off. But she'd known what she was getting into. When she'd taken a job in data analytics for the local professional baseball team, the San Diego Tide, she knew it'd be a challenge.

"I will buy the lighter fluid," she half joked and envisioned her and her sister dressed like cat burglars breaking into Tide Field to set it ablaze. She finished off her champagne with a smile.

"Girls, no one is burning anything down," Vera said, like the threat might have been real. Both of her daughters shared a fiery spirit; Piper was just a bit more transparent about it.

"We are *kidding*, Mom," Piper said, and snuck a wicked wink at Emmy in the mirror. "Oh! Actually, a much more important topic: Em, who are you bringing to the wedding?"

Emmy would rather have been arrested for arson than discuss the dreaded Plus One topic. She mournfully looked into the bottom of her empty champagne glass. "Natasha, another?"

Piper frowned at her avoidance. "You can't keep putting it off, Em. The wedding is in three weeks, and I won't have my MOH show up stag."

"I draw the line at pronouncing 'MOH' out loud," Emmy said. She'd asked her sister to translate MOH the first time she'd texted it, and Piper explained it was shorthand for maid of honor. After helping with the initial dress search, the engagement party, the bridal shower, and weighing in on Piper's ever panicked texts over chiffon versus charmeuse, fondant versus ganache, rose versus blush, Emmy's only MOH responsibility left between today's final dress fitting and the big day was throwing the bachelorette party. And, unfortunately, finding a plus one for the wedding.

Seeing as she didn't date, she had no candidates. No front-runners. No one who owed her a favor. And it wasn't a casual *Hey, wanna come to my sister's wedding this weekend?* It was *Hey, could you book a plane ticket and fly to Cancún to hang out with people you've never met in a remote location for several days?* Who was going to say yes to that?

The thought of hiring someone à la rom-com trope had admittedly entered her mind on more than one occasion. But with her luck, she wouldn't have Dermot Mulroney sweep her off her feet but probably someone who'd steal her passport to sell on the black market and leave her stranded in Mexico. The prospect was grim. And she honestly had no qualms over showing up solo to Piper's wedding, but she knew doing so would incite a bridezilla meltdown, and no one needed that.

"I am the bride, and if I want to call you my MOH, I will call you my MOH," Piper said as if to reinforce Emmy's thoughts. "But also—"

Emmy was halfway through an eye roll when the tone of her sister's voice stopped her. A secret hid inside it, she heard it tittering on the edge of Piper's quick breath. "Also what?" she asked, fearing the answer.

Piper grimaced in her reflection. She bunched her ballooning skirt in her hands and held it like a security blanket. "Jacob is on the guest list." She flinched like Emmy might leap up and attack her.

Emmy's hearing had gone offline, and she wondered if she might have been losing her mind, because no way—*no way*—did her sister just tell her that her ex-boyfriend was coming to her wedding. "*What?*"

Piper held up her hands, still facing the mirror with her back to Emmy. "I know. I'm sorry. But he's Ben's cousin's plus one. They started dating recently, and she RSVP'd with him as her guest. *Believe me* I lost it when I saw it, Em. I will uninvite them if you want me to, but that won't be a great foot to start out on with my in-laws . . . I mean, you know if it was someone on our side, she'd be dead to me and scratched off the list."

Emmy was still reeling. She hadn't seen or talked to Jacob in over a year. Not since he'd told her she was too obsessed with her career, and if she wanted a future with him, she'd have to give it up. Literally. He'd said *me or your job* in a moment that felt so misogynistically surreal

Emmy sometimes still wondered if it had really happened. If maybe she'd wake from some bizarre fever dream to find the guy she'd fallen for was not in fact a controlling jerk but rather the supportive partner she'd thought she'd known. Alas, Jacob had said those words to her, *me or your job*, among other mean things about how she'd die alone if she married her career, and Emmy had chosen her job. And, consequently, had given up on dating.

She hadn't regretted her decisions—to ditch him and not date—for one second. Until right now. Suddenly the thought of running into him with his new girlfriend had her veins tight with anxiety. He couldn't see her alone and dateless because then he'd think he was right about her, and she would not give him the satisfaction. Not to mention, she still battled the teeny tiny voice in her head that crept out of the dark in her low moments and tried to convince her he *was* right. She could hear it growing louder as she thought about showing up to a wedding of all things—the epitome of romantic commitment—by herself. She didn't think she would care so much until the situation was right in front of her.

Emmy gave her sister a steely glare in the mirror. "Are you specifically telling me this while you're standing there in a five-thousand-dollar dress so I don't murder you?"

"Maybe?" Piper's voice came out a squeak. "Seriously though, I will take one for the team and uninvite them if you want me to."

Yes, please fizzled around Emmy's mind like an angry firecracker, but she couldn't put her sister in the position of offending her new family. She could be the bigger person. She could handle seeing her ex. She could . . . find a date.

"No, you don't have to do that," she said warily. "But thank you for offering."

Piper sagged with visible relief. She waved her hands. "Don't worry. When you show up with someone else, he'll see you've moved on, and everything will be fine."

"Also!" Their mother took the opportunity to chime in. "If you find a date, that could be a step toward starting something serious, Emmy. You know you're—"

"If you're about to remind me how old I am, I'm going to stop you right there, Mom."

Vera paused with her mouth open and then sighed. "That's not what I was going to say. You are still so young, Emmy. What I was going to say is maybe this is a good opportunity to spend some time away from work and getting to know someone."

"So in a year from now, we're planning *my* wedding, and you don't have a spinster daughter on your hands anymore?" Emmy said with a frown.

"Emmy, stop it. I just think you put an awful lot of energy into your career, and maybe if—"

"I like my career. Speaking of—" She waved her phone at them in a signal she needed to check her email, a routine they were well accustomed to. She wasn't really going to check it; she just didn't want to talk about her lack of a love life anymore. She thumbed at her screen, and it took all her strength not to open Instagram and search for Jacob's new girlfriend. She did *not* care enough to look.

Her eyes landed on her texting thread with Axe Murderer and a smile bent her lips. Emmy glanced up at her mother and sister to see they'd fallen into a critical discussion of what fresh flowers would be pinned into Piper's hair and decided they did not need her input.

She wasn't sure what she expected to get in return, if anything, but before she could stop herself, she tapped out a message to Axe Murderer.

> So, you still haven't told me what you did to get fake numbered.

She hit send and bit her lip, surprised at the hope blooming in her chest that she'd get a response.

A quiet gasp slipped between her lips when the typing dots almost instantly appeared. Her heart nervously trilled at the thought of what he was going to say. Maybe he'd tell her to go away. Maybe he'd make another bird-band pun. Maybe he'd ask who she was because he'd deleted her number after their mistaken exchange and had already moved on.

She stilled in anticipation when his message appeared.

> Honestly, I'm not the best at connecting with people. I obviously misread the situation.

It was not the answer she expected. She blinked a few times at his surprisingly vulnerable response. The fact he'd been so open rather than passing her question off with a joke softened something already well on its way to melting in her chest.

> Well, your faux pas worked in my interest because now you're connected to me. 😊

> Happy to be here. It was also the first time I'd gone out in ages.

> Oh? Why so?

> Mostly super busy with work.

She quietly snorted to herself. A kindred spirit.

> Relatable.

> What do you do for work?

She hesitated because the reaction she got from men was reliably one of two things: intimidation or an uninvited download of mansplained baseball stats and facts because they automatically assumed they knew more than she did. Both options reliably killed the conversation because they either backed away in fear or she wiped the floor with them with knowledge.

She couldn't say why, but she wasn't ready to lose Axe Murderer for any reason, and especially not over her job, so she decided to be vague.

> I'm a data analyst downtown.

It was the truth. The ballpark sat squarely among the skyscrapers and a stone's throw from the waterfront. A downtown office could have meant any number of things. Maybe she worked in pharma or at a bank or at one of the zillion microbreweries dotting San Diego like constellations. He didn't need to know she was an analyst for the Tide.

> Who takes care of your chihuahuas while you're away?

She frowned at the message, not following, until she remembered she'd joked about being an old lady with three dogs and a parrot.

> Cawly Rae, of course.

> Ah, a singer and a dog sitter. Truly a jackdaw of all trades.

A small chuckle snuck from Emmy's lips.

> I would ask what you do for work, but I'm pretty sure you're an ornithologist with all these bird-band puns.

> Speaking of. *Clears throat* Mötley Crow, New Kids on the Flock, Bawk the Moon.

A full laugh burst out of her mouth.

> Why are you so good at this?

> I may have been preparing.

> Oh, so there's a list?

> Perhaps.

> Does that mean you were expecting this conversation to continue?

> I hoped it would. 😊

The little smiley face drew a mirroring one from her in real life. The warm, soft thing in her chest fully spilled open.

> Me too.

Chapter 3

Emmy went to work with a smile on her face on Monday morning. She felt like she had a secret weapon in her pocket. A tiny bright spot by the name of Axe Murderer that she could fire off a message to if she needed a boost.

They'd continued texting throughout Sunday once Emmy had escaped the bridal salon and survived lunch with her mother and sister. His messages had brightened her weekend chores and nearly made her forget about the pending disaster of her ex being a guest at her sister's wedding. She'd laughed at more bird-band puns while she folded laundry and was so distracted by their conversation that she almost bought almond milk instead of oat at the grocery store. They hadn't told each other their real names or anything identifying at all. She knew he worked downtown too, he was her age, had a big family, and he did in fact prefer regular milk to either almond or oat. Although part of her wanted to, she held back pushing too hard for fear she might crush the fledgling wings of whatever was hatching between them. She knew they were flirting with each other but calling it that put too much pressure on the situation. She wanted to keep it simple. After all, she didn't date.

"What are you smiling about, Jameson?" Gabe Olson greeted her when she walked into their office. As was customary, he sat on the edge of his desk in the cubicle neighboring hers like some kind of Abercrombie gargoyle. He had an affinity for pastel-colored polos that tightly cuffed his biceps. (Emmy vowed never to look at his arms. Someone so infuriating was not deserving of such nice arms.)

His teeth literally *sparkled* when he smiled, and his dark hair was always gelled into a neat wave she wanted to flick tiny wads of paper into just to see if they'd get stuck.

At the sight of him perched on his desk's corner, long legs stretched and ankles crossed, Emmy's morning glow instantly dimmed. He may have been visually appealing, but she reminded herself he did things like stick tape over her computer mouse's sensor, tell her meetings had been moved so she'd show up late, and often ate her—*clearly marked*—leftovers in the communal fridge.

In truth, all the men she worked with did things like that to one another. It was a bizarre bonding ritual—and maybe she should have been thankful they included her in the pranking at all, but Gabe seemed to single her out more than the others. Not to mention, he had a reputation for being cutthroat; his nickname around the office was Gabe Ruthless, and it was a well-known fact he'd do anything to win. There was even a rumor he'd gotten another analyst fired years ago because he was in his way for a promotion. It had happened before Emmy joined the team, back when Gabe was still an intern. She trusted him as far as she could throw him, and seeing as he was over six feet of solid ex-baseball player muscle, that distance was about two inches.

Nevertheless, Emmy was well versed in working with difficult men and knew how to handle him. She rounded into her cubicle and dropped her tote on her desk. "I'm not smiling anymore, thanks to you."

Gabe dropped his face into a dramatic puppy dog pout and leaned over their half wall. She would have sold her left kidney to make it a full wall. "Aww, come on. You were happy for a minute there. Did you have a good weekend? What did you do?"

As a rule, she didn't talk about her personal life at work, though Gabe always seemed interested. Other than when she occasionally grabbed lunch with her boss, Alice, and savored the rush of feminine energy as rare as oxygen on Everest, Emmy kept anything other than baseball analytics close to her chest. Part of that was because she was one of two women in the whole department and one of maybe fifty in the whole organization. She worked in Boys Town and had learned to be a chameleon. She could talk like them, drink like them, argue like them. It was the price of admission to her career. In all the years of doing it, she had partly become one of them.

She wasn't about to tell Gabe Gargoyle Olson she went to her sister's wedding dress fitting—he didn't even know her sister was getting married. If she was going to do that, she might as well tell him she spent Saturday on the couch with cramps radiating up to her eyeballs too.

She sincerely thought about doing it for a second because surely he'd recoil in horror and regret even saying hello to her.

But she opted not to share. Instead, she sat in her chair and ignored him. She reached for her computer glasses and turned on her monitor.

"Silent treatment, great way to start the week," Gabe said, still leaning over their wall. He altered the pitch of his voice and pretended to mimic her. "'My weekend was great, thanks for asking, Olson. What did you do?'" He shifted back to his normal voice. "Oh, how nice of you to inquire, Jameson. I went to my grandma's birthday party and entertained my nieces and nephews while their parents drank enough booze to drown a small village."

A reluctant laugh punched its way out of Emmy's throat. She chewed her lips to hide a smile. No fraternizing with the enemy. Especially not today.

Another member of their team waltzed around the corner carrying a tray of to-go coffees.

"Good morning!" Pedro Torres sang in his buoyant voice. He wore his customary plaid button-down, glasses, and lanyard looped around his neck. "One for you," he said, and handed a coffee to Gabe. "One for you," he said, and passed one to Emmy. "Is Alice here yet?"

"Torres, it's a little late in the game to start kissing ass, you know,"

Gabe said, and sipped his drink. He immediately frowned. He smacked his lips and gagged like a cat with a hairball. "Does this have almond milk in it again?"

"Yes," Pedro said, and marched for his desk across the aisle from Emmy's and Gabe's.

Gabe dropped his coffee in the trash bin. "Milk comes from cows, not nuts."

"Heathen," Pedro said with a smirk.

It was not the first time Gabe had rejected his offering. They argued like brothers.

Emmy rolled her eyes at the scene. "Thank you, Torres," she said, and happily sipped her drink. Everyone called one another by their last names like in a locker room; the reflex was ingrained in her. "This was very kind of you." She could have added that she'd prefer oat milk next time, but she did her best to reinforce their good behavior. She was honestly a little surprised he'd remembered to buy her one too.

The fourth member of their little nerd quad slipped in the door with his customary head bob greeting. "Sup?" Silas Ishida said, and directed it mostly at Gabe and Pedro.

Pedro held up his coffee like the Statue of Liberty's torch, and Silas seamlessly grabbed it from his hand as he passed, nodding in thanks.

The four of them worked in a windowless, sometimes overheated cubby belowdecks at the ballpark. While fans only saw the players on the diamond, the perfectly cut grass, the jumbotron, the peanuts and beer and seventh-inning stretch, the organization had hundreds of people split up into an executive team, accounting, marketing, communications, guest services, operations, and—the department where Emmy worked—research and analytics working at the stadium in a suite of offices out of sight.

The room Emmy shared with three men, a wall of whiteboards scribbled with equations, and a fake ficus tree branched off a long underground hall somewhere behind home plate. Inside that room, they ran numbers, analyzed mountains of game data, wrote algorithms, built predictive models, all to help the team managers make decisions. Trades, batting orders, pitching rotations, who got called up from AAA and who got sent down.

So, you're like, the Moneyball *guy?* a particularly bro-y dude had said to Emmy on a truly awful date back when she used to attempt to socialize.

Rather than explaining she had advanced degrees in computer science and statistics, could write code with her eyes closed, and drew complex predictive models in her sleep, she'd blinked and said, *Sure, something like that.*

That bro turned out to be one of the ones who tried to educate her on baseball. They never had a second date.

Marrying math to her favorite sport was a dream come true. She lived and breathed baseball. Even if she didn't watch every game, the haul of data—RBIs, OBPs, walks, hits, strikeouts, pitch counts—that flooded her desk allowed her to reconstruct a game from start to finish. It was all a giant math equation, and the only variable was the human performance. She *loved* her job, despite the daily upkeep of living in Boys Town. She often got asked things by colleagues and peers like whether she was sure her results were correct, or to list her qualifications, or where she went to school, or how she got interested in data analytics in the first place—things none of her male colleagues were ever asked. And often she was asked these things in a room full of mostly men, as if she had to prove her right to be breathing the same air. It was exhausting, and sometimes she wanted to scream, but nothing fulfilled her the way crunching baseball stats did. It was her calling, and she simply had to do it.

Unfortunately, she had to do it with a bunch of boys who often acted like she was the tagalong little sister no one wanted around.

Luckily, a senior analyst position had opened up down the hall—literally. The office was down the hall and had an internal-facing window. And if Emmy won the job, she'd at least have the peace and quiet of her own four walls at the stadium.

As it stood, their team worked a nine-to-five routine. They did the grunt work of cleaning and analyzing all the data into a digestible format for the higher-ups. The promotion to senior analyst would mean working during games, traveling with the team. It would be a major change, but it was a change Emmy craved like the first bite of a ballpark hot dog. Earning that position would put her one rung higher on the corporate baseball ladder, in a place where even fewer women had ever set foot. After a round of interviews and presentations, their boss Alice, the assistant director of research and analytics, was going to submit two candidates to the department director to make a decision.

Emmy knew Alice was on her side. She'd pulled her under her wing the day she stepped in the door. Emmy was almost certain she'd make it to the final round—they were due to find out in mere minutes—but after that, she couldn't say what might happen.

She guzzled a long sip of her coffee as the sound of clicking heels approached from down the hall. Alice's calling card. Emmy never wore heels to work. She didn't like them to begin with, and one more thing to remind everyone she was an imposter in Boys Town would not work in her favor.

Alice always wore heels, and Emmy had to assume it was because she didn't care what anyone thought.

"Oh good, gang's all here," Alice said from the doorway. She and the director only occasionally traveled with the team. They spent most of their days deep in the bowels of the stadium entrenched in strategy sessions. Today, Alice wore a smart navy skirt suit and patent slingbacks. Baseball ran in her blood the same way it did in Emmy's. Her great-uncle was among the first Black players to join the major leagues.

Most people in the organization had some tether to the sport.

Gabe was an all-star pitcher in college; Silas's cousins played professionally in Japan; Pedro had been obsessed with the sport since childhood; and Emmy . . . well, Emmy's connection to the sport was one of the personal things she didn't discuss at work. Among her colleagues, only Alice knew because Emmy had gotten weepy after one too many happy hour beers on an important anniversary, and she was the only one not afraid to ask the Only Girl why she was crying into her Blue Moon.

Emmy could tell by the look on Alice's face now she was about to deliver the news they were all waiting for right then and there. No need for a special meeting or even to close the door.

People tended to get to the point in their industry. Conversations that uprooted lives in a snap happened on the regular. (*Sorry, kid. We're sending you back down.* Or, *You're being traded to the Cardinals. Hope you enjoy St. Louis.*) Emmy sometimes felt bad the numbers she produced were the driving force behind these decisions and often had to distance herself from thinking too hard about what they meant. But still, there was no real sense in beating around the bush.

"After careful consideration, I've made my decision as to who's moving on to the next round for the senior analyst position," Alice said.

The four of them stared at her in anticipation. Emmy's heart beat double time.

Alice pointed at her and Gabe like she was calling them out of the dugout. "Jameson, Olson, you're moving on. Torres, Ishida, keep up the good work. Final decision will be made at the end of the month."

The air in the room hung tense for several seconds. Emmy vibrated with simultaneous joy and frustration. She couldn't say she was surprised it was she and Gabe, but she'd *hoped* it would be anyone other than him. The battle was already lost, and the idea of losing to Gabe Olson—again—made her want to scream.

Pedro eventually broke the silence with a loud exhale. "Well, glad that's over, huh? Congrats." He gave Gabe one of those dude-bro half-hug backslap things as if he'd already won and as if Emmy wasn't standing right there too.

"Thanks," Gabe said.

"For sure. And I guess fair warning to watch out, Jameson. Now that you've got Gabe Ruthless on your tail here," Pedro said, and nodded at Emmy. *"You've heard the rumors,"* he stage-whispered like they were in a horror film.

Emmy frowned, and Gabe scoffed.

"Rumors, Torres," Gabe said, and slapped him on the back.

"Sure. Tell that to poor Mikey Walker," Silas chimed in with a sly grin. "Last I heard, he's selling solar panels after you got him fired."

Gabe shook his head with a half smile but made no further comment.

"We should go out this weekend to celebrate," Pedro said. He directed the statement at Gabe and Silas, in indication the invitation extended to Silas too.

"That's a great idea!" Alice chimed in from the doorway where she still lingered. "I'll buy you all a round of drinks for the work you've put in so far."

They all turned to her. Despite Alice's smile, Emmy felt like she was crashing a party that hadn't even happened yet. The three men awkwardly shifted their weight while Emmy stared at her feet. To her surprise, it was Gabe who broke the silence.

"That would be great. Thanks, Alice."

"You bet. Friday night. I'll be in touch." She swept out the door with an efficient nod.

Emmy could feel them looking at her, and before the awkward tension made her say something that would make it even more awkward, she followed Alice into the hall.

"Alice!" she whispered as she hurried to catch up to her. She was already halfway back to her office, her clicking heels snapping off the floor.

"What's up?" she said when Emmy caught up. "Congrats, by the way."

"Thank you," Emmy said, still flustered. "Why did you do that?"

Alice's face flattened into a frown. "Move you to the next round for the promotion? Because you deserve it."

A warm rush of pride washed over Emmy, but now was not the time. "No, not that. Why did you offer to buy us drinks?"

Alice arched a knowing brow at her. "Because they wouldn't have invited you if I hadn't. They were halfway done making plans already."

"Yes, but I don't want to hang out with them."

"Emmy, that's not the point. You know how things go around here. Hell, I taught myself to golf so they'd stop making decisions on the course without me. I'm pretty good now." She proudly tilted her head.

Emmy grumbled, knowing the proverbial *they* Alice referred to meant all the men they worked with, but really, men in any corporate setting. She'd been around long enough to know if she didn't purposely insert herself in extracurricular activities, she'd get left out. Most of the time, that was fine with her, because her liver quivered at the mere thought of a pub crawl through the Gaslamp, surely the night out that Pedro would have planned. But on more than one occasion, she'd heard her team talking about the round of golf they'd played with the director, or she found out they had critical information about an upcoming trade she didn't because they'd learned about it over drinks she hadn't been invited to. Those were the times being the only girl worked to her disadvantage the most. Alice was right: Emmy needed to insert herself so she wasn't left out—yet another thing that required extra effort. With a promotion on the line, face time with her colleagues was probably a good thing.

"It'll be fun," Alice said, and softly punched her in the arm as she began to walk away.

Emmy tried for a smile, but it came out more of a grimace. She suddenly needed a break from it all, which did not bode well, seeing as it was only minutes into Monday morning.

She left the hall and headed for the communal kitchen. On her way there, she opened her group chat with her parents and Piper and shared the news.

I made it to the next round!

Piper instantly responded, surely still in her sweatpants and working from home. She wrote content for tech companies and had worked completely remote for nearly five years now. Their mother, a nurse at a VA center, would be slower to respond, and their father, a nearly retired accountant, was more likely to call her later than respond to a text, though he'd told her he always read them.

Woo hoo! **Piper wrote.** You and who else?

Gabe Olson.

KICK HIS ASS.

Emmy laughed out loud at her sister's message as she reached for a bag of crunchy cookies from the snack rack. Aside from the snacks, the small kitchen with golden walls held two round tables usually littered with crumbs, a set of uncomfortable chairs, a coffee station, a fridge with fermenting leftovers no one except Emmy ever cleaned out, and a microwave that often smelled like reheated Thai food thanks to their department's communal favor.

"Smiling again, Jameson?" Gabe said from behind her.

She slightly jumped and turned to see him entering the kitchen with his own smile.

Her smile dropped into a frown. "Did you follow me in here?"

"Of course not," he said, and joined her at the snack rack. His cologne swirled around her when he lifted his arm to reach for the rack. He always smelled like someone had zested an orange over cinnamon bark and amber. The zip of citrus was strongest in the morning, like now, and faded to a warm, spicy scent as the day wore on. She knew the profile so well because she sat beside him all day, and the fresh, leathery fragrance did something heady to her that she did not care to admit to. He grabbed a bag of salted rice cakes, and she snorted a laugh. "What's funny?" he asked.

"You're so desperate to hide the fact you followed me that you're *pretending* you came in here for food, and now you have to eat that sorry excuse for a snack."

Gabe scowled at her as if it weren't true. "For your information, I *love* rice cakes."

Emmy folded her arms and blinked at him. "Prove it then. Eat them."

"I will," he said with a cocky tilt of his head. He pulled the bag open and plucked out a sad little wafer. He popped it in his mouth and noisily crunched. "Mmm, these are *so* good."

Emmy watched him with a satisfied smirk. "You know what's better than a rice cake?" she said over the sound of tearing her little bag open. "A cookie." The mini chocolate chip biscuit made an even more satisfying crunch because she knew he was eating something far inferior.

They stared each other down, each chewing their respective snacks. A muscle twitched in his jaw with every bite, drawing her attention to the chiseled nature of his face. He had chocolaty brown eyes and obscenely full lashes. Like the kind she'd pay someone at a salon to glue to her lids. His chin had an annoying dimple in it, and his cheekbones may well have been arches in a cathedral. The symmetry of it all was simply unfair. And then there was the rest of his body that Emmy had to force herself not to look at because *wow* he was in shape, and how dare he wear shirts that so specifically showcased his arms? It was rude—*he* was rude. And there would be no fraternizing with the enemy!

Gabe blinked like he'd been studying her just as intently. Then he cleared his throat like he might have been choking on a rice cake. When he managed to find his voice, he said, "I really came in here because I wanted to say congrats. On making it to the next round."

"Oh," she said, thrown again. Was this some kind of backhanded trick to make her lower her guard? An attempt at weakening her walls so he could swoop in and steal her job? Just in case, she wasn't going to let on she was suspicious of him. "You too."

"Thanks." He popped another rice cake in his mouth and crunched it. "Sorry I'm going to have to beat you though."

Emmy kicked herself and glared at him. She should have known he was putting on a front. "You're such an ass, Olson."

He grinned at her. "Hey, you never told me what you did this weekend."

"Because it's none of your business."

"Sorry," he said at the bite in her voice. "Just trying to keep things friendly."

She snorted. "We are not friends."

He ate another rice cake. He folded his arms over his broad chest and gave her a rather unfriendly stare. "I said friend-*ly*, not friends. There's a difference."

Emmy finished her cookies and folded her own arms. "You're right, there is. We're colleagues and tolerate each other at best."

"Well, now we're more than colleagues."

"Oh?"

"Yeah. We're competitors." He narrowed his gaze and lowered his voice. He moved a fraction closer to her and brought his disarming scent with him. "And I don't lose, Jameson."

Emmy glared at him, holding her ground. He was trying to

intimidate her, and she would not let him have the satisfaction. Nor would she let on she thought he'd already won the promotion.

In that moment, she decided she was going to fight tooth and nail. Hell or high water, reputation be damned, she was going to do whatever it took to beat him.

She stepped closer and lowered her own voice to a menacing growl. She was a solid nine inches shorter than him, but with the way he flinched, she knew she'd made her point. "Well, that makes two of us, Olson, so this should be interesting then, shouldn't it."

A grin curled his lip. "Indeed, it should be." He found one more rice cake in his bag and crunched it in her face.

She scoffed with a roll of her eyes and stepped around him. She walked back into the hall, ready to return to her desk, when she got a text.

Her mother had responded.

Fantastic news! She added a little confetti emoji.

Emmy smiled at it and saw her most recent message from Axe Murderer below it.

> The Flamingo Lips like The Flaming Lips, get it?

Last night, she'd used the *Ha Ha* reaction at his latest bird-band pun instead of texting back because he'd sent it at nearly 11 p.m., and she knew they'd have texted all night if she didn't end it and go to sleep.

Now, before she could allow herself to overthink if sending him a message about her good news was too much when they hardly knew each other, she wrote one and hit send.

> This week is off to a good start! Good things happening at work!

He almost immediately responded.

> Congrats! Me too!

> Really? That's awesome! Congrats!

He hit the heart reaction, and Emmy's heart took a swan dive to her toes and back.

Did he just *love* her message?

It didn't mean anything, she hurried to convince herself as her face heated. The heart reaction was a step above the thumbs-up for *like*, and good news on the job front was worth a heart. Maybe he was simply excited. She couldn't blame him. She was excited too. And he was probably busy and needed to get back to work, much like how she'd ended their conversation the night before so she could sleep. It wasn't anything to read into.

But she knew, even as she tried to convince herself differently, that the little heart would be bouncing around her brain all day.

Chapter 4

Axe Murderer: Favorite movie?

Oof. Too many to list.

What? Everyone has a favorite.

What's yours? If you say a Tarantino film, I might "lose" your number.

What's wrong with Tarantino?

Is that what you were going to say?!

. . .

Wow, Axe Murderer. Things were going so well.

Don't hold it against me.

Redeem yourself, then. Favorite book?

Oof. Too many to list.

> Fair.

> I take it you like to read given your polite acceptance of my dodge.

> Accurate. I couldn't pick one either, so I'll give you a pass. As long as you aren't secretly a pretentious Lit Bro who worships the Jonathans and pooh-poohs romance as a genre.

> I don't even know what half of that means, so chances are slim I fall into that category.

> Good.

> Best concert you've ever been to?

> Ooh, good one. My parents took us to see the Rolling Stones when I was little. It was amazing.

> I bet. You must have cool parents.

A sharp pain lanced Emmy's heart at the family memory. She'd opened the door herself without even thinking, a door she kept closed.

"Um, Em? Are you going to put that down anytime soon?" Her best friend, Beth, cut her text conversation short.

Emmy looked up to see her sitting next to her, one eyebrow raised. She'd met Beth Coolidge in a computer science class freshman year of college. As a software engineer for a biotech company,

Beth too knew what it was like to live in Boys Town. She wore slip-ons and jeans and lanyards at work, downplaying anything feminine about herself, but unlike Emmy, she turned into a glamazon outside of business hours. Winged eyeliner, tumbling blond beach waves, chest out and chin high. This early evening, she wore a candy red maxi dress that turned heads while she walked, and a pair of platform sandals fit for a Spice Girl. Not exactly baseball game garb, but Beth was Beth. The two of them sat next to each other sipping margaritas high up in left field at the ballpark.

The exclusive patio nearly had a bird's-eye view of the field with the city skyline peeking in from outside the stadium. Beth had all but begged Emmy to meet her downtown for happy hour, and when Emmy asked for a rain check yet again because she was working late, Beth compromised by showing up at the game. She'd sent Emmy a Let me in text, to which Emmy, still in her office, responded Where? in confusion, and then received instructions to meet her at the ticket gate. Guilted into hosting her guest, Emmy met Beth at a side entrance and grabbed them both wristbands before heading to what Beth referred to as "the best seats in the house."

Arguably, the best seats in the house were behind home plate, or in one of the private boxes, but neither was an option, seeing as they showed up when the game was already underway.

First pitch had been at 5:05, which meant they were somewhere near the fifth inning now, but Emmy had been so distracted by texting Axe Murderer she'd lost track—which was saying something. She didn't even know the score.

She glanced at the towering scoreboard across the field and saw the game was tied.

"Sorry. I lost track of time," she said to Beth and set her phone on the bar in front of them. The narrow railing facing the field dropped straight into the lower decks below them.

"Thank you," Beth said with a flip of her silky hair. "I came here to hang out with you, not watch you crunch numbers on your phone.

You can't constantly work, you know. I mean, it's awfully telling that the only way I can have a happy hour with you is if I literally come to your place of employment. You don't see me hanging out in the server room at my office after hours, do you?"

A pang of guilt hit Emmy like a foul ball. Her history of skipping out on Beth's invites was well documented, and when they did go out, Emmy was notorious for checking scores and updating stats between conversations. "No. But to be fair, my place of employment is a lot more entertaining than yours," she said, and nodded out at the field.

Beth gave her a frosty glare. "You know what I mean."

"I'm sorry. But if it helps, I wasn't working."

"Oh?" Beth asked with a curious tilt of her head. "Were you talking to someone? Is your sister having another bridezilla meltdown?"

Emmy snorted. "Thankfully, no. But the night is still young."

Beth let out a breezy breath and reached for her margarita. "Thank goodness for that." She lifted it and tapped it against Emmy's with a dull, plastic clunk before they both sipped. "So, who is it then?"

Emmy smacked her lips against the tart pucker of the citrusy tequila. The evening summertime air hung thick with the signature smells of the ballpark: hot dogs, beer, spicy tacos from the booth behind them. Laughter and conversation bubbled around them. The next batter's walk-up song blared through the PA system, and fans cheered. Despite sitting in an enormous, wide-open space, the focused attention on her best friend's face narrowed Emmy's world to a private little bubble.

"Are you not going to tell me?" Beth asked with a flirty shake of her shoulders.

Emmy fidgeted and took another sip. "You're going to think I'm weird."

"Em, I've known you for over a decade. I *know* you're weird."

A laugh popped from her lips. "Fine. So, the other night I got a text from an unknown number. It turned out to be this guy who someone had given a fake number to at a bar the night before. He thought I was her. I explained I wasn't, and now we've been texting for the past five days." Emmy buried the end of her sentence with another gulp of her drink.

Beth blinked wide. "Wait. Someone fake numbered this guy, and the number happened to be yours? What are the chances?"

"I know, right?"

She could see Beth trying to mentally calculate the literal chances of randomly landing on a ten-digit combination of numbers that happened to belong to a specific person. Emmy had tried it herself, and the answer was: astronomical.

"It's weird, right?" Emmy said, embarrassed she'd finally confessed to someone. At least that someone was Beth. "It's totally weird."

"Not necessarily," Beth said with an astute shake of her head. "Something like 80 percent of relationships start online or via digital messaging these days." She leaned in and lowered her voice to a conspiratorial whisper. "I should know, because I'm part of that statistic." She winked.

Emmy gasped. "Does that mean you met someone?!"

"Shhh!" Beth said, and flapped her hands to quiet her. "Maybe. I don't know yet. But we had a promising date last weekend."

"Oh! Is this Mustache Guy?"

"*Ugh.* No. Mustache Guy didn't get a callback. I'm on to Nose Ring Guy now. I wasn't sure I was into it at first, but he's got a whole Lenny Kravitz vibe going, and I don't think there's a soul on earth who'd kick Lenny out of bed for eating crackers."

"Well then," Emmy said with an approving nod.

Just then, the batter roped a single out into right field, and the crowd erupted, startling Emmy from their conversation. She joined in the clapping and eyed the scoreboard, knowing exactly how that hit would change his stats.

"Yay, sports!" Beth hollered from beside her. She threw her arms in the air and bounced around in her seat. The man sitting next to them eyed her tumbling hair and the tight outline of her dress. She might as well have been a blinking siren amid all the jeans and ball-caps and jerseys. Emmy knew her enthusiasm was genuine, despite Beth having told her on more than one occasion that she didn't understand baseball, didn't want Emmy to explain it to her, but was happy to cheer along.

The crowd continued cheering to the next batter's walk-up song, riding the momentum. Davey Hollander, the center fielder. Emmy knew from studying his stats all season that chances were low he'd get on base. A sequence of numbers cascaded through her mind. She knew against a right-handed pitcher with a runner on and one out, he had a 60 percent chance of striking out, and if he got a hit, it would most likely be a grounder straight into a 6–4–3 double play that would end the inning.

Still, she hoped against the odds.

"So, who is he?" Beth asked, drawing Emmy's attention back to their conversation. "Text Message Guy."

Emmy kept one eye on the field, lifting her shoulders in a shrug. "That's the thing: I don't know."

"Is that safe? I mean, there are a lot of creepers out there."

"I know there are, but I honestly don't get that vibe from him. Like, at all. When I'm talking to him, it's like I'm . . ." She trailed off and gazed out to the field below. It may have been the booze or the atmosphere or perhaps that her thoughts had strayed to Axe Murderer, but everything—the lights, the grass, even the dirt—looked twinkly and soft. Glowing.

"Like you're what, Em?" Beth cut in, and Emmy had no idea how long she'd been staring in a daze.

She snapped back to focus, only narrowly pulling herself from the gauzy dream. She met her friend's eyes and confessed something she hadn't even admitted to herself. "It's like I know him. Like I *want* to know him. I don't know. I can't really explain it, but I've never felt so comfortable talking to someone before. Is that strange? I mean, I don't even know his name." She sincerely looked to her friend for advice. Beth was the dating app expert; of the two of them, she knew most about text communication. The only reason Emmy hadn't come to her earlier was because she wanted to keep Axe Murderer as her own little secret.

Beth shook her head. "I don't think it's strange. A connection is a connection, regardless of when or how."

She should have known her best friend would understand.

"Unless he murders you, then I take it all back. And I will hunt him down and kill him."

Emmy leaned in and whispered, "I saved his name as Axe Murderer in my phone, so if anything happens to me, that's how you find him."

Beth threw her head back, laughing a warm, generous sound that made a few people look over. Their attention was quickly pulled away by the sound of a ball cracking off a bat. The crowd roared in delirium while the runner on first took off. To Emmy's shock given Hollander's stats, the ball stayed in play, narrowly skipping by the shortstop out into left field. It allowed the runner to score, putting them in the lead, and left Hollander on second base with a double.

"Huh," Emmy said, impressed.

The crowd continued to cheer while the next batter approached the plate.

"Do you have a date to the wedding yet?" Beth asked in another reroute of conversation, paying minimal attention to the activity on the field. "I can't believe he-whom-we-do-not-speak-of is going to be there."

Emmy palmed her face with her hand. "I know. And no, I don't. Can I borrow Lenny?"

"I don't think I'm willing to share. But why don't you ask your texting guy?"

The thought had honestly occurred to Emmy, but she hadn't let it grow to more than a blip on her mental radar. Because that was absurd. Right? She couldn't ask this guy—this *stranger*—to be her date to her sister's wedding when they had never even met before. Could she?

But when she thought about it, she knew him better than anyone else she could get to know in the time between now and the wedding, so he was less stranger than it might seem.

"I don't know, Beth. That might be a little *too* weird."

Beth shrugged a shoulder. "Get to know him more. Ask him to meet in person. If you're still into him, see if he's willing to go with you. I mean, a trip to Cancún with a bunch of free booze? Who's going to turn that down? Speaking of, I am still willing to be your plus one. I've kept my calendar clear, just in case." She pressed a hand to her chest like she was humbly offering up her services. "I am willing to make the sacrifice."

"That's very generous of you."

"Always happy to help. So, what's up with work? You and Gabe going to duke it out for the senior analyst title?" Of course Beth knew every detail about the bane of her existence.

Emmy squared her shoulders, feeling confident. "Yes, and I am going to win."

"That's my girl. Screw all these boys who think they run the world."

"Screw 'em," Emmy said, and tapped her margarita once more. The sound made her remember she had another pending night out to plan for. She only had so many in her system; she'd need at least two days to recharge her introvert battery after this simple happy hour with Beth. "Except, *ugh*." She threw her hand to her face again. "I'm supposed to go out and celebrate with them this weekend. My whole team. Alice set it up."

Beth smirked at her. "So that's what it takes to get you to go out? Your boss has to mandate it?"

Emmy smirked back at her. "She thinks it's a good idea I hang out with them. Some kind of team bonding thing, I guess."

Beth sourly frowned into her drink.

"I agree," Emmy said. "*And*, the worst part is I'll have to make nice with Olson in public."

"You know you can call him by his first name with me. This isn't the dugout dungeon you all work in."

"Sure, but calling him by his first name humanizes him, and the last thing I want to do is think of Gabe Olson as a human—especially when my plan is to destroy him at work."

"Killer," Beth said with an approving grin.

They decided to share nachos and another round of margaritas. Beth lasted until the seventh inning before she lost interest in the game and decided her maxi dress was in fact not suited for the chill of a nighttime ball game after all.

Emmy was ready to head out too; she could see the rest of the game play out in her stats app anyway. By the time she made it home, she was ready for pajamas. The drinks and pile of food had gone straight to the sleepy center of her brain. She kicked off her shoes inside her front door and peeled off the sweater she'd thrown over her blouse to fight the brisk seaside air. She fished her phone from her back pocket and saw she had two messages from Axe Murderer.

A warm flush curled into her cheeks as she immediately tapped her screen to open them. The first showed a ten-minute gap between it and the previous message he'd sent about her parents being cool.

Sorry. Family a hot button?

He'd waited another ten minutes before messaging again.

> Bird Girl? Did I mess up?

Emmy leaned her elbows on her kitchen island and chewed her lip, feeling bad for leaving him wondering.

> Sorry! I was out at happy hour with my friend. Just got home.

She bit her lip again, wondering what he'd been thinking the whole time she'd gone silent. She normally didn't want to talk about her family, but for whatever reason (two margaritas? the nachos?), she found herself willing to crack the door open a few inches.

> And you didn't mess up. I honestly had to go because I was being rude to my friend by texting you instead of hanging out with her. But you're kind of right. My family is a sensitive subject . . .

She smiled when his typing dots bounced into place.

> Whew. Thought I lost you. And I hear you on the family thing. Mine is . . . complicated.

> Oh? What's your brand of dysfunction? I'll tell you mine if you tell me yours.

A daring thrill zipped through her. She hardly talked about her family issues even when pressed, and here she was volunteering them to a man she'd never met. She set her phone down and headed for the cabinet to find a glass to fill with water.

When she made it back to her phone, she saw his typing dots still bouncing. He was either writing a novel or rethinking and restarting

multiple times. When the message finally popped up, she concluded
it had been the latter given its brevity.

> My brand of dysfunction is disappointing
> my parents. They had a vision for my future
> that didn't pan out, and they remind me of it
> constantly. Your turn.

She made it to her bedroom and peeled off her jeans. She sat on
her bed in her underwear and offered him a small sliver of her heart.

> We had a family tragedy when I was a kid,
> and I entered the profession that kind of tore
> us apart.

It was far more complicated than that, but any more detail would
launch a Google search campaign that would inevitably result in him
finding out her name, and their secret little bubble of anonymity
would pop.

> Wow, had to go and one-up my dysfunction,
> Bird Girl. I'm just the prodigy who blew his
> chance, but you're a full-on defector over
> there. How Game of Thronesy of you to turn
> on your own family.

Emmy giggled, which she assumed was his intention. At the same
time, her chest felt cracked wide open.

> Well, you know what they say.

> What do they say?

She paused and laughed again.

> I have no idea. I was hoping you might know.

> Sorry to disappoint. I've got nothing, but I'm happy to be in the Screw Up Kid Club with you.

> It's an honor. We SUKC.

> Good one.

> Thank you.

> Speaking of judgy parents, mine think I'm being too picky about dating and wasting time I could be finding someone.

> Umm, are they in cahoots with mine? Because same.

> Maybe this is how all parents of thirtysomethings act.

> There must be a faction plotting against us.

> Surely.

Emmy softly smiled at her phone, feeling another thread of the bond tying them together tighten. The list of their commonalities kept growing and growing.

He sent another message.

> So, what's your hang-up? You told me
> back at the start that you don't date mostly
> because of your job. Is that the only
> reason?

Emmy felt the vulnerable door she'd walked through earlier straining on its hinges as he opened it wider. Just like her family issues, she didn't talk about her relationship issues much either, but somehow, she felt comfortable sharing both topics with him.

She confessed something she hadn't told anyone other than her innermost circle.

> I had a bad experience with my ex. Long
> story short, he thought I was too focused on
> my career and made me choose between it
> and him. I chose it. It probably makes me a
> terrible person, but I don't regret it. I love my
> job, and I figured that was going to be the
> response no matter who I date, so I just kind
> of gave up.

His dots didn't appear for long enough that Emmy worried she'd scared him away with her honesty. Her heart leapt when they popped up.

> First of all, what an asshole.

She laughed out loud.

> Thank you, I agree. Villainizing women for
> loving their careers is one of society's worst
> pastimes.

I agree, that is a terrible take. I love my job, and no one has ever told me I'm too obsessed with it and should be doing other things with my time.

Exactly. Double standard. And to have it so bluntly thrown in my face by someone I trusted and cared about kind of poisoned the well for me.

I am sorry that happened to you. Anyone who gives you an ultimatum like that is not worth your time anyway.

Again, she agreed with him, but at the same time, she felt the niggling fear she could never fully quiet darting between the folds of her brain. With Jacob, anger had helped her say *screw him* and easily give up dating. But in her loneliest moments, sometimes she worried if all the mean things he'd said to her were true. She'd never expressed the fear to anyone before, and somehow, the man on the other side of her screen drew the honest truth from her fingertips.

Sometimes I'm afraid he was right. He told me I'd die alone if I married my career.

He said that to you? Seriously?

Seriously.

His dots disappeared for a few moments, and Emmy wondered what he was thinking.

> Sorry, what I really want to say right now might *actually* implicate me in a crime, and I know you have me saved in your phone as Axe Murderer, so I had better err on the side of caution here. But what a capital A Asshole!

Emmy snickered a laugh.

> I will destroy any evidence, don't worry.

> Thank you, but I'm still keeping it PG, just in case.

A smile jumped across her face at the thought that this person she'd never met was ready to come to her defense. The knowledge drew more honesty out of her.

> The truth is, I do want a connection. I'm just afraid I'll never be able to find someone who understands.

> I mean, I think that's everyone's fear, right? That we're all too weird for anyone to love? But that's obviously unfounded. Look at all the weirdos out there in happy relationships. You just have to find the right person who will understand and share your priorities.

Emmy thought about his words and knew there was truth to them. It was just that the *finding* element of that equation involved a lot of trial and error. And her last error had burned her badly enough to need a break.

He came back with another message.

> But also, your ex is a sample size of one. You said you're a data analyst; you know there are better guys out there simply by probability. Do not let him bias your perspective.

Emmy laughed again and felt her face warm.

> Are you a better guy, Axe Murderer?

> Yes.

> Okay. Then why are you single? What's your hang-up?

> Honestly, I think people are turned off by the reality of me once they get to know me.

> Well, you are obviously getting to know the wrong people then.

> You flatter me, Bird Girl. But people tend to have this perception of me, mainly because of how I look, that I'm going to be a certain type of person. And then when I'm not, they aren't interested.

Emmy blinked at his message, not sure what to make of it. *Certain type of person?* She wasn't sure where to go next, so she went with a joke.

> Wait, who am I talking to here? Are you a movie star? Is this Ryan Gosling???

First off, if this was Ryan, do you really think I'd cheat on Eva? That woman is a goddess.

Agreed. Good point.

But no. Not a movie star. An athlete. Before they get to know me, most people think I'm a dumb jock, which is an egregious stereotype on its own. Some of the guys I used to play with were the smartest people I know. There are more kinds of intelligence than just book smarts.

Emmy found herself surprised and even more curious. She noted his use of the past tense—*used to play with*—so assumed she wasn't talking to a professional athlete.

I completely agree. What did you play?

Baseball.

She sat straight up.

Really? I was at the game tonight!

No way! You're a fan?

It's my favorite sport!

(*And my job,* she thought about adding but held back.)

Damn, Bird Girl, if you get any more perfect, I don't know what I'm going to do.

Emmy almost dropped her phone as a warm wave washed over her. She tingled all the way to her toes. He'd called her *perfect*. She was cartwheeling sitting still. She fought to compose herself and pulled their conversation back on track before she did something reckless like ask him to meet for a nightcap.

> So, this perception vs. reality thing. Explain more, please.

> Ah, yes. Well, the athletic résumé attracts a certain kind of person, let's say. And in case you haven't noticed, I'm actually a huge nerd.

> A point in the win column if you ask me.

> Well, you're in the minority. Most people want a good time with the himbo jock, and that's just not me. They lose interest when I start nerding out about anything deep.

> I love a good nerding out.

> See, again. Minority.

> You said it yourself earlier: don't let sample size bias your perspective. The nerdily inclined exist aplenty.

> You're right, I did say that. But I've unfortunately got more than a sample size of one to go off here. Plenty of dates have tanked thanks to my inability to connect.

I think you're being a little hard on yourself.

You're talking to a man who was fake numbered, remember?

Again, point in the win column. For me.

He paused, and Emmy wondered if he was smiling like she was.

You're right. This is an unexpected connection.

I see what you did there.

Just stating a very favorable fact.

Emmy could feel the anticipation crackling between them long-distance. Was one of them going to take the leap and suggest they meet? Her thumbs tingled with the urge to tap out the letters, but the nervous tick in her heart held her back. It was too much. She didn't want to ruin what they had yet. And besides, it was getting late.

Favorable, indeed. I've got to go to bed. Sweet dreams, Axe Murderer.

A pause passed, and she would have paid good money to know what he was thinking before he came back with,

Good night, Bird Girl.

Chapter 5

The next day at work, Emmy joined her team in the conference room for a staff meeting with Director Allen. They were going over a trade prospect analysis Emmy had put the finishing touches on the day before. With the trade deadline approaching, she was buried and stressed about taking time off for her sister's wedding.

Of course Piper decided to get married in July when the entirety of major-league baseball was hurtling toward career-changing decisions backed by the data Emmy was personally responsible for analyzing.

She pushed thoughts of the wedding aside and focused on the task right in front of her. Unfortunately, Gabe Olson was also right in front of her because he'd sat in the chair directly across the table from her. He wore a buttery yellow shirt today that drew out the golden hue in his skin. He had a ballpark tan just like she did: arms, face, and neck a few shades darker than everything else. But she fully suspected Gabe Olson was one solid shade of SoCal bronze under his shirt, probably from jogging along the beach.

She nearly winced at the sudden image of Gabe Olson jogging shirtless and sweaty in the sand as it bounced through her mind. Where did *that* come from? She shook it away and turned her attention to the front of the room where Director Allen stood. He was in his early fifties, had a PhD in statistics, a neat part in his graying hair, and a pair of wire-framed glasses.

He stood in front of a data dashboard Emmy had built projected on a screen. The dynamic visualization of numbers and charts was the end product of hundreds of thousands of data points the R&A team compiled and crunched. This specific one contained data on the top five players up for potential trade and the players they were considering trading them for: position, stats, contract status, and attached budget. The back-end database that populated the information was updated daily what with a new game's worth of numbers constantly pouring in.

"Vasquez, what do we know about him?" Director Allen said, and pointed to one of the prospects the team was considering trading for. All the numbers were right there, but Emmy knew he liked to have it described along with any extra commentary for context.

She took the cue to answer. "In his third year with Pittsburgh. Was a second-round draft pick. Bats over three hundred when hitting cleanup. Solid slash line otherwise. Based on the numbers, he's a top prospect."

"Hmm. Who else wants him?" Director Allen asked.

"San Fr—" Emmy started, but Gabe cut her off.

"San Francisco, Arizona, maybe Cleveland."

Emmy shot him a glare for talking over her. He had a knack for either stealing her words or repeating exactly what she had just said. His voice often got heard over hers one way or another.

"The numbers are solid," Gabe said. "Players like him, coaches like him. He'd be a great addition in more ways than one. Management should move on him if we want him."

"Thanks, Olson," Director Allen said. "I'll keep that in mind."

Emmy squeezed the pen in her hand until the plastic whined in protest. She nearly snapped it. It was instance number ten thousand where she and Gabe had said the same thing, and he'd gotten credit for it. Sometimes she wondered if she needed to light her hair on fire or maybe stand up on the table and shout, because creating impeccable dashboards and being able to spew stats like a fire hose wasn't enough.

"How's Hollander looking?" Director Allen asked about their own player they were considering trading.

Emmy jumped in before Gabe could speak again. "Not great. He's slashing one twenty-five, two fifty, and two hundred flat," she said in reference to his batting average, on-base percentage, and slugging percentage, the three stats that told everything about a hitter. "He's put up three errors in ten games, and he—"

"Came in clutch last night." Gabe cut her off again. "His double in the fifth scored the go-ahead run."

Emmy gnashed her teeth, both that he'd interrupted her again and that he'd explained a fact she was well aware of. She'd seen Hollander's at bat with her own eyes at the game. "Sure, but that was a fluke. His averages tell a different story."

Gabe dismissively shook his head. "This is just his pattern. He'll bounce back. I suggest removing him from the list altogether."

Emmy scoffed. "Seriously? He's dead weight right now. Not producing at the plate, making errors in the field. If you ask me, he should be first on the list."

"I disagree," Gabe said, and defiantly cocked his head. Their conversation had picked up a cadence like they were arguing alone and not in a room full of their co-workers and higher-ups.

"Based on what?" Emmy said.

"A feeling."

"A *feeling*? Olson, you're staring at the data, and you're telling me you want to make this decision on a *feeling*?"

"Yeah. And maybe if you'd ever been on the field, you'd feel it too."

Emmy paused midbreath like he'd punched her. The room went painfully quiet. She was quickly reminded they weren't alone. Everyone was suddenly staring at her, her Only Girl status on full display.

So. He was going to play that card, then.

An awkward tension rippled around the room. Alice, Pedro, Silas, and the pair of analysts from the finance department uncomfortably shifted in their chairs. Somehow, Emmy found the strength to maintain her composure. She cleared her throat.

"I may not have field experience like you do, but I understand that data don't lie. If you want to make multimillion-dollar decisions based on *feelings*, go make movies."

He stared back at her, and she swore she saw one corner of his mouth twitch up.

"Okay, well, there's still time until the deadline, so we'll see how his numbers move around," Director Allen said. "Who's next?"

Emmy reluctantly broke her eye contact with Gabe, silently wishing she could channel the fury burning in her gut into melting him with her gaze. She turned back to the dashboard. "O'Haron," she said, and launched into his details.

The meeting followed a predictable pattern of numbers and stats being thrown around, names being moved up and down, Emmy emotionally detaching herself from all of it rather than thinking about how decisions made in this small room could cause a whole family to move across the country. But the players had signed up for it when they entered the league, so it was all part of the process.

By the end of it, Gabe had cut her off three more times. She knew by the depth of the indent in her hand from squeezing her pen in angst. His all-time single-meeting record was six times, and that poor pen had snapped.

When the meeting was over, and everyone went to leave, they arrived at the door at the same moment. Gabe cast her a glance and then stepped in front of her.

Emmy scoffed. "Cut me off every chance you get," she muttered.

He heard her and turned back with a glower.

"You really are ruthless," she muttered again.

He stopped walking, and she almost ran into his back. When he turned, his face was cool. "No, I'm committed. And I told you: I don't lose."

She opened her mouth to snap back with some frosty retort, but Alice stepped into the hall and saw their standoff.

"Jameson, lunch?" she asked.

Whether Alice was throwing a desperate lifeline to save her or to prevent her from publicly tearing into her co-worker with a stream of obscenities worthy of an HR visit, Emmy couldn't be sure. But she took the excuse to make an exit.

"Sure," she said, and followed her toward her office. She brushed past Gabe and intentionally held her breath so as not to inhale a waft of his cologne.

"Don't let him get to you," Alice said once they were inside her office. Emmy could hear echoes of Gabe making lunch plans with Silas and Pedro out in the hall.

She was about to defend that no one was getting to her, but Alice saw right through the denial on her face. "Well, it's hard when he's always doing it on purpose."

"And that's exactly why he does it. He *knows* it bothers you, so don't let it. Or at least don't let it show." She looped her purse over her shoulder and dug around in it for her sunglasses even though they were still underground. She put on the gold Gucci frames and looked like a total badass.

"How do you do that?" Emmy asked.

"What?"

"Not let anything get to you."

Alice shrugged and headed for the door. "Years of practice. Eventually, you just realize stressing over it is not worth it. Come on, I'm starving, and it smells like socks down here."

Emmy followed her back into the hall where the men were still chatting by the conference room door. The director stepped out and nodded at Gabe.

"Olson, a word?" He started down the hall in the opposite direction without waiting for Gabe to acknowledge, but of course Gabe instantly cut off conversation and followed him. Emmy momentarily thought of running over and tripping him. Maybe letting loose a bucket of baseballs on the floor to roll under his feet. Finding a bat to do some real damage.

Her facetious thoughts of sabotage made her hurry along to catch up with Alice going the other way though she longed to follow and hear what they were discussing. The director was probably inviting him for a round of golf to talk about the *feeling* he had about Hollander.

"Alice," she hissed with a glance over her shoulder. "Are the rumors about Olson true? Did he actually get someone fired?"

Alice cast her a sideways glance. Her giant sunglasses blocked out her eyes and brows, but Emmy could tell she was frowning at her. "I'm not at liberty to say."

Emmy almost tripped. That was basically HR speak for *yes*. "Holy shit," she muttered to herself. She and Alice arrived at the elevator, and Emmy threw one last glance over her shoulder to see Gabe stepping into Director Allen's office. Their eyes connected for a long beat, and in it, a tingle bristled Emmy's spine.

Apparently, he *was* ruthless.

Well, in that case. She would be too.

Chapter 6

Piper: Got a date yet?

Piper's pushy little text message buzzed around Emmy's mind like an angry bee all day on Friday. Even with everything else crammed into Piper's brain—the dress, the venue, the caterers, the marriage license, the menu, the officiant—the chance she'd forget about her sister's plus one was about as good as, say, randomly guessing someone's phone number. Although she knew Piper was asking in part to help spare Emmy the humiliation of showing up alone in front of Jacob.

She had not *not* stalked Jacob's social media for evidence of his new relationship, but she also hadn't dwelled on it. She'd allowed herself five minutes for a rabbit hole into his life without her and found out Ben's cousin was a cute blond dental hygienist named Katie. Surely she had a profession with more of a work-life balance than watching and analyzing 162 baseball games in six months. Emmy had nothing against Katie; that was unfair. But she had half a mind to DM her and let her know just what a tool her new boyfriend was. Alas, she'd resisted and decided the most satisfying move would be to show up to the wedding looking happy and fulfilled and prove Jacob wrong about being alone.

Which, unfortunately, meant she still needed to find a date.

She'd responded to her sister's text with a vague *Working on it* and threw herself into a day at the office. Alice had decided they were going out in the Gaslamp Quarter that night after work. The home game started at seven, which meant their time at the office would bleed right into a night out in the surrounding bars near the park where the game would be on every TV.

Emmy had gone home between the end of work and the start of the game. She wasn't sure what had come over her, perhaps her sister's insistent reminder she was down a few runs in the plus one game, but she decided to channel Beth and actually dress up to go out. Sure, she was still in Boys Town, whatever. But at least with a game going on down the street, the bars and lounges would be flooded with all sorts of people to take the focus off her dressing up for once.

She picked out a little black dress with a scoop neck and short sleeves. She attempted the winged eyeliner thing with modest success and painted her lips shiny pink. Given that she knew there'd be a fair amount of walking involved, she skipped heels and went with a pair of Chucks. She threw a small crossbody purse with a gold chain over her head and stashed her phone, wallet, keys, and lipstick in it. She'd left her curly hair loose and knew it would continue to grow throughout the night thanks to the humidity. The whole look was a little punk rock, but she liked it. She didn't sincerely *plan* on finding a date to her sister's wedding, but she thought the effort might give her a leg up.

When Emmy arrived at the bar Alice designated as the night's starting point, the crowd already spilled from the doorway. She fought her way inside among all the jerseys and T-shirts, the backward hats, and pitchers of beer. She spotted Alice, Pedro, and Gabe near the bar half watching the game on a TV and half laughing about something. Alice still wore heels and a power skirt like she'd come straight from the office. Pedro also looked how he always looked, but Gabe had ditched one of his Easter polos for a jersey that hung open over a tight white tee. His hair was still neatly sculpted, and he too wore a pair of Chucks with jeans. Emmy could see his perfect smile glowing from across the bar like a beacon in the dim light.

A funny thing happened in her chest at the sight. And then she remembered his comment in the staff meeting and decided the sensation was preemptive heartburn from all the booze they were about to make her drink, and she went back to despising him.

In the game, someone got on base and sent the bar into a cheering tizzy. The echo from the actual stadium a block away pounded like drums Emmy could feel in her bones. It sent a thrill zipping across her skin.

She walked up to her colleagues and stood behind them. "Hey," she greeted.

"Hey," Pedro said, distracted by the game and only glancing at her. Then, like a cartoon character, he did a double take and turned back around. "Jameson? Is that you?"

Emmy rolled her eyes. "Of course it's me."

Pedro managed to shove his bulging eyeballs back into his face and smile. "Holy shit, I didn't even recognize you."

Emmy fought to control the red she felt rising in her face. At least the bar was dim. She made knowing eyes at Alice, who gave her a tight smile. "Can I get a drink, please?"

"Of course," Alice said. "First round is on me." She turned to the bar with her hand up.

Gabe quietly cleared his throat from beside Emmy. She turned to him and saw a strange look on his face. A little like he was being stung by a thousand bees at once. "Jameson," he said with a tight nod.

"Olson," Emmy responded with a narrowed gaze. He smelled good again, damn him. Even in the grimy bar with competing odors of beer and fried food, his scent curled into her nose like orange cinnamon stick tendrils reaching out to grab her.

She took a deliberate step back and bumped into someone.

"Excuse me," the person said politely.

Emmy turned to see it was Silas, and he too was doing a buggy-eyed cartoon double take at her.

"Damn, Jameson. I didn't recognize you. You look . . . different." He said it as if he could not put his finger on why.

"Yes, we've established that already, Ish," Pedro said, and helped Alice hand them both shots.

Alice raised her shot glass to the center of the small circle they had formed. "To everyone's hard work so far and a great rest of the season."

They all clinked and drank. Whiskey. Alice's favorite. Emmy fought not to squeeze her face too tightly as she swallowed. She slammed her glass on the bar and exhaled. Gabe did the same, and his arm brushed against hers for a hot second. They both wore short sleeves, and the skin-on-skin contact made Emmy break out in goose bumps. Or maybe that was the liquor.

Gabe cleared his throat again and stepped back to where he'd been standing.

"Well, that's it for me. Have a great night, you guys. Don't get too carried away," Alice said. She waved at the bartender again and made the universal motion of *check please.*

"What?" Emmy asked. She stepped toward her and lowered her voice. "You're leaving? We just got here."

"I have to go back to the park," she said as she scribbled her name on a tab.

"*Alice*, you can't leave me here with them!" Emmy hissed. "I never would have come if I'd known you—" She cut herself off, realizing she'd been tricked.

Alice casually shrugged, not looking at all guilty. "You're already out. Try to have some fun. Bye, guys," she said to the other three with a wave.

"Thanks for the drink, Alice," Gabe said. "Have a good night."

Alice bobbed her head at him in acknowledgment and then slipped into the crowd like a stylish little fish.

"Traitor," Emmy muttered in her wake. She turned back to her three companions and considered making an excuse for why she needed to leave too, but she saw a glint in Gabe's eye. Something that looked like a challenge. As if he was daring her to see the night through. She knew in one blink if she left, it would be admitting defeat, and she was not about to lose to him. Again.

"Another round?" she said with a cocky tilt of her head.

His lip twitched the same way it had in the conference room the other day. As if he *liked* it when she challenged him. The thought sent a surprising thrill tingling her spine.

"On me," Gabe said as if he had accepted her acceptance of his challenge.

They went with beers, and Emmy was thankful for being able to slowly sip instead of gulp something that tasted like an oak barrel lit on fire.

"Well, that worked out for the best," Pedro said, and wiped the foam from his lip. "No shade to Alice, but her hanging around would have ruined the surprise I have planned for later." A mischievous secret hid in his voice.

Emmy, Gabe, and Silas all looked at him in interest.

"A surprise sounds intriguing, Torres, but the last time I went along with one of your surprises, I ended up in Tijuana at two a.m.," Gabe said.

"Yeah, and I was wearing someone else's pants," Silas said with a flash of his eyes.

Emmy couldn't stifle her giggle. She'd heard stories about that night they'd headed for the border. Something about a dare and a donkey and the best tacos in TJ. The details were hazy, but she hoped, at least for her sake, that Pedro's surprise was nothing of the sort.

Pedro gulped his beer and rolled his eyes. "Relax. No international travel involved this time."

"Then what is it?" Gabe asked.

Pedro shot them a coy grin. "You'll have to wait and see. Another shot to go with these beers?" He already had his hand raised to flag the bartender.

To Emmy's surprise, any *only girl* awkwardness faded away quickly, and soon they were just . . . hanging out. Of course, the copious amounts of alcohol they were drinking didn't hurt in aiding the situation, but still. She was pleasantly surprised to be enjoying herself.

Somewhere around the fifth inning, they got tired of standing and decided to venture in search of a bar with open seats. It was a tall order given the crowd out and about for the game, but Pedro possessed a certain charm that worked in their favor. That was, he could talk his way into anything. The sidewalks teemed with fans, music, cheering. The whole neighborhood turned into a giant block party during home games. An electric booze-and-asada-filled current hummed through it all like lightning.

Although Emmy had ordered as many drinks as the guys had, she wasn't finishing them all like they were. They were equally drunk; it just took her less to get there given she wasn't a six-foot-something, broad-shouldered ex-baseball player who wore jeans like he was doing them a favor. Or was that just Gabe Olson and not every man in their group?

She realized somewhat ashamedly that she'd been staring at his ass in front of her the whole time they'd been walking down the street. She almost tripped when she glanced around to make sure no one had seen. Mortified and in need of a distraction, she pulled out her phone. The little glowing screen danced before her eyes in a blur, but she immediately saw she had an unread message from Axe Murderer. She hadn't heard it ding inside the noisy bar.

> Exciting Friday night?

Her face instantly split into a smile.

> Meh. Out at a work thing. I'd rather be at home.

Hey, me too. To both.

Does your work thing involve guzzling booze
to keep up with your co-workers?

Actually, yeah.

Ha! I thought that was only something
women had to do to be one of the guys.

It's all bullshit if you ask me. I'd never judge
anyone for not wanting to drink.

Noble of you. Are you drunk right now?

Emmy bit her lip, wondering if that was too far. It felt borderline
You up?

Unfortunately.

Why unfortunately?

Because I'm old and know I'm going to feel
like shit tomorrow.

A laugh leapt from her throat. Loudly enough that Gabe and Pedro turned around to look at her. She wanted to climb a nearby tree and hide.

"What's so funny, Jameson?" Pedro asked.

Emmy tucked back her hair that had gone billowy and frizzed in the humid night air. "Nothing."

He frowned at her, his eyes glazed behind his glasses and his cheeks flushed. "With you and Olson grinning at your phones like idiots, I feel like I'm being left out of a joke."

She noted then Gabe had his phone in his hand too, the little screen casting a blue glow on his face. At least she wasn't the only one not fully present.

Gabe locked his screen and shoved his phone back into his pocket. He clapped Pedro on the shoulder. "You're not missing anything, Torres. Now, let's keep this night going."

The second bar was just as loud as the first, but it at least had couches. Pedro watched one like a hawk and swooped in when a group got up to leave. Soon, the four of them sat crowded around a low table littered with empty glasses and juiceless lime wedges. The game was, of course, on every TV.

"Aw, what are you thinking, skip? He's got plenty left!" Silas bellowed at the nearest TV.

Emmy glanced up to see the manager jogging out of the dugout to make a pitching change. She had to agree with Silas: the guy they were taking out for the guy they were putting in wasn't the best move, at least statistically.

"Maybe he has a *feeling*," Emmy said snidely.

Gabe heard the remark that was intended for him and shot her an arrogant glare. "Feelings are valid, Jameson."

They'd sat next to each other on the cramped couch, so when she turned sideways toward him, her knee brushed his thigh. All the booze slowed her reactions. It took her a hot second to pull away and gain her bearings. "Okay, if they are so valid, and we live in a quantitative world, how do you factor them in? Y equals mx plus b, *plus* your *feelings*?" she said with a snort, proud of her supremely dorky joke.

Both Pedro and Silas laughed, and it made her heart fizz with satisfaction.

Gabe rolled his eyes. "It's probably more of a moderation effect, but let's not split hairs."

"Oh, *please*, let us split hairs. I want you to write me an equation that accounts for your baseball spidey senses, since, as you have pointed out to everyone"—she paused and gestured at the group—"I don't have them. As someone who's never *been on the field*, I want to see evidence for how they factor into your models." She found a fresh napkin on the table and the pen the previous party had left sitting on their check tray and sloppily shoved both at his chest.

Gabe scoffed and let the bundle fall into his lap.

Emmy gave him a sad puppy dog pout. "Aww, do you not know how, Olson?"

Pedro snickered. "Drunk Jameson is sassy. I like it."

Emmy looked over to see Pedro and Silas grinning at them, and a wave of embarrassment hit her. At the same time, a wave of badly needing to pee also hit her.

"Be right back," she said as she pushed herself up out of the low couch to stand. She slightly wobbled and noticed Gabe shoot out his hand to steady her. He didn't make contact, but he held it there like a safety rail just in case. "I'm fine," she said on a low breath with a flush in her cheeks.

She wound her way through the crowded room thick with hot air and bodies and turned the corner to find, of course, a line for the bathroom. With a sigh, she leaned against the wall rattling with the bass line pulse of the music next door. While she waited, needing to cleanse herself of the tang of Gabe's arrogance, she pulled out her phone to continue her conversation with Axe Murderer.

You can't be old because we've already established we're the same age, and that would mean I'm old.

He responded as if he'd been waiting for her.

Well, then I can at least take comfort in knowing you'll feel like shit tomorrow too.

Chances are high.

What's your favorite hangover cure?

Greasy food and reality TV. Preferably something spicy and trashy, respectively.

Isn't all reality TV trashy?

Gasp How DARE you. But yes, most of it is, and that's why I love it.

I'm not big on reality TV, but greasy, spicy food is my love language.

The thought of suggesting they meet for breakfast to cure their mutual hangovers temptingly swam through Emmy's mind. The opportunity to take their strange relationship to the next level had just leapt into their laps. Or perhaps they had subconsciously put it there as they were both looking for a way to naturally take the next step and meet in real life.

Reluctance washed over her. What they had, as bizarre as it was, was perfect. Inside her screen, he was everything she didn't know she wanted: funny, sincere, understanding, thoughtful, honest. And she couldn't help thinking he thought the same about her. She didn't want to risk ruining anything by disrupting what they already had. Even if a piece of her ached to make him LOL in real life, to hear the sound of his voice. To touch him.

She was suddenly hot standing in the cramped hall. She squeezed her thighs together, but that only made the need to pee feel worse. She needed another distraction.

> I haven't heard any bird-band puns lately. Hit me.

> I thought you'd never ask. *Ahem* The Beak Boys, Snoop Duckk, and The Pecksies.

> Hmm. Not your best work.

> Well, I did warn you I'm drunk.

> Fair.

"Hey, are you going or what?" someone said, and pulled Emmy out of her reverie.

"Huh?"

A leggy woman with thick dark hair, a cat eye Emmy could only dream of, and a Tide jersey nodded at the bathroom door. "It's open."

"Oh! Sorry. I was distracted," she said, almost dropping her phone when she tried to shove it in her purse.

The woman laughed a warm, throaty sound. "You've got it bad, girl."

Emmy wasn't sure what she had, but she pushed open the bathroom door and locked it behind her. Her feet stuck to the floor inside the small red room that was overcompensating with air fresheners to the point it made her eyes water, but it served its purpose. She washed her hands after and made her way back out into the bar.

"Jeez, Jameson, did you fall in, in there?" Silas joked when she plopped back down on the couch.

She cast him a glare and reached for the beer that had been refilled in her absence.

"I was going to come looking for you if you didn't get back out here and save us from Olson. This fool hasn't stopped staring at his phone since you left." He lunged forward and tried to reach for Gabe's phone, but he yanked it away. "Who are you even texting, dude? Got a new girlfriend?"

"Shut up, Ish," Gabe said, and shoved his phone in his pocket.

Silas only laughed. "She must be special if she can tear your eyes away from the game. You're usually over here running stats on a napkin."

Gabe glowered at him and reached for his beer.

Silas let it go but only because someone hit a home run, and the bar erupted in delirium. Everyone was high-fiving and screaming. The noise from the stadium shook the ground. An inning later, the game ended in a victory, and they shared another round. And then another for good measure.

They eventually left the bar in pursuit of Pedro's surprise. The game might have been over, but outside, the lively night was just getting started. Spirits were high, inhibitions low. Everything sparkled and spun with the special communal joy that only sports could incite.

Pedro had aimed them toward the ballpark. Halfway there, he drunkenly looped his arm around Emmy's shoulders and attempted to whisper but really just loudly slurred into her ear. "Listen, Jameson. Do us all a solid and beat Olson for this promotion, mmkay?"

Emmy, surprised both that he was dangling off her like they were best friends and that he was apparently rooting for her, turned her head toward him. "What?"

"I mean, I like the guy, but—" He glanced over his shoulder to where Gabe walked behind them. "He gets *everything*, you know what I mean?"

Emmy snorted a laugh. "Torres, I am the last person on earth you have to tell that to."

"Okay, fair. I just mean it would be nice to see someone else get a chance for once. And if that someone can't be *me*, then I would rather it be you. You're pretty badass, you know?"

Emmy almost tripped. In shock and because his unsteady weight swiveling against her was like trying to hold up a drunk telephone pole. She cast him a flat frown. "Who *are* you?"

Pedro chortled a belly laugh that made Emmy laugh too. "I am your very drunk co-worker who is being way too honest right now. And since I've started, might as well keep going and tell you that you intimidate me."

She arched a surprised brow at him.

Pedro glanced over his shoulder again and then stage-whispered into her ear. "And don't tell him I told you this, but I think you intimidate Olson too. That's why he can be such an asshole to you sometimes. Gabe *Ruthless*, amirite?"

There was too much alcohol in her system for Emmy to fully un-pack what Pedro had said to her; she'd have to revisit it later, but one part stuck out and pushed a niggling question to the front of her mind.

"Did he really get Mikey Walker fired?"

Pedro took a sobering breath. His voice came back serious. "Lis-ten, I only know what *I* know, but back when it happened, they were branching off the R&A department to be its own thing. Walker and Olson had interned together, and they were both up for a full-time role. And then one day, Olson had a meeting with Alice and the di-rector, and the next day, Walker was gone. For good."

"Shit," Emmy muttered, her fear of Gabe's ruthlessness only am-plified by all the drinks.

"Shit, indeed," Pedro said. "I think under that Captain America exterior beats a cold heart. But I guess that's kinda necessary if you want to win all the time."

Emmy glanced over the shoulder Pedro wasn't dangling off and saw Gabe a few paces behind them tapping at his phone again. His phone's light carved up his face into dramatic shadows that made him look even more menacing.

She turned back to face forward. "Well, I guess I'll just have to put an end to that winning streak, won't I?"

Pedro threw his head back and cackled a loud laugh. "That's the spirit. Use that fire to take him down."

Emmy smiled to herself and vowed she would.

When they eventually stopped walking, it was way past Emmy's bedtime, and they were nowhere closer to her bed that she desperately wanted to collapse into.

"Uh, why are we at the park?" Gabe asked exactly what she was thinking.

Silas lingered behind them with a female companion they'd somehow picked up over the course of the night. She had pink hair, a dozen earrings, and combat boots and was, by all standards, smoking hot.

"Hello," Emmy said to her with a friendly wave.

She silently waved back with a smile.

Pedro cleared his throat with a dramatic flourish and held out his arms. "We are here, dear friends and colleagues, because I have a surprise for you." He checked his smartwatch and then turned around to look at the set of handle-less doors behind him that only opened from the inside. He'd led them to a maintenance entrance at the ballpark. The stadium lights were off, the crowd had dissipated. They were basically in a creepy back alley that would have set Emmy's nerves on edge if she wasn't with a group of people.

"What is it, postgame trash duty?" Gabe said with a chuckle.

Emmy could tell by the sway in his shoulders and the crooked grin on his lips he was drunk.

"No," Pedro said sourly. "We are not picking up trash. Someone in Facilities Management owes me a favor, and I decided to cash in on it." Pedro shimmied his shoulders and gave them a wicked grin.

Emmy gasped at the same time Gabe chuckled a warm belly laugh.

"No way!" he said excitedly.

A similar excitement thrummed through Emmy. Facilities Management meant keys to the ballpark, and keys to the ballpark meant access to places they were supposed to have permission to go.

Like the field.

"Yes way," Pedro said with a proud grin. Right then, the doors behind him opened a tentative crack. A head appeared from inside and looked out at them. "Right on time," Pedro said.

A tall man with dark eyes and hair whom Emmy might have recognized if not for all the booze gave them a nod and waved them in. "We've got to do this quick if we're going to do it," he said.

"Oh, we are most certainly going to do it," Pedro said, and stepped inside.

The rest of them followed into the dim hallway and closed the doors like a tomb sealing shut behind them.

"If you get in trouble for this, it wasn't me who let you in," the man who had in fact let them in said and then disappeared into a shadowy doorway.

Emmy spent every day at the ballpark, but somehow being there after hours and in a restricted zone flipped the mundanity into a daring thrill. She excitedly shoved her way forward and squeezed Pedro's arm. "Can we go on the field?!"

He shot her a flat, sarcastic stare. "No, I broke us into the park to hang out in our office."

Emmy squealed in delight. "This is the best surprise ever!"

They crept through the catacombs of the stadium like the cast of *Scooby-Doo*, peeking around corners and scurrying past cameras. Eventually, they made it onto the field. The sheer scale of it humbled Emmy every time. On the rare occasions she got to put her feet on the grass, scuff the dirt, *feel* the energy of forty-five thousand fans in the seats, she fell in love with the sport all over again. It was no wonder little kids dreamed of one day going pro.

She caught sight of Gabe jogging out to the mound. They'd scooped up a few gloves, bat, and ball on their journey. Gabe tossed the ball to Pedro as he backpedaled, and then caught it when he threw it back. Silas and his pink-haired companion wandered into the out-field to lie in the grass and stare up at the sky.

Emmy wondered if they'd had more than just drinks.

"Let's see what you've got, Gabe Ruthless," Pedro cheered as he jogged to home plate, punching his mitt.

"First off, Babe Ruth was left-handed," Gabe said from the mound, in reference to his nickname's origin.

"Always a buzzkill with the facts, Olson," Pedro said. "Come on, let's see it." He squatted behind home plate as Gabe warmed up his shoulder.

Emmy looked on from the third base line, leaning on their filched bat like a cane.

Gabe stretched out his arm a little more and then went into a windup. The ball flew from his hand with surprising precision given everyone's state and landed with a sharp smack squarely in Pedro's glove.

"Woo! Okay, *okay!*" Pedro sang and stood to throw it back. "The Bambino's still got some heat."

Gabe caught it with a smile and kicked at the dirt. He shook out his arm, ready to go again. The second pitch flew by even harder.

"*Owww!*" Pedro howled with a laugh when he caught it. "You were all-state in college, right?"

"Yeah," Gabe said with another shake of his shoulders. He was warmed up now.

Emmy snorted without even meaning to. "Of course you were," she muttered.

"What's that?" Gabe asked.

She kicked the bat so it swung up onto her shoulder and cocked a hip. "I said *of course you were* all-state in college. I bet your alma mater has a shrine dedicated to you."

Gabe scowled at her as Pedro hollered again.

"Uh-oh! We've got a heckler!"

Emmy used the bat to point at Gabe. "Did you put that on your résumé? *College baseball legend* turned stats nerd? It'll take more than history with the sport to get this promotion."

Gabe shook his head. "You talk a big game, Jameson."

"Oh yeah? I also swing a big game, Olson." She twirled the bat around like a baton and gave him a cocky grin.

"Is that a challenge?" he said with an arched brow she could see even from the sidelines.

"Maybe it is."

Gabe puffed out his chest and threw the ball into his own glove with a close-range snap. "All right, how about this: You get a hit off me, and I'll step aside for the promotion."

Emmy gaped at him, unable to stop her mouth from falling off its hinges.

Pedro cackled from home plate.

Based on the grin stretching Gabe's lips, he was serious.

"You are *that* confident that you'd risk your job?" Emmy said, still blinking in shock.

"Yep," he said, and pointed at the plate. "Go on then. One at bat to see who gets it."

A laugh escaped Emmy's mouth. "I don't know whether to be offended by your lack of faith in me or thankful for your arrogance for giving me this opportunity to so handily destroy you—with an audience." She walked to home plate with the bat in her hand, ready to show him.

"Yeah, yeah, yeah," Gabe said. "Let's see what you've got, Jameson."

Behind the plate, Pedro was grinning like a fool. "This keeps getting better and better."

Emmy squared up in the batter's box and kicked at the dirt, more thankful than ever she'd worn sneakers and not heels.

"You always been a lefty?" Gabe said with a curious hitch to his voice. As if he was suddenly recalling only ever seeing her write with her right hand in the office.

She swung the bat a few times to warm up her arms and hips. "Only in the batter's box. Stop stalling and let's do this." She'd played a few seasons of softball in school, but most of her experience came from days in the backyard as a kid. Her ambidexterity was directly inherited from her dad.

"Okay, you asked for it," Gabe said in a taunt.

"Just throw it," she called back. She squared herself and took a deep breath, trying to remember the last time she'd even swung a bat.

With the stadium lights off, all they had to work with was the surrounding buildings glowing down on them. A marine layer had mottled the sky in a patchwork of gray. Even so, she narrowed her eyes on the ball in his hand. He turned it inside his glove, lining the seams up with his fingers to make it spin a certain way.

Good thing she knew how to read a fastball.

He went into his windup, and Emmy fought to focus through the long lines of his powerful body bending and angling for leverage. She would never admit it—especially to her colleagues—but one of the perks of working in men's sports was getting to watch men do sports. The precision bodies cut like diamonds from all the training. The explosive yet graceful movements. The sheer power of it all. She kept such thoughts locked up with other unprofessional ones—like how good Gabe Olson looked standing on the pitcher's mound right now. Even if he wasn't in the game anymore, he still looked the part.

Gabe turned to face the third base line and then brought his left knee to his abdomen, spring-loading his limbs to explode with motion. The giant step forward he took left his jeans tight on his thick thighs and his broad chest flexed through his T-shirt. Emmy blinked in the split second he was fully extended with his right arm out behind him, ball gripped in his hand, and legs nearly in the splits, shamelessly storing the image in a part of her brain she did not know craved such a view of him until that exact second. Before she knew what happened, the ball sailed past and landed with a sharp smack in Pedro's glove.

"Shit," she hissed as Gabe cackled.

"You know, Jameson, you might want to swing if you're hoping to hit the ball. Strike one!" he called.

Emmy forcibly snapped out of the haze watching him had put her in and reminded herself she had a job to do. "Shut up and throw it again," she demanded as Pedro threw the ball back to him.

"As you wish."

He went into his windup again, but this time she was prepared. Braced for the mesmerizing motion of watching him hurtle a ball with laser precision like his body was a perfectly tuned instrument. He planted his front foot into his wide stance, stretching his limbs as far as they could go, and rocketed the ball at her. The pitch sailed by with just as much speed as the first but sank hard at the last second. She swung, but it was embarrassingly late.

"Strike two! Trying to send that one to Mexico, Jameson?" Gabe roared with laughter. He bent over and slapped his knees. "Might as well hand me the job now."

Pedro stood from his crouch to throw the ball back and whispered, "Dude, I thought we had a deal. *Beat him*, Jameson!"

"I'm *trying*!" she said back.

"He's probably going to go tight on the inside," Pedro muttered. "Belt high."

"Hey! What's all the whispering?" Gabe called. "No conspiring at the plate."

"We're not conspiring!" Pedro called. "We're discussing who's going to take care of the ficus when Jameson moves into her new office."

"Isn't that tree fake?" Gabe said.

Pedro squatted back down and clapped his glove a few times. "All right, batter up, batter up! Two strikes, here we go!"

Gabe rolled his eyes and worked his shoulder again. He bent over and let his arm dangle like a pitcher on TV. His open jersey loosely flapped at his sides; his T-shirt offered the slightest peep of his collarbone at the neck hole given the angle. Emmy thought she saw a slight wince when he straightened to start his windup again, but she couldn't be sure from so far away.

She lasered her eyes on the ball, shaking off all distraction, and could tell from the way it left his hand this time that it was a four-seam fastball. Inside, belt high. Just like Pedro said. In the blink of an eye, she adjusted and angled her hips. She started swinging a split second sooner than last time, and when the ball cracked off the bat and went flying out into right field, she could have done a backflip.

"YES!" Pedro hollered. "Well done, Jameson!" He clapped her on the back and shook her shoulder with a squeeze.

Gabe leaned over with his hands on his knees, staring out into right field as if he couldn't believe what he'd seen.

Silas popped up from where he'd been canoodling with his friend to retrieve the ball and toss it back in. Gabe caught it, still in shock.

"Welp, we'll miss you, Jameson. Promise you'll come back and visit from your new office," Pedro said.

Emmy watched Gabe out on the mound looking stung and stunned. They'd had a bet, and she'd won, but she knew if he took himself out of the running, she'd never live down that she only got the job because he'd given it up, and she wasn't about to stand for it.

She swung the bat back up onto her shoulder. "How about a second wager?"

Gabe's head snapped up to look at her.

She started walking out toward him on the mound. "How about if *you* get a hit off *me*, then our first bet is void, and we go back to normal."

He tilted his head and the stunned look morphed into a sly, cocky grin she knew well as he watched her approach. "Are you sure you want to make that bet, Jameson? I'm pretty sure I could get a hit off you with my eyes closed."

She glared at him and shoved the bat at his chest. "Yes, I'm sure. I want to beat you on merit, not the swing of a bat, because I *deserve* that job."

He flinched at the force of the bat pressing up against him, but he took it with another smug smile. "All right, let's do it." He removed his glove with the ball cupped inside and handed it to her.

They swapped places, Gabe taking a few swings as Emmy threw a few pitches to Pedro. She definitely couldn't throw as hard as Gabe; he had at least thirty pounds of muscle on her. And sixty feet, six inches—the distance from the pitcher's mound to home plate— was a hell of a distance once she was staring it down. But she could throw as accurately. The ball landed smack in Pedro's glove every time, even if it was getting there at a fraction of the speed Gabe had thrown it.

"Not bad, Jameson," Gabe said. "How about we make it interesting, and you have to buy another round when I hit one of these lobs out of the park?"

"If you hit this out of the park, I will buy you a new car, Olson," she said, and stepped back for her windup.

"*Ooh*, deal. Cherry red is my favorite color."

Emmy gave him one final glare and hurled the ball as hard as she could.

Of course he made contact on the first swing. Except it wasn't a mile-high home run. It was a line drive. Straight into her thigh.

She couldn't even blink between the time the ball left her hand, when it hit the bat, and when it smashed straight back into her leg. It was like the fastest pinball ricochet of all time except ten times the size and flying at a hundred miles an hour. A moment of stunned silence passed before the pain set in. Emmy looked down in slow motion and saw a furious red imprint the shape of a baseball stamped into her thigh just below her dress. And then she fell back on her butt and thought she might die.

"*Emmy!* Oh my god, are you okay?!" someone shouted into the night. She wasn't sure who since none of them ever called her by her first name. The sound of hurried footsteps thundered toward her. She was going to get trampled by the stampede where she lay flat on her back. She couldn't tell what hurt more: her leg, her butt from hitting the ground, or her pride.

Her leg. It was definitely her leg.

"Emmy! Emmy, I'm so sorry! Are you okay?"

There was the sound of her name again. Who was saying it? She didn't put two and two together until Gabe's face was hovering over her, creased in concern and framed by the night sky.

"Holy shit, Olson, you *nailed* her!" Pedro cried. "I didn't think you'd resort to physical violence to take out the competition."

"Shut up, Torres," Gabe snapped at him.

Emmy tried to sit up. Her thigh had burst into flames, she was sure of it. The whole limb was dead weight, too stunned to receive signals from her brain to move.

"Don't get up yet," Gabe said, and gently pressed his hand to her shoulder.

Two more faces appeared above her: Silas and the girl with the pink hair.

"Did you hit your head?" Pink Hair spoke the first words Emmy had ever heard her say.

Emmy shook her head and tried to sit up again. "No. Just my butt when I fell. Ouch!" she cried when Pink Hair touched her leg.

"Dude, you can, like, *see* the imprint of the ball's stitching," Pedro said.

"Not helping, Torres," Gabe muttered.

"What are you doing?" Emmy asked Pink Hair as she probed her leg. "Who are you?"

"This is my girlfriend, Mae," Silas said.

"You have a girlfriend?" Pedro asked as Mae pushed him out of the way.

Apparently, Emmy wasn't the only one who didn't talk about her personal life at work.

"Yes. She's an EMT," Silas said.

Emmy winced with another gasp of pain when Mae squeezed

her thigh. "I doubt anything is broken, but you might want to get an X-ray just in case. Otherwise, it will bruise like hell but heal in time," Mae said.

Emmy risked a glance at her leg that was already turning purple. She had a particularly nasty comment ready to hurl at Gabe, but when she looked up and saw the pure anguish on his face, the utter remorse, she swallowed it.

"Jeez, Olson. You look like *you're* the one who just took a line drive to the leg," she said.

"Emmy, I am so sorry. That was a total accident, you have to believe me."

There was her first name again. The sound of it on his lips did something funny to her chest that she might have spent more time thinking about if it weren't for the flaming pain radiating out from her thigh into every cell.

She snorted as Mae scooped her hands under her arms and helped her to sit. "Yeah, I know it was an accident. Like you have that good of aim."

She expected him to smirk, but the concerned crease folding his brow wouldn't budge.

"Here, let's help her up," Mae said. "Do you think you can walk?" Emmy felt the other woman's strong arms boost her off the ground. Surely Mae was accustomed to maneuvering bodies as an EMT, but a second set of hands grabbed her and finished the job with far less effort.

"I got her," Gabe said, and suddenly, Emmy was vertical, feeling blood fight its way to her head and trying to balance on one leg. "Give me your arm." He looped her arm over his shoulders and had to stoop over to support her given their height difference. It was all very awkward and inefficient, but it occurred to Emmy that other than a handshake the day they'd met and the occasional and accidental arm or knee graze, she'd never really touched Gabe Olson before.

The heat of his firm body was a welcome balm in the night that

had grown cool and foggy. She could feel tiny calluses on his palm
where he gripped her wrist on the arm looped over his shoulders.
Their hips kept bumping off each other like buoys with every delicate step. They were making far less progress than the struggle was
worth, but Emmy found herself unwilling to move out of his grip.

"Thank you," she muttered to him, embarrassed for having been
taken out by a baseball and by how much she liked the feel of his
body against hers. She would erase this night from memory for both
reasons.

"I'm so sorry," he said again.

"You can stop apologizing. It was an accident," she said through
gritted teeth. Her left leg was still useless. Its only function seemed
to be throbbing in furious pain.

They'd made a pitiful amount of progress back toward the dugout
when Pedro whipped around from in front of them.

"Um, guys? We gotta go." He pointed up at the field level, where
lights had flicked on. Someone was marching down the stadium steps
with a flashlight.

"Oh shit," Silas hissed from behind them.

Everyone in the group took off running for cover. Emmy felt
Gabe's momentum shift forward on the same instinct, but her body
dangling at his side stopped him.

"I can't—" she said with a shake of her head. "This is as fast as I
can go."

He glanced down at her like a soldier who'd just been told to *save
yourself* by a fallen comrade. His jaw clenched with a determined grit.

And then he scooped her up into his arms.

"What are you doing?!" she yelped in surprise.

"Saving our asses. Hold on."

He began to jog to keep up with the others. He held her against
his chest tightly enough that the bouncing was minimal, but each
time she bobbed against him, it stirred something deep in her belly.
With her arm still looped over his shoulders, she could feel the con-

tours beneath his shirt pressing into her side. Just as she'd always imagined, his chest and abdomen were firm as a slab of rock. Without her permission, her eyes traced the line of his jaw. The way it smoothly connected to his throat inches from her face. The way she imagined it would smell if she touched her nose to it. Oranges, leather, spice. She clung to him tighter, suddenly needing to ease the involuntary burn radiating in her own chest, and she swore she could feel his heart beating against her.

"If you ever tell anyone about this, I will murder you," she threatened, horrified by all of it.

"Don't worry. As long as you don't tell anyone I beaned you with a baseball, I won't tell anyone you needed me to carry you off the field."

She scoffed. "I don't *need* you to do this. You picked me up before I could stop you."

"Kinda looked like you needed me," he said with a grin.

She rolled her eyes in annoyance, knowing he was one hundred percent right and secretly enjoying it.

They made it into the dugout where he carefully carried her down the stairs. He didn't set her on her feet until they were deep into the hidden hall they'd snuck in through. The others had disbanded to take cover elsewhere.

"Can you walk on it?" Gabe asked, only slightly out of breath from carrying her through their escape.

Emmy chanced putting weight on her leg and immediately winced. "Not really."

"We should get you some ice."

"We should get out of here. I don't think getting caught trespassing will bode well for anyone to get promoted."

"True. Want to split a ride home?"

She arched a brow at him from where she'd taken to leaning against the cool concrete wall. He was chewing on his lip and still looking worried. A slow smile spread over her face. "You feel guilty, don't you? That's why you're being so nice to me."

He combed a hand through his hair that had lost some of its hold and huffed. "Of course I feel guilty, Emmy. I could have seriously hurt you. Thank god it was your leg and not your head."

The thought hadn't occurred to her until that moment. *Yikes.* She could have been unconscious in an ambulance rather than goading him over his guilt trip in an underground hallway.

"Well, it wasn't my head. It was my thigh. And if you were going to whack me with a ball anywhere, we can be thankful it was someplace that could take the hit. The only better option would have been my butt."

His lips twitched at the corners. A flush pinked his cheeks like he was suddenly thinking about her butt. "Are you still drunk?"

"I certainly think so. Otherwise, I would not be handling this situation very well. I might have hit you with the bat."

He quietly laughed and swiped his hair again. "You know, your hit was really impressive."

She narrowed her eyes. "Why do I feel like you are actually complimenting yourself right now?"

He laughed again, and Emmy found herself enjoying the sound and concluded she had to be really, *really* drunk to be getting along with Gabe Olson.

A door clanged shut somewhere in the distance, and they both jumped.

"Come on. Let's get out of here," Gabe said.

They hobbled their way out of the ballpark and found a rideshare. Gabe made sure Emmy got to her building's door safely, and once she assured him she could handle the elevator *and* she owned a bag of frozen peas to use on her leg, he let her go.

It wasn't until Emmy had made a snack, drunk a gallon of water, and collapsed on her couch with said frozen peas on her leg that she managed to look at her phone. She had an unread message from Axe Murderer from a few hours before. Given the night's events, she couldn't even remember where their conversation had left off. Based on his message, she quickly recalled she'd told him his most recent bird-band puns weren't up to snuff.

> Hootie and the Bluefinch, Doja Catbird, Cawmilla Cabello.

Emmy instantly smiled and laughed.

> Much improved.

Guilt prickled at her for messaging so late, but it dissolved as soon as he responded.

> Why are you still up?? I thought you went to bed at like 10.

> I told you, I was out with co-workers tonight.

> Until 1am?!

> God is it that late?

> Yes, we are well into regretting our life choices tomorrow territory now. And I guess I shouldn't be talking because I just got home too.

> Tsk-tsk, Axe Murderer. Did you score any more fake phone numbers tonight?

> No. I'm in an exclusive fake number texting relationship already, so not looking anymore.

> You mean with ME?!

> Who else, Bird Girl.

She knew they were just drunk bantering but couldn't fight the warmth spreading slow and thick in her chest.

> Well, I am honored. Shoutout "Lacey" for the bait & switch that started it all.

> She did me a solid.

His dots disappeared, and Emmy's eyes drooped closed. The strong current of sleep was ready and waiting to pull her under. She popped back awake when her phone buzzed again.

> But in all seriousness, I've never talked with anyone the way I'm able to talk to you, Bird Girl. These past several days have been the best I've had in a long time.

A slow smile unzipped across Emmy's face. She was tired and tipsy, and he was making her feel all sorts of warm and fuzzy to the point that a confession she'd hardly admitted to herself bubbled to the surface.

> Wanna know a secret?

> Desperately.

> You're my favorite part of every day.

Her eyes fluttered closed again, and she let the warm, heavy feeling of having told him the truth sink her into the couch. Another buzz popped her awake again.

You're mine too.

The pain in her leg had almost disappeared. She smiled again. She managed to hit the heart reaction to *love* his message before she fell asleep.

Chapter 7

The color of Emmy's bruise when she woke the next morning landed somewhere between the *Exxon Valdez* oil spill and a strawberry. On close inspection, it looked pixilated. As if the blood vessels had burst and frozen in place. And Pedro was right: she could in fact see the ball's stitching imprinted on her leg. It was nearly a tattoo. Needless to say, it was hideous. At least the pain pounding her muscle and bone like a jackhammer with every movement took her focus off the fact that her head was full of cotton and screaming with a hangover.

She usually spent at least part of Saturdays working from her couch, but her throbbing body quickly informed her there was no chance of that happening today.

Showering was herculean but helpful. By the time Emmy hobbled to the couch, hair wrapped in a towel and coffee mug in hand, she wanted to drop a bomb on whoever was daring to buzz at her door.

The building's security system synced with her phone. She pulled open the app to see a black-and-white video of the entrance. She frowned at the sight of none other than Gabe Olson. He held a takeout bag in one hand and chewed his bottom lip, looking nervous. He knew where she lived thanks to them sharing a ride last night, but she couldn't fathom why he'd shown up at her door on a Saturday morning. Making him sweat out the wait for her response gave her a small bit of satisfaction.

Simply curious, she pressed the button to answer his call. She could see him, but not the other way around. "Olson? What are you doing here?"

He visibly jumped at the sound of her voice. He eagerly leaned into the wall, drawing his face closer to the video screen and, consequently, the camera. At least he looked puffy and haggard with a hangover too. She would have been even more annoyed if he'd shown up with his standard magazine model glow. "Hey! Hi. I was in the area and thought I'd stop by with breakfast. You know, in case you were having trouble getting around this morning."

Emmy's frown deepened, wondering if this was some kind of trick.

"I'm not trying to trick you, Jameson," he said, like he'd read her mind. "This is a sincere gesture." He held up the bag with a crooked smile. It softened Emmy into a more pliable form. Or perhaps it was her growling stomach that did the trick.

"What's in the bag?" she asked.

"Best chilaquiles in Old Town."

Her mouth watered. She was not going to turn down her favorite breakfast food. Even if it was being hand-delivered by her archnemesis.

"Fine. Bring it up."

She caught the flash of his grin as she hit the button to unlock the building's front door. While she waited, she sat back and gazed out her living room window, a little dazed Gabe Olson was on his way up to her apartment. She'd slept until nearly 10 a.m. The morning sun was well on its way to brightening another perfect SoCal day. If she hadn't been hobbled by a co-worker, she might have taken a stroll to the farmers' market before getting to work.

And then it hit her all at once that *Gabe Olson was on his way up to her apartment*.

She jolted upright, nearly spilling her coffee. "Oh shit!" she hissed. She pushed up off the couch and untangled the towel from her hair. With the most accuracy she could muster for a shapeless, wet object, she hurled it down the hall toward her bedroom. She looked down at her outfit: pajama shorts and a Fall Out Boy T-shirt, standard Saturday morning garb, and considered changing. But then she realized she didn't *really* care what Gabe Olson thought about her appearance when he was the one showing up unannounced on a weekend morning after a night out getting smashed.

And besides, her shorts put her spectacular bruise on full display, and she didn't mind the idea of giving him a reminder of why she was laid up on the couch to begin with.

She kept her apartment tidy, but she hadn't yet put away signs of her 1 a.m. arrival. Her Chucks sat by the couch, laces tangled like noodles. Her purse spilled over on the coffee table from when she'd upended it in desperate need of lip balm while icing her leg. The kitchen island still held a plate and knife smeared with peanut butter from when she'd made toast before bed in an attempt to sop up the liquor still floating her brain.

As quickly as she could, she scooped the contents of her purse back inside and set it on her island, wiped crumbs from the granite and put the plate and knife in the sink, kicked away the towels mopping up Tom's still-leaking sink from the floor above, and twirled her damp hair up into a sloppy bun. She tossed her shoes by the front door right in time to hear her doorbell ring.

She limped over and took a breath, bracing herself for the oddity of seeing a co-worker outside of business hours. It was like seeing a teacher at the grocery store or a dog walk on two legs.

When Emmy opened the door and saw Gabe Olson standing there in the flesh—gelled hair, tight tee, boat shoes, and a pair of shorts—a funny feeling fluttered in her chest. He stared back at her for an oddly gentle moment. And then his eyes dropped to her leg.

"Oh, *damn*. Look at that thing!" he said in greeting.

Emmy frowned. "Good morning to you too."

He responded with a half grin. "Sorry. It's just impressive, that's all."

"Again, why do I feel like you're complimenting yourself?"

"I'm not. I promise. Token of my penance?" He held out the bag with a guilty grimace.

The smell of chilaquiles hit Emmy like a truck. She almost started to drool. She took the bag and noted the weight of multiple to-go containers inside it. "I accept. Also, if this is from Old Town, you weren't in the area; that's miles away. Also also, why are there two servings in here?"

The guilt on his face only multiplied. "I may have gotten something for myself too."

"Ah, well. You shouldn't have handed it over then. Mine now."

He scoffed. "Jameson, come on. Give it back or invite me in."

She suspiciously narrowed her eyes at him. "You really want to come in and eat breakfast with me?"

Gabe squeezed the back of his neck with a shrug.

"Wow, you must feel *really* guilty," she said, and dropped her hand from where she'd been holding the door. "Going all the way to Old Town for food then volunteering to hang out? Fine. Come in, I guess."

He followed her inside and let out a low whistle. "Wow, nice place."

Once they passed her office / guest room, the entryway of her corner apartment gave way to an open living room / kitchen area with floor-to-ceiling windows on each wall. The view was half the reason she lived there.

"Thanks," Emmy said, and placed the bag on the island. She had no room for a dining table, so all her meals took place seated at the barstools lining her island. Well, there, or on the couch in her pj's.

"How's the leg?" Gabe asked as she gingerly sat on a stool with a wince.

"Not great but better than last night."

"I'm still really sorry."

She untied the take-out bag and lifted out the top carton. "Yeah, I can tell." The smell wafted out in a mouthwatering tease: eggs, tortillas, salsa, onions—chorizo if they were lucky. She noted when she opened the box with a smile they were, indeed, lucky. "For the record, I will take this form of apology any day."

Gabe pulled his own box out of the bag and fished out plastic forks for each of them. "Noted, though I don't plan on smashing any more line drives into your legs."

"Appreciated," Emmy said around a luscious bite. "Good thing my maid of honor dress for my sister's wedding is long, otherwise she'd hunt you down herself for ruining the aesthetic she's had planned since she was twelve."

Perhaps it was the food distracting her or her still thriving hangover or the fact Gabe Olson was sitting at her island sharing breakfast with her, but she didn't realize she'd breached her *no personal stuff* rule until the words were out of her mouth.

"Your sister is getting married?" he asked with an interested tilt of his head.

"Yes," she said, suddenly feeling vulnerable and exposed.

"Huh. I don't think I even knew you have a sister."

"Yeah, well, I don't talk about my personal life much at work."

"No, you don't. I didn't even know you were left-handed until last night."

"Only in the batter's box," she reminded him. "And I'm not the only one who keeps personal things to themselves. Did you know Ishida has a girlfriend?"

A muffled laugh pushed out around the bite he was chewing. "No. Not until last night. Did you?"

"No idea. She was nice."

"She was."

They chewed in silence for a few beats. She wasn't about to give him the pleasure of knowing, but these were quite possibly the best chilaquiles she'd ever had.

"What about you, Jameson?" he asked. "Are you seeing anyone?"

Emmy almost choked at his question. Not only were they sharing breakfast in her apartment, now he was asking her about her relationship status. As with many things with Gabe Olson, the question felt like a challenge. He was going to somehow one-up her by saying he was dating Miss Universe or something. So, in a reflexive move of self-preservation, she told him a half truth.

"Yes. Kind of. It's still very early, so nothing official yet." Her face burned at the mention of Axe Murderer.

He turned to her and finished his bite. A tiny spec of salsa clung to his lip.

"What?" she asked. "What's that look?"

He shook himself like he was snapping out of a haze. "Oh, nothing. It's just, well, I'm at that stage too."

"Oh?" she asked, ignoring the confusing twinge in her chest. It was probably heartburn again. She was eating spicy food after all.

"Yeah," he said. "Still very early. But, like, kind of awesome."

A rare glimpse of vulnerability flashed over his face. Emmy saw it come and go like a wave scurrying onshore only to recede back into the tide. Something about it felt familiar though she couldn't say why. The most vulnerable she'd ever seen Gabe Olson get was when the Tide had made the playoffs. Admittedly, they'd all gotten a bit misty-eyed that night.

"That's cool," Emmy said for lack of a better response. She simply could not believe she was discussing love lives with Gabe Olson. She stabbed another bite. "Do you want it to be official?"

"That's rather personal."

"You're the one who brought it up."

"Fair," he said, then filled the air with a contemplative pause. "I don't want to say, because I don't want to jinx anything."

Emmy normally would have rolled her eyes because the seriousness of his tone matched with a silly superstition like jinxing was worthy of an eye roll. *But.* She admittedly felt the same way about Axe Murderer, so she gave him a pass.

"I get that."

They ate in silence again, and when Emmy took a swig of her coffee, she realized he had nothing to wash down his breakfast with.

"Do you want some coffee? Juice?"

"I'll take some coffee, sure."

Emmy shifted to slide off her stool and immediately winced.

He popped up when she made a pained sound. "I'll get it. Sit tight."

She was in no position to protest, so she lowered herself back to sitting. "Thanks. Mugs are in that cabinet." She pointed and watched him circle the island into her kitchen. His shirt was tight enough she could see the muscles in his back. She gobbled another bite of chilaquiles for distraction.

"You know, if it's any consolation, my shoulder is wrecked from last night," he said as he chose a pod from her K-Cup selection. "You're not the only one who got hurt."

She tilted her head in question. "From pitching?" As soon as she said it, the image of him lunging on the mound hit her in a place that would have made her sit up and cross her legs if not for her injury.

"Yes." Gabe moved his shoulder in a circular motion and squeezed it with his other hand.

"You threw, like, five pitches."

"Yeah, well . . ." He trailed off with a sad shrug. "That's what happens when you have a career-ending injury and then get drunk and go act like it never happened to try to impress your co-workers."

Emmy slowed her chewing and looked at him in surprised interest. "Wait, what?"

His coffee finished brewing with a gurgle, and he turned around to gather it. "I played ball in college, right?" He turned back to face her from the other side of the island. He propped himself on his hands in a way that popped out the muscles in his arms.

"Yeah . . . ?" she said with an upward inflection, curious to know where he was going and needing a distraction from the sight of his arms. His personal life was as mysterious as hers.

"Well, I was also a cocky piece of shit in college who thought he was invincible. I got in a car accident and broke my collarbone." He reached for his shirt's collar and pulled it aside, revealing the contoured curves of his muscular shoulder and part of his chest. Emmy almost gasped at the visible scar cutting a three-inch line over his skin like a little railroad track. "Changed everything," he said with a single shake of his head.

Emmy reeled. Several pieces shoved their way into place. "Is that why you——?"

"Never went pro? Yeah. Well, assuming I could have made it, but the chances were looking good. Kind of let down the whole family. It was my parents' dream to see me play professionally." His face bent into a sad shape Emmy could tell was well worn.

"Wow, Gabe. I'm sorry."

His sadness shifted into something softer and warm.

"What?" she asked at the curious new look on his face.

"I don't think you've ever called me by my first name before."

A heat wave washed over her. She hadn't even realized she'd done it, and it brought back the memory of how she'd liked the sound of her first name coming from his lips last night, which then, of course, made her think about his lips. She quickly deflected with a scoff. "That's because you all have trained me to only use last names at work. I bet half the people in the organization don't even *know* my first name."

This pulled a tiny laugh from him that Emmy hated to admit she liked the sound of too. "That's probably true. I guess it's just part of the culture."

"Boys Town," she muttered into her coffee mug before she took a sip.

"What's that?"

"Nothing. There's milk in the fridge if you want it for your coffee, but fair warning: it's oat milk."

He scrunched his face into a sour pinch. "I'll pass. I take it black anyway."

"Black like your soul."

He threw his hands to his heart and dramatically pouted. "You wound me, Jameson."

She sputtered a dramatic sound, half grinning despite herself, and spun on her stool to lift her leg. With both hands, she pointed at the inkblot on her thigh. "You *literally* wound me, Olson."

Gabe blushed in shame, and Emmy couldn't help noticing his eyes trace the outline of her thigh from her hip to her knee. He bit his lip, and she dropped her leg.

"Sorry. Bad joke," he said. "Anyway, my arm is out of commission for a while."

"Well, good thing there isn't a pitching contest involved in getting promoted at work."

He smirked at her, but it was half-hearted. Beneath the customary sass, she could see the vulnerability she'd glimpsed before. For some inexplicable reason it compelled her to expose some of her own vulnerability.

"My brother played baseball," she said quietly.

Gabe turned to her with an intrigued look. "I also did not know you have a brother."

"Had," Emmy said on a near whisper.

"What's that?"

She took a breath and forced herself to walk through the door she'd opened. "I said *had*. I *had* a brother. He died when I was a teenager."

His face fell into a look of sincere sympathy. The kind that stabbed right at her wounded heart, and one of the main reasons she didn't talk about Josh much. "I'm so sorry, Emmy."

"Thanks. My love of the game comes from him. He was older, and I grew up watching him play. He and my dad were always playing catch in the backyard, and I used to make them let me join." She softly smiled at the memory even though it had grown faded and blurred.

If she looked hard enough, she could see Josh's smile, feel his big hand mussing her hair, smell the leather of his old glove he gave her. But if she looked too hard, she saw too much, and her heart circled back around to hurting. His injury, his recovery, the struggle she didn't understand—the struggle none of them understood, honestly—until it was too late.

"What position did he play?" Gabe asked, and she appreciated the question much more than the one she usually got: *How did he die?*

"Shortstop. He was one of those ballerina-on-the-field types."

"Ah, yes. I know those. The ones who can catch anything and look good doing it."

A warm smile lifted Emmy's face. "Yep, that was Josh!"

Gabe did a double take. His eyes bugged out and then zigzagged over the island like he was putting pieces together before he looked up at her. "Wait, your brother was Josh Jameson? *Josh 'JJ' Jameson?* How did I not know that?!" He looked more disappointed in himself for not making the connection than in her for not telling him about it.

She shrugged a shoulder. "Because I don't talk about it."

"Um . . ." Gabe trailed off, and she knew he was remembering headlines from over a decade before.

SUPERSTAR SHORTSTOP'S BRIGHT FUTURE CUT SHORT

JOSH JAMESON REMEMBERED FOR HIS BRILLIANCE ON THE FIELD

ALL-STAR ROOKIE FOUND DEAD OF OVERDOSE AT 23

Those headlines simplified the truth about how Josh had hurt his back making one of those highlight-reel-worthy catches and had been prescribed painkillers to recover. And how those painkillers woke a sleeping darkness in his brain that consumed him. The news didn't cover how Emmy's mother begged him to end his season and go to rehab, or how her father pushed him to fight through it, and how this drove a wedge between them. Or how Emmy and Piper, only sixteen and thirteen at the time, couldn't understand why their beloved older brother had become someone else. How his moods darkened, and his temper grew short, and why he'd call them in the middle of the night from the road, leaving slurred messages about how much he loved and missed them, and had they watched the game on TV that night? *Of course* they had. They watched every game just to see him. He always winked at them from the batter's box. And then one day, he wasn't there. Someone else took the field at shortstop, and her parents got a call Josh had been found in his hotel room that morning. And then, he was gone. Just like that.

Emmy's mother disowned the sport. Her father retreated into himself, taking blame for pushing his son to keep playing, having no idea he was driving him deeper into his addiction. Piper took their mother's side, shattered by the loss. Emmy shattered too. Into a million tiny pieces she could only begin to put back together by devoting herself to the one thing she and Josh loved most. Baseball.

She felt Gabe eyeing her, not really sure how to come back from delving into her painful past. In fairness, she didn't know either. And that was part of the reason she avoided the topic.

He eventually cleared his throat and nodded at the TV she'd left playing across the room. "What were you watching?"

She turned to see a shot of an attractive couple handcuffed to each other while struggling to assemble furniture. "*Name Your Price*," Emmy said.

Gabe circled back around the island to his stool. "Is that the reality show where they make people do shitty things for money?"

Emmy snorted a laugh. "Yeah. I love this show. In this episode, these exes are trying to live locked in the same house together for a month for a million dollars. He's an actor, and she's an entertainment writer, and they had this big dramatic breakup that went viral a while ago."

They swiveled their stools to face the TV as they finished breakfast. They forked mouthfuls and laughed at the contestants' misfortune as they tried to tolerate each other through a series of increasingly intimate challenges under the same roof.

When the episode ended, a wave of sleepiness hit Emmy, thanks in large part to her full belly and the fact she'd slept in a mostly drunken stupor the night before and needed real rest. She yawned, and Gabe took his cue to leave.

"I should get going," he said, and it struck her as odd all over again he was even in her apartment to begin with.

Had she really just had breakfast with Gabe Olson? Was she perhaps still asleep and drunk dreaming? Was he about to go sailing in his boat shoes and shorts?

"Got a boat to catch?" she joked and nodded at his shoes.

He combed a hand over his sculpted hair and quietly laughed. "Actually, yes. My cousin owns a charter company that does tours of the bay. One of his crew had to travel to go help with a family thing, so I've been stepping in as his replacement."

"That's generous of you."

He casually shrugged like it was no big deal. "Yeah, let's just hope I don't lose my breakfast into the bay after last night."

"Seasickness isn't a very good quality in a sailor."

"Indeed, it is not." He scooped up both of their empty cartons and found her trash can at the end of the island. "Thanks for the coffee."

"Thanks for breakfast."

"Sure—oh! I almost forgot." He reached into his pocket and pulled out a folded napkin. "The equation you wanted to see."

Emmy unfolded the paper square she'd shoved at him last night and saw a complex string of Greek letters and mathematical symbols written in ink. She recognized the equation as one they used to calculate a player's overall standing, except Gabe had added a new term that weighted the score differently.

"I figured out how to quantify my feelings," he said with a sly grin. "Feel free to run that model on Hollander and see what you get."

A mix of emotions crashed inside her. Surprise he'd dragged work into their otherwise pleasant conversation, annoyance this was a smug display of his signature one-upping, and most of all confusion, because she admittedly found a man handing her a math equation he'd invented at her request unbearably hot, and the fact that that man was Gabe Olson left her unsure what to do with the flutter in her chest.

Sass seemed like the safest route given all of the above. "I will," she said with a skeptical tilt of her head.

He smiled at her. "See you Monday."

"Bye," she said with a small wave.

Gabe let himself out, and Emmy limped back over to her couch. She deflated herself with a heavy sigh and reached for the remote to select what would keep her company for the next several hours. The desire to get her laptop and run his model flitted through her, but her hangover squashed it. She could get to it tomorrow. She'd landed on a dating show with an absurd but addictive premise when her phone pinged with a message.

Axe Murderer.

With an instant smile, she opened it.

> How are you feeling today?

> Like shit, as expected.

> Same. At least I had some greasy, spicy food to sop it up.

> Same! And now I'm bingeing *exceptionally* trashy reality TV.

> Sounds like your dream day.

> The only thing missing was a text from you 😌

Happy to provide my services. How was your night? Is the hangover worth it?

Is it ever? But you know, all things considered, it was a good night.

I take it you weren't expecting it to be?

Not really. Honestly, I tend to struggle with my co-workers. I don't really fit in, but my boss has been encouraging me to try harder.

I get that. I struggle with everyone. I spent my formative years playing competitive sports with a group of built-in peers, so I never really had to try to build relationships. Now I'm not good at it. At least that's what my therapist says.

Emmy softened at his vulnerable message, feeling special he was willing to share with her.

I think you're pretty good at whatever we're doing here.

Again, you are the exception, Bird Girl. The one-in-ten-zillion chance "Lacey" made up a string of numbers that happened to belong to you is the best luck I've had in a very long time. Maybe ever 😊

MVP "Lacey"

Bird Girl?

Yeah?

What ARE we doing here? (Not all-caps
shouting at you, just impatiently waiting
for the day they implement italics in
text.)

Emmy quietly laughed as she thought about how to respond. She
knew he didn't mean what were they doing commiserating about
their hangovers. He meant what were they doing texting each other
a hundred times a day. They were getting to know each other. They
were flirting, obviously. Being vulnerable. Spilling their hearts. Having deeper conversations than Emmy had had with anyone in a long
time, maybe ever. Denying they were doing *something* would have
been an insult to her feelings.

And yet.

She knew despite the way her heart took off galloping every time
she saw his name, the safety barrier of the screen was what was allowing her to be so open. Without that, she wouldn't have the guts to
tell him half the things she had—and she liked telling him things and
didn't want to do anything to jeopardize it.

We're taking it slow.

A decent pause passed before he responded, but when he did,
Emmy's heart settled.

Okay 😊

She smiled at the smiley face and saw him continue to type.

> Well, I'd happily stay here and talk to you all day, but I have to go get ready for the family stuff I volunteered for. Happy recovering, Bird Girl.

> Have a good day, Axe Murderer.

She rethought the heart—it was a big leap from a smiley face—but her thumb tapped it before her mushy brain could stop it. Her nerves over sending it dissolved as soon as he *loved* it with his own heart reaction.

On Sunday, despite her insistence she needed to catch up on work after her day of recovery, Emmy found herself at a yacht club in La Jolla. One with yawning windows overlooking the crashing waves and a view of Scripps Pier darting out into the cove like a trestled needle. If she looked closely enough, she'd probably see dolphins frolicking in the surf. It was someplace she never thought she'd be, but that was before her sister had gotten engaged to the West Coast version of a Rockefeller.

Ben's family had biotech money. *Loads* of it. The Carmichaels were cliffside-mansion, Tahoe-ski-lodge, fifty-foot-sailboat, blue-blood-with-a-surfer-tan rich. It was only fitting Piper would marry a prince, and Emmy was as thankful for Ben's levelheadedness as she was for his humility in the face of such obscene wealth.

He drove a Jeep and wore Levi's and played beach volleyball.

He also had champagne brunches at yacht clubs and made gooey eyes at her sister while he twirled the tumor-size family heirloom engagement ring he'd given her around her polished finger.

Piper had invited Emmy to join them that morning (more like in-sisted she join and guilted her over working too much), and by the third time they leaned in to rub noses and sweetly murmur about how they *couldn't wait to be husband and wife in two weeks,* Emmy pulled out her phone to text Axe Murderer.

> SOS. Family thing is killing me right now.

> Shall I send in the cavalry? Bob Marley and the Quailers, The Storks, Sheryl Crow.

Emmy sputtered a laugh and disguised it with a sip of her mimosa.

> Sheryl Crow isn't a pun. That's just her name.

> You're right. That one is a throwaway.

> Do better, Axe Murderer . . .

> You caught me off guard.

> Why? Are you being tortured at the hands of your insufferable relatives too?

> Not today. I'm actually on my way to the ball game.

Emmy sat at attention. A fleeting thought of heading to the ball-park and somehow geolocating him in the sea of fans by his cell phone ping swept through her mind. But that only happened in mov-ies, right? She *did* have someone in IT who owed her a favor but cashing it in on this might lead to too many questions.

The thought of telling Axe Murderer she worked at the park and could get him all sorts of special access if he wanted flashed through her mind too, but that would be *way* too revealing. All he'd have to do was look up the front office directory and narrow down the list of the few dozen women among the hundreds of employees to find her.

But *did* she want him to find her? Was it time?

"Oh my god, are you working?" Piper scolded and interrupted her thoughts.

"What? No," Emmy jerked her head up and said too quickly.

Piper suspiciously eyed her reaction and then grinned. "Then you're texting him again, aren't you?"

Emmy reddened. She had reluctantly widened her circle of trust about Axe Murderer to include her sister and was suddenly regretting it based on the mischievous look on Piper's face.

"No, I'm not," Emmy said.

Piper gave her a dismissive eye roll and turned to Ben as if their pending marriage meant the circle by default included him too. "Babe, Em met this guy because someone fake numbered him at a bar, and the number happened to be hers. Now they've been texting for, like, over a week because they are *perfect* for each other. Isn't that weird but also really cool?"

Ben tore his eyes from his fiancée's face for the first time all brunch and smiled at Emmy. "No way! What are the odds?"

"Actually, they're—" Emmy started to say because she had run the numbers again and had something slightly more precise than *astronomical* to report now, but Piper cut her off.

"Isn't it sweet? I'm *obsessed*." She suddenly gasped and bounced in her seat. "*Ooh*, Em! Invite *him* to the wedding!"

Ben's smile widened. They looked at her like a pair of golden retrievers, tails practically wagging.

Emmy set her phone on the table with a sigh. "I can't do that."

"Why not?" Ben said with a tilt of his head in perfect golden retriever fashion. His sandy hair even flipped over like an ear.

"Because it's . . . complicated."

"What's complicated about it?" Piper said. "You need a date and you're *clearly* into this guy based on the look on your face every time you text him. Sounds simple to me!"

"I agree," Ben said with a nod. "I think you should go for it, Em."

Emmy glared at him, for once not appreciating his reflex to appease his future wife. "You're just saying that to keep her happy."

He leaned back in his chair and threw an arm around Piper's tanned shoulders left bare by her sundress. "Yes, as is my duty."

Piper squealed a joyful little sound and leaned in to rub his nose with hers again.

Emmy thought she might choke on the syrupy emotion gushing out of them at lethal levels. "You guys need to dial it back. Seriously. I know you're getting married in two weeks, but the sweetest thing in here should be the crullers." She picked up the sticky pastry on her plate and took a bite. The glaze was called something pretentious like *Amalfi lemon zest*, but it was divine. She washed it down with another gulp of mimosa and did almost choke when her sister snapped out her hand and grabbed her phone.

"Fine. *I'll* invite him for you."

It might have been the fastest Emmy had ever moved in her life. She dropped her mimosa flute, knocking it over into Ben's lap, and reached for her phone in Piper's hands. Her nimble fingers had already started typing by the time Emmy ripped it away.

"Piper! No!" Her shrill cry turned a few heads as Piper jerked back.

Ben popped out of his seat to deal with the spilled drink and politely waved at the guests of his same ilk looking on as if he'd brought two heathens to brunch. Surely his parents would hear about their abhorrent behavior.

"Jeez, Em. Chill out!" Piper said. Her face flushed with embarrassment.

Emmy's heart was pounding so hard her hands shook. Adrenaline shot through her body like lightning as she assessed her sister's damage. The message to Axe Murderer had at least been cut off, but what did exist of it would be hard to explain.

We should

Her speeding heart sank. The statement had an obvious ending, and she could only imagine what thoughts were running through Axe Murderer's mind right now. If she had snatched her phone away one second later, Piper would have successfully finished the invitation: We should meet.

Axe Murderer's typing dots didn't appear, and Emmy wasn't sure what it meant. Was he panicking like she was? Was he . . . hoping? Her stomach flipped with worry on both counts.

She convinced herself he hadn't replied because he was busy. Perhaps driving to the ballpark or picking out his lucky jersey to wear.

She glared at Piper. "I can't believe you did that."

Her sister's face was still an embarrassed pink, probably because people were still staring. "You didn't have to overreact, Em," she scolded under her breath.

Ben was still standing and blotting his pants with one of the embroidered napkins thick as a sail. "I'm going to run to the restroom and give you two a minute. I'll be right back." He pressed a kiss on the top of Piper's head. She gazed up at him with an apologetic look and mouthed *Sorry*. He mouthed back *It's fine* and softly smiled before he walked away.

Guilt punched Emmy in the gut for making a scene. "I'm sorry," she said to Piper once they were alone. "I didn't mean to cause a scene, but you shouldn't have done that."

Piper pinched the stem of her champagne flute and twirled it between her fingers. "I'm sorry too. I shouldn't have grabbed your phone, but I was only trying to help."

"Well, let's hope you didn't cause irreparable damage," Emmy replied with a sigh. She glanced at her phone again. Still no response.

Piper laid her hand out palm-up on the table in a show of penance. "Em, what's the big deal? You like this guy, right? Why don't you just ask him to meet?"

Emmy twisted her lips, battling wanting to tell her the truth and fearing how desperate it might make her sound. But if she could be stripped down and vulnerable with anyone, it was the person she used to take bubble baths with as a kid. "Because everything so far has been perfect, and I'm worried if I meet him in person, it won't be anymore. Not to mention, I don't know how I'd have time to start something with someone given work and the promotion and the fact that—"

"If you're about to say you *can't have both*, I have to stop you right there. Just because that dickwad Jacob told you that was the case, it doesn't mean it's true. I mean, you spend hours every day texting this guy already, so in a way, you've already figured out how to have both."

Emmy paused, not having thought of that. Piper was right: she did spend a fair chunk of each day tapping away at her phone screen with Axe Murderer. But even then, the convenience of texting was different from being in a relationship. They could come and go around their schedules with no commitment or pressure. Even with the undeniable connection they had, what would happen if he didn't like how she prioritized her time in real life?

"I don't know, Piper. What if meeting him in person ruins everything?"

"But what if it doesn't?" Piper said with an excited flash of her eyes. "What if it's even *better* than what you have right now?" She glanced over her shoulder and leaned in. She lowered her voice and spoke out of one side of her mouth. "I mean, I don't know what kind of sexting you've been getting up to, but you know, the real thing can't really compare."

"Piper! Ew!" Emmy said with an embarrassed laugh. "Please don't ever talk to me about sexting again. You are my *baby sister*!"

She threw up her hands with a grin. "What! I'm only speaking the truth!"

Emmy had a mind to wad up her napkin and throw it at her but surely that would earn them another scandalized glare from the nearby diners. Instead, she let out a long breath and felt honesty bubbling up to the surface. "I guess I'm just . . . scared."

Piper's face grew as serious as Emmy had ever seen it. She leaned in again, lowering her voice once more. "Em, you think I'm not scared? You think I'm not *fucking terrified* of this world I'm marrying into?" She picked up a shiny silver fork. "Is this a dinner fork? A salad fork? I have no idea! And this shit *matters* to these people! I don't know what I'm doing half the time and always worried I'm going to say the wrong thing, but you know why I'm still here? Because I love Ben. He's worth every second of it. I may be scared, but I know he's got my back no matter what." She reached out and gripped Emmy's hand. "Maybe your guy is scared too, and the two of you have to make the leap together. And when you do, you'll realize there's actually nothing to be afraid of because you've got each other's backs."

Emmy stared at her little sister in awe. She'd never heard her express such feelings about the world Ben lived in. Given her princess obsession dating back to childhood, she'd always assumed Piper was born ready to step into the glass slippers. Looking at her sitting across from her now with sun-kissed skin, a beachy blowout, diamond studs in her ears, and a classy Sunday dress, Emmy couldn't help but see the little girl she used to play dress-up with. At the same time, Piper looked like a grown woman who knew exactly what she wanted.

Emmy squeezed her hand back, feeling a rush of affection for her and a sense of wanting to protect her from anything she might be afraid of. "For the record, you don't look scared," she said. "You look like you belong." She meant it as a compliment, and based on the glowing smile on Piper's face, she took it as one.

"That actually means a lot to me to hear. Thank you."

"Thank *you*. For saying all that. How'd you get so smart?"

"I have a good role model," Piper said, and squeezed her hand again as Ben returned.

"Are those new pants?" Emmy said when he approached. She'd been fully prepared to apologize for making him look like he'd had an accident, but in place of the awkward crotch stain she expected, she saw a pair of navy chinos he had not been wearing when he left the table.

"Yes. I had a fresh pair in my locker." He kissed Piper's head again on his way down into his chair.

"Ah, yes. As one does at a yacht club," Emmy said, and toasted him with the fresh mimosa their waiter had set on the table.

Piper shot her a glare before she shifted into a grin. "Speaking of *boat stuff*," she said, and shimmied her shoulders. "I am *so* stoked for next weekend."

Ben lovingly tucked her hair behind her ear, showing off the rock of a diamond stud he'd given her as an engagement gift. "Next weekend? Oh, right. The bachelorette party."

"Yes!" Piper sang and clapped her hands. "Emmy booked us a booze cruise. The besties and I will be partying on a boat all night. No boys allowed." She booped him on the nose and scrunched up her face.

"Please just don't end up needing me to bail you out in Mexico," Ben said with a teasing sigh and a glance at Emmy.

Emmy held up her hands in innocence. "I am not the captain. I'm only the party coordinator."

"And it's going to be one hell of a party," Piper said, and bounced her brows before diving into her fresh mimosa.

Chapter 8

We should
    We should
We should

Emmy spent most of the next week rereading the half message her sister had sent. Axe Murderer hadn't responded, and the thought she'd scared him off only confirmed her fear that meeting in person was a bad idea.

At the same time, work had become grueling. With the trade deadline fast approaching, they were buried day in and out. Requests would come down from the GM to their director, who'd then pass them to Alice, who'd pass them to the data analysts, and Emmy, Gabe, Pedro, and Silas would hole up in their cave cranking out predictive models to aid in decisions. Emmy still hadn't had time to run Gabe's *feelings* model, although she was curious about it. Trying to outdo each other and earn as many gold stars as possible, they stayed later than everyone else. Even with the office empty, they remained, glassy-eyed and glued to the dim glow of their computer screens. He returned from a long lunch one day clearly having gotten a haircut, and because he stayed late to make up for it, Emmy stayed late too. She refused to throw in the towel before him and ended up leaving the ballpark near midnight three nights in a row. It paid off when Alice commended her latest report in a department meeting, which earned her an approving nod from Director Allen.

The consequent icy glare from Gabe was a cherry on top, but in truth, all of it served as distraction from worrying she'd ruined things with Axe Murderer.

By the time she collapsed in bed on Friday night, Emmy thought she was too tired to do anything but sleep. Her leaping heart quickly corrected her when she got a message from Axe Murderer.

> So, I've spent all week wondering if there's an end to that last text . . .

She sat straight up with her heart in her throat and blinked at her screen. Her hands trembled. She had no idea what to say. She'd figured if he ever responded, he would gloss over that text, and they'd pretend it never happened, like eating an entire cake by oneself or spending a whole paycheck on a new handbag. Directly confronting it had not entered her mind as a possibility. Was he bringing it up because he knew what the message implied and wanted to go there? Did he *want* to meet her?

The thought broke a clammy sweat over her skin. She almost went into cardiac arrest when he sent another message.

> I've also been wondering if it was a butt dial and you've been trying to figure out how to backtrack it.

The sigh of relief that escaped Emmy could have inflated a blimp. She found herself smiling softly at her phone and much more relaxed about talking to him since he'd given her an out.

> Hey. Sorry for the silence. Work has been wild this week. But you're right. My sister actually sent that message. She took my phone to write to you and managed to text that before I stopped her, and I wasn't sure how to come back from it.

Her heart had eased into a calmer rhythm, but it quickly picked up pace again when he didn't immediately respond. What was he thinking? What was he going to say?

Eventually, he came back with:

> You told your sister about me?

Emmy quietly laughed.

> That's what you took from all that?

> Yes. I mean, it's kind of a big deal.

He was right. It was a big deal she'd told anyone about him.

> I guess you're right. I did tell my sister. And my best friend.

> Wow. Not to sound full of myself, but TWO people know about me?

She blushed and pulled her knees up to her chest, grinning like a schoolgirl at a sleepover.

> Yes.

> Well, I am honored. And if we're making confessions here, I have to tell you that THREE people know about you.

Her pumping heart positively soared to the moon.

> One-upping me, I see. Who are these 3 people?

> My sister, my mom, and, oddly, my barber.

His mom? His *mom* knew about her?!

A literal squeal snuck from Emmy's throat, and she was glad no one was there to hear it. She composed herself to send back another message.

> Wow. Barber. That's a big step.

> Indeed.

She tapped her thumbs on the sides of her phone, not sure what to say next. She'd been reluctant to admit what they had was more than just a texting thing, but it was clear it was. They'd both told important people in their lives about each other. Emmy may have been out of the dating race, but she knew that meant they were already beyond casual.

And she knew in the past week of silence, she'd missed him.

Her phone buzzed with another message.

> So?

> So, what?

A measurable pause passed. Emmy's mind filled it with a thousand tiny pricks of nerves. She felt herself standing on a very high ledge with one foot dangling out over the deep expanse below. The thought of falling in was at once terrifying and thrilling, and he was poised to push her. She was almost certain she knew what he was going to say. And sure enough, he delivered.

Should we meet?

And with that, she felt herself fall. Gravity pulled her down at the same time something far more amiable lifted her up. The tug-of-war left her twisting and turning in indecision over the potential outcomes: hit the ground or hope he caught her before the bone crush.

She thought about what her sister had said. They had to jump together, and he had just jumped.

But the thought of joining him stilled Emmy with too much fear.

She hadn't planned to meet anyone. She was buried at work—and trying to get promoted on top of that. Her sister's wedding was in a week, and she still had to make it through the bachelorette party this weekend and find a date. Yes, asking Axe Murderer to be her date was a solution glaring at her with the obviousness of a sunburn, but what if that turned out to be a disaster? What if she felt no in-person attraction when she saw him, and then she was stuck with him for a long weekend nearly three thousand miles from home and having to explain to everyone how they'd "met" and navigate what was sure to be a painfully awkward situation for all involved?

Again, she heard her sister's words: What if it was better than what they had texting?

Her data-driven brain tried to write an equation to figure out if that could possibly be true. Given what she knew of him, what was the probability their experience would enhance if they took it to the next level? Yes, he was charming, funny, thoughtful. He was obviously close with his family despite what he'd told her about his parents' dashed hopes for his future. He knew his way around a pun like no one she'd ever met. And on that note, he was easier to talk to than anyone she'd ever met. But was that because all their communication had been through a screen? Would their chemistry translate face-to-face?

Emmy was about to open a spreadsheet and assign numerical values to her pro/con list and literally write an equation to determine next steps when another text came through.

> No pressure. Sorry. The timing finally felt right to me seeing that my hang-ups are communication and finding a connection, and we've established we're pretty on fire with both of those things.

Emmy softly smiled at his sincere and accurate message.

> You're right, we are 😊

> But . . . ?

She sighed and knew she could be completely honest with him.

> But this is perfect. I don't know about for you, but talking to you is the best thing in my life right now. Aren't you worried things will get ruined if we take it to the next level?

> See, when you say things like "the best thing in my life right now" it makes me want to scour the city door-to-door until I find you.

Emmy chewed at the smile on her lips.

> There are a lot of doors in this city.

I am a tenacious man.

And a patient one.

Indefinitely.

The conversation paused for a few moments. Emmy wondered if he was waiting for her to change her mind. He eventually came back with a long message.

But listen, I don't mean to pressure you. Honestly. I know your hang-ups are harder to work through than mine. (If I ever meet your ex, trust that I will have choice words for him!) So, I will be ready when you are. But please know it's taken enormous strength not to even ask for a picture of you. (Hint hint.)

She quietly laughed in relief when she realized he wasn't going to push her. And she had thought about the picture thing—she longed to know what he looked like, but crossing that boundary was nearly as hazardous as meeting in person. Exchanging photos would shake the status quo of what they had, and clearly, given her reflex to turn their relationship into a math problem, she was not ready to disrupt anything. Yet at least. And thankfully, he knew that without her having to tell him.

Thank you.

Of course, Bird Girl. I'm here. And I'll tell you where to find me IRL if and when you want to know. 😊

And with that, Emmy turned over and went to sleep feeling like there was no way he'd ever let her crash when she eventually jumped.

Saturday night brought the event that had been in the making nearly as long as Piper's princess wedding fantasies. The bachelorette party. Knowing her sister would want the penultimate step before she officially became a Mrs. filled to the brim with stereotype staples—booze, boas, Team Bride sashes, a veiled tiara, phallus-shaped everything—Emmy went all out.

She, Piper, and eight of Piper's closest friends—five bridesmaids and three co-workers who'd been invited to the wedding—made for a party of ten at a downtown restaurant. Emmy had shelled out extra for a private room, thankfully, because the noise reached a deafening level after the first round of drinks. Ten women in dresses and heels with a rainbow of party favors with Piper as the all-in-white star of the show were hard to miss. Once they'd all showered her with praise and envy (*Look at that rock! My god!*) and gift bags of see-through lingerie that was too scandalous to give her at the bridal shower, they piled into rideshares to make their way to the harbor.

Emmy had booked three hours on a boat that would ferry them around the bay, from the Coronado Bridge over to Point Loma and back. It had an open bar, snacks, a playlist she'd carefully curated and transported on an iPod to hand over to the crew, and their own private, floating dance floor.

The only hiccup in the otherwise perfect night was the wind. San Diego Bay sat nearly entirely protected from open water given its shape, but as soon as they stepped onto the correct pier in the harbor, all ten of them glommed together into a huddle with a shiver.

"Are there heaters on this boat?" Piper asked as she squeezed herself against Emmy. The two of them brought up the rear of the pack, clacking along the dock toward their boat behind the fragrant cloud of feather-boa-draped, laughing women in front of them.

"Yes," Emmy said. It was something she'd confirmed with the company in the event of this exact scenario. She knew her sister would not want to sully her bride-to-be outfit—a strapless white minidress with a lace bodice—with a jacket simply because they were going out on the water. The day had been warm, but a wind had whipped up and turned even the bay a little choppy.

"Good," Piper said with a clatter of her teeth. Emmy worried she was unhappy about the weather despite it being out of anyone's control, but then she lit up and squealed at the sight of the boat bobbing alongside the dock. "Oh my *god*! It's *perfect*!" She hopped a little skip as they fell in line behind the other women making their way up the gangplank.

Their modest-size charter—it comfortably fit thirty people; Emmy wanted plenty of room to move—floated alongside the pier trussed up like a little Christmas tree. At her request, the crew had outfitted it in sparkling lights and streamers. A banner with gold letters exclaiming *Congrats, Piper!* hung over the covered dance floor section at the stern. Bundles of balloons hung like shiny grapes from the ceiling and poles.

"It does look perfect," Emmy said with a smile.

Piper squealed again and squeezed Emmy's arm. "Thank you *so* much, Em. I love it! You are the best MOH ever!"

The reflex to roll her eyes surprisingly did not hit Emmy at her sister pronouncing the acronym. She was too wrapped up in the night's spirit and honestly having a great time.

"You're welcome, Pipes."

They boarded the boat, and Emmy glanced back at the city behind them. The wind at least was keeping the marine layer away, leaving the downtown lights glittering in an array of heights and colors. The moon lazed in a thick crescent above it. The USS *Midway* loomed gargantuan and mighty at the next pier over. The historic aircraft carrier and museum permanently docked in the bay made their boat seem comically small by comparison, and at seeing it up close,

Emmy wondered as she did every time how something so large even managed to float.

"Welcome aboard, ladies," a voice called from up ahead. "Please, make your way to the front of the boat for some safety instructions before we get underway."

They followed instructions, *oohing* and *awing* and clinging to one another for warmth and support as they left dry land for the wobble of water. Emmy had intentionally worn block heels for that exact reason. She wasn't about to snap an ankle or fall overboard in stilettos because she'd had a few drinks on a boat. Judging by the communal sway of the other women and the strength with which her sister gripped her arm, she was pretty far behind the rest of them on drinks anyway. Which was also part of the plan. Someone had to make sure the night went off without a hitch, and as MOH, that duty fell to her. But on the outside, she looked the part for the party.

Her sparkly emerald-green cocktail dress hugged her curves and had a daring slit up her thigh. She'd braided her hair into a wreath with a few dangling tendrils, knowing the ocean air would frizz it into a cloud if she didn't take precautionary measures. She'd donned a purple feather boa and carried a tote bag with the rest of the party favors she'd saved for after dark and the iPod with the playlist. She was *ready*.

Except, when she and Piper fully stepped onto the boat, she froze in shock.

"Oh my god." Emmy gasped at the sight of a man in a tight black polo up ahead. She knew those arms. And that hair. And that charming smile he was giving everyone who walked past.

What the holy hell was Gabe Olson doing on her sister's bachelorette party boat?

Emmy blinked in complete shock several times, trying to make sense of what she was seeing. She wasn't drunk enough to be imagining it. It was him.

The urge to hide hit her like a truck, but there was nowhere to go unless she dove overboard, and she'd spent way too much time on her hair and makeup for that. Out of desperation, she tried to seal herself to the boat's cabin wall but only succeeded in nearly tripping her sister behind her.

"Whoa! What are you doing?" Piper said, and reached out to balance herself.

"Sorry," Emmy hissed. "It's—" She cut off and leaned over to peer down the walkway toward the front of the boat as far as she could without being seen.

"It's what?" Piper said, and leaned over too.

Emmy's heart was positively pounding, and she suddenly wished she'd partaken in the dinner cocktails as much as everyone else to numb the shock of seeing her co-worker in the absolute least expected place on earth.

How was this even happening?

She nodded toward the bow of the boat. "That guy up there? The one in the black shirt? That's Gabe Olson. From work."

Piper's face folded in confusion as she leaned to look. Then her eyes popped wide. "Wait, *that's* Gabe Olson? That absolute *thirst trap* standing up there by the captain?"

"Yes! Stop staring." Emmy clawed at Piper's arms to pull her back.

"Sorry. It's just, you never mentioned he's a total smokeshow. *Damn*, Em. I pictured some stats nerd with questionable hygiene and smudged glasses. More like Gabe the *Babe*." She was practically drooling.

"Piper!" Emmy said. "Remember your fiancé? Ben? And that your pending marriage to him is the impetus for this party?"

Piper tore her eyes away and shook herself. "Right. Sorry. But what's your work nemesis doing on my party boat?"

Emmy was wondering the same thing. Was it some kind of prank? Had he followed her? Why would he even do either of those things?

And then she remembered what Gabe had said to her that morning they had breakfast in her apartment.

"His cousin owns a charter company, and Gabe's been helping out

because one of the crew is away dealing with family. Oh my god."
She knocked her head back on the cabin wall as the pieces clicked
into place. "I had no idea it was *this* charter company. Pipes, I'm so
sorry."

Piper frowned. "What are you apologizing to me for? I don't have
a problem with the guy unless he's being mean to you, in which case,
I'll shove him overboard if you want me to."

The tempting idea spun a circle in Emmy's mind. The thought of
Gabe Olson bobbing in the bay on a chilly night was rather appealing. But if he was on the boat in an official capacity, assaulting a crew
member was probably grounds for losing her security deposit.

"No, that won't be necessary."

Piper squeezed her hands with a smile and shrug. "Fine. Then let's
ignore him and have a good time."

Emmy wasn't sure how she was supposed to have a good time
while trapped on a boat with Gabe Olson—especially since the
thought of him seeing her wearing one of the glow-in-the-dark penis
necklaces she'd ordered for the occasion made her want to curl up
and die.

But her sister vibrated with excitement beside her, ready to get
the party started. And Emmy would not ruin her sister's party.

She took a deep, determined breath and continued walking. "Okay."

They joined the rest of the women, who'd flung themselves on the
cushioned seats lining the open deck at the bow like a pride of feral
cats. Emmy couldn't help noticing them all staring at Gabe and the
captain and all but licking their lips. Honestly, she couldn't blame
them.

The captain wore a captain's uniform complete with epaulets and
a white cap. On closer inspection, Gabe's shirt had the charter company logo stitched over his heart. The sleeves still cuffed his arms in a
way that made Emmy bite her lip. He otherwise wore black pants and
the same boat shoes he'd had on in her apartment when he'd come
over for breakfast the previous Saturday.

She wondered if it was physically possible to go three hours on a small boat without running into him. Chances did not seem high.

The third member of the crew was a stocky woman with sleeve tattoos and a pixie cut. She wore the same shirt as Gabe and an apron, which Emmy assumed meant she was the bartender.

"Ladies, welcome aboard," the captain said. "I'm your captain, Carl. You can call me Captain Carl." He held out his arms in welcome and smiled at them all. Emmy immediately saw the family resemblance. Even if he hadn't been standing beside Gabe, it was there in his winning grin, his dark but sparkling eyes, his arched cheekbones. The Olson family ran flush with good genes. She could tell Carl was older, maybe by a decade. He wore signs of a sea life on his face: crinkles at the corners of his eyes, sun-darkened skin, a peppering of gray in his stubble. Every bit of it worked in his favor.

After his introduction, the flock of women responded with a flirty chorus of, *"Hi, Captain Carl,"* followed by bubbling giggles.

"Hello," he said with a chuckling laugh. "I'll quickly introduce the rest of the crew here. This is Gloria, who will be helping you with food and drinks." The woman gave a friendly wave and smile. Carl gripped Gabe's shoulder and shook it. "And this is my first mate, Gabe."

The sound of his name drove a sharp spear of reality into Emmy's brain. Until that moment, she'd still hoped it was a bizarre hallucination and Gabe Olson wasn't actually standing ten feet away from her looking like an ad for luring a bunch of horny women onto a booze cruise. But alas, that was exactly what was happening.

"Hi, Gabe," the chorus sang, and Emmy felt a confusing stab of . . . what, jealousy? She couldn't be sure, but when Gabe gave them a shy wave and full on blushed, her belly flipped in a surprising and traitorous way.

"Hi, ladies," he said.

Captain Carl clapped his hands. "Okay, so a few safety instructions before we head out. You've probably noticed the wind picked up tonight, so things are a little choppy out there. I'll keep us close to the shore to limit too much motion, but please be extra mindful of using the rails and watching your step. We don't want anyone going overboard because then Gabe will have to jump in after you, and that would mess up his hair." He reached over and tried to muss Gabe's signature gelled wave, but Gabe fought him off with his arm. Someone wolf whistled and a few others cheered like the idea of being rescued sounded appealing.

That same stab hit Emmy again.

Captain Carl laughed. "I'm kidding. But in all seriousness, we're here to keep you safe while you have fun tonight. So, some ground rules . . ."

They all listened as he described safety instructions and demonstrated how to use a life vest. Emmy had sat with Piper in the back of the crowd, and she kept her eyes on Gabe during the whole presentation, praying he didn't notice her. By some miracle, he didn't.

She thought she was in the clear and could spend the rest of the night avoiding him, until Captain Carl said, "All right, that about covers it. Now, where's the maid of honor who planned this whole thing? We need that playlist so we can plug in and get moving."

A cheer rose from the boozed-up bridesmaids ready to continue the night as all heads swiveled to Emmy.

Piper pushed her up out of her seat and hollered "She's right here!" to cheering.

The moon suddenly shone on Emmy like a spotlight. The universe narrowed to the short distance between her and Gabe, and if she thought perhaps he wouldn't recognize her in a dress and heels because he only ever saw her at work in jeans and computer glasses, she was sorely mistaken. She couldn't tell if his look of shock was due to her appearance or simply the utterly unbelievable coincidence they were on the same boat. He blinked like imminent roadkill. His lips popped open. No one except her noticed how intently he was staring at her, and to his credit, he kept the sheer shock contained.

"Excellent," Captain Carl said. "If you'll just share that list with Gabe here, we'll get underway. Ladies, the boat is open."

The group collectively threw their arms in the air with a cheer.

Gloria stuck her hand up as well. "Follow me to the bar!" she called over the sound, knowing exactly what they all wanted.

The group filed into line to make their way to the back of the boat, where the dance floor and drinks waited. As they cleared out, the space between Emmy and Gabe got emptier and emptier, with fewer excuses for not interacting.

Piper noticed. She squeezed Emmy's arm before she followed the rest of their guests, leaning in to quietly speak. "Offer still stands to push him overboard. Let me know if you need me."

Emmy chortled a strangled laugh, tempted again. "Thanks. But I'll be fine."

"Good. Because I'm going to go get shit-faced." She winked and sauntered off.

And then it was only Emmy and Gabe staring at each other from across the bow.

He seemed unable to peel his eyes off her. She felt them touring her bare legs and the slit in her dress. They bounced up to her face, and he swallowed hard. "Hey." His voice came out gravelly and half there. He cleared his throat and started again. "Hey. I didn't know you were part of this party tonight."

"Hey," she said back, absolutely thrumming with awkwardness. "You didn't tell me your cousin owned this charter company."

"I didn't think I had reason to," he said, still looking stunned.

They kept staring at each other, adrift in a strange space in so many ways.

"So," he eventually said. "The music."

"Oh, right," Emmy said, honestly having forgotten they had a job to do.

He waved her over. "Follow me."

She followed him toward the main cabin where he turned into a small enclave lit up with a wall of radio and PA equipment.

"iPod?" he asked, and held out his hand.

She fished it out of her tote bag, momentarily mortified when it tangled on a glow-in-the-dark penis necklace she frantically shoved back down inside. From the tiny laugh that escaped his lips, she knew he'd seen it. "Here you go," she said, a bit flustered, and presented it to him.

"Thank you." He plugged it in and tapped the screen. "Which playlist?"

"There's only one on there." She'd purchased the device specifically for this purpose because she liked the idea of gifting it to her sister after the fact as a keepsake from the night.

"Got it," he said, and hit play.

When throwback Britney blared out of the speakers to a roaring cheer, Gabe and Emmy stared at each other. A sense of embarrassment curled inside Emmy's belly; she wasn't sure why. There was nothing inherently embarrassing about Britney or booze or penis necklaces, but somehow all those things in front of Gabe Olson made her want to leap into the bay and swim to Mexico. Maybe it was because professional boundaries governed their relationship. He'd toed that line when he brought her breakfast after clobbering her with a baseball, but that was different. This was him seeing her fully exposed on a night out with friends and fully embracing the femininity she worked so hard to shield them all from at work.

As if he were reading her mind, Gabe gave her a shy but sincere look. "Emmy, um. I know you're here for your sister's party and this night is supposed to be fun, so just ignore me, okay? I'll stay out of your way."

She appreciated him saying it and felt a twinge of guilt for being so obvious in her discomfort.

"Thanks," she said. She turned to join the party when a thought made her turn back. "Oh, could you—?" She cut off, embarrassed by the request.

"Could I what?"

Her face had become a lit fire again. She desperately needed to visit Gloria at the bar. "Could you please not tell anyone at work about anything that happens here tonight?"

"Hey," he said, and pretended to twist a key in front of his lips. "What happens on Captain Carl's boat stays on Captain Carl's boat."

Despite herself, she laughed in relief. "Thank you."

"Enjoy the party."

Emmy did enjoy the party. At least until she heard the unmistakable sound of someone puking halfway through.

She'd limited her own alcohol intake as the responsible older sister while the bride and everyone else got hammered. They'd danced, they'd belted 2000s pop classics, they'd eaten cupcakes with purple penis sprinkles. With the boat's heaters and all the booze, they'd created quite the cozy little island on their dance floor. Outside of the pocket, the wind whipped and left the water restless with whitecaps. Emmy didn't realize how much the boat was rocking until she left the dance floor to head to the bathroom.

On her way back, she heard the telltale retch and splash of someone hurling overboard. The thought of ignoring it tempted her to keep walking, but what kind of MOH would that make her if she didn't hold back someone's hair in her moment of need?

Gripping the handrail, Emmy breached the pocket and braved the chilly air on the starboard side of the boat. She looked both ways when she entered the walkway—forward, toward the bow, and backward toward the noisy party—and expected to see one of her sister's scantily clad friends losing her dinner over the rail, but instead she saw someone else.

"Olson?" she asked toward his dark shape slumped over the rail. Gabe held his forehead in one hand and leaned on his other forearm. Spray from the rough water splashed up onto him. He turned at the sound of her voice, and even from a distance, Emmy could see the complete misery on his pale face.

"*Oh god,*" he muttered and leaned back over the rail. "Please don't watch me puke, Jameson."

The agony in his voice drew her toward him. "Are you okay? Do you need something?"

He squeezed his eyes shut like it was taking all his strength not to heave again. "Yes, I need this boat to stop swaying and I need you to please leave me alone."

She reached across the walkway to the rail he was leaning on and firmly gripped it. He was right; the boat was swaying out here. "You know," she said as she carefully inched her way toward him, "it's much less choppy back where we are."

"Yes, but I told you I'd stay out of your way." He spoke through gritted teeth and then blew out a long, slow breath.

Emmy jerked back in surprise. "Wait. You're out here puking because of *me?*"

"No. I'm out here puking because I get seasick."

She reeled in further confusion. "Then why . . . are you on a boat?"

The poor guy deeply inhaled and squeezed his eyes shut, not in frustration but in an effort to soothe his illness. "Because Carl needed my help." He rushed out the words in a single stream before breathing deeply once more.

Again, she inched closer. Her hand gripped the rail half a foot from him. "You mean you volunteered for this job knowing you'd get sick?"

"I was hoping I wouldn't, but yes. It's not usually this rough out here." He squeezed the rail again as they hit a wave and a splash of mist leapt up to greet them.

Emmy reeled for a whole different reason. "Wow. That's incredibly selfless of you."

"Maybe, but I'm starting to rethink it. *Oh god.* Please don't stay here for this." He leaned over the rail again, and before she could stop herself, she reached out and pressed her hand to his back and gently rubbed.

"Hey, you carried me off the field when I couldn't walk. This isn't as bad as that."

"Jameson, this is like, *a million times* worse. Please."

She continued to rub small circles on his back and noticed the terrain was as muscled and firm as expected. "You know, I thought you were just being dramatic about getting sick when you mentioned it that morning in my apartment."

"I wish."

"Have you always gotten seasick?"

"Yeah—that's what kept me out of the navy, unlike Carl."

"He was in the navy?"

"Yes. He's not just a tourist cruise boat captain."

"Oh, so he's like, a *captain*, then."

"Right."

"Well, I think it's really sweet of you to lend him a hand despite your condition."

"Why are you being so nice? How drunk are you right now?"

"Unfortunately, not at all. Someone has to Big Sister this party, and it looks like my services are needed beyond the gaggle of smashed bridesmaids back there, lucky for you."

"What services?"

"You haven't puked since I've been out here, have you?"

He pushed himself up to standing straight and faced her. In her heels, Emmy's eyes hovered closer than normal to his. His eyes were bloodshot and his face pale and clammy but, *damn it*, he was still so good-looking. How dare he, truly. If she'd been the one hurling over the rail, she'd have been a frizzy, sweaty, ghostly white nightmare. Probably with puke in her hair. But Gabe Olson even made seasickness look good.

"You're right, I haven't since you've been out here." He glanced back like he'd only then noticed her palm rubbing circles on his back.

She stopped the motion and dropped her hand. She awkwardly smiled at him. "Well, glad I could be of help."

He did his best to muster a grateful smile, but it came out more of a grimace.

The boat hit another wave, and they both stumbled. Her footing slipped out from under her, and she slid straight into him. The firm wall of his body stopped her, and before she could get her feet back under her, she was pressed against him with his hands gripping her upper arms.

"Sorry," she muttered.

"You all right?"

"Yeah. Who knew a boat in heels would be a bad idea." She stiffly laughed.

"Um, I think everyone knows that, Jameson."

When she looked up at him and frowned, she found a cheeky grin on his lips. "Glad to see you're feeling well enough to insult me, Olson."

He fully smiled at her, and she realized only then they were still standing chest to chest.

"You going to let go of me now?"

A deep flush filled Gabe's face with all the color the seasickness had robbed from it. He dropped his grip and took a step back. "Sorry."

Emmy didn't have time to process the curious feeling of regret brought on by his sudden absence before they hit another wave. They mirrored each other in gripping the rail, and while it only sent Emmy slightly stumbling, it drained Gabe's face again and put a miserable crease between his brows.

Emmy reached out and patted his arm. "Come on. Come sit with me. You'll feel better. It won't be weird. Well, I mean, there are tiny purple penises everywhere, but what are you going to do on a bachelorette booze cruise?"

He weakly laughed. "You sure?"

"Yes. Just keep in the corner so they don't think you're a stripper or something. They're pretty rowdy right now."

He laughed again. "Duly noted. And, Jameson? Can this little episode be a secret too?"

She pretended to twist a key in front of her lips like he'd done earlier. "Captain Carl's boat rules."

"Thank you."

They spent the rest of the cruise sharing a couch at the back of the boat, Gabe sipping ginger ale and Emmy promising everyone who came and asked her to dance she'd be right there, and then never getting off the couch because they forgot after a minute anyway. Gabe quietly laughed every time she lied, and it became a running game to see if anyone would remember she'd made them a promise. No one did, and by the time they returned to the dock, half the party was passed out and the other half declaring the night was young and making plans to continue in the Gaslamp instead of going home.

Thankfully, Piper was in the pass-out camp, and Emmy would not have to supervise any more debauchery because she, too, was ready to peel off her party outfit and climb into bed.

Captain Carl stood at the top of the gangplank as they deboarded and bid each of them good night. Gabe stood at the bottom back on the pier looking profoundly thankful to be on solid ground and held out a hand to help each of them off the boat.

By that point in the night, Piper walked barefoot with her shoes dangling from one hand and her veil tiara slipping from her messy hair. Emmy had her propped against her hip, nearly dragging her like a rag doll, until they hit the end of the gangplank and she saw Ben there waiting for her. Emmy had texted him a heads-up to come collect his bride to put her to bed.

At the sight of him there in his jeans and windbreaker and floppy hair blowing in the breeze, Piper gasped and took off running for him. *"Baaaby!"* she shouted, drawing out the word.

"Oof," he grunted when she leapt into his arms. Piper wrapped her

long legs around his waist and smashed her lips to his. "Hi there," he said between kisses.

"Oh my god, babe, we had *so* much fun, but I missed you," Piper slurred and kept kissing him like she'd been away at sea for years.

Ben struggled to hold her and simultaneously remain on his feet after her near tackle. "Yes, that's great, Pipes. I missed you too. Honey, your dress is kind of short for this—? Okay." He did his best to shield her butt with his hands as she clung to him and kept kissing him. Luckily, it was only Emmy left with a view from behind as she was the last one off the boat. Gabe stood behind her and politely averted his eyes.

"Piper, you're flashing the pier," Emmy said as she paused to scoop up her tiara that had fallen on the concrete.

Piper untangled her legs from her future husband and slid down his body to stand with a wobble. "Sorry," she said with a coy bite of her lip.

Ben smoothed his rumpled clothes and kissed her head. "Sounds like it was a good party?"

"It was the *best*," Piper said, and swung around to grip his shoulders. She dangled from him once more. "And get this," she said, turning around to sloppily point at Gabe. "This is Emmy's co-worker. The guy from work who she *hates* and who always takes stuff from her that she deserves because he's a dude and she's a girl. His cousin owns the boat, so he's randomly here. But it wasn't that bad? I don't know. I kind of lost track. I'm sleepy. Can we go home now?" She said it all in a mortifying spray of drunken babble, and Emmy wanted to shove her off the dock.

She felt her face turn red and couldn't bear the thought of turning to see the look on Gabe's.

Ben, ever polite and easygoing, laughed it off and extended his hand. "Please excuse her; she's had a lot to drink. I'm Ben. Nice to meet you."

"Gabe," he said, and shook Ben's hand.

"Well, sounds like it was a great night. I better get her home." He gave them another breezy, Prince Charming smile and then scooped Piper up into his arms.

She squealed in delight and kicked her bare feet. "Good night, sister! Thanks for the party! I love you!" she called down the dock as she left Emmy standing there in the wake of her damage.

Part of Emmy wanted to keep walking and pretend it had never happened. But a bigger part of her, one prickling with guilt and shame, forced her to turn around.

Night had completely fallen. The lights out on Coronado twinkled in the distance. Only a few boats bobbed on the water. The pier sat quiet other than the soft rush of nearby traffic and the sound of Emmy's own heart beating in embarrassment.

Gabe watched her from close by, an unreadable look on his face.

"I'm sorry she said that," she offered. "She's really drunk, and I don't . . . um. I don't hate you." The words were feeble and strained, and she surprised herself by saying them at all, but as soon as she heard them aloud, she knew they were true.

She didn't hate Gabe Olson.

He, on the other hand, looked unconvinced. And that somehow made what her sister had said all the worse. He gave her a stiff nod. "Okay, Jameson. Have a good night." Then Gabe turned and marched back up the gangplank to help clean up their party.

Chapter 9

By Monday evening, after a day of awkward silences and side-eyes from Gabe all day at work, Emmy had changed her mind about meeting Axe Murderer. Her sister's wedding was in five days, and she could not face her ex without a date. It may have been her guilt over putting that look of hurt on Gabe's face on Saturday night, but she wanted redemption. Seeing as how he was avoiding her like the plague at the office so she couldn't even apologize, her best bet for pulling her mood out of the gutter felt like setting up a meeting with someone who currently held her in high regard. Someone who, as she still thought of him, might have even considered her perfect.

All that perfection might come crashing down when they met, but at least it existed in some capacity.

But if she was going to do it—actually take the leap and agree to meet—she couldn't do it alone. Not to mention, she'd complicated matters by waiting so long to invite him. With the wedding this weekend, her suddenly agreeing to meet might come across as a little too convenient, and she didn't want that. No. She needed coaching. She needed help. So, Monday night after work, she invited over her resident dating app and digital communication expert for dinner and drinks.

Now, against the backdrop of Emmy's living room windows, Beth paced with a glass of wine in her hand. They'd plotted a plan of action, and Beth was reiterating it like a general giving battle orders.

Emmy sat cross-legged on her couch taking deep breaths and intently listening.

"Okay, so. Since the wedding is now short notice and a travel commitment, you need to lead with that. Obviously, you guys are going to need to meet in person before you bring him as a guest, so it will be a natural progression." Beth sipped her red wine that was the same color as her leggings.

"But what if he wonders why I waited so long?" Emmy asked, her voice full of nerves. "The last conversation we had was me telling him I'm not ready to meet, and now I'm asking this enormous favor of him at the last minute."

Beth held out a hand, considering. "True, but you said he said he's willing to go door-to-door to find you, so I somehow doubt he won't jump on a romantic getaway."

"Favor," Emmy corrected.

"Mm-hmm. Call it what you want," Beth said with a casual flip of her hand. "Now, let's do this."

Emmy took a steadying breath. "Okay. Where do I suggest we meet?"

Beth held up a finger and sipped her wine again. "Someplace public, obviously. Neutral territory. Safe. I mean, the guy's name is Axe Murderer, so there's a chance this could all still go to shit."

Emmy frowned at her. "That name was a joke."

"You invited me over for my expertise. Take it or leave it."

"Fine. I agree. Public and neutral is a good idea. How about Balboa Park?"

"Perfect."

"But he's not going to murder me. I know him too well for that now."

Beth did a little shimmy dance on her way to the couch. "Well, then let's do this so you can get to know him even better." She sat beside Emmy and encouragingly nudged her with her shoulder.

Emmy took a deep, full breath, centering herself for one of the most frightening things she'd ever done, and unlocked her phone screen. She tapped the message icon with a shaking thumb.

"Come on, you can do it. Just like we practiced," Beth hummed in her ear.

Emmy braced herself and typed out the message they'd planned.

> Hey, Axe Murderer. So, I need a favor. Absolutely no pressure to accept, but I need to travel to a wedding this weekend and I'm wondering if you'd like to come as my date.

She hit send and immediately locked her screen and threw her phone across the room.

"Hey!" Beth cried and went to retrieve it from the armchair where it had landed. "That wasn't part of the plan!"

Emmy flopped over and buried her face in a throw pillow. She groaned into it. "*Ugh*, Beth! I can't do this! What am I *thinking*?" She wanted to take it back. She wanted to unsend the message and pretend it had never happened.

Beth clucked, and Emmy felt the couch shift when she sat back down. "Well, you have to do it now because he already responded."

Emmy sat up with a start. The pillow had filled her hair with static that left strands floating eerily beside her head like she'd been electrocuted. "He did?"

"Yep. Now unlock this thing so we can see the rest of the message." She shoved Emmy's phone in her face so she could see the message preview. Her heart lifted at the sight that at least the first few words weren't an immediate no.

Emmy took the phone and unlocked it. Beth rested a calming palm on her arm that was visibly shaking with nerves.

"You're doing great, Em."

Emmy took another breath and opened the message.

> Hey, Bird Girl. I've missed you. This certainly
> sounds intriguing. 😊

Emmy read it and immediately turned to Beth to interpret.

"Um, he *missed you*? Em, if you don't land this guy, I will," she said from where she leaned over her shoulder.

Emmy huffed a little laugh, feeling her heart swell at his message.

"But this is good," Beth said. "He's happy to hear from you and he's interested. Smiley face is a good sign; *missing you* is obviously a good sign. Keep going."

With a nod, Emmy turned back to her phone and tapped out the next message in their plan.

> I've missed you too. Sorry for the short
> notice, and I know this is coming across as
> suspiciously convenient on my end, but you'd
> be doing me a huge favor.

> I'm happy to do you a favor.

They both inhaled matching sharp breaths. Beth squealed and gripped Emmy's arm. "See, I told you!" she whispered, like Axe Murderer might somehow hear them.

"Okay. Okay!" Emmy said, trying to gather herself and suddenly brimming with excitement more than nerves. She let out a little yelp when her phone whooped with another new message from him.

> When you say travel . . .

She bit her lip, hoping the distance wasn't a deal-breaker.

> Yeah, about that . . . The wedding is in
> Cancún. I totally get it if that's out of the
> question on such short notice.

Beth clucked and swatted her arm as soon as she hit send. "Stop giving him an out! He's ninety percent there already!"

"Sorry."

His typing dots appeared, and Emmy stopped breathing.

> Cancún? I think I could swing that. But, Bird
> Girl, you realize this means we're going to
> have to meet, right?

"YES! Yes! Yes! Yes!" Beth cheered and shook Emmy's arm so hard she almost dropped the phone.

The grin on Emmy's face was equally large and delirious. She rode the thrilling high to push through the more immediate and intimidating next step.

> Yes. I do realize that. And I want to. Maybe
> tomorrow? Then we can discuss travel
> plans.

> That sounds perfect. Where?

Beth punched her arm with another excited gasp. "*Oh*, that's a good sign! Letting you choose! He's not going to murder you!"

Emmy would have rolled her eyes if she wasn't positively vibrating with nerves. She knew the perfect location in Balboa Park. Someplace public but intimate. Safe but picturesque. Easily accessible but off the beaten path.

> The Botanical Building at Balboa Park. By the lily pond.

> Sounds perfect. Around 7?

> See you there.

Emmy collapsed back against the couch with a profound exhale. The buildup of nerves from the past weeks rushed out of her in a giant and welcome whoosh for clearing the obstacle that had had her spiraling. She could feel a new set of nerves prodding their way closer, but she'd deal with those tomorrow.

She shot off a text to her sister: Wedding date secured. And then added the most significant event she'd had in a long time to her calendar.

Axe Murderer @7pm Balboa Park

Of course Tuesday turned into a marathon of never-ending work. The day passed at an achingly slow pace, all because Emmy couldn't wait to get to the end of it. At least Gabe's sour mood seemed to have lifted. Even though he hadn't voiced it, she thought maybe he'd forgiven her for the scene on the pier. Or at least gotten over it. He was remarkably amiable while their team pounded away at their keyboards all day. He even found her a new marker when the one she tried to use on the whiteboard was dried out.

And then he tried to tell her the equation she'd written was wrong, and, when he leaned in close enough, she *might* not have moved the uncapped marker in her hand, to rub against his shirt without him noticing. Whatever. He had a dozen more pastel polos where that one came from.

Emmy had taken Thursday, Friday, and Monday off, which was not ideal given the trade deadline and the race for a promotion, but Piper's wedding had been on the books for over a year, and she'd cleared her time off with Alice ages ago. That meant she was working extra hard for three days this week before she jetted off to Mexico for five.

But her attention had waned. She couldn't stop thinking about Axe Murderer and their pending date. What would he look like? What would his voice sound like? Would she get the same butterflies in her stomach she got every time he texted her when she finally saw him in person? The gravity of the step they were taking threatened to consume her in a pit of nerves, but she wouldn't let it. Instead, she held on to the thrilling sense of hope her sister would be right and knowing him in real life would be even better.

Once they clocked out for the day, Emmy headed home to change. The ballpark, Balboa Park, and her apartment all existed within a two-mile radius. She had plenty of time to make it from one to the other to the next before her meeting at 7:00, but she wanted enough time to put on the outfit she and Beth had chosen the night before and fix her hair from pulled-back office bun to something a little more flirty and free. She could have easily walked to the Botanical Building from home but didn't want to undo all the work she'd done and show up frizzy and sweaty in the warm evening air. When she was ready, she summoned a rideshare and set off feeling like she was seconds from exploding in a supernova of nerves and excitement.

What would he be like? What would he think of her? Would they kiss?

The final thought made her dizzy. Physical contact felt like an enormous leap after only texting, but she'd have been lying if she didn't admit she'd thought of it over and over in the past weeks.

She popped a mint from her purse into her mouth just in case.

When she arrived at the park, her driver dropped her as close as possible to the Botanical Building. Balboa Park sprawled like a lush green jewel amid San Diego proper. A network of walkways and trails, the park housed several museums, theaters, event centers, the famed San Diego Zoo, and acres of open lawns for sunbathing, picnicking, throwing Frisbees. This late on a Tuesday night, the museums and gift shops had closed, but patrons still strolled the paths in the twilight air.

Emmy turned onto El Prado, the main walkway with an enormous fountain at one end and the iconic California Tower at the other, and felt her heart rate pick up. She glanced around at everyone passing by, wondering if any of them could be Axe Murderer.

The tall man with a goldendoodle; probably not since he'd never mentioned a dog.

The fit jogger dripping with sweat and wearing earbuds; she hoped not since she'd rather he didn't show up to their first meeting needing a shower.

The man with sleeve tattoos pushing a stroller; she *really* hoped not because a kid would complicate matters more than she was prepared for.

She decided to stop speculating and wait for the reveal once she got to their intended location.

When she turned toward the Botanical Building, the lily pond stretched out before her like a long, reflective carpet. Palms lined the walkways on either side, and flowers popped in pockets of color. The domed building sat at the other end of the pond, flanked by lawns. She'd chosen the place for its scenic beauty and centralized location, and now as she approached a bench to sit and wait for Axe Murderer, she couldn't help feeling the symbolism of following a path to an endpoint.

The time had come.

Emmy sat on one of the empty benches in front of the building and gazed at the pond. The palm trees rustled. The sky had faded into a milky blue that would soon twinkle with stars. The warm evening hummed and buzzed around her. Despite her nerves, she felt remarkably content.

Until she heard a familiar voice.

"Jameson? Is that you?"

She turned to see Gabe Olson standing beside the next bench

over, looking dapper in a button-down with a small bouquet of flowers in his hand.

"Olson?" she said, and had the increasingly routine feeling of wanting to hide from him because he'd caught her doing something vulnerable. "What are you doing here?"

He looked over his shoulder and then sat on the other bench. "Uh, I'm meeting someone here. What are you doing here?"

"Same," she said, and crossed her legs. She'd worn strappy sandals and a flowy floral-print dress that fluttered around her ankles. She gathered the skirt when it fell open at the slit and she felt his eyes momentarily flash to her bare legs. "Don't tell me your other cousin is a curator at one of these museums or something," she said, and turned slightly away from him. He'd already seen her at the bachelorette party. The last thing she wanted was Gabe Olson infringing on her meetup—especially if it didn't go well.

Oh god, what if Axe Murderer showed up and turned out to be a catfish who lived in his mom's basement, and Gabe witnessed her humiliation firsthand? The thought made her want to submerge herself in the lily pond and never resurface. She would become one with the koi.

Gabe huffed a small laugh. "Um, no. I don't have any cousins who work at this park. I'm here to meet . . . a date."

She turned to him in interest. "Oh yeah? The mystery girl you didn't want to jinx by confessing you wanted it to become official?"

"That would be the one."

"Well, with the flowers, the shirt, the romantic location"—she paused to sweep her arms at the view—"I have to say this looks pretty official."

He shyly smiled. "I guess you're right. Still hoping not to jinx anything."

"Hmm. Well, the night is young, Olson. I wish you luck."

He snorted a laugh. "Thanks."

They went back to sitting silently, and Emmy really wished he'd go away. Why did he have to pick *that* bench? Seriously, what were the odds he'd chosen the same location as she had for a meetup? It seemed astronomical. And yet, there they were. Again. *She* could get up and move, but she didn't want to miss Axe Murderer showing up, and she'd gotten here first. If anything, *he* should leave so she could have the space to herself.

Emmy nervously checked the time on her phone to see it was five after seven. Nothing in their history suggested Axe Murderer was anything but punctual. She hated to think something had happened to him—or worse, he'd changed his mind and she was being stood up.

The latter thought bottomed out her belly and almost made her feel sick.

She side-eyed Gabe and wondered if he was judging her for being stood up. How mortifying. She and Beth had not rehearsed this scenario. She didn't know what to do. She couldn't bear the humiliation, so she pulled out her phone to text Axe Murderer in a fit of panic.

> I'm here 😊

Her heart beat like a frantic drum. Her hands had begun to sweat. But she calmed when she saw his dots immediately appear.

> Me too 😊

Her head popped up to look around. Aside from her and Gabe, she only saw a family with a toddler playing on the lawn and the sweaty jogger having stopped to stretch.

> Where?

> By the lily pond. Right in front of the building.

Emmy stood and did a full three-sixty turn to look for him. The fantasy palette of twilight sky, stucco, lawn, and rainbow of flowers blurred by. But she didn't see anyone new. It was on her second rotation that she noticed Gabe standing too, phone in one hand, flowers in the other, and an expression of stupefied shock on his face.

"What?" she asked.

He silently blinked at her, looked down at his phone, and then looked back up at her.

The realization hit Emmy with the force of an atomic bomb. In a blink, the world as she knew it ceased to exist.

Chapter 10

I t's *you*?!" Emmy screeched in disbelief.

"It's YOU?!" Gabe echoed, always having to one-up her.

She suddenly couldn't breathe. She might never find oxygen again. The earth was crumbling to bits beneath her. Up was down. Inside was out. *Gabe freaking Olson was Axe Murderer.*

"No," she said out loud. "No, no, no. This is not possible. It can't be you!"

"It can't be *you*!" he cried.

Birds took flight from a nearby tree at the shrill sound of their voices. The family playing with their toddler scooped him up and moved farther down the lawn.

Emmy couldn't even feel her feet on the ground. Reality was shredding to pieces before her eyes. She went full Sally Field in *Mrs. Doubtfire* on him. "The whole time? *The whole time?!* THE WHOLE TIME?!"

She wanted to sink into the earth. She wanted to drown in the lily pond. She wanted to break into the Air & Space Museum and launch herself to Mars on one of the old rockets.

"*You're* Bird Girl?" Gabe said, and gaped at her as if he was still collecting the pieces and needed her to confirm.

Emmy didn't know how to respond other than to hold up her phone. "*You're* Axe Murderer?!"

They showed each other the other half of their shared conversation, and sure enough. Every box on her screen that was blue was gray on his, and the other way around.

"No!" Emmy screeched again. She stamped her foot and balled her fist. She felt shocked and betrayed—by who or what, she couldn't say—but most of all, she felt *humiliated* Gabe Olson had been on the other end the whole time. All the things she'd told him. All the jokes, the secrets—the vulnerability she'd never shared with anyone else.

"No!" she snapped once more. Then she stepped toward him and shoved a finger in his face. "I swear, Olson, if this is some kind of sick joke."

He held up his hands and stepped back. "Emmy, I *swear* I didn't know. I had *no idea* it was you."

She shook with nerves, nausea, utter terror over it all. "This is impossible. What is even happening right now? I think I'm going to throw up." She gripped her face in her hands and took a deep breath.

"Here, how about we sit down?" Gabe said, and gently reached for her.

"Don't!" she snapped.

He recoiled in fright.

"Sorry. I'm just— This is . . . I can't—"

"Yeah. Same," he said, and sank onto the bench where she'd been sitting.

Emmy felt so raw and exposed. She wanted to burrow into a hole and never come back out. Gabe Olson of all people knew things about her—*intimate* things—no one else knew. The shock might never wear off. She couldn't even look at him. "I'm so embarrassed," she muttered and held her face in her hands.

"*You're* embarrassed?" Gabe said with a note of incredulity. "*I'm* the one who was given a fake number that started all this!"

Emmy popped up out of her hands. "*That's* what you care about right now? How about the fact I've poured my heart out to you, not knowing it was you!"

"Same for me!"

They were arguing like they might at work. Like someone had flubbed an equation and threw off everyone's projections. The lines between work and personal and reality and cyberspace had blurred into disordered chaos. It was enough to make Emmy's head spin. She desperately wanted to go home and lie down.

"Look," she said. "Along with the baseball bruise, the bachelorette party, and the seasickness, how about we pretend this never happened?"

He turned to her with a pained look that was at once tortured and pleading. "Yes, I think that's for the best."

"Okay," Emmy said in relief. "Although—shit. I still need a date to my sister's wedding." She palmed her forehead again. All her plans were falling apart in such spectacular fashion.

"Your sister who had the party on my cousin's boat three nights ago?"

"Yes."

He shook his head with a small laugh. "This is all so obvious in retrospect. Like, *embarrassingly* obvious."

Emmy glared at him. "I'm glad you think this is funny, Olson."

"I'm not laughing at you, Jameson. I'm laughing at how fucking obtuse I've been—we've both been. It was right there in front of us the whole time. Think about it."

Even if he was right, even if all the pieces had been right in front of them, it was not *obvious*. Because never in a million lifetimes would Emmy think she could get along with Gabe Olson the way she did with Axe Murderer. She didn't even want to think about it. She didn't want to think about how she'd been flirting with her co-worker from mere feet away, because she knew she'd most certainly texted Axe Murderer in Gabe's presence more than once. The idea of it was simply too mortifying to dwell on.

She popped up from the bench, suddenly unable to be in his presence for a moment longer. She was going to expire from humiliation. "I have to go."

"Emmy, wait—" he said, but she was already walking away.

She beelined along the lily pond, heading back toward El Prado so she could get to a parking lot and into a rideshare as soon as possible. She summoned a ride but at least waited until she was out of his line of sight before she lifted her phone to call Beth.

Beth answered on the first ring, having been on standby in the event of an emergency. "Oh god, you're calling me. Why are you calling me? Please don't tell me this means you've been kidnapped."

"Worse."

"Worse? Like, mom's-basement-catfish worse?"

"Like, 'Meryl Streep just pursed her lips in *The Devil Wears Prada* catastrophe' worse. I'm coming over."

"Oh no. What do I need to uncork: white or red?"

"Tequila."

"Shit, Em. Okay. What happened?"

"I'm still in too much shock to explain it. I have to tell you in person."

"Okay. I'm here."

Twenty minutes later, Emmy sat on her best friend's couch staring at a Princess Leia Funko Pop figurine perched on a busy bookshelf draped in houseplants. Beth sat next to her in leggings and a hoodie, jaw unhinged.

"Gabe. As in, Olson. As in, Gabe Olson," Beth said for at least the tenth time.

"*Yes!* Saying it over and over isn't going to change that fact, Beth!"

"Sorry! I'm just . . . Are you sure? Like *sure,* sure?"

Emmy tore her eyes from the quirky little Star Wars parade on her friend's bookshelf and leveled her with a glare. "Yes, I am sure."

"And it's not a prank or something? The guys in your office aren't, like, ganging up on you for some reason?"

"That would be incredibly mean, even for them. And no, it's not a prank. He was as genuinely shocked as I was." She could still see Gabe's face from the park. The gaping confusion and utter disbelief—

an image she was sure he now had burned into his memory too but starring her.

"Wow," Beth said. "That's . . . Wow. Can't say I saw that one coming. So what happened?"

"We made the discovery, and then I basically ran away."

"You ran away?"

"What was I supposed to do, stand there feeling naked and wallow in it? I had to get away from him. Oh *god*, and I'm going to have to see him at work tomorrow." She grabbed a fluffy throw pillow and buried her face in it. She felt her friend's warm hand land on her back and rub.

"Well, at least you'll be gone for the wedding for a few days after tomorrow," Beth said.

Emmy groaned and lifted her face. "Don't remind me! Getting a date was the whole point of this, remember?"

Beth smoothed down Emmy's hair that had gone wiry from static. "No, the point of this was meeting the guy you've been crushing on for weeks. Having a date to the wedding was going to be an added bonus."

"Well, both of those things are now moot," Emmy said, and frowned at her.

"Are they?" Beth's voice was cautious and soft, and Emmy did not like her implication.

"What does that mean?"

Beth stood up from the couch and splayed her hands like Emmy might throw something at her. "Hear me out. I'm just the messenger, so don't shoot, but do you think maybe . . . this all means something?"

Emmy *really* didn't like her implication. "Means something like what?"

Beth hesitated and then spoke cautiously. "Maybe it means you guys have a connection. A real one."

"No, I have a connection with Axe Murderer, not Gabe Olson."

"You realize they're the same person, right?"

"No. They are not the same person. The person I see at work every day is *not* the same person I text all the time."

Beth sat back down and placed a hand on her knee. "Em, are *you* the same person when you're texting him?"

"I—"

Her sentence jammed in her throat. She paused because when she stopped to think about it, she realized the answer was yes. She did keep certain things from Gabe because their relationship was primarily professional, but that didn't mean she was fake around him. More like guarded and mindful of boundaries. With Axe Murderer, however, all her guards were down. If Gabe had gone one level deep, Axe Murderer had been ten levels deep, but both of them were dipping into the same well.

Beth gazed at her like she recognized the conclusion she'd come to. "All I'm saying is, it's not nothing that you've been so open with him all this time. There's obviously something there, so maybe don't be so quick to shoot it down."

Despite herself, Emmy considered it. She would have been lying to deny there was something between her and Axe Murderer. Discounting the past several weeks and pretending none of it had happened would be a disservice to her feelings. But how could she possibly reconcile that fact with the reality of Gabe Olson being the single most infuriating man she knew?

She thought back to the earnestness on Gabe's face when he'd first arrived at the park. He'd brought Bird Girl flowers, and that was about the sweetest damn thing she could think of. And as long as she was being honest with herself, she could admit there had been instances in the past few weeks where she'd seen unexpected sides of Gabe that had brought out unexpected responses in her. Like how the feel of his body against hers when he carried her off the field sent her blood looping in all sorts of ways. And how pleasantly surprised she'd been to enjoy sharing breakfast with him. And how utterly selfless she'd found his volunteering to help his cousin in the face of certain seasickness.

And then there was the truth she'd never admit to anyone—not even her best friend—about how his annoyingly perfect hair and gorgeous smile and goddamned sculpted arms had always, from day one, put a flutter in her belly and a flame in her blood.

She scoffed aloud, disliking the whole perplexing situation. "You realize what you're saying, right?" she said to Beth. "You want me to give *Gabe Olson* a chance."

Beth shrugged her shoulders up to her ears. "Sure, why not?"

"*Why not?*" Emmy sputtered. "I can list about ten thousand reasons *why not*. First—" She held up her fingers to start counting, but Beth cut her off and gently pushed her hands down.

"Before you do that, how about we think of all the reasons this is a *good* idea instead?"

Emmy narrowed her eyes. "Name me one."

"Well, aside from the fact he could still go to the wedding with you and solve your date problem, I can say with the utmost certainty in the decade of our friendship, I have never seen you this into someone before. Seems like a pretty good reason to me."

"I'm not *into* him," she said on reflex.

Beth snorted a laugh. "Em, *yes* you are. At least you were until about an hour ago when you found out who he really is. But that shouldn't change anything, in my opinion. You were ready to fly to Mexico with Axe Murderer; why should Gabe Olson be any different?"

Emmy felt like she had been smacked with a heavy dose of reality, and she didn't like it. Beth made good points. Emmy had been gung-ho about meeting Axe Murderer and taking him to the wedding. She'd been willing basically sight-unseen. Granted, when she saw the sight, she ran away screaming. But maybe Gabe was just the packaging around the real person she'd gotten to know. Maybe Beth was right. Maybe she *should* give it a chance.

She honestly couldn't believe she was even considering it.

She picked at a thread on the throw pillow. "Well, there's a very good chance he never wants to talk to me again, so that might make things difficult."

"I doubt that's the case," Beth said astutely. "Who knows, maybe he's getting a pep talk from his BFF right now, too."

Emmy rolled her eyes with a blush. She swatted the pillow in angst. "How can I ever come back from this though? What's the conversation starter after a cataclysmic revelation like that? *Hey, I know you actually hate me now that you know it's me, but still wanna be my date to the wedding?*"

Beth took the pillow from her so she didn't pull it to pieces. "He doesn't hate you. And you said Axe Murderer is the easiest person to talk to you've ever met, so just talk to him like that! Pretend you're texting!"

Emmy sighed and gazed back at Princess Leia on the bookshelf. If she was going to convince Gabe to be her date, she had one day to do it before she left for the wedding. It was either that or hire someone off Craigslist. Neither option was appealing, but she got the sense her sister would be less likely to murder her if she brought the hot first mate to her wedding than if she brought a total stranger who might himself possess homicidal tendencies.

"Fine. I'll talk to him at work tomorrow. But, Beth, *no one* hears about this, okay? We are the only people who know Axe Murderer and Gabe Olson are the same person, and I want to keep it that way—especially from my sister. If I do anything to take the focus off her big day, she'll lose it."

Beth gave her a knowing grimace. "My lips are sealed."

"Thank you. I should go. I have to start packing."

Beth rose with her off the couch to walk her to the door. "Open mind, Em," she said with an encouraging pat on the shoulder.

Emmy grumbled and headed into the hall. When she made it outside to walk the few blocks back to her place, the urge to text Axe Murderer hit her hard. Not because she now knew who he was—actually, the fact she *did* know was what stopped her—but because he had been her source of comfort for the past few weeks. He'd been who she turned to when she needed a laugh, a distraction, a bird-band pun. And right now, she could have used all three of those things.

Maybe Beth was right. Maybe there *was* something there. Maybe it was worth exploring, and maybe a few days in Mexico with Gabe Olson would give her a chance to.

That was, if he ever spoke to her again, let alone agreed to go with her.

When Emmy headed into work the next day, she assumed it would be a painful day of thousand-yard stares and avoidance. Gabe might have even called in sick just to dodge her. She already had a list of a million things to do before she left for five days, and finding time to squeeze in a desperate, humiliating-in-more-ways-than-one chat with Gabe made it all the more complicated. She braced herself for the onslaught when she walked into their office, but to her brief relief, she found it empty. She set down her bag and headed to the kitchen to load up on caffeine before fully starting her day.

It was there her relief evaporated, because there was Gabe standing at the counter in one of his cool shirts—minty green—stirring oat milk into a mug of coffee.

Emmy froze in her tracks. She'd worried about what she would feel upon seeing him again after the big reveal—a suffocating wave of embarrassment that would surely drown her on dry land—but instead, she felt . . . something else. A curious warmth pooled out low in her belly, in her chest, into her face.

Goddamn it.

"I thought you took your coffee black," she said to distract herself from the confusing yet pleasant way her body was reacting to seeing him.

He turned at the sound of her voice and dropped his stirring spoon in surprise. It splashed into his mug and caused him to need to lick his finger. "Emmy!" he blurted when he pulled it out of his mouth. "I-I mean, *Jameson*. Good morning."

His genuine fluster made her feel more flustered. And the flush in his cheeks only amplified the one burning hers. She glared at him out of reflex and self-preservation and headed to the coffee station to make her own drink. "Good morning," she said with her customary terseness.

And then she remembered with a sigh she needed a favor from him and needed to rein in her reflexes—all of them.

As her K-Cup gurgled and squirted into her mug, she felt his eyes on her back. She was in her standard office garb: jeans, blouse, lanyard looped around her neck. A hot pang zipped through her when she remembered the way he'd looked at her in her dress last night, how his eyes had lingered on her bare legs when her skirt tumbled open around her knees.

Her coffee finished brewing, and she turned to see him still standing by the fridge with the oat milk on the counter. She had no choice but to venture into his orbit to use it.

"I thought you hated milk not from cows," she said as she reached for the carton.

He casually sipped his coffee, apparently having recovered from his earlier fluster, and shrugged. "I figured I'd see what all the oat milk fuss was about."

Emmy sipped her own coffee and eyed him over her mug. "And?"

His mouth twisted into a wobbly line that made her acutely aware of how soft and lush his lips looked.

She immediately took another gulp for distraction.

"I guess it's not terrible," he said.

A silence ballooned between them. Strained and awkward and so huge, Emmy knew popping it would startle them both.

But she did it anyway.

"So, last night was . . ."

"Fun?" he offered when she couldn't find the right words to finish her sentence.

For a brief moment, her reflexes made her worry he was mocking her with a call back to the text that started it all. But then she saw a gentle smile curve his lips and realized he was simply as uncomfortable as she was. As nervous that this new territory was going to blow up in their faces and leave everything irreparable.

She quietly laughed, feeling the tension loosen. And then he laughed too, and it fell away altogether.

"Listen," Emmy said, and leaned on the counter beside him. "I'm wondering if—and you have every right to say no because I know this is all kind of absurd and ridiculous—but I'm wondering if . . . you'd still be willing to go to the wedding with me." She bit her lip and nervously watched his reaction.

A look bloomed over his face, tangling on itself somewhere between surprise she was asking and sincere contemplation like he might say yes. "Really?"

She desperately leapt on the opportunity. "Yes! I will buy your plane ticket and everything. *Please.*"

He softly chuckled. "You don't have to do that." He set his coffee down and stroked his jaw. "I guess I just thought, you know, you were never going to talk to me again after last night, so I'm a little surprised."

Emmy blinked at him in relief. "I thought *you* were never going to talk to *me* again, so I'm surprised you're even considering this." She leaned back and looked at him with a narrowed gaze as if to check he wasn't pulling a trick. "You *are* considering it, right?"

He smirked at her, and a flash of the Gabe Olson she knew well peeked through. The one who relished any opportunity to lord something over her. But a softer version chased him away. "Yes, I'm considering it."

"*Really?!*" Her hand shot out and gripped his forearm of its own accord. He didn't shake her off, so she left it there.

A grin spread his lips. "Desperation is a new look on you, Jameson. I kind of like it."

She rolled her eyes and dropped her hand, afraid she'd misjudged the whole situation and he'd been playing her from the start.

Gabe looked amused. "Sorry, old habits die hard. I'm just messing with you. Yes, I will come with you to your sister's wedding in Cancún."

Emmy's heart lifted, but she eyed him with great caution. "Not messing with me now?"

He held up his hands in surrender. "Not messing with you, promise. But can I be there by Friday? You're right this is short notice, and I have some things to take care of before leaving."

"Yes!" Emmy almost jumped on him again. "Yes, that's perfect. The rehearsal dinner is at five. Any time before that is fine. And we have the hotel until Monday, so you can stay as long as works for you."

"Cool," he said with a nod. "Can you text me all the information?"

And just like that, he invited the awkward elephant right back to the party. Because Emmy Jameson did not have Gabe Olson's phone number. But Bird Girl had Axe Murderer's.

Emmy pursed her lips. Nerves coursed through her body like an army of ants. "Yes, but about that. I think it would be best if you come to the wedding as you, not . . . the other guy. We don't have to tell anyone who you really are. There will be fewer questions that way." She bit her lip and awkwardly looked away.

She felt his eyes studying her. The nervous ants started dancing in a conga line. Then he nodded in understanding. "Oh, right. Because you told your sister and your best friend about me. Well, the other me."

"Right."

She silently thanked him for not mentioning what her sister had said about Emmy hating him the night of her bachelorette party.

He stroked his jaw again like he might have been remembering it. "Yeah, sure. I can do that."

"Thank you—and. Shit," she mumbled, suddenly drowning in embarrassment again. She set her coffee down so she didn't spill it in her fluster. "I was going to tell you this anyway—well, the other you—but that was before we realized . . . And now—" Her words were messy and jumbled, and she wanted to melt through the floor, but Gabe was looking at her with sincere interest.

"Tell me what?"

Emmy took a breath, knowing she needed to be honest with him because this tidbit would be an unfair bomb to drop on him three thousand miles away from home. "The reason I'm so desperate to have a date to this wedding is because my ex is going to be there."

The interest on Gabe's face bent into a frown while one brow flicked up. He almost looked protective, and it made Emmy tingle. "The one who told you to choose between him and your career?"

It took her a moment to remember that when she'd told Axe Murderer that information in confidence, she'd been talking to Gabe.

God, he knew so much about her. She felt like she had secrets popping out of her like confetti. She fought to maintain her composure and not dissolve into a puddle of shame. But he wasn't looking at her with any judgment, but rather, concern.

"Yes, that ex is going to be there," Emmy confirmed.

"Why?" He asked a very legitimate question.

"Because he's my brother-in-law's cousin's plus one. My sister can't uninvite them; it's a whole thing." She was mumbling again, rushing out words in a flood of embarrassment. She threw her hands over her face. "It's just . . . I can't have him show up and see me there alone and think he won." She listened to the sound of her breath bounce off her palms, her nervous pulse racing, until she felt his hands circle her wrists. He gently pulled her arms down so he could see her face.

"Hey. I promise you he lost, Emmy."

They stared at each other for a heart-thudding moment that made Emmy forget to breathe. It sounded like something Axe Murderer would say in text, and there was Gabe saying it to her face.

They're the same person. She heard Beth's words again.

She didn't have time to fuse the two men she knew into one being before Silas appeared at the kitchen doorway.

"What's going on in here?" he asked when he came to an abrupt stop at the sight of them.

Both Emmy and Gabe startled and looked up to see him approaching. Emmy flushed at the suspicious look on his face, feeling like they'd been caught and had *We've been having a secret texting affair* written across both their foreheads. Not to mention, Gabe was still holding her wrists.

He quickly let go.

Silas blinked a few times and then grinned. "You guys are supposed to hate each other. Why are you in here looking all chummy?"

They obviously could not answer him honestly.

Relief flooded through Emmy when Gabe reached out to slap him on the back. "Jameson was just showing me the wonders of oat milk. That's all. Turns out, you all are onto something." He left the kitchen casually sipping his coffee.

Silas looked at Emmy with an arched brow.

She simply shrugged, thankful Gabe had come to her rescue in multiple senses: for covering about their conversation and for agreeing to be her wedding date.

Now all she had to do was figure out how she was going to handle being in Mexico all weekend with her archnemesis turned anonymous pen pal who made her heart flutter. No big deal.

Chapter 11

When Emmy arrived at the palatial oceanfront resort in Can-cún, she expected to find her sister in a state of prewedding preparation: focused, slightly jittery, maybe a little unhinged, but overall glowing and bride-to-be happy. Never in a million years did she expect the look of sheer terror on Piper's face when she met her in the marble lobby.

Instantly, Emmy's mind flitted to grave disaster: Ben had jilted her thousands of miles from home, and they'd need to find a place to dump his body, and then she'd spend the rest of her life evading arrest for his murder.

But she knew that couldn't be true because she could see Ben plain as day right in front of her putting his expensive private school education to use by having a spirited conversation in rapid Spanish with one of the hotel employees. For once, his Prince Charming demeanor had slipped. His face had reddened, and he kept stroking a frustrated hand through his hair while the other rested on his hip.

Piper stood off to his side looking both like she'd seen a ghost and like she was going to burst into tears. The warm greeting Emmy had expected—a hug, maybe a celebratory margarita shoved into her hand—was markedly absent, and instead of embracing the tropical air and letting herself sink into the spirit of the weekend, she fought to control her suddenly speeding heart at the look on her sister's face.

"What's wrong?" she asked, and dropped her bag.

Piper and Ben had arrived earlier that morning on a different flight. First class, obviously. Emmy had taken a later flight where she sat smushed up against the window beside an overly friendly middle-aged couple on an anniversary trip who did not get the hint she didn't want to chat, even when she put on noise-canceling headphones and tried to listen to an audiobook.

Piper sniffed once and spoke in a tear-clogged voice Emmy could tell teetered on the edge of full-blown panic. "They double-booked the venue."

Emmy's speeding heart stilled as she had a vision of her sister's perfect dream wedding collapsing like a building. She could tell from the look on Piper's face that of all the services Emmy could have provided in that moment—join in the argument with Ben as backup, offer to torch the hotel, maybe lead a smear campaign against the resort on social media—what Piper needed most was a hug.

"Oh, Pipes. I'm sorry," she said, and wrapped her in her arms.

Piper took a shuddering breath and let out a brief but loud yelp of a cry. "This is a disaster."

Emmy gently pushed her back and firmly held her shoulders. "Hey, no, it's not. We're going to figure it out, okay?"

Piper sobbed again, and Emmy reeled her into another hug. She caught Ben's eye over Piper's shoulder and could tell his conversation wasn't going well.

He held up a hand to the employee he was speaking with, someone in a suit and tie with a name tag who had to be high up, and nodded. He stepped away and joined her and Piper.

"Hey, Em," he said in a weary voice. He reached out and gave her a half hug before circling his arm around Piper's waist. She leaned into him.

"So?" Piper asked. "What's going to happen?"

Ben let out a long breath. "Well, their suggestion is we sit together with the other wedding party and discuss if anyone is willing to change plans."

"*Change plans?*" Piper squawked in a voice closer to Bridezilla.

"We've been planning this event for literally a year, and they want us to just *change plans*?"

"I know," Ben said, and gave her a calming kiss on the temple. "It's ridiculous, and they will be giving us a serious discount after all this, but since both weddings have people flying in and can't easily be rescheduled, they are trying to do what they can. We could swap days and have the wedding on Sunday instead of Saturday, or they can accommodate another location on the property for the event."

Piper squeezed her face in her hands. Emmy could feel a tantrum brewing, and for once, she didn't blame her at all. When she dropped her hands, her face had bloomed red. Her voice came out a harsh hiss. "Ben, no! I don't want to change anything! We've been dreaming of this for months!"

"I know, Pipes! And we're going to figure it out. I'm not going to let anything ruin this weekend, I promise. Just . . . take a breath, okay?" He inhaled his own deep breath and blew it out as he stroked his hands up and down her arms left bare by her white romper. Emmy watched in wonder as he basically diffused a bomb simply by touching her.

Piper matched his deep breath and leaned her forehead into his shoulder. "Sorry, it's all the stress. It has me really emotional. I just wanted everything to be perfect."

"It will be, okay?" he said, and wrapped her in a hug. "We're going to fix this. Your sister is here now; the sun is shining. We're getting married in two days." He pulled back and lifted her hands to kiss the backs of both sets of knuckles. His lips spread into a soft grin that managed to pull a mirroring one from Piper. "I love you," he said.

"I love you too," she responded, sounding dreamy and pacified.

Ben kissed her forehead again. "Why don't you head over to the room to relax, and I'll stay here and see what we can do."

"Okay," Piper said with a nod. "Em, your room is under your name. Text me when you're settled."

"I will," Emmy promised and then watched her sister glide off toward a hallway like she'd just had the best massage of her life. Once she was out of earshot, Emmy turned to Ben. "You are a magician. Do you have, like, sedatives in your palms or something? Where were you when we were teens fighting over everything?"

Ben softly chuckled and stroked his chin. Then he let out a big sigh.

"So, how are you going to fix this?"

He squeezed the back of his neck and shook his head. "I have no fucking clue." Hearing Ben curse, a sound as unnatural as "Jingle Bells" in July, put the situation into crisp perspective. "The other wedding is coming in today, too. Their rehearsal dinner is tomorrow at five, and their ceremony is Saturday at the same time as ours. It's like an exact copy paste of our events—*and*, their party is huge, so all the rooms are booked. Everything is at max capacity."

Emmy was still struggling with the shock of things derailing so quickly, it took her a moment to register what he'd said.

"I'm sorry—you said all the rooms are booked?"

"Yes. At least *that's* not overlapped with the other wedding because this is the only hotel around for miles. Everyone's room reservation is fine, it's just the wedding venue that's double-booked. God, what a nightmare." He scrubbed his face again, and Emmy tuned out whatever he said next because all she could think of was her plan dying on the vine.

Her room had been booked for ages; Piper blocked a whole wing for the bridal party back in February. Given that she wasn't exactly keen on sharing a hotel room with Gabe Olson, she'd planned to sneak down into the lobby and book him his own before he got there. But now Ben was telling her the place was at max capacity for the weekend. Which meant unless she convinced Gabe to sleep outside on a lounge chair, they'd be sharing a room. For three nights.

". . . so, I don't really know what other options there are." Ben was still talking, but she was far away wondering what Gabe Olson wore to sleep in, and if she'd remembered to pack her floor-length bathrobe because no way was she wearing anything more revealing than that in front of him.

Ben checked his watch. "My parents should be here soon. Maybe my dad can . . . I don't know." He sighed, and Emmy mentally filled in the blank with *throw some money at the problem*.

"Hey, if it saves the wedding, I'm all for whatever it takes."

"The wedding will be saved one way or another, don't worry," he said with his Prince Charming smile back in place. "I won't let anything upset Piper."

Emmy gave him a genuinely warm smile. "I'm glad she's marrying you, Ben."

"Me too." He flushed a sweet shade of pink. "I'm going to go talk to the manager some more. Can you help keep Piper calm through all this, please?"

She held up jazz hands and smiled. "I don't have the narcotic touch like you, but yes, of course."

"Thanks, Em."

He left her alone to head to the front desk, and she realized that through all the mayhem, neither of them had asked her where her date was and why she'd arrived by herself.

She swallowed down the story she'd spun about him joining her tomorrow and took the easy—for now—pass.

At the front counter, a woman with thick dark hair and an impeccable white uniform beamed at her.

"Hi. Checking in for Emmy Jameson?" Emmy said.

The woman nodded and typed something into her computer. Emmy took a moment to take in the grand scale of the lobby. Burbling fountains anchored each side of the entrance, and a towering, thatched roof reached like a pyramid over the round center of the room. Out the back entrance—an open-air arch crowded with deeply green palms leaning in as a frame—she could see the aqua blue of a swimming pool and a bevy of lounge chairs and umbrellas.

The woman called her attention back by setting a pair of pink elastic wristbands on the counter. She lifted one and pointed to the little plastic square with the resort's logo on it attached to the band. "Here is your room key," she said in a thick accent.

Emmy nodded and slipped both bands around her wrist for safe-keeping.

The woman then produced a map of the property. Emmy had seen photos of it already, of course, but according to the map, it was way bigger than she'd realized. "We have four shuttle stops on the property," the woman said, and circled the lobby and three more stops along what looked like a pathway winding through the sprawling grounds. "You are in room 2247. Oceanfront king," she added, and circled the end of a building facing an illustrated strip of beige sand and then a blue swath of sea.

Emmy initially smiled with a nod, thankful her sister had booked her a room with a view, but quickly backtracked her thought when she registered the latter part of the description.

"King?" she asked the woman.

"Sí." She nodded with a smile.

Emmy's smile morphed into a tight line as her pulse leapt in her throat. "As in, one bed?"

"Sí," the woman said with another smiling nod. "One big bed."

A hot bloom of color raced up Emmy's neck. "No. I need two beds." She held up two fingers. "Dos camas, por favor."

The woman's smile faltered, and she tilted her head in question.

Emmy's nerves twisted around inside her like eels. The mere idea of sharing a room with Gabe Olson had her spinning, let alone having to share one with only one bed. And now she was having to negotiate her way out of it in a language she hardly knew beyond high school instruction. She glanced over her shoulder to see if Ben could come help translate, but he and the manager had disappeared. Desperate, she leaned back over the counter and began babbling to the clerk.

"Listen, I'm here for a wedding, and my date is coming tomorrow.

We are not a couple. In fact, we don't even really like each other. Well, I guess that's not entirely true. I *do* like one version of him, but that's not the version who's coming to the wedding. The guy who's coming is my co-worker, and he's doing me a favor. We can't share a room with only one bed because that is crossing so many boundaries I might as well report myself to HR right now. Please. I need a room with two beds." She held up two fingers again. "Better yet, I need two rooms. Can you help me with that, please?"

The woman blinked at her, clearly not having followed her ramble. Still smiling, she held up one finger. "One bed. One room. The hotel is full."

Emmy grimaced and realized it was less of a language barrier and more the fact there were simply no other rooms.

"Well, can I switch with someone? Someone here by themselves who doesn't need two beds?"

The woman shook her head with another polite smile. Emmy had to credit the hotel management for training their staff to maintain such composure in the face of whining tourists. "We don't have any more rooms. The shuttle is ready for you now."

Resigned to her fate, Emmy sighed. She looked over her shoulder to see a fancy golf cart with a luggage rack outside the front entry-way. A young man in a white shirt and khaki shorts stood by waiting. "Gracias," she told the woman and gathered her map.

She rolled her suitcase across the lobby with her heart beating uncomfortably hard. She had a few choice words for her sister for booking her a room with a single bed because Piper knew she wasn't going to find a date until the last minute, and anyone she invited to come would *not* be someone she was comfortable sharing a bed with. And now that someone was her co-worker. Her archnemesis. Her . . . secret pen pal crush.

"*Argh!*" Emmy yanked her suitcase over the curb to the waiting golf cart.

The bellhop flinched and looked frightened.

"Sorry," she muttered.

He recovered with a pleasant smile. "Bienvenidos. Room number?" he asked in heavily accented English.

Emmy dug for the map she'd shoved into her jeans' back pocket. She needed to get out of the denim ASAP as she was starting to sweat in the aggressively humid air. "Um, 2247," she told her driver as he hoisted her bag up into the luggage rack.

He nodded and circled around to sit behind the wheel. Emmy climbed into the back seat and held on to the handrail. The cart had no seat belts, but she couldn't imagine they'd be driving very fast over the small, paved pathway that unspooled before them. He hit the gas, and they lurched off.

The warm air rushed by like a blast from an open oven. The sweet smell of guava and palm and sea salt pushed in on Emmy in a rush, and she remembered she was in paradise. They passed a blur of green on either side as they zoomed through the jungly landscape toward the water. A golf course briefly sprang up to their left in a finely manicured streak of lime green. She glimpsed a swimming pool in flashes of aqua on the right. They'd been driving for at least five solid minutes when Emmy realized it was no wonder they escorted guests around by shuttle; it would have taken her ages to walk this far with her luggage.

Her driver eventually stopped in front of a white stucco building with a tile roof. Emmy could see the Caribbean Sea, a glittering shock of teal water, straight through the building's breezeway. It momentarily stole her breath.

"Bienvenidos," her driver said again. He smiled at her and hopped out to grab her bag.

Emmy climbed out of the cart and felt the sun mercilessly beat down from above. With the humidity, she felt like an insect being burned under a magnifying glass. She only had thoughts of getting into her air-conditioned room and stripping down to one of the cot-

ton sundresses she'd packed. Or putting on her swimsuit and jumping in the pool.

"Gracias," she told him, and dragged her bag toward the building's entrance. It had no exterior doors or windows. Simply big, open
holes painted with blue trim that allowed the thick air to freely
move in and out of the lobby and halls. The elevator deposited her
on the second floor, and when she unlocked her door and saw a king-
size bed plush with dreamy white linens framed by the teal sea, all the
blood in her body took a funny loop.

It was stunning and utterly romantic.

She dropped her bag and immediately cranked the AC as low as
it would go. Then she peeled off her jeans and flopped on the bed in
her underwear. She lay there like a starfish, reaching for either end of
it to gauge how big a king-size bed really was and trying to think of a
remedy for the situation.

She could go yell at her sister for booking her a room with one
bed, but her job was to help keep Piper calm, not start a fight. There
were no more rooms, and there was no other nearby hotel. Their
resort was several miles down the coast from Cancún, where all that
existed were insular mega resorts specifically designed for guests to
never have to leave. She knew from Piper's planning that the all-
inclusive property had a grocery store, a laundromat, a golf course, a
spa, eight restaurants, three pools, a private beach, two gyms, gift
shops, two clothing stores, a daycare, a wedding venue, and, somehow, no spare rooms with two beds.

Was this really happening? In approximately thirty hours, was she going to have to share a hotel room with Gabe Olson? Granted, it was a
beautiful hotel room with an absolutely stunning view, but even with
the sunken tub, minibar, and TV big enough to be seen from space,
it still only had one bed.

It struck Emmy then that she needed to warn him. If their roles
were reversed, she'd want to know what she was walking into because
otherwise, it might have felt like a trick. And they were on shaky

enough ground with their dual identities that she wanted to be transparent about the situation so he wouldn't think she was trying to pull one over on him.

She reached for her phone. The last text she'd sent Gabe was the name and location of the hotel. Other than that, the conversation between Axe Murderer and Bird Girl had died days ago.

The thought put an ache in her chest.

She checked the time to see it was lunchtime in California. She imagined him sitting at his desk next to her empty cubicle. Or maybe he had gone out to grab a bite with Pedro and Silas. Or maybe he was studiously pounding away at his keyboard and skipping lunch to make up for the time he'd lose by coming to the wedding for her.

Before she could talk herself out of disrupting him further, Emmy typed out a message and hit send.

> Hey. Made it to the hotel. So, bit of a situation . . .

Her heart positively leapt when he instantly responded. She tried not to read into it.

> Glad you made it. What's going on?

> Well, turns out the hotel double-booked the venue this weekend. There's another wedding happening at the exact same time.

> Oh shit. Really?

> Yeah. My sister is freaking out. My (almost) brother-in-law is talking to the hotel manager trying to fix it.

Yikes. What's going to happen?

Not sure, but the double book isn't the only problem.

She nervously bit her lip, afraid to say the next part.

Oh?

With two weddings, the hotel is completely full. I was planning to get you your own room, but there aren't any available. So we're going to have to share.

She immediately locked her screen and laid her phone on her chest, breathing deeply. She wasn't sure if it was the thought of sharing a room with him or worry over how he was going to react that had her pulse hammering. She gasped when her phone buzzed.

Well, I don't snore.

Her face bent into a smile.

I do.

Really?

No. But I've been known to talk in my sleep.

Ah. Well, I look forward to learning Emmy Jameson's deep, dark unconscious secrets.

> You already know my biggest secret.

> What, that you have an affinity for musical bird-related humor?

Emmy laughed out loud, and the sound startled her. Why was talking to him through text so easy? It was like no time had passed; nothing had gone wrong. They hadn't imploded their perfect relationship by taking it to the ill-informed next level.

> No, pun master. I meant your identity.

> We need to expand your horizons if my identity is your biggest secret. I'm looking forward to what kind of trouble we can get into in Mexico.

Emmy's heart flipped over with a delicious little bump. The feeling made her forget she was texting Gabe, not Axe Murderer.

Beth's words floated back to her. *They're the same person.*

She knew that was objectively true, but she still could not fully wrap her mind around it. Especially with the curious floating feeling his saying he was *looking forward* to joining her had filled her body with.

> I look forward to it too. I've got to go. I didn't buy an international plan, so these texts might be costing me like 50 cents apiece.

> Stay. I'll Venmo you.

She smiled again, finding herself pleased he wanted to keep talking.

Aren't you at work?

Yes, but everyone else is at lunch.

Aw, are you having a sad desk lunch all by yourself, Olson? 🙁

Alas, the price I have to pay to be able to jet off to Mexico on short notice, Jameson.

That, or Torres insisted on Thai takeout for the hundredth time this month, and you don't like fish sauce so were looking for an excuse not to join.

How do you know I don't like fish sauce?

Emmy felt like she'd been caught doing something she wasn't supposed to. Put to a test, she could list several facts about Gabe Olson she'd collected over the years, mostly by osmosis. Working in close quarters with someone tended to reveal their quirks and preferences. Like how he liked his coffee black, linked paper clips into chains when he was thinking hard, always chose the green marker when he wrote on the whiteboard, and had mentioned on more than one occasion he actually found fish sauce too potent despite the office's general affection for Thai takeout.

You've mentioned it before. Down with fish sauce; down with oat milk.

True on the first, but I'm reformed on the second, remember?

> Oh, right. I forgot you've come over to the oaty side.

> Happy to be here.

> We're up to like $15 in texts here . . .

> The price of an oat milk latte, how appropriate.

Emmy snorted a laugh and realized she couldn't put a price on the way texting with him made her feel. She didn't care how high her phone bill got.

> But I'll let you go. Back to work anyway. See you tomorrow.

> Thanks again for doing this. It means a lot to me.

> You're welcome. Oh, actually one more thing—

> Yes?

> The ex situation. We didn't really get a chance to talk about it . . .

Her belly bottomed out with worry over what he was going to say at the same time a wave of embarrassment washed over her that they needed to discuss it at all.

> Right. That.

> What's his name?

> Jacob.

> Do you want me to do anything?

She tilted her head in confusion, unsure what he meant.

> Do anything?

> Yeah, you know like in movies. Like pretend to be your boyfriend or anything.

"Oh!" she said out loud with a breathy laugh. She could somehow feel Gabe blushing through the phone. Her own rose-colored face made her think of how sweet he'd looked when he'd shown up in the park with flowers for Bird Girl, and here he was being sweet again. At the same time, her blood raced liquid hot through her veins. *Did she want him to be her boyfriend?* The question felt too loaded to approach, even facetiously.

> Not gonna lie, I thought you might offer to punch him in the face.

> I mean, I will if you want me to.

Emmy snort-laughed, knowing he was joking.

> Not necessary. And no, you don't have to pretend to be anything. My sister confirmed he's only coming to the ceremony and reception, so it's not like we'll be hanging out with him all weekend.

Got it. You're the boss.

I am. Get back to work!

See you in Mexico, Bird Girl.

Emmy set her phone aside with a sigh. That had gone better than expected, but the same as their whole complicated situation in general, there was a difference between what they said in text and facing it down in real life. She'd warned him they'd have to share, but they still had to . . . actually share.

With a nervous tumble of her stomach, she sat up to prepare.

The room was spacious but clearly not designed with privacy in mind. Aside from the closet, bathroom, and balcony, there was nowhere to hide unless she built a fort out of sheets over the small dining table in the corner. No, this room was designed for intimacy. People didn't book an oceanfront king with creamy linens and fluttering curtains to *not* touch each other inside it.

At least the toilet had its own little closet-size door, but the rest of the bathroom—a palatial sweep of brown marble and glass with a drive-in shower stall and a tub big enough to swim laps—screamed romantic getaway. The wall above the bathtub even had a set of shutters that opened into the bedroom facing the bedside, in case one lover wanted to watch the other bathe.

By herself, the room was glorious. Opulent. A much-needed escape into indulgent luxury. But the thought of Gabe's presence inside it with her—his cologne, his warmth, the way they would inevitably bump into each other despite their best efforts—had her hot with nerves. Or perhaps hot with something else that she couldn't look directly in the eye.

Thoroughly intimidated, Emmy silently cursed her sister for sentencing her to such a fate and then set about unpacking.

She hung her clothes in precisely half of the closet and used exactly one-half of the dresser drawers. In the bathroom, she placed her toiletries around one of the two sinks and then reached in again to cluster them tighter when she saw her facial cleanser had crossed the midline toward the other side. She struggled to imagine someone who always looked as put together and perfect as Gabe Olson using such pedestrian things like toothpaste and deodorant, but in one short day, all his personal effects would be on display alongside hers.

The fact secretly thrilled her.

She may as well have rolled a strip of tape down the center of the room to mark it his and hers, but she was satisfied with her work once finished.

As instructed, she pulled out her phone to text her sister.

> I'm settled. Where are you?

Piper responded within a few seconds.

> Villa 2. You can walk from your room. Bring your suit.

Of course they had a villa. Emmy silently wondered if it had a spare room she could escape to and leave Gabe their room to himself.

Once she had slathered herself in sunscreen, stripped down to a bikini and loose cover-up, and thrown her phone, water bottle, and wallet into a tote bag, she found the map the woman at the desk had given her. Villa 2 sat to the north of her building and somehow even closer to the sea.

Emmy broke the seal of her air-conditioned room and stepped back into the hallway. Her flip-flops pleasantly smacked the tile as she returned to the elevator, much more comfortable in her loose and flowing clothing now. Outside, the sun still beat down from above, but a gentle breeze cooled the ocean side of the building when she got there. The Caribbean rolled and tumbled onto the shore to her right, the color palette completely different from anything back home. The powder-white sand and crystal water were almost hard to look at for being so vibrant. Her brain could hardly process the colors. Lounge chairs and umbrellas dotted the beach with sunbathers basking in the heat. The sweet, thick smell of coconut and cream threaded into the misty air, either from the cocktails melting in sandy glasses, the oil and sunblock, or the actual coconuts growing on trees.

It was *Wish you were here* postcard perfect, and Emmy found herself smiling.

She followed a path to the end of her building and saw a small cluster of stucco houses in a shady grove of palm trees. Each had its own walkway and enough space between the next to allow privacy. Villa 2 hid behind a lush garden. Emmy almost didn't see the hand-painted address tile thanks to the crash of flaming pink bougainvillea draping the front doorway. Birds-of-paradise poked their spiky little heads in every direction like a curious flock beneath the front windows, and a forest of squat palms brushed her legs as she made her way up the path.

She could not even fathom what Ben and Piper were shelling out per night for this place.

When Emmy reached for the doorbell, because of course there was a doorbell, she noted a second hand-painted tile below the one marking it Villa 2. *Bridal Villa.* She smiled again.

She half expected a butler to open the door, but instead, it was her sister. Barefoot and wearing a gauzy white cover-up over a pink bikini and holding a tumbler with clinking ice.

"Hi. Um . . . *wow?*" Emmy greeted. "And here I thought my room was nice."

Piper casually waved her hand and welcomed her in. "Yeah. At least we don't have to share the bridal villa with the other wedding couple too."

Emmy followed her into a space equally as beautiful as the outside. Kitchen, living room—actual doors closing off bedrooms. Everything was marble and sandstone, the beach out the back doors clearly private, and to top it off, they had their own pool. A peanut-shaped puddle three shades bluer than the teal sea just beyond it.

"Piper, this is incredible," Emmy gushed.

She expected another dismissive *this is my life now* hand wave, but instead, she heard a hard sob that pierced her right in the heart.

Emmy immediately dropped her bag and pulled her sister into her arms. Piper was taller, so her chin landed on Emmy's shoulder. Still, Emmy cradled her against her like a little sister and stroked her hair. She saw over her shoulder Piper had set up camp at the breakfast bar, a slab of icy marble, with a bottle of tequila and bag of Takis.

"Everything is going to be all right," she promised her. "Mom and Dad are on the way. Your dreamboat fiancé is out there walking to the ends of the earth to make you happy. Your friends are coming. Everyone will be here together, and it will all work out."

Piper shuddered in her arms and said something Emmy was not at all expecting. "I wish Josh was here."

Oh.

Mention of their brother stunned Emmy into silence. A hot wall of pain slammed into her and nearly closed off her throat. She suddenly couldn't breathe.

Piper pushed back and wiped her eyes. "I'm sorry. I've been thinking of him a lot lately because I hate that he can't be here for this. I was doing okay with it, and then things went wrong with the hotel, and it was like the last straw. This dam broke loose, and now I can't stop."

Piper had always been so free with her emotions. She didn't hold them back but instead embraced them, even when messy and inconvenient. Emmy didn't have that skill. She swallowed hers down and left them festering and sometimes cancerous inside her. It was how she'd coped with their brother's death as a teen, thinking she was being strong rather than doing herself a disservice, and the habit had lingered.

But here, in this beautiful place with her beautiful sister crying in her arms over their shared loss, she felt herself break. She stopped fighting the pain she kept at bay whenever she thought about Josh and let it in. It ripped through her, shattering her like glass, but her sister's arms around her helped hold her together.

She squeezed Piper tighter. "I wish he was here too," she said thickly. Tears had welled up her throat and pushed out her eyes.

They held each other, crying, in a shared moment of sorrow. They hardly ever talked about their brother, but Emmy quickly remembered the hole that plagued both their hearts felt slightly more whole when they were remembering him together.

Josh was permanently twenty-three in her mind. Curly hair the same color as hers, a big, generous smile for everyone because he just plain loved people. She had trouble envisioning him close to forty, as he would have been now if he were still alive, but she imagined he'd still be smiling. Maybe coaching his kid's Little League team by now.

Piper chortled a soggy-sounding laugh and pulled back to wipe her nose. She found a box of tissues on the countertop. "God, he was such a dork. I miss him so much." She dabbed her eyes with a wet smile.

Again, so free with her emotions. Emmy tried to be as brave. She forced her voice to come out around the hard lump jamming her throat. "He'd probably be married to, like, a supermodel by now."

Piper huffed another laugh. "Yeah, with, like, five kids and a mansion in Malibu. Tom and Gisele predivorce."

"He'd have half his own baseball team."

"Maybe a reality TV show."

"A podcast, surely."

"A spokesperson deal with Subway."

"Two World Series rings and a Golden Glove."

"A charity for abandoned turtles."

"The cover of *Men's Health*."

"A late-night appearance with one of the Jimmys."

"An invitation to the Met Gala."

"What? No, he was never fashionable enough for that."

"I mean, if he's married to Gisele and hawking sandwiches on TV, he's probably got a whole team of stylists at his disposal."

"True, but professionals can only take you so far, and Josh would never be avant-garde enough to wear something other than a classy tux."

"Oh, he totally would. Don't you remember that Halloween when he dressed up as David Bowie? Full Ziggy Stardust makeup?"

Piper narrowed her eyes in thought.

"You were probably too young," Emmy said, recalling Josh had been in high school then, which would have put Piper in preschool still.

They both sighed, wrung out from imagining the life their brother would have had. The bittersweetness of it left Emmy feeling full and empty at the same time.

"Can I get some of that?" she asked, and pointed at the bottle of tequila.

"Help yourself." Piper pointed to the cabinet nearest the sink in the kitchen. "Glasses are in there."

With fresh drinks in hand, they ventured out onto the back patio. Privacy hedges shielded either side of the pool deck and small grassy yard and edged up to the sand. There, a pair of lounge chairs under a thatched umbrella with a table pointed out to sea. The scene was a Corona commercial come to life.

Piper sank into one of the cushy chairs under the patio's pergola laced with more tropical flowers and vines, and Emmy peeled off her cover-up and slipped into the pool. The cool water swallowed her the same way she swallowed her icy drink: with a refreshing and necessary gulp. She swam the width of the pool and rested her arms atop the opposite wall. Her gaze hovered at sea level. The only thing between her and the curling waves was a short stretch of lawn and sand. She turned back around to face her sister.

"Piper, this is kind of absurdly amazing."

Piper sighed and rested her chin on her hand. "It was supposed to be anyway."

Emmy swam back to the other side of the pool. She climbed out and sat in the chair opposite her sister. Sunlight cut through the pergola, leaving them striped with dark and light bars. Birds chirped, waves crashed. Emmy felt the cares of normal life melting like the ice in her glass. "No, it is—and it will be. No matter what. Even if you have to get married in this backyard, it will be perfect."

Piper sighed again like she didn't believe her. She ran her fingertip painted the color of a ballet slipper around the rim of her glass. "I know I sound like a spoiled brat, but I had a vision. And this is not how it was supposed to be."

Emmy sipped her drink. She'd found a fruity juice in the fridge to cut the tequila. The combination pinched her tongue with a delicious tartness. "Well, maybe we should forget about what was *supposed to be* and enjoy what is. Sometimes it's the unexpected changes that turn out for the best."

Piper eyed her with an arched brow. "That's a very un-Emmy thing to say. What's gotten into you? Also, where is your date?"

A rosy glow warmed Emmy's cheeks. She thought she might need to jump into the pool again. The truth was, what had gotten into her was a curious optimism over what was going to happen when Gabe showed up. Yes, of course she was still thrumming with nerves over the prospect, but something in the air, the water—maybe aided a *tiny* bit by the tequila—had her feeling a new kind of anxious. A not altogether unpleasant kind.

"He'll be here tomorrow."

Piper perked up. "Really? Like, a real person? Not a Canadian Boyfriend situation?"

Emmy rolled her eyes. "Yes, a real person."

"Who is he?"

Now Emmy buried her face in her drink. This moment had been

inevitable since Gabe had agreed to come—actually, since she'd asked Axe Murderer to come. But Piper didn't need to know the latter detail.

"It's Gabe," she quietly muttered into her glass and sipped.

"Who?" Piper leaned in like she didn't hear. She would not let up.

Emmy set her glass down and grumbled. "It's Gabe. Olson. From work."

Her sister's face changed with the speed of a cuttlefish's colors from shock to suspicion to a scheming satisfaction. "Well, that's a surprise. I thought you didn't date, and here you are dating a co-worker—and one you don't like, at that. Although you did look pretty cozy at my bachelorette party."

"We are not dating."

Piper continued to grin at her. "No? Then what exactly are you doing that has him willing to fly to another country for you?"

Emmy considered, because that was an excellent question—and one Gabe himself had asked her weeks ago. She still did not know what they were doing, but she couldn't deny the existence of the little butterflies flapping curious wings inside her at the thought of him joining her.

But they still had boundaries. She could not date her co-worker.

"We're not crossing any lines. He's just doing me a favor."

"Mm-hmm," Piper hummed like she didn't believe her. "And what if you did cross a line? Would that be so bad?"

"Yes," Emmy said emphatically. "Because I like my job."

At this, Piper's smug little grin faltered at the edges. She sighed and reached her hand across the table, reading her sister like a book. "Em, how many times do I have to tell you? Just because your jerk ex told you that you can't have a career and a relationship doesn't mean it's true. You don't have to put up your defenses all the time. Also, still sorry Jacob is going to be here. I can poison his flan if you want me to."

Emmy quietly laughed at the same time a well of hot, familiar

anger surged up inside her. It had dulled over time but was still read-
ily present. "You don't need to poison him."

"No, because seeing you with a hot date will ruin his weekend
enough on its own," Piper said with a flirty wink. She squeezed
Emmy's hand and took on a sober but encouraging tone. "But seriously, you don't have to choose between your job and a relationship.
I know baseball was your and Josh's thing, and I know your job makes
you feel close to him." Her voice wobbled and a soggy sob slipped
from Emmy's mouth. Piper squeezed her hand tighter. "But I also
know you could be the commissioner of baseball someday—literally
running the whole damn show—and it's not going to bring Josh back.
He'd want you to have a life outside of your job, Em."

Emmy gaped at her wise little sister, floored all over again. Piper's
ability to cut straight to the heart of the matter never ceased to
amaze her. It was true: her job made her feel close to her brother, and
she kept pushing to succeed at it as if making it all the way to the top
would somehow fill a void. But maybe all that pushing was coming at
the expense of other aspects of her life.

"Stop being so smart; you're stealing my thunder as eldest sibling."

Piper giggled and wiped a stray tear from her eye. "So, Gabe the
Babe Olson, huh? Whatever happened to asking Texting Guy?"

A hot pang of guilt hit Emmy like she'd been caught. "Oh, that . . .
got complicated."

Thankfully, she didn't have to elaborate because Ben, bless him,
appeared at the back door.

"Pipes? Are you out here?" He slipped outside and slid the door
shut to keep in the precious refrigerated air.

"Yes," Piper said. "Please tell me you fixed everything."

Ben circled the table and kissed the top of her head. "Not everything, but I did get them to comp some massages at the spa to help
deal with the stress. One for each of you starting in a half hour, if you
want them."

Emmy polished off her drink and set the glass on the table. "Earning husband points already. I'm in."

Piper looked less certain, but Emmy stood and reached for her hand to make the decision for her.

"Come on. Let's go get pampered."

Piper followed with a half-hearted sigh.

Emmy's own heart took a tumble when she found her phone inside and saw she had a text message from Axe Murderer. Not having thought to change his name in her phone, she threw a glance at her sister to make sure she hadn't seen.

But Piper was too distracted to notice.

Emmy's heart took another tumble when she opened the message.

> You can add this text to my tab, but just checking in to say I got an earlier flight. See you tonight.

Chapter 12

Emmy could hardly relax through her massage. She could hardly greet her parents when they arrived. She could hardly hold a conversation with Ben's parents when they all gathered in the villa's backyard for the pre-prewedding casual dinner. All she could think of was Gabe Olson on a plane coming closer by the minute.

He was scheduled to touch down at 8 p.m. local time, which would be 6 p.m. body clock time thanks to the time difference, which would mean they would be *awake* when he got there and have to figure out what the hell to do for several hours before they could then figure out how the hell to share a hotel room with one bed.

There wasn't enough cool Caribbean breeze, beautiful scenery, or piña coladas to calm Emmy down now. She'd thought she'd have another day to prepare before he descended on her. But no. In true Gabe Olson fashion, he'd pulled one over on her and left her spinning.

Admittedly, the spinning was half lusting and concentrated in her lower abdominal region, which was *highly* confusing and *not* helped by the piña coladas she kept downing in an effort to stop all the spinning but that only made her spin more. She had half a mind to text Beth ABORT MISSION and have her come get her.

But.

Amid all the spinning and mingling with family and a few friends who'd arrived early, the worried creases on Piper's face had started to lift. Emmy even caught her full-on smiling a few times, laughing with her future in-laws, and she wasn't about to do anything to ruin it.

So Emmy kept her spinning to herself as she too mingled and laughed. A veritable tornado ripped around inside her, but on the outside, she performed her MOH duties with grace.

That was, until her phone pinged with an I'm here message from Axe Murderer.

Emmy had lost track of time in the festivities. Night had completely fallen. The moon shone on the inky sea like a spotlight. Someone had lit the torches lining the yard and sent the air dancing with flickering flames.

She checked the time on her phone to see it was after nine, which meant Gabe's I'm here text indicated he was already at the hotel and not still at the airport, having just landed in Mexico.

Her heart leapt into her throat. Her hands began to sweat. Her time for preparation shrank down to minutes if she was lucky. She was half drunk and all the way panicking. Through her dizzy haze, she tried to figure out what to text him back. Should she invite him to the villa? Meet him at the room? Go for a nightcap at one of the bars?

But it turned out she didn't have to do any of that, because Piper materialized at her side and pinched her elbow.

"Em," she said, and nodded toward the back of the house.

Emmy looked up to see Gabe standing there at the door, loose shirt partway unbuttoned, shorts, boat shoes. The flickering flames cut his face into dramatic shadows, arching his cheekbones even higher and leaving his dark eyes glittering.

Oh. He meant *here*, here.

"*Easy*, girl," Piper said when Emmy sagged against her. She hadn't even realized her knees had given out. Her body was responding to him in the same way it had when she'd seen him in the office kitchen the morning after the big reveal, which, somehow, was only yesterday. It knew before her brain did, and on a deeper level, that she wanted to see him. Badly. Piper pushed her back up to standing with a laugh.

"Sorry," Emmy said as a heat wave engulfed her. "I've had a few drinks."

"Mm-hmm," Piper said, like she didn't buy that as the reason Emmy had suddenly turned to jelly. "Go make him feel welcome." She gave her a little shove.

Emmy almost tripped on the edge of the lawn where they'd been standing. The space between her and Gabe expanded into infinity and somehow disappeared all at once. Without the context of their normal life around them—the office, the ballpark, their home city—a million cues to signify how things were *supposed to be*—the world shrank to only them in a completely free new territory. He watched her the whole way while she walked toward him, as if his eyes were reeling her in on an invisible string. The rest of the party faded away: sounds of laughter, the soft music pumping from the house's exterior speakers, the gentle splashing of someone kicking their feet in the pool. All she could hear were the waves and the sound of her own thundering heart.

And then, his voice.

"Hi."

"Hi."

"You look nice." His eyes took a polite tour of the flowing floral dress she'd put on for dinner. It hugged her chest and draped openly around her legs. She wore a pair of wedge sandals with it.

"You look . . . here," she said, still stunned and a bit overwhelmed by his presence. He'd obviously freshened up after his flight, and the smell of him reached out to grab her with a heady hand.

Gabe laughed, and the warm sound sent her chest fluttering. "Yes, here I am. I hope it's okay I came earlier than planned. I got an alert for an open seat and took it."

"Of course it's okay. I'm glad you made it. How'd you know where we were?"

"The front desk told me. I went to the room first, and when it was empty, I figured I'd find you all at the villa."

"Good thing you aren't an actual axe murderer swindling informa-tion out of innocent hotel clerks to find me," Emmy said, and sucked her piña colada's straw. It was easily her fourth of the night.

"Good thing." He gave her a cheeky grin. "So, this place is incred-ible," he said in a change of subject and looked around appreciatively.

"Ah, yes. Did I forget to mention my brother-in-law's family is filthy rich?" Emmy said with a facetious grimace.

"You may have overlooked that detail."

"Apologies. But don't worry; they are all super nice."

"I would hope so."

Emmy sucked her straw again until it made a sputtering sound. "So," she said, trying to embrace the awkward situation they were in by poking fun at it. "Wanna meet my whole family?"

Gabe snorted a laugh and sweetly blushed. "Yes, but could I maybe get one of those first?" He pointed at her empty glass.

"Oh, indeed. I need a refill anyway."

She led him into the house where the magically bottomless blender held a fresh batch of creamy frozen booze. Emmy honestly didn't know who kept making the drinks, but they were damn good at it, and she wasn't about to stop them.

Back outside, drinks in hand, she introduced Gabe to her parents, Ben's parents, Ben's brother and his wife, and two of Piper's friends who'd been on the bachelorette cruise but thankfully had either been too drunk then or were too drunk now to recognize First Mate Gabe. The introductions were pleasant but brief, with most everyone tired from travel and promising to catch up more over the coming days.

Soon, the party was over and the bride- and groom-to-be kicked everyone out so they could go to bed. Emmy and Gabe made their way back toward their building along the paved path. The tropical night hummed with chirps and buzzing. Waves crashed in the dis-tance, and palms rustled. The jungle came alive with a new set of sounds after dark.

"How was your flight?" Emmy asked when the silence between

them became too obvious to ignore. She was a hair past tipsy and now into drunk territory, which had been intentional because she didn't know how else she was going to be able to fall asleep in the same room as Gabe Olson.

"It was fine," he said. "I had an aisle seat." He'd been nothing but charming and friendly at the party, but now that it was only the two of them, Emmy sensed a wall had risen. He was guarded with an almost painful effort.

"Love an aisle seat," Emmy said, trying to lighten the mood. "Good for the legs." She kicked her foot out in front of her, pointing her toe, and tottered off-balance.

"Careful," Gabe said, and reached out to steady her. His warm hands gripped her bare arms and sent a wave tingling through her.

She tittered and put her foot back on the ground. "Thanks. Those piñas were strong. I don't even know who was making them. The Ghost of Piña Colada Present."

"You are drunk."

"Indeed. Are you not?"

"Not as much as you, Bird Girl."

Emmy playfully gasped and held up a hand to her ear. "Do you think we can hear birds?"

"If we're quiet, probably."

"Then stop talking."

"I'm not talking."

"Yes, you are."

"Well, now we both are."

"But you're talking more—" Emmy cut off with a loud shriek and all but jumped into his arms.

"What! What is it?!" he shouted and squeezed her close.

But Emmy was already laughing. She pointed to the leafy grass beside the path where a thick, spiky iguana grumpily looked at them like they were interrupting his night. "It's just an iguana. I saw its tail move out of the corner of my eye and thought it was a snake." Her cackle echoed off the building and out to sea. Drunken tears dotted her eyes.

Gabe looked down at her with a narrowed gaze, and she realized they were perfectly modeling the famed clinch pose from romance novel covers. Her hands pressed into his chest, and one of his arms wrapped around her shoulders and the other, her waist. She'd even jerked her knee up on reflex lest the not-snake try to slither over her exposed toes.

"Sorry," she said, and removed herself from his grip. A tiny smile twitched her lips at his momentary reluctance to let her go.

Gabe cleared his throat and shoved his hands into his pockets. They started walking again. "So, what's on the docket for tomorrow?"

"Negotiations, apparently."

"Oh?"

"Yes. Since the hotel screwed up so royally, their suggestion is both wedding parties sit together to come to some kind of agreement about how to share. My job is to keep my sister from combusting. *Speaking of my sister . . .*" Emmy said, and spun on her toes to face him, continuing to walk backward. She'd wanted to clear the air since that night on the bachelorette cruise, and she was drunk enough to have the courage to do it right now. "I still feel really bad about what she said that night on the boat. I don't hate you, Gabe. It wasn't true."

He blinked at her, looking caught off guard. Then he let out a long breath that surprised her. "I think it was partly true."

"No, it wasn't. I promise. I mean, sure, you make me want to scream and throw things sometimes, but I don't *hate* you. I—"

He held up a hand to stop her and stopped walking. "That's not the part I meant."

This time, she blinked at him in confusion.

"She also said I take things from you at work all the time, and the truth is, *I've* felt bad ever since." A look of sincerity softened his handsome face. "I know it can't be easy being the only woman all the time, Emmy. And I know we can act a little *boys' club* sometimes. Between that and what you texted me about feeling like you don't fit in, I'm really sorry if I've ever made you feel like you weren't part of the team. Like what I said the other week about you never having been on the field; that was a real jerk thing to say. You're one of the smartest people I've ever met, and you absolutely deserve all the same things I get, if not more. I'm going to be more sensitive to how you are treated—by everyone—from now on. I promise."

Emmy's mouth fell open. She blinked in shock. It was like he'd read lines from a script titled *The Exact Right Thing to Say to Emmy Jameson*. When she managed to close her mouth, she cleared her throat and found her voice. "Thank you. That means a lot to hear, actually."

"Well, I mean it."

"Good."

They continued walking in silence for a few more moments.

"Scream and throw things, huh?" Gabe asked, and shot her a sly grin.

She flushed over the admission she'd made. "Only on your best days."

Gabe laughed a warm, throaty sound and turned into the breezeway of their building.

Emmy's heart kicked up a notch because they were now one elevator ride away from the inevitable.

"You swindled an extra room key out of the front desk too, I see," she said, and nodded at the band around his wrist.

He lifted his arm as the elevator arrived. "Yes. Celia was very generous."

"I'm sure she was," she said, casting him a sly grin.

"What's that face for?"

"Oh, nothing. I'm just sure you shamelessly sweet-talked your way into that key, because I never gave them your name at the front desk."

He scoffed as they stepped into the elevator. "Are you accusing me of being a flirt, Jameson?"

"If the shoe fits, Olson," she said as the elevator doors closed and lifted them off the ground. The small space made her aware of every breath. She felt his heavy gaze on her. It sent a signal straight to the pleasant burn low in her belly that had been growing hotter all night.

"It goes both ways, you know," she said.

"What does?"

"I get it now. Because of what you texted me, I know why you are the way you are at work. The whole *formative years in a competitive sport* thing. Makes total sense why you always want to win and have trouble connecting with people."

Gabe went quiet, and Emmy worried she'd overstepped. But then he half turned to her with a look that was at once shy and scorching and said, "Except with you."

Her knees wobbled again, and she leaned against the wall for support. He held her gaze while the corner of his mouth twitched up. The metal box was suddenly hot and small in the most delicious way.

"Tell me what you're thinking," she said with a rush of drunken bravery.

He fully turned to her and leaned in close enough that she pressed her back to the wall behind her. The cool metal sent a shiver rippling through her. His lips parted and his voice came out a near growl.

"I don't think that would be a good idea right now." The words uncoiled from his tongue like a velvet rope that wrapped around her. He had her in a choke hold and he wasn't even touching her.

She thought of making a joke about him flirting with her like she'd accused him of doing with the desk clerk, because *holy fuck*, but she couldn't form words. His dark eyes burned inches from hers. She'd stopped breathing. Her pounding heart and the ding of the elevator arriving were the only sounds.

Emmy shook her head, coming back into herself. "Well, knowing you, whatever you were thinking was probably an insult."

He quietly laughed and then sighed. He followed her out of the elevator and down the hall. Emmy was suddenly bone-tired and hoped they could sort out the sleeping arrangement without too much fuss. Maybe she'd just pass out on the bed, and he'd have to deal with it however he deemed suitable.

A blast of frozen air greeted them when she opened the door. She quickly noted the addition of his belongings neatly unpacked alongside hers.

"I used the rest of the closet and drawers, if that's okay," he said.

"Of course. I left them empty for you." A watery yawn suddenly hit her. She covered it with the back of her hand.

"You must be tired," he said, and headed toward the bed. He sat and removed his shoes.

Gabe Olson shoeless. Who knew the sight would make her dizzy.

"*You* must be tired. You worked today and then flew here. All I did was travel then get a massage and drink my weight in piña coladas."

He grinned and stood up to reach for the dresser drawers. He moved so comfortably while Emmy stood there feeling as agitated as a beehive full of rebels trying to kill the queen. He pulled an old T-shirt out of the drawer, one with *SDSU Baseball* branded across the chest, and she had her answer to what Gabe Olson wore to bed: old alma mater tees. Well, at least that was what he wore to bed in the presence of a half-drunk female roommate of very complicated relation.

"I'm going to get ready for bed," Emmy said, and escaped to the bathroom. She'd stashed a set of pajamas in there earlier in the event of this exact scenario and thanked her past self for it. Once she'd brushed her teeth and scrubbed off the minimal makeup she'd put on for dinner, she changed into her own pj's: a T-shirt and comfy sports bra along with a pair of cotton shorts. She'd deemed it suitable for sharing a room with a very attractive male roommate of extremely complicated relation.

When she returned, ready to negotiate the bed issue, she found the room empty.

"Gabe?" she called into the space she could already see every square foot of. He wasn't in it.

"Down here." His voice came from the floor on the other side of the bed.

Emmy frowned and crawled up on the bed that she noticed was now without a few pillows and the top blanket. "What are you doing?" she asked when she found him on the floor in a makeshift nest with said missing bedding and his phone propped on his chest.

"Going to sleep."

"On the floor?"

"Yes. You can have the bed."

She frowned deeper. She knew the bed would be a tricky situation, but she figured they'd construct some kind of barrier or take shifts. She never thought he'd volunteer for the floor.

"No," she said plainly.

"Why not?" He looked up at her like a cuddly teddy bear wrapped in white linen. The T-shirt hugged his broad shoulders and chest. A lock of his hair curled over his forehead.

Emmy sat up on her knees. "Well, for one thing, the floor is marble, and that's not even remotely comfortable. You won't be able to walk in the morning."

"It's not so bad," he said with a shrug.

"You're a terrible liar. Come on. This bed is gigantic. There is plenty of room for both of us." She patted the fluff beside her.

"Emmy, I'm fine. I'll stay down here."

"No, you won't because you'll be uncomfortable all night, and I'll be up here *worrying* about how uncomfortable you are all night, and neither of us will get any sleep. Get up here." She scooted back and started building a barrier down the bed's middle. "I'll make a wall if that makes it better. We can call down for more pillows."

"I don't think there are enough pillows in the world . . ." he muttered. He was still on the floor, and she could hardly hear him over the sound of rearranging the bedding.

"What was that?"

"Nothing. I'll be fine down here."

She finished building her barricade and reached over to snatch the blanket off him.

"Hey!" he called.

"Olson! Stop being such a stubborn ass and get up here!"

His head popped up at the bedside. He eyed her pillow wall with suspicion. She'd constructed it on top of the sheets and climbed into her side of the bed already.

"It's the best I can do," she said, and pointed at it. "Your side; my side. Now, let's sleep. We're going to need all our energy tomorrow to prevent Bridezilla Meltdown."

He eyed the pillows with another moment of hesitation and then decided he was satisfied. "I've heard those are the worst meltdowns," he said, climbing onto the bed.

"Life-threatening, really." Emmy felt the mattress dip under his weight. She rolled slightly toward the middle of the bed where the pillows stopped her. "See? Already working." She patted the wall.

He'd settled on top of the sheets and curled onto his side facing away from her. "Good night, Jameson."

"Good night, Olson." She clicked off the light and plunged them into darkness.

Emmy's heart nervously thrummed as they settled into the silence. She was acutely aware of him beside her. She could hear every breath, feel every movement. It took a fair amount of time for her heart to eventually calm into a relaxed rhythm. Sleep had almost pulled her under when his voice softly called her back.

"Emmy?"

The sound snapped her out of her haze. Her whole body became alert again as if he'd flipped a switch inside her. "Yeah?"

"Can I please have a blanket? It's really cold in here."

"Oh!" she said with an embarrassed laugh, not having realized she'd hogged them all. "Yes. Sorry. I turned the AC all the way down when I got here earlier." She removed the blanket she'd stolen from him and threw it over to his side.

"Thank you."

She listened to him settle beneath it and considered suggesting he climb under the covers with her. But that might have been one step too far into a direction they'd never be able to turn back from.

"Good night, Gabe," she said.

"Good night, Emmy."

The next morning, Emmy woke alone. She wondered if it had all been a dream, but the pillow wall was still intact, and Gabe's side of the bed was neatly made up with the blanket. His phone was gone from the nightstand and in its place, a piece of hotel stationery with a word scrawled in his familiar handwriting.

Running.

She reflexively rolled her eyes, because of course he would get up at—she turned to check the clock—8 a.m. on his first day of vacation to go for a run. She had half a mind to pull the sheet over her head and sleep off her sugary sweet hangover for two more hours. But she quickly realized his absence meant she had free rein to use the bathroom without worrying about sharing, and that might have been exactly why he'd gone out for a run.

Not wanting to waste the opportunity, she threw back the sheet and quickly padded into the bathroom. The icy floor made her both shiver and thankful that she'd convinced Gabe to sleep in the bed for fear he would have frozen to death on the marble. She basically ran through a steaming shower and took care of all necessary business in record time. She'd just flipped off the blow-dryer when she heard a knock at the door.

She walked into the hall to peer out the peephole and saw Gabe on the other side.

"Forget your key?" she asked in greeting when she opened the door.

She almost staggered back at the sight of him in a tight gray tee, black shorts, and a pair of red running shoes. Sweat clung to the ungelled hair around his face, flipping it out in chaotic little curls. Dashes of rosy pink colored his cheeks. He towered over her where she stood barefoot.

"Hey. No," he said, slightly winded, and swiped a hand through his damp hair. She saw his key right there on his wrist next to his smartwatch. "I just wasn't sure what you'd be doing in here and didn't want to barge in." He glanced at her outfit and softly smiled. "But I see you've taken advantage of being alone."

"Yes, um. Thank you," she said, and stepped aside to let him in.

"Of course." He passed her and somehow smelled like a tropical beach and not someone who'd just run several miles on one. The view from behind was even more distracting. The nylon shorts hugged his ass in a way that put jeans to shame. The sweat-dampened shirt carved out the muscles in his back.

She found herself forcefully having to pull out of a daze. "I can return the favor. I was about to head down to breakfast."

He found a water bottle in their minifridge and set about gulping it. "Great. I can meet you there after I shower?"

Emmy was suddenly hot and possibly a bit bothered. There was no way she could sit in the room knowing he was naked on the other side of the bathroom wall. She needed to make an exit well before that scenario.

"Sounds good. We'll be in the lobby restaurant."

"See you soon."

Gabe began untying his shoes, and she quickly grabbed hers along with her phone and sunglasses.

"See you." She slipped out the door still shoving on her sandals and steadied herself with a deep breath on the other side.

Once she had her head on straight, she made her way to a shuttle stop and rode back to the main lobby. The bright day already hung thick with humidity and enormous puffy clouds. She'd scrunched her hair into a tight bun and could already feel it fighting to expand itself.

Piper had instructed her to meet at the lobby breakfast buffet, and Emmy found her there with Ben looking resort bridal chic and like she was ready to stab someone with a fork.

"Hey," Emmy greeted when she joined their table. "Everything all right?"

Her sister sat across from her over a plate of papaya and scrambled eggs with her eyes drilling into a party at a nearby table. "That's *them*," Piper muttered.

As Emmy sank into her chair, she glanced across the terrace—a sun-splashed patio overlooking one of the enormous swimming pools—and saw two men sharing breakfast, one of them staring daggers right back at Piper.

"Them who?" Emmy leaned in and whispered. A waiter appeared and poured her a glass of water that instantly started sweating in the heat.

"Café?" he asked.

"Sí, por favor," Emmy said quickly as she tried to get a read on who her sister was assaulting with her eyes. "Piper, who are you looking at?"

"*Them*," Piper said again. "*The other wedding.*"

Realization dawned on Emmy. She glanced over her shoulder again to notice the men were her age, one of them with dark features and a painfully stylish hairdo, and the other, the one waging ocular warfare with her sister, fair and blond. They looked American, based on what exactly, Emmy couldn't tell, but she somehow knew it. The dark-haired one reached out and squeezed the blond one's hand and whispered something with a nod in their direction, prompting the blond one to scoff and look away. From that one interaction, Emmy got the sense they shared the same dynamic as Ben and Piper: one was cool and levelheaded, and the other a firecracker.

"Gary and Cary," Piper seethed like the two had personally conspired to ruin her wedding.

"Their names rhyme?" Emmy said. "That's cute."

Piper scoffed. "They are not *cute*, Em. They are the enemy and must be stopped!" She picked up her fork and stabbed it into a juicy slice of papaya.

Emmy made wide eyes at Ben, who scrubbed his face with a hand and sighed. "Well, what are you going to do? Battle for the wedding venue?" she asked, and sipped her water.

"If it comes to it, yes," Piper said, and narrowed her eyes.

Ben heaved another breath and lifted his napkin off his lap. "Piper, you are not *fighting* them for the venue."

"Why not? I could totally take Cary. We're the same size."

Emmy snorted, and Piper shot a death glare at her. She grimaced and decided to go fill a plate with breakfast.

When she returned with sliced fruit and an omelet, Piper and Ben were deep in hushed conversation.

"So, what's the deal?" Emmy interrupted. "How is this going to go down?"

Ben sat forward with his elbows on the table and folded his hands like he was in a board meeting. "We're meeting with the manager at nine thirty to see what can be worked out." Piper scoffed. "And *everyone is going to behave*," he said over the sound.

Emmy glanced over at Gary and Cary again. The blond one—who she gathered was Cary given Piper's comment on being his same size—was still glaring like he fully planned to out-zilla Piper during the showdown. "Well, this should be fun," Emmy said. "How do you know their names?"

"Because Gary, *who is a very nice person*," Ben said, emphasizing the words, "came over and introduced them. They are from LA. They got engaged around the same time we did."

"Oh, that's nice," Emmy said, and speared a pineapple wedge.

"It's not *nice*," Piper said with a glower. "Don't take their side, Em. I need you."

"There are no sides, Piper. It was a mistake, remember? It's the hotel's fault, not theirs. So you can stop staring at them like they ran over your foot." She waved her fork at her to refocus her attention.

Piper only glowered deeper.

Ben sighed again. "Where's Gabe?" he asked, and sipped his coffee.

"Oh, he went for a run this morning, so he's still in the room showering. He'll be here soon." Her face ignited to rocket launch temperature at the word *showering*. She sipped her own coffee and wished it was iced instead of hot.

Ben checked his watch. "Well, you might have to catch up with him later because I could really use you in this meeting in a few minutes." He tilted his head toward Piper with a pleading look on his face.

"Happy to help," Emmy said, though she was dreading it. She wasn't a great mediator, and with the way Piper and Cary were glaring at each other, she felt like a warthog about to be torn apart by two lions.

What she needed was an ally on the other side. Another neutralish party who could help negotiate without the emotional investment of being the bride or one of the grooms. How she was going to find one of those in the next fifteen minutes, she had no idea.

Emmy settled into her breakfast and tried to keep her nerves at bay as the pending meeting drew nearer. To compound that, Jacob could arrive at any moment given they were so close to the wedding. She was cautiously keeping her eyes peeled for a flash of blond surfer hair and an entitled smirk roaming around the property. She didn't want to run into him at all, but especially not without the buffer of Gabe there for support. So far, she was in the clear.

Soon, they were all back in the lobby. Team Piper & Ben and Team Gary & Cary awkwardly milled around the plush armchairs near the registration desk. Each side had gained a few more supporters:

Ben's brother and aunt; Gary's mom, based on the resemblance; a few members of the bridal parties. A small crowd had gathered, and Emmy felt like they were the Sharks and Jets about to throw down in a tropical paradise.

She was nervously wringing her hands, trying to think of an opening argument for equitable division of the venue, when Gabe appeared at the lobby entrance.

The calming wave that washed over her at the sight of him was not subtle. It muted the surrounding chatter, dulled her nerves. Narrowed her senses to only the space he occupied and cradled her there with him.

"Hey," he said with a warm smile when he approached her. "What's all this?"

The freshly showered smell of him flooded over Emmy. She took a small step back only to prevent herself from shoving her nose into the contours of his chest left visible by his partly unbuttoned shirt. He wore his boat shoes again and another pair of shorts. His hair was without any of its standard gel and was left curling over his forehead in rebellious little loops.

Vacation looked good on Gabe Olson. Very, *very* good.

"It's, um . . . the other wedding," Emmy managed to mutter. She needed to pull herself together, both to stop ogling her co-worker and so she could stop the Bride/Groomzilla war about to break out.

Gabe bounced up onto his toes to look into the crowd. When he landed back on his heels, his arm brushed Emmy's and then stuck there in a pleasantly tacky bind, as if the humidity wanted to glue them together. He markedly did not move it. "That's the other couple?"

Emmy markedly did not move her arm either.

"Yes. Gary and Cary from LA. Ben met them and says they're nice, but Piper is ready to go full *American Gladiators* with Cary for the venue. We are waiting for the manager to show up to start the discussion. He's late."

Gabe grimaced. "Well, I'd probably be late too if I was walking into this mess," he muttered. And then, "How can I help?"

Emmy turned to him, noting their arms were still glued together and doing nothing about it. Looking into his dark eyes quieted her nerves all over again. "You can keep me calm while I keep my sister calm."

"Done. What else?"

"Umm, manifest a second venue on the property? Teach my sister a valuable lesson about sharing? Find a mediator to help everyone get out of this alive?"

Just then someone called his name.

"Gabe?"

They both turned to see a harried-looking man with a duffel looped over his shoulder and a backward LA Lakers hat. He wore a gold watch and had a bright and startlingly familiar smile.

"Wait, *Henry*?" Gabe said in shock.

The man dropped his bag on the lobby floor and threw out his arms. "Dude! What are you doing here?"

Before Emmy blinked twice, they were embracing in a tangle of backslapping and matching grins.

"I'm here for a wedding!" Gabe said excitedly. "What are you doing here?"

"I'm here for a wedding too! I'm the best man!" Henry cried.

"No way!" Gabe turned to Emmy with surprised joy all over his face. "This is my cousin Henry from LA. Henry, this is my girl— I mean, my co-work— I mean my . . . Emmy. This is my Emmy." He stroked a hand through his messy hair and blushed.

"Nice to meet you," Emmy said, and felt her face warm at his charming fluster.

My Emmy. Her heart grew three sizes.

"Oh, is this the girl? The one your mom said you're wild about?" Henry asked with a wide grin.

"*What?!*" Gabe screeched and turned a burnt shade of red. "My *mom* told you about her?"

"No, dude. *My* mom told me about her. *You* told your mom, she told *my* mom, and now like half of LA knows. What did you expect to happen?"

"Oh Christ." Gabe buried his face in his hands.

"Anyway, good to see you, man!" Henry slapped him on the back again. "Small world to run into each other like this."

"Yeah, what are the odds," Gabe muttered, still recovering.

Emmy felt her own cheeks flaming. She knew his mom knew about her, but not his extended family. And, *wild about?* That would take *at least* two couch and wine therapy sessions with Beth to sort out later.

"I need to find Cary," Henry said, and craned his neck toward the crowd. "I just got here—dude, my flights, I can't even." He shook his head in dismay. "But I guess there's some kind of drama going on? I don't know. His texts have been getting progressively more incoherent. And violent . . ." He looked down with a grimace and thumbed his phone.

"Wait, Cary?" Emmy said.

"Yeah, you know him too? Wait, are you guys here for the *same wedding?* How wild would *that* be! I mean, I know some of Gary's friends, but not a ton, so there's totally a chance we've never met and we're all here for the same reason."

The man spoke a hundred miles a minute. Emmy was tempted to put her hand over his mouth just to get a word in. She noted Gabe instantly adapted to the same style of speech. She'd never seen him around his family other than Captain Carl and wondered if all the Olsons spoke like auctioneers around each other. Listening to them talk was like watching popcorn kernels in a kettle with the way they jumped around.

"No. We're here for the other wedding," Gabe said.

"Other wedding?" Henry asked.

"Yeah. Emmy's sister is getting married, and for a second, when you said you were the best man, I thought you might be *Ben's* best man, and that would have been—"

"Ben?"

"The other groom. Well, one of the grooms, I should say."

"There are a lot of grooms."

"There are. The hotel double-booked the venue this weekend. We were just down here trying to—"

"Oh, shit! *That's* what Cary has been freaking out about?" Henry thumbed his phone again. "Ah, I see it now." He nodded and tilted the screen to show Gabe. "I didn't get all the twins and wedding rings and knives and skulls before. But now I do. Makes sense."

"Totally. So, it's kind of a disaster, and we're trying to figure out—"

"*Time-out!*" Emmy shouted. She stepped between them and made a T shape with her hands.

They both stopped blabbering and looked at her.

"First of all," she said, turning to Gabe, "how many cousins do you have?"

"A lot. I told you I have a big family."

"We have, like, fifteen on our side alone," Henry chimed in.

"Second," Emmy went on, "*he* is the best man in the other wedding?"

"It would appear so, yes."

"Reporting for duty," Henry said with a salute.

Emmy couldn't believe it. Her wish had come true. Gabe had manifested an ally for her. Someone from the other side she could lean on for help negotiating.

"This is perfect," she said. She threw her arms around Gabe and squeezed him in a hug. "I think you just saved my sister's wedding." She kissed his cheek and left him standing there stunned.

His mouth popped open like he'd lost his cool and didn't know where to find it.

Emmy didn't have time to help him find it. She had a wedding to save.

"Come on," she said, and grabbed Henry's arm to head into the bedlam. "We're going to fix this."

Chapter 13

"I owe your cousin dinner back in LA," Emmy said as she sank into her chair next to Gabe with a contented sigh.

"I think it's just as fair to say he owes *you* dinner." He helped scoot her chair in, which was completely unnecessary but indulgent and appreciated. His arm brushed her bare shoulder, and his hand gripped the seat very close to her thigh.

After the morning's negotiations, Gabe had gone golfing with Henry while Emmy spent the afternoon at the pool with her sister and the bridal party. Still no Jacob sighting, and Emmy was so wrapped up in the spirit of the festivities she'd all but forgotten he was due to arrive at all. They'd all cleaned up for the rehearsal dinner they were now attending on the same terrace where they'd had breakfast.

What about a boat? Those had been the magic words during the negotiations. Emmy had thought of it, inspired by the bachelorette party she'd thrown. Luckily, Gary thought it was a great idea: thrilling, unique, memorable—everything they wanted their wedding to be, heightened to a new level. Together with Henry's help, he'd been able to convince Cary to agree to hosting their ceremony and reception on a chartered boat, courtesy of the hotel, in exchange for getting to use the landlocked venue for their rehearsal dinner tonight, while Piper and Ben got the venue for their ceremony and reception. That was why the Carmichael-Jameson party had been relocated to the lobby terrace—the second-largest space aside from the venue— for rehearsal celebrations. Piper had been willing to compromise if it meant she still got to get married beachfront and dance all night under the swaying palms, and Emmy had heaved an enormous sigh of relief.

"You both pulled off an amazing feat," Gabe said, and slowly removed his hand from the back of her chair. His fingertips grazed her shoulder blades and sent a thrilling zap straight to where her thighs met.

Emmy lifted her wine for reprieve. "That's largely credited to my skill for negotiating with difficult men," she muttered into her glass. Cary had been hard to win over.

Gabe gasped in mock scandal and pressed his palm to his chest. "Was that comment in reference to *me*, Jameson?"

"If the shoe fits, Olson," she said in a cheeky tone.

Under the table, he lightly stepped on her foot with his shoe.

"Ow!"

The lines between who they were behind their screens and who they were face-to-face had blurred so much they'd nearly dissolved. They'd gotten braver about touching each other. Little nudges, arm grazes. Swatting away bugs that may or may not have been present but served as excuses to brush fingertips against skin. Emmy took the liberty to playfully punch him in the arm for stepping on her foot.

"Ow," he quietly said, like it actually hurt. He reached up and squeezed where she'd hit him and rolled his shoulder back.

"Oh! Sorry," Emmy said, regretting it at the pained look on his face. "Are you all right?"

He shook his head once with a half grimace, half smile. "I'm fine. It's my own fault. Too much shoulder motion today."

"From golfing?"

"Yeah."

Through his opened top buttons, she glimpsed the scar on Gabe's collarbone where he'd been screwed back together years before. He'd told her he'd had pins and a plate put in his shoulder, and the thought made her knees weak in the worst way. She cringed again at seeing a piece of the scar now.

"I'll have to take it easy tomorrow," he said. "Maybe a pool day while you're getting ready for the wedding."

"I mean, they probably have a sports masseuse on hand at this place if you want a massage . . ." Emmy muttered and glanced over her shoulder.

Gabe was still gripping his arm right as Emmy's parents returned to their seats across from them. They'd been up mingling as mother and father of the bride. Piper and Ben were doing the same while everyone finished off their dinners before dessert was served.

"Gabe, sweetheart, are you all right?" Emmy's mother asked in concern when she noticed him holding his arm.

Emmy sucked in a breath and stilled with worry. Vera and Frank Jameson were the *last* people to talk to about a sports injury.

Gabe glanced over at the sound Emmy made and raised a brow at her sudden rigid posture.

Of course he had charmed the pants off her parents. Her mother was already calling him sweetheart, for goodness' sake. They were *thrilled* she'd brought a date, even though she'd introduced him as a friend. The doting looks on her mom's and dad's faces made Emmy want to throw herself in front of the oncoming bus that would surely smash the pleasantries to bits by bringing up any reminder of her brother.

"He got stung by a bee," Emmy covered.

"Just now?!" Vera asked with wide eyes and looked around like there might have been more bees ready to attack. But there weren't. Only a long table with a centerpiece runner made of palm and plumeria and tea light candles. Glittering wineglasses and champagne flutes sweated in the sinking sun. Dishware clinked.

"No, when he was golfing earlier," Emmy went on, her face flaming as the lie snowballed.

Gabe side-eyed her.

"Golfing?" her dad piped up. "Hey, we should play a round tomorrow!" Grayed at the temples and curly haired like Emmy, he was all smiles and welcome.

"You don't have time tomorrow, Dad. We have to get ready for the wedding starting at noon."

Her father waved his hands. "Oh, how long can it take to put on a suit? I won't want to get dressed too early anyway in this heat." He tugged at his shirt, a tasteful short-sleeved button-down Piper had approved. She'd forbidden anything floral printed or too loud. "What do you say, Gabe? We could fit in a morning nine?"

"Oh, um . . ." Gabe said, still squeezing his shoulder and now looking at Emmy for advice.

"He can't either," Emmy blurted again. "He has . . . a thing with his cousin."

"Your cousin in the other wedding?" Vera asked, and delicately cut into the piece of fish artistically draped over her dinner plate.

"Yes," Gabe said, still eyeing Emmy. "We're, um . . . going fishing?"

"Hey, now *there's* a sport!" Frank cheered. "The billfish down here will pull you overboard if you're not careful."

"I thought Emmy said you get seasick?" Vera added.

"She did?" Gabe said, and quickly recovered. "I do! I meant we are going fishing off the pier."

"Well, I'd certainly have time for that," Frank said, lifting his wine-glass in a toast. He gave Gabe a lippy smile and sipped.

Right then, one of Emmy's aunts came up behind her parents and wrapped them in a boisterous hug.

Emmy took advantage of their distraction and leaned in to whisper to Gabe. "*Fishing?* Why are you such a bad liar?"

"Why are we lying to your parents about bees?" he hissed back.

"Because sports injuries are a very, *very* touchy subject for my family. It's how my brother—" Her throat choked up with tears, and she couldn't say any more. Apparently, she didn't want to talk about it either.

Gabe read the truth in her eyes. She could see him remembering the conversation from that morning they'd had breakfast in her apartment and putting the pieces together. He stopped holding his shoulder and reached for her hand on the table. He squeezed it and gave her a soft smile. Then he turned to her parents, who'd been freed from the embrace of Aunt Mary and smiled again. "Frank, I'd love to go fishing from the pier with you tomorrow morning."

Emmy almost cried at the delighted twinkle in her dad's eye.

He lifted his glass in a toast again. "Well then, it's a date!"

Emmy felt her mother's eyes on her hand clasped with Gabe's. She didn't want to let it go, but she also didn't want to have the conversation she could sense brewing in her mother's mouth.

"So, I hear you two are competing for the same promotion at work?" Vera said exactly what Emmy was expecting. She knew how seriously Emmy took her job, even if she didn't exactly approve of said job, and she was rightfully wondering why she was crossing personal boundaries with a co-worker, even if she was perennially lobbying for Emmy to find a partner.

Emmy would rather have gone back to talking about fake beestings and sports fishing. Work had been a distant memory for the past day and a half, and she was not ready to invite it to the party now.

"Um, we are, yes," Gabe said with a gentle laugh, still holding her hand. "And Emmy is stiff competition. Your daughter is really remarkable. I've learned a lot from her." He gazed over at Emmy, and she almost fell out of her chair.

Now he was reading from a script titled *The Exact Right Thing to Say to Emmy Jameson's Parents.*

On cue, Vera and Frank both lit up. Their enthusiasm admittedly caught Emmy off guard. Any talk of her job often left everyone looking for a change of topic.

"That's our girl," Frank said, his eyes shining. Of the two of them, he'd always been more supportive. "She's gotta be tough as hell to work in men's sports. No offense to you, of course."

"None taken," Gabe said. "And she is tough. One of the toughest people I know." His lips quirked like he was thinking of a secret. "She deserves everything."

Emmy swallowed a hard, hot lump in her throat that struggled to go down thanks to the force with which her heart was beating. She looked over at her mother to check if she was satisfied with the answer she'd been fishing for. Based on the glow on Vera's face, she was.

Wrapped up in the spirit of it all—the sun melting in the sky, the decadent meal, sounds of her loved ones near—Emmy couldn't have been blamed for thinking it really did matter what her parents thought of Gabe. That their opinion of him would need to extend beyond this weekend and reach back into real life. It didn't, because this was just a favor, and she and Gabe were just co-workers. But imagining they were more felt too easy in this golden paradise with his hand wrapped around hers and him saying all the right things. She quietly longed for this version of life to become reality.

"How'd you get into baseball, Gabe?" her father asked as the wait-staff began clearing plates for dessert.

Emmy tensed again, nervous about skirting the dark-edged topic. Gabe felt it and gently smoothed his thumb over her hand in small circles.

"I pitched in college," he said. "But I also majored in math and went to grad school to get a master's in statistics, so here I am. Now I love the strategy of it all. The way it's one giant formula." He flashed them his million-dollar smile, and Emmy silently thanked him for leaving out the part about his career-ending injury.

"Ah, I thought I recognized an ex-player," Frank said. "You've definitely got the reach." He lifted his hand as if to demonstrate how tall Gabe was. "Have you ever considered coaching?"

"Actually, I'd love to get back on the field," Gabe said. Emmy turned to him in surprise. "Not as a player, of course. But on the training staff. It's always been a bit of a dream."

Emmy squeezed his hand at the small ache in his voice. She wasn't sure her parents could hear it, but she did. She knew what he ached over.

Their conversation then turned to the wedding and tomorrow's schedule. It would be a full day of preparation and celebration. It had been so long coming, Emmy was both thrilled for it to finally happen and eager for it to be over with.

As she sipped the final drops of her final glass of wine of the night, she caught sight of her sister radiating joy across the terrace. Piper laughed with her head tilted back, dark hair cascading over her shoulders and shining in the candle- and moonlight. She wore a white jumpsuit and a glittering wreath necklace that looked like icicles dripping from her throat. Another Carmichael family heirloom, certainly. The night had, miraculously, gone off without a hitch. Sure, they were crammed into a smaller space than planned, but that made everything all the more intimate.

Her sister was happy; her parents were happy; she was happy. The moon was full, and Gabe Olson was stifling a yawn beside her and looking ready for sleep.

"Bedtime?" Emmy asked.

"It was a long day," he said, and wiped the tiny tear that had pinched out of his eye.

"Well, tomorrow is going to be even longer."

"Maybe for you. I'm just a plus one freeloader."

"I believe you made a fishing date with my dad, and you can't break a promise to Frank Jameson."

"I wouldn't dream of it." Based on the honest glint in his eye, she could tell he was serious.

She smiled at him and then nudged his knee. "Come on. I think we are safe to make an exit right now."

They slipped away from the party without any fuss and headed for the shuttle stop. As they whizzed through the grounds in a golf cart, Emmy grew increasingly aware of Gabe's presence beside her. She'd been aware of it all day. And if she was completely honest, she was always aware of it. In any space they shared, whether it be an office, a hotel room, a dinner table, a zippy little golf cart, he was like an anchor pulling her in. A sun around which she orbited. She'd never realized how aware of him she was until she'd started paying attention.

When the shuttle deposited them outside their building, a breeze blew through the archway leading to the beach like a hand beckoning them. The salty air curled over Emmy's face and shoulders, fresh and inviting, and made her want to stay in the open a while longer before she was back someplace where Gabe's presence and her thoughts over what to do with it would overwhelm her.

"Want to go for a walk?" she asked, and nodded toward the path leading to the beach.

"Sure," he said with a nod.

They passed through the building and out into the dark on the other side. Except for the tiny ground lights lining the path every ten feet or so, the only light came from a few balconies glowing above them, the villas dotting the distance, and the moon on the water. They walked in silence for a while, and Emmy let the rush of the waves soothe her nervous thoughts. They'd been inching closer and closer all day, in many senses, and she wasn't sure how close they might continue to get.

"You don't actually have to hang out with my dad, you know," she said when they stepped off the paved path and into the sand. The beach was empty and bleached black and white by moonlight.

"Of course I do. I want to."

She looked over at him and felt a warm smile spread across her face. "Well, be careful. He might try to adopt you."

Gabe snorted a laugh. "Frank and Vera Jameson seem like pretty cool parents, so I might take him up on the offer."

"Back off, pal. They're mine." She playfully nudged him with her elbow.

He laughed again and stumbled a step sideways in the sand.

Emmy thought back to their conversation with Henry that morning in the lobby. Well, *his* conversation with Henry that she had to forcibly insert herself into because they wouldn't even pause for a breath. "What's your mom's name?"

"Rose," he said with a small smile.

"And your dad?"

"John."

When he didn't say anything else, she wondered if he was uncomfortable talking about them. "What are they like?" she asked, somehow knowing he'd open up to her, even if that was the case.

He softly smiled again, but it looked almost sad. "They're the best. My parents did everything for me. They paid for every baseball camp and traveling team when I was a kid. They came to every game." He huffed and swiped his hand through his hair. "They gave me the best shot, and I crashed and burned—literally." He squeezed his shoulder again and shook his head.

Emmy stopped walking and turned to him. "I don't think that's fair to say. You've done pretty well otherwise. And besides, if you'd kept pitching, you'd be old by baseball standards now. Maybe even staring down retirement. I mean, sure, you'd probably be sitting on an obscene mountain of money with a bunch of trophies and rings, but your glory days would be behind you. I think you've got a lot of glory left in other ways, Gabe Olson." She poked him in his uninjured arm and smiled.

He looked at her for a few beats, considering, and then softly smiled back. "Thank you."

"It's the truth," she said, and kept walking. He followed her for a few silent paces. The waves invisibly crashed off to their right; trees rustled to the left. "What you said to my parents at dinner, is that true? I didn't know you wanted to be on the training staff."

He shrugged. "It's a long shot and will probably never happen, but it's kind of a dream. If I can't be *on* the field, it's as close as I can get."

Emmy considered it with a tilt of her head. "Well, I think you'd be a great coach. And you would be traveling with the team."

"Yes. And doing early workouts and ice baths and weight training—for them, not me." He said it like it thrilled him.

"You sound way too excited about all that."

"It is exciting."

"Sure, if you like your limbs falling off by your late twenties."

"With the right training, they won't."

"Whatever you say, Coach."

They walked a few more paces without talking. The silence between them grew increasingly comfortable.

"You know what I've been thinking about?" Gabe eventually said.

"What?"

"All the times we overlapped without even noticing it."

Emmy glanced sideways at him. "What do you mean?"

"I mean all the times we were texting each other and didn't catch on. Like that night we were out with Torres and Ishida and complaining about being at a work thing when we'd rather be home and we were *with each other* at the work thing."

An awkward, embarrassed laugh popped from Emmy's throat. "Goes to show what kind of company we are, I guess."

"And then the next day when I brought you breakfast, and you texted me you were recovering from your hangover with spicy food and reality TV when I'd literally just brought you spicy food and left you watching reality TV."

"Yeah, that was pretty bad. And that day early on when we both told each other we got good news at work, and we'd come from learning about the promotion minutes before."

"I think we were even in the same room for that one."

"And when you told me you were helping with a family thing, and then I ran into you helping with your cousin's boat the next week."

"Also painfully obvious."

"And when you told me about your parents' dream for your future and then showed me your scar days later. I definitely didn't put two and two together."

Their laughter fell to a simmer, and Emmy regretted broaching the serious topic. "Sorry, that one's not as funny as the others."

Gabe paused walking and reached for Emmy's arm. They'd stopped on the sand a few feet from the path's edge. The powder had cooled to soft white dust in the dark. She turned to him and could see in his eyes he was about to walk through the door she'd opened.

"Emmy, I'm really sorry about your brother. I didn't know what to say when you first told me in your apartment that day, and I obviously hadn't put two and two together to know that was the family tragedy you'd texted about. I should have realized it's a sensitive subject for all of you and steered clear of it tonight."

She gave him a sad half smile. "It's okay. You don't need to know what to say. *I* don't even know what to say, and it's been fifteen years." She let out a big breath and gazed out at the water. The sea rolled like an inky black blanket with a shimmering streak of moonlight. The sight of it, an endless expanse, and the feel of Gabe beside her, his warmth, his steadiness, drew words from her mouth with a whole host of feelings she normally kept locked up. A pair of silent, giant tears budded out of her eyes and rolled down her cheeks. "I do okay with it most of the time. It's just things like this—life events—that really hurt because he's not here." She turned to look at him and found a sincere crease of sympathy between his brows. "And that's so unfair." Her voice dissolved into tears. Hot, angry, aching tears. She hated how much it hurt still. That the price of loving someone was carrying the pain of their loss forever.

"Emmy," Gabe said on a soft breath. He wiped her tears with his thumbs and then pulled her into his chest. He held her there while she quietly sobbed, gently swaying with the breeze, and letting her empty out all her feelings. She hadn't cried so hard in years. The smell of him, the warmth of his sturdy embrace, it drew emotion out of her like a toxin. She cried into his chest until she had nothing left. Until she was drained and only upright because he was still holding her in his arms.

She pulled back and wiped the tearstains on his chest. "I ruined your shirt," she said in a clogged voice.

"You didn't ruin anything."

"I invited you to Mexico to cry all over you. Probably not what you expected. You have such nice shirts. I'm sorry." She smoothed her hands over the fabric she'd soiled.

"I have plenty more, don't worry."

"Stop being so nice to me."

He kissed the top of her head.

She stilled in his arms.

"Sorry," he said, stiffening. She could feel his heart beating harder in his chest.

She tilted her head to look up at him. The moonlit night sky framed his face. His lips hovered inches away. All she'd have to do was push up on her toes to kiss him. "You don't have to be sorry," she whispered.

He blinked his long lashes and gazed down at her. Time seemed to slow. It became sand slipping through an hourglass at half speed, and Emmy could feel every grain. He moved closer, and her eyes had started to flutter closed when a shout in the dark snapped them apart.

"*There* you are!" Piper squawked like a gull. She appeared from the walkway dangling off Ben's arm. Both of them looked boozy and exhausted. "I've been looking all over for you!" Piper sang and launched herself at Emmy.

"Uh, hey, Pipes," Emmy said, trying to recover from her sudden appearance and nearly being tackled.

"Hey," Piper said. "Ready for bed?"

"Umm, sure?"

"Great. Let's go." She grabbed her arm and started pulling her toward the villas.

Emmy shot a desperate look at Gabe. "My room is that way."

"Not tonight, it's not," Piper said, and kept dragging her. "I'm not sleeping by myself down here, and I obviously can't sleep with Ben."

"Obviously?" Emmy nearly tripped as she tried to keep up literally and figuratively.

Piper stopped yanking on her and pivoted to face her. She was barefoot and holding her shoes in one hand. Her white jumpsuit looked wrinkled and ready to be peeled off in exchange for pajamas. Her lipstick was smeared outside the lines of her lips like she'd made out with her fiancé on the drive back from dinner.

Emmy glanced back at Ben to see, indeed, red smudges painting his dopey grin.

"*Obviously* I can't sleep with Ben because we can't *see each other* tomorrow until I walk down the aisle," Piper explained in a tipsy tirade. "And how are we going to not *see each other* if we wake up together?" She smacked the heel of her hand on her forehead and then grabbed Emmy's arm again. "So it's you and me tonight, sis. Let's go. We need our beauty sleep."

Emmy stumbled after her, tripping in the sand, and throwing another desperate look back at Gabe. "Um, see you tomorrow, I guess?" she called.

"Good night!" Gabe called with a wave. She could see the disappointment on his face even from far away.

"Piper, chill out. I'm coming," she protested when her sister nearly pulled her arm from its socket. "Where is Ben sleeping if you're kicking him out?"

"I don't know, with his brother. Or with your boyfriend. He'll figure it out."

"He's not my boyfriend."

Piper let out a loud, drunken honk and cackled. "*Okay*, Emmy. Whatever you say."

When they made it to the villa's walkway, Piper pulled her along the path. She stopped at the door and turned around to face Emmy. Her face was suddenly sobered. "Emmy, the truth is, I'm getting married tomorrow, and I feel like tonight is the last night I'm a kid, so I want to spend it with you."

There on the doorstep of a seaside Mexican villa under a full moon, Emmy's heart cracked wide open. Her tears returned, and she threw her arms around her sister.

"I love you, Piper."

Piper stiffened in surprise, unused to her emotionally reserved sister being so open, but she quickly softened and wrapped her arms around her. "I love you too, Em. Thank you for being here. And for fixing everything. Sorry I took you away from your boyfriend tonight."

Emmy pulled back and wiped her eyes as she rolled them. "He's not my boyfriend."

"Keep telling yourself that," Piper said, and booped her on the nose.

Inside, they got ready for sleep. Emmy borrowed a tee to sleep in and used a spare toothbrush from the hotel. They were settled into the same bed, facing each other like they used to when they'd stay up late and swap secrets as kids, when Emmy felt an overwhelming need to tell her sister something.

The moment Piper had interrupted between her and Gabe was one of the realest things Emmy had ever felt, and telling Piper the truth about him would make everything real. And there in the dark, bundled in a king-size princess bed sharing air with her lifelong confidante, she wanted it to be real.

"Pipes, I have to tell you something," she whispered.

"Hmm?" Piper sleepily hummed.

Emmy was suddenly ten years old again with her head on her sister's pillow.

"Gabe *is* Texting Guy."

Piper pulled in a tiny, sharp breath. "What? Really?"

"Yes. We had no idea until the other day. I *did* invite Texting Guy to the wedding, and it turned out to be him. We were both completely shocked. Isn't that wild?"

Emmy chewed her lip, waiting for her sister's judgment. The

pounding in her chest made her realize how important knowing what Piper thought of the situation was to her.

"No, that's . . . perfect," Piper said on a dreamy exhale. "You're perfect. Good night, Em."

Emmy closed her eyes and fell asleep with a smile.

Chapter 14

In the morning, Emmy woke to a firm swat on her butt. She peeled open her eyes to see her sister hanging over her with a half-deranged grin and pink jelly stickers beneath her shining eyes.

"Wake up! I'm getting married today!" Piper bellowed and shoved off the bed. She ran out of the room barefoot with her silky white bridal robe fluttering in her wake.

Emmy sat up with a groan but couldn't deny the excitement bubbling in her heart.

"Breakfast is coming in twenty minutes, and the girls will be here at ten!" Piper shouted from the kitchen, where Emmy heard the distinct pop of a champagne bottle.

She'd just swung her bare legs over the bed's edge when Piper reappeared with two champagne flutes blushing pale orange. *A dash for color* was how Piper had always preferred the orange juice in her mimosas.

"Good morning," Emmy greeted when Piper handed her a flute.

"Good morning. Cheers." Piper clinked her glass and sipped.

Emmy sipped the fizzy bubbles and smiled. "Happy wedding day."

"Thank you. I have something for you." She set her flute on the nightstand and swept off to the walk-in closet.

A walk-in felt like overkill for vacation to Emmy, but the likes of people renting the villa probably traveled with a closet's worth of luggage anyway. At least it had plenty of space for Piper's ballooning ball gown to hang.

Piper returned with a gift bag and presented it.

"What's this?"

"It's your MOH gift." She sat on the bed next to her and excitedly watched her open it.

Emmy pulled out a short, silky robe the same champagne color as her bridesmaid's dress.

"To wear while we get ready," Piper said.

"Thanks." Emmy slipped it on and felt the luxurious sleeves brush her arms like silk gloves. She reached deeper in the bag and found a small jewelry box. Her eyes popped wide when she opened it to two dazzling diamond stud earrings.

"To wear with your dress," Piper said with a smile.

Emmy gaped at them. "Are these *real*?"

"Yes. Don't go swimming in the ocean with them, please."

Emmy turned to her sister and realized today was significant in more ways than one. Piper was getting married, yes, but she was also transitioning from a single girl to a woman who gifted multicarat jewels. Her life was becoming one with Ben's, fully, and some things would never be the same.

"Thank you," Emmy managed to squeak out.

"Of course. They're bigger than all the other girls', don't worry," Piper said, and pushed up off the bed.

Emmy snorted. "I wasn't worried." She shoved her hand back into the bag and felt a small card tucked into an envelope. Piper had scrawled *My Sister* on the front of it, and with a sudden thick lump in her throat, Emmy decided she was going to read it later.

The villa was soon overtaken by an elaborate room service spread—eggs, fresh papaya, passion fruit, waffles, endless mimosas—a gaggle of squealing bridesmaids, and photographers. Hair and makeup began promptly at 11 a.m. to fit everyone in before pictures and then the ceremony. Before she was committed to being glamorized for the rest of the day, Emmy still needed to escape to her room to get her dress and shoes.

She narrowly slipped through the throngs of matching silky robes, excited giggles, and the bachelorette playlist pumping from the house's speakers and snuck outside. The sun splashed brilliantly from above, saturating all the colors into a dazzling, vibrant tapestry. Sand, sky, sea. Thick, puffy clouds hung offshore, rimmed soft gray at their bottoms, and Emmy hoped any rain would hold off.

She dashed back to her building and rode the elevator, feeling light and bouncy thanks to two mimosas and the thought of seeing Gabe on this happy day. At their door, she knocked, and when he didn't answer, she swiped her wristband and poked her head in the door.

"Gabe?" she called.

Only silence responded.

She slipped inside to find the room empty and a note on the dresser.

Gone fishing.

Emmy quietly laughed at the little drawing of a fish with bubbles coming from its mouth and smiled at the thought of him spending time with her dad. She had no idea what they were going to *do* with any fish they caught, but that wasn't really the point.

She opened the dresser to retrieve her bra and dreaded shape-wear then turned for the closet to gather her dress. On her way, she noticed the pillow wall had been deconstructed and one side of the bed slept in.

Her side.

The pillow she'd slept on the night before was indented and the one next to it crushed like it had been hugged all night. She picked up the crushed one and pressed it to her nose. It smelled like him—and her, because the night they'd shared the bed, she'd spent the whole time holding that pillow between her arms.

Her heart stuttered and she smiled. She wished she had more time to dwell on it, maybe lie down and hug the pillow herself, but she needed to get back to hair and makeup.

She gathered her dress and threw all her necessities in a tote. Before she left, she scribbled a note below the *Gone fishing* one.

Gone to get made up. See you at the ceremony. Xo.

And then, the wedding was upon them.

Emmy had been so wrapped up in getting ready, posing for ten thousand preceremony photos, and fulfilling all her last-minute MOH duties, that she really didn't see Gabe again until the ceremony.

She walked down the aisle, a stone pathway scattered with white rose petals, arm in arm with Ben's brother, the best man. It wasn't until she stopped at the archway exploding with palm leaves and tropical flowers and turned around to face the guests that she saw Gabe sitting among them. He'd donned a soft gray linen suit with a white shirt and styled his hair into its customary wave. Like most of the guests, he wore sunglasses to combat the late-afternoon sun, but even behind the shades, Emmy could feel his eyes on her.

She gave him a tiny wave and mouthed *Hi.*

He waved back and moved his mouth in shapes Emmy interpreted to say *You look incredible.*

She quietly laughed and gathered her satin skirt to step into position as maid of honor. Gabe's words felt like a suit of armor when she caught a glimpse of a familiar face in the crowd. Jacob sat five rows back on the groom's side. Emmy didn't make eye contact with him, but she felt his eyes on her. His gaze landed differently than Gabe's; something cooler and probing, perhaps laced with curiosity. Luckily, she had too much else to focus on to pay any mind to it. Namely, holding her bouquet as instructed (belly button high, tilted forward), trying not to sweat in the sun (impossible), and remembering to take Piper's bouquet when she handed it to her and then hand it back to her before she returned down the aisle (no pressure; don't ruin the photos).

The other bridesmaids fanned out behind her in matching dresses, all of them lined up inches from where the pool deck ended and the beach began. Only Emmy's dress was of a different cut, hugging her chest and leaving her shoulders bare save for two thin straps. The long skirt was slit to her thighs on either side and let the gentle and merciful breeze move around her legs.

When her sister walked down the aisle, Emmy didn't stop the joyous tears from blurring her eyes. She held Piper's bouquet and listened to her and Ben exchange vows. Then there was an enthusiastic kiss, ecstatic cheering, and ten thousand more photos.

It wasn't until cocktail hour, after she'd gotten lost in the billows of Piper's skirt as she bustled it for her, that Emmy finally had a moment to catch her breath. And in that moment, Gabe slid up to her and handed her a fizzy pink drink, which she eagerly sipped.

"Thank you," she told him and clinked it against the matching one in his hand.

"You're welcome. You look amazing."

The pink fizz tingled her tongue in a dangerously delicious tequila-laced bite. "Thank you. So do you."

He kept staring at her like he was seeing her anew and couldn't stop looking. It put a hot flare in her already warm cheeks.

"So, are you relieved of all maid of honor duties now that they've said I Do?" he asked.

Emmy scrunched her face. "Not quite. Still have to make a speech. And probably a hundred other things Piper will think of to ask me to do before the night is over."

"Hmm. Is dancing on the list?"

"Let's hope not."

"What if it's with me?"

She stilled with her glass pressed to her lips, poised to sip again. "Are you asking me to dance, Gabe Olson?"

"Indeed I am."

"There's no music."

"Well, I assume there will be later."

"I might be drunk later."

"A prerequisite for dancing, naturally."

She playfully smiled at him over her glass and took a much needed sip. The thought of twirling around in his arms or bumping and grinding or even doing the robot—whatever they were going to get up to based on the mischievous grin on his lips—had her dizzy already.

"Fine. I'll save a slot on my dance card for you."

"Much obliged," he said with a little bow.

Emmy laughed, and when it came time to dance later, she was a little drunk, and he was, to absolutely zero surprise, an excellent dancer. Much better than her, and honestly hard to keep up with.

"Why are you so good at this?" she asked as he spun her around and reeled her back in as Van Morrison crooned a classic love song.

He pressed his hand warmly into her lower back and held the other up to lead her around the dance floor. "Would you believe my parents enrolled me in ballroom lessons as a kid because it was supposed to help with athletic performance?" He dipped her over backward and used the move as an excuse to pull her against his chest.

She laughed, dizzy with joy. "You know, I absolutely believe that."

"I'm a proud graduate of Señora Sanchez's Junior Dance Academy."

"The one in East Village?"

"The very one." He dipped her over again as she giggled. With her vision turned upside down she caught a glimpse of Jacob swaying with his date nearby.

"What's wrong?" Gabe asked when he pulled Emmy right side up and noticed she was no longer smiling. His face dropped in concern.

The music transitioned into a bouncy salsa-pop song with a heavy beat. Bodies around them started shimmying and shaking to the new sounds.

Emmy glanced over her shoulder without responding and felt Gabe follow her eyes. He stiffened at the sight of Jacob staring at them.

"Is that him?" he said under the song, obviously having figured it out.

Emmy nodded.

As soon as she did, Gabe sharply pivoted and led them across the floor—straight toward Jacob.

"What are you doing?" she whispered. She tried to plant her feet and stop, but he was holding her too tight and moving too fluidly. They were basically tangoing right at him. "Gabe, stop it!"

"Just relax."

She could do nothing of the sort. Not only were they gliding directly toward disaster, but everyone was staring at them because Gabe was moving like he'd waltzed off the *Dancing with the Stars* stage. He stepped and pivoted and dipped like it had been choreographed, and Emmy was along for the ride, somehow a nimble ballerina in his arms.

"What are you going to do?" she nervously asked.

"I told you I'd have choice words for him if we ever met," he said. Before she could react, he shifted to grip her hand and reeled her in to his chest. Then pushed her hip hard so she spun out with their arms fully extended, linked by their hands.

He'd spun her directly at Jacob and his date, and for a frozen moment, Emmy's eyes locked on Jacob's from a foot away. Jacob watched her with a stunned look on the face she'd been familiar with once upon a time. His blue eyes studied her as something unspoken passed between them. She couldn't be sure what all their silent conversation contained on his part. Maybe surprise. Maybe intrigue. Maybe, she was happy to believe, a little bit of regret. On her end, it was . . . nothing. An absence of feeling. Where she thought she would feel angst and anger, she felt pure neutrality at seeing him again. Which was relieving and supremely satisfying. Especially when

Gabe skillfully reeled her back in and then dipped her over right in front of him. The steps couldn't have been more perfectly placed.

"Jacob?" Gabe asked, and nodded at him once they were upright.

"Yeah?" Jacob said with a confused frown.

Emmy worried what was going to come out of Gabe's mouth next, but he gave Jacob one of his devastating million-dollar smug smiles and said three words. "Big mistake. Huge." Then he twirled Emmy like a top and moved them back across the floor.

She was nearly crying with glee by the time he stopped spinning her. "Did you just *Pretty Woman* him?"

"I told you: choice words," he said, and pulled her flush against him.

Emmy cackled under the moonlight and let him continue to spin and sway her body. They didn't run into Jacob again, and Emmy wondered if (hoped?) he was off sulking in defeat. For how worried she'd been about seeing him, it ended up not being a big deal at all. Thanks in no small part to Gabe. His presence was buoying her in so many ways.

Later, when it came time for her speech, Emmy left the crowd misty eyed. Then she shared a dance with her dad and a few with her sister and Ben in a mob of bouncing bodies belting lyrics to "Good as Hell" and "Uptown Funk." By the time the cake came out, the air had thickened enough to erase all the stars and started to tingle with electricity. The first clap of thunder rolled in around the time most guests had shed their shoes and moved to the sand for nightcaps anyway. Gary and Cary's boat was visible lurking offshore.

Piper found Emmy at the edge of the party and slung her arm around her shoulders. She kissed her cheek with a contented sigh, resigned to their fate. "Well, it was perfect while it lasted."

Emmy turned to her with a smile, happy to see her surrender to Mother Nature. "It was."

They watched the storm clouds roll closer until a playful drizzle turned into big, juicy drops that sent everyone scattering for cover. Gabe grabbed Emmy's hand and towed her under the nearest bar's thatched roof.

"We should catch a shuttle before this gets too bad!" He nearly had to shout over the sudden downpour. The sky had cracked open.

"I think it's already bad!" Emmy shouted back.

Globs of water pummeled into the sand and slapped the swimming pools. Emmy's feet were already soaked in her strappy heels, and the hem of her dress lapped up water like a sponge. She gathered her skirt up around her knees as Gabe took off his jacket and held it over their heads as a shield. The warm smell of him enveloped her in a heady rush.

"I don't think that's going to last very long!" she yelled and pointed to his thin jacket.

He shrugged with a smile. "Come on!"

They hurried off into the rain toward a shuttle stop as buckets of water poured down. Gabe's jacket was soaked in seconds and became more of a limp curtain than an umbrella. Luckily, the hotel staff had jumped into action, and a line of golf carts waited at the nearest stop. They hurtled themselves into one and told the driver their room number.

"This is ridiculous!" Emmy shouted with a cackle. "I've never seen rain this hard in my life!" She slid across the wet bench seat into his hip as they took a corner.

"Me neither!" he said, and threw an arm around her to keep her in place. He gripped the handle hanging from the ceiling with his other hand.

Emmy shivered against him. Unlike home where the rain was often stinging and cold, here it was warm and thick, each drop a plump bulb that popped on contact. But the warmth of Gabe's body pressed up against hers made her all the more aware she was getting soaked. The cart had no doors and a roof really only to shield out the sun. It was no match for a torrential downpour.

"At least it waited until now!" Emmy said, and stuck her hand out into it. Fat drops pelted her palm.

"Yes, could have been worse," Gabe said right as they hit a hard bump that bounced them off their seat.

Emmy let out a yelp and gripped his thigh with both hands. "What was that?" she shouted. Their cart skidded sideways and came to a stop halfway off the path. She glanced over the edge to see what had happened, but only saw a river of rainwater rushing over the pavement.

The driver hopped out and inspected the cart, then shouted over the rain, "Flat tire!" He climbed back in and unclipped the radio hooked to his belt before speaking into it. He waited for a response and turned back to Emmy and Gabe. "Wait for maintenance," he said, and waved the radio at them.

Rain continued to slam down around them. It pounded the roof of the cart and splashed up off itself where it had begun to flood the path. Emmy looked forward through the half windshield and saw their building glowing in the distance. It was at least a hundred yards away still, but the alternative seemed to be drowning in a golf cart while they waited for a repair.

"Want to make a run for it?" she asked Gabe.

He laughed at first but then realized she was serious. "We'll get soaked!"

"We're already soaked!" She flopped the soggy entrails of her dress onto his lap.

He looked down and then he shook his head with a wry smile. "Okay, if you say so, Jameson."

"I do," she said, and gripped his hand. "Gracias!" she shouted to the driver as she yanked Gabe out of the cart behind her.

The flood washed over her toes, and she gave up any notion of caution after two steps. They were instantly soaked. She held her skirt and clutch in one hand and Gabe's hand in her other and ran.

"Don't slip!" Gabe shouted from behind her.

"Don't trip!" she shouted back.

They kept running, splashing a path through the storm and getting absolutely drenched. Emmy's hair fell from its artfully braided bind and slapped at her back. Her dress clung to her like a second skin. Gritty rocks and sand pushed their way between her toes and into shoes she'd probably have to throw away.

She heard Gabe chuckling behind her and glanced back to see him tilting his head toward the sky. The clouds had stolen all the moonlight and left them only with the interspersed lamps buried in the palms lining the path. Even in the dim glow, she could see his shirt was soaked and completely see-through. He held his jacket looped over an arm.

Emmy released his hand and came to a stop in the middle of the pathway. They were twenty or so yards from the building now. She held her arms out and leaned her head back, letting the warm rain shower down over her. Gabe stopped next to her, and she felt his eyes on her.

She looked over at him, wet to the bone and chest heaving from running. He was looking at her with a heat unlike anything she'd felt before. A need.

Through the pouring water, the heavens crashing down all around them, she felt it too. An ache deep in her chest only he could soothe.

Emmy stepped toward Gabe and watched the rain drip off the ends of his hair and cling to his long lashes. He was doing nothing to stop it, to shield himself or keep dry. His singular focus was her and only her.

Her heart thundered in her chest. The lightning sparking in the distance could have been channeling into her fingertips.

"What were you thinking in the elevator the other night?" she asked. The rain nearly drowned out her voice, but by the sudden flash in his eyes, the flare in his nostrils, she knew he heard her.

He stepped closer, nearly eliminating the space between them. She could feel the heat of his body, the literal steam rising off him in the rain. He searched her face with his dark eyes and spoke in a low rasp. "I was thinking I wanted to kiss you until you forgot how to breathe."

Emmy nearly collapsed. The nerves sending signals to her legs might as well have been hit by a line drive all over again. She'd thought it might have been something of the sort, but she hadn't let herself hope. Now she knew, and it took all her strength to remain upright long enough to ask him another question.

"Do you still want to?"

Gabe stepped even closer, nearly chest to chest now, and reached for her face. Water streamed off their noses, dripped from their hair. His eyes continued to search hers, a pair of embers in the dark, as he softly cupped her cheek and brushed his thumb over her lips. "More than anything."

Emmy could not take one more second of not knowing what it felt like to kiss Gabe Olson.

She pushed up on her toes and pressed her mouth to his. He instantly leaned into it, cupping her face with both hands. She gripped his wrists and heard herself softly moan. The release was more than she could have imagined—more than she knew she'd needed. An uncoiling of something so tightly wound, she would have snapped if they'd denied themselves any longer. His tongue swept over hers, wanting more, and she realized in a hot rush that she'd been wondering what Gabe Olson tasted like for years.

Sweet. Warm. Perfect.

He wrapped his arms around her back to pull her closer and lifted her off the ground in the process. She happily pressed her body into his, enjoying being squeezed. He was firm, with arms like steel, but warm and gentle at the same time.

She threaded her arms around his neck and kissed him deeper, her heart pounding out *more more more*. The pouring rain had all but disappeared. It was only them, standing in a downpour with the bubble of their kiss as their own personal umbrella. The world could have ended, and Emmy wouldn't have noticed or cared.

Gabe eventually pulled back and pressed his forehead into hers. "Hi," he said in a low voice.

"Hi," Emmy said back.

They stayed that way, pressed together and staring deep into each other's eyes for a long moment.

"We're getting very wet," Gabe said with a small laugh.

"We are."

"Should we go inside?"

"Probably a good idea."

They released each other and continued on the path, no longer running because there was no point, but still holding hands. When they reached the building's breezeway, Gabe pulled on her to stop.

"Emmy, wait."

She turned back to him. They were the only ones around. Everyone else had the sense to come in out of the rain ages ago. Each of them dripped a small pool at their feet. Gabe's shirt clung to him, completely transparent. Emmy's chest had risen into peaks plainly evident through her dress. Her hair hung in a soaked tangle dripping down her back.

"I don't think I can go in there," Gabe said.

She looked at him in concern. "Why not?"

He took a breath and stepped toward her, searching her eyes again. "Because I don't want this to stop, and going in there with you is going to make it very, *very* difficult to stop."

Her heart took a bounding leap and all her blood refocused to the deep core of her belly.

He didn't want it to stop.

And neither did she.

She pressed a hand to his chest. "Why does it have to stop?"

He looked down at her pruned fingers splayed over his soaked shirt. There were dozens of reasons they should stop, but neither of them seemed to be able to name one.

Gabe looked back up at her, eyes hooded but still glowing. "I guess it doesn't have to."

Emmy's pulse leapt. Her fingers twitched where she touched him. A million thoughts sped through her mind. She honestly couldn't tell if this was the best or worst idea she'd ever had. "How about this?" she said. "Same as with the baseball bruise, the bachelorette, the seasickness, the texting—basically all of this: What happens in Mexico stays in Mexico?"

Gabe considered for a few beats but looked like he'd made his mind up ages ago. Maybe before he'd even boarded the plane to come meet her. "Always one for logic, Jameson," he said with a nod. Then he gripped her hand and pulled her toward the elevator.

Chapter 15

Once they made it to the room, they toweled off as best they could. Emmy squeezed out her sopping hair and took off her ruined shoes. Gabe wrung out his jacket and hung it over the shower wall then removed his shoes and socks. All the while, Emmy was acutely aware of his every move and every beat of her heart.

They met back at the foot of the bed, and a sudden shyness fell over them. As if having time to cool from the sprint through the rain brought their senses back online. But when Emmy met his eyes, he was still staring at her with the same hunger as before.

"Emmy," he said softly, and her nervous heart trilled at the sound. "I don't want you to think I came here with any expectations, but I am prepared. I have condoms." He nervously watched her and bit his bottom lip as he waited for her reaction.

Emmy stared back at him. The air between them thickened and strained. Her heart beat in every cell down to her fingertips. Knowing he was prepared broke something loose inside her. A deep, dark well of desire that had always been there but bound up and buried. She hadn't had expectations either—in fact, she was mildly in shock over it all still—but staring down the opportunity, she knew there was no chance she wasn't going to sleep with this man.

"Thank god," she said, and reached for him.

He smiled when she kissed him. "Glad we're on the same page," he slurred against her lips.

"Very much. Same page. And I'm totally healthy."

"Me too."

"Good." Her words became broken and hurried. Now that she knew where they were headed, she couldn't get there fast enough. She pressed herself against him, hungry for more of what she'd felt outside. Hungry to chase the pulse pounding in her chest, her throat, between her legs and threatening to consume her whole if she didn't answer its call immediately.

But Gabe had other ideas. He reached up and gently removed her hands from where they'd clawed into his wet hair. He pressed them between his own and held them in front of her to kiss her fingertips. "Slower. Please. If we're only going to do this once, I want it to last."

The heated look in his dark eyes melted her bones. She trembled with anticipation at the promise in his velvety voice. God help her, she was going to have sex with Gabe Olson, and it was going to be good.

She slowly nodded.

He nodded back and hooked his fingers under her jaw to tilt her mouth to his. The slow, deep kiss spread through her like ink dropped onto parchment, seeping out to her every edge as she greedily absorbed it. He had her spinning, sparking with thrill, and he'd hardly even touched her.

Correction: she was going to have sex with Gabe Olson, and it was going to be *fucking amazing.*

They kissed for a sublime eternity. It turned out that smart mouth of his was even smarter when he wasn't using it to talk. He swept her tongue with his and used his teeth to graze and nip. He sucked her lips and alternated between feathering his fingers over her jaw, her throat, her chest, and squeezing her nape and tangling her hair. His chest, warm even through his wet shirt, pressed into hers and put his heartbeat close enough to feel. His arms found their way to her waist, bracing her back, holding her tight. His firm thigh moved deliciously between her legs.

Gabe Olson kissed with his whole body, and it was divine.

A moan escaped her throat, and he mistook it for impatience. Or perhaps it was his own impatience that prompted him to step back. She'd felt the bulge in his pants pressing into her. "Enough of this?" he asked, cupping her face in his hands. He smoothed his thumbs over her swollen lips.

Speaking felt foreign after using her mouth for other purposes for so long. "No. Just more of the next thing, please," she said, and reached for his collar.

Her fingers were still damp from the rain and their wet clothes. She helped him unbutton his shirt, and when they got it off, she took a moment to appreciate the landscape of his chest and abdomen. It was just as defined and tanned as she'd imagined it under all those cool shirts. Firm and toned with a smattering of dark hair that gathered into a little trail disappearing into his waistband.

"What you expected?" he playfully asked when he caught her staring.

"Better," she said, desire filling her as she reached for his pants. She caught the matching desire in his face as he leaned forward to reach behind her for her dress's zipper.

When they got them undone, they each stepped out of their respective garments and stood to face each other.

Emmy felt a pang of embarrassment when Gabe's eyes popped wide at the sight of her.

"Good lord, what are *those*?"

She looked down and realized he was staring at her Spanx. "Oh. What, you've never seen shapewear before?" she asked with a hand on her hip like she was modeling them.

"Uh, not of this industrial grade, no. How have you been breathing all day?" The look of genuine horror on his face made her laugh.

"Women only need eighty percent of the oxygen men need. Didn't you know that?"

He reached for her hips, smoothing his hands over the tight spandex spanning from her thighs all the way to under her strapless bra. "How do we get them off? Are we going to need scissors?" He twisted her side to side with a serious look on his face like he was trying to solve a puzzle.

Emmy sniggered. "No, but since they're wet, I might need some help." She shoved her thumbs into the top band and began to peel the Spanx down.

"Happy to be of assistance," Gabe said, and dug his fingers in to pull.

They got them down to her hips, her lungs joyously refilling to fuller and fuller capacity with each breath, before they *really* had to tug. It was a hundred times worse than a wet bathing suit.

"What's the point of these things?" Gabe asked with a grunt and a yank. He'd sunk to his knees for better leverage, leaving his breath warm against her bare belly. "I'm not a fashion expert, but I think your shape is perfect without them."

Emmy blushed and wiggled her hips side to side with another shove. "Thank you, but since my sister picked out unforgiving, shows-everything satin for her bridesmaids' dresses, I needed something to help smooth everything out underneath. If I wasn't wearing them, you'd have seen my underwear all day."

"You're wearing underwear under these things too?"

"Yes."

"That's unfortunate," he said with a cheeky grin. "Almost there."

Emmy leaned forward to shove them over her butt right as Gabe yanked hard on the front. The force of both made her lose her balance and fall forward over his shoulder into the perfect fireman's carry position.

"Ah, well, this is convenient," he said as he hooked his arm over the back of her thighs.

She squealed when he stood with her body draped over his shoulder. The room turned upside down, and her wet hair dangled down his back. "Put me down!" she said through a laugh.

"Gladly." He dropped them both onto the bed and finished pulling her Spanx from where they'd landed at her ankles. He was down to his boxers—a pair of tight gray shorts that clung to his muscular thighs—and she, her underwear and bra. Everything was still soaked. "Much better," he said, and crawled up over her. He supported his weight in a way that flexed his triceps into rounded bulges Emmy could not resist reaching up to squeeze. She let out an appreciative moan that was equal parts lust and relief for finally getting full access to her secret obsession. *Goddamned sculpted arms.* Gabe smiled at the sound she made when he leaned down to kiss her.

She pushed her hands into his wet hair and kissed him back. Her heart pounded that she was kissing Gabe Olson in her underwear on a bed. As if reaching to calm it, he trailed his fingertips over her chest. Really, it did nothing to calm her but only made her heart race faster. He traced her collarbone and the swell of the tops of her breasts before he moved his palm to cup one. He brushed his thumb over her bra. Her nipples were already hard peaks thanks to the rain, but his touch made them stand at attention in a different way.

"All your clothes are so restrictive today." He slid his hands under her back to reach for her bra's clasp.

"You have no idea," she said, and arched up so he could undo it.

The release of the tight elastic felt heavenly. Emmy inhaled the deepest breath she'd been able to take since that morning and was so relieved she forgot she was now topless in front of Gabe Olson, and he was staring at her bare chest like he'd fallen into a trance.

The reflex to throw her arms over herself hit her, but the reverent look on Gabe's face stopped her. He looked like he wanted to devour her whole.

"What you expected?" Emmy managed to ask in a steady voice.

He grinned, and it filled her with radiant confidence. *"Way better."*

She grinned back. "Always have to one-up me."

Gabe sank his mouth over one of her breasts, circling her nipple with his tongue, and any remaining sense of shyness vanished. They both wanted this, and even if it was a onetime thing, it was going to be worth it.

They pushed down the sheets and rested against the pillows. He lay at her side and kissed her, deeply, while they explored each other with their hands. The dips and grooves of hips, the firm planes of thighs and stomachs, the soft swell of her chest and the length of him growing increasingly hard between them.

Once she was dizzy from making out, he slipped his hand between her legs and pressed against the silky fabric of her underwear.

"Tell me what you like, Emmy," he whispered like it was a secret he desperately needed to know. The sound of his voice fizzed through her like champagne.

She canted herself into his palm, nearly trembling at his touch, and fully giving over to him. "I like it when you say my name. My first name."

"Emmy. Emmy Emmy Emmy," he purred into her throat. "What else do you like?" he asked as he pushed her underwear aside and slipped his finger over and then inside her.

She gasped and felt her body deliciously clench around him. "That," she managed to whisper.

"Yeah?" he darkly hummed and smoothly slid it back out before joining it with another.

A second gasp rushed out of her. She reached up to grip his arm so she didn't explode.

"This too?" His thumb joined the party and began to circle over her most sensitive part.

She nodded. Little sparkling stars pricked behind her closed eyes.

"You're so soft, Emmy. So perfect," he murmured and kissed her neck. His teeth grazed her pulse leaping in her throat. "Tell me what else."

Her whole body pulsed with need. The way he was taking his time, studying her like there'd be a test later he planned to ace, was a divine kind of torture. Her mind was nearly blank. Right now, she couldn't think of anything else beyond the fact that his touch was the single most pleasurable thing she'd ever felt. How could it get any better? But the hunger in his voice, the need to make her feel more and the promise that he could, made her want to give him more and gave her the courage to ask for it.

She thought of his perfect smile. That dazzling grin. Those lips.

"Your mouth," she said. "I want to feel your mouth on me."

She felt his smile against her throat before he shifted his weight and moved down her body. He slid her underwear off and then positioned himself between her thighs. With a hot hand, he lifted her left leg to press a kiss into the inside of her knee. And then another one, higher up. And then another and another and another until he reached the apex of her thighs, and she reared against him. His mouth pressed into her, his tongue sinking like a hot blade into butter.

"Holy shit," she gasped and fisted the sheets.

She expected a quip from him. A gentle jab at her unfiltered outburst, but she looked down to see him completely consumed. Eyes closed, lashes fanning. A deep flush in his cheeks and a knit between his brows like he was concentrating and appreciating in equal measure.

She'd been wrong about his hands. *This* was the most pleasurable thing she'd ever felt.

Gabe Olson: baseball star, brilliant, hot as hell, *and* good in bed. Of course.

"*Of course you are,*" she accidentally murmured out loud, lost in a thick haze.

"What?" he paused to ask. The brief absence of his lips left her aching and desperate.

Emmy looked down again to see an image that would be burned into a very special part of her memory forever: Gabe, coal eyes burning, hair a mess, halfway feral, and looking up at her from between her thighs with a reverent gaze and a tiny quirked smile.

She smiled back at him. "I said, *of course* you're good at this too."

His smile grew like she'd confirmed what he expected. And then he showed her just how good he was at it until she was trembling on the edge of a cliff with a wave down below she knew would consume her completely.

"Come here," he said in the moment before she was lost to the sea. The sudden pause didn't crash the wave, but it left her reeling. The raw ache between her legs only grew hotter and sharper.

"What?" she asked, and noted the desperation in her own voice.

But Gabe was already moving. He'd stood off the bed to remove his boxers and retrieve one of the condoms from his suitcase. When he tore open the wrapper and set about rolling it onto himself, Emmy only then got a look at the whole package. He was all muscle and long limbs. His hips jutted out from two indented grooves she imagined sinking her fingers into, maybe her teeth. Her gaze traveled down, and her eyes popped wide as she added one more large thing to Gabe Olson's list of impressive personal qualities. There was a joke to be made about him swinging a big bat, but she was too consumed to make it. He returned to the bed to settle with his back against the headboard and reached for her.

He pulled her over onto him, gripping her hips to set her on his lap so they were chest to chest. He was giving her full control, letting her take the lead. It was unbearably sexy. The full length of him pressed into her belly, and she heard him suck a sharp breath through his teeth. "I want to feel you closer. Is this okay?" he asked, his voice deep and low and aching with the same need burning in her own veins.

It was more than okay. She was ready to do anything he wanted. "Yes," she said with a nod and wrapped her arms around his neck. Her knees pressed into the mattress on either side of his legs.

He lifted her with his hands on her hips, and she relished the flex of his arms, the muscles moving in his back, as he positioned her above himself. She reached down with one hand to guide him, and he slid into her, slow, hard, like a missing piece.

A gasp tore from her throat as she gripped the back of his neck. She'd never been filled so fully, and the slight pinch of exquisite pain lit something dark inside her on fire. The same as when they'd first kissed in the rain, her heart pounded out *more more more*.

"You good?" he paused to ask.

"*Oh* yeah," she panted, nearly delirious with thrill.

He grinned at her like he knew exactly what she was thrilled about, before his forehead fell to her shoulder. She felt him shudder. "You feel so perfect, Emmy," he breathed into her rosy skin like he was under a spell. His lips worked a trail around her jaw and back to her mouth.

She clung to him while he gripped her thighs with his strong hands and buried himself inside her. The feeling filled her in more ways than one. Chasing the heat roaring through her veins, she moved her body with his, lifting her hips and sinking back down in a steady rhythm. The wave they'd abandoned came rushing back, and soon Emmy was poised to fall into an endless oblivion and pleasantly shocked to be there with him. At one moment, she found herself smiling into his kiss.

"What?" he asked when he felt it.

"We're having sex," she said with a small laugh, completely wrapped up in it but still unable to believe it was actually happening. "You and me."

He smiled back and lifted his hand to tangle in her mussed hair. "Yeah, we are. And I think we're pretty fucking good at it." He drove his hips up with a sharp stroke and made her gasp again.

"I think so too." She arched into him and kissed him hard. Hard enough to bring back the sparkling pricks behind her eyes. Soon, she was dizzily approaching the ledge, ready to fall and get swept under by the rushing current. She pressed her forehead into his and squeezed her thighs around him, still feeling him deep inside.

"Come for me, Emmy," he growled into the hot air between them.

Even his breath on her skin felt like electricity. Her nipples pinched anew as she crushed herself against his body that had turned slick with sweat. "I want to hear you. I want to feel you. I want all of you."

His words were her undoing. The wave caught her, pulling her under into a deep, dark current that had her tumbling through space and time, ceasing to exist beyond physical sensation, and fighting for air so she didn't black out.

"Yes. Fuck yes," he panted over the sound of her desperate gasping like it felt just as good for him. He scattered kisses over her shuddering body and loosened his grip to allow her to arch and buck and yank on his hair. It lasted forever. An infinite spiral of him holding her as she shattered to pieces, their bodies one unified being.

Once the brunt of the wave passed, she slumped against him and rippled with aftershocks. He softly stroked his hand down her spine, unzipping her into a melted puddle. The gentle moment didn't last long before he pulled her off him and laid her beside him on the bed.

"You're so incredible, Emmy," he hummed and climbed over her. He nudged her legs apart and slid back inside her. Emmy jolted with a renewed sensation of having been lit on fire.

"You. Incredible," she managed through a heady haze. She could hardly speak.

His breath puffed against her neck. He gently skimmed her throat with his lips and then began to move his hips with slow, deep rolls.

Just like looking at him in person, Gabe Olson didn't have a bad angle in bed.

Emmy sucked in a hard breath, bracing herself for more, and marveling that her body was capable of processing so much sensation. The wave had begun to build again already. Or maybe it had never stopped crashing, she couldn't be sure.

But she could be sure that Gabe Olson on top of her was the most beautiful thing she'd ever seen. His messy, still rain-wetted hair fell forward, and his cheeks had gone rosy. A determined focus burned in his dark eyes as he moved his body against hers with more speed, their stomach muscles tightening together and lungs heaving for air. At the same time, he looked like he'd transcended into a realm where all his fantasies were coming true.

Emmy burned white hot thinking *she* was one of his fantasies. That he'd secretly dreamt of this moment like she had, and now that they were here, he realized any fantasy paled in comparison to reality.

She smoothed her hands over his broad back, his shoulders, up into his tangled hair, soaking it all in and making permanent memory out of it. It was all perfect, topped only by the gorgeous, ragged sound that ripped from his mouth when he finally lost himself and shuddered against her, completely undone. She clung to him, absorbing every quake, every gasp, the feel of his damp skin breaking out in goose bumps. The combination of it all plus the sound of him murmuring her name like a prayer shoved her right back over the cliff into another wave.

When they pulled apart and turned on their backs, breathing hard, the gravity of what they'd just done, all the lines they'd crossed, settled over Emmy in a haze. Nothing would ever be the same, she knew that, but when she thought about it, nothing had been the same since the day she met Gabe Olson anyway. Perhaps the inevitability that had been chasing them all along had simply finally caught up.

She lay beside him and welcomed the new territory, though she found it confusing, because where did they go from here?

As she wondered, Gabe seemed to come up with an answer.

"There is no—" he said, and paused to catch his breath. "Fucking way—" Another heave of air. "We are only doing that once."

Emmy laughed and rolled over into his chest. She pressed a kiss into the firm muscle and smoothed it with her hand. His heart still thundered inside. "Well, we agreed to keep it in Mexico, and we're technically still in Mexico for another day, so."

In a rush of movement, he grabbed her hand and kissed it. "Brilliant logic as always, Jameson." Then he reached for the sheet and threw it over them, scooting his body down and dragging her with him into a warm cloud of a tent.

Emmy squealed and savored the feel of his mouth already pressing more hot kisses into her chest. She could tell by the hunger in his touch, the need they had awoken in each other, that they would not be getting any sleep tonight.

Chapter 16

They, indeed, got no sleep. That was why it took all Emmy's strength to peel her eyelids open and then immediately snap them shut against the blazing sun when someone dared knock on their door and wake them the next morning.

Gabe was face down into the mattress beside her, arms flung out and hair sticking up in every direction from her yanking on it all night. The sheet half covered his perfect ass, and two of the pillows had landed on the floor.

Emmy sat up and shamelessly tugged the sheet to expose all his perfect ass and cover her chest.

The sight of Gabe Olson sleeping naked was criminally stunning. His long legs, his grooved back. That perfect, rounded real-life peach emoji she'd gripped in her palms multiple times last night. She could have stared at him for the rest of time. It took more strength than she knew she possessed to tear her eyes away.

She left him sleeping and assessed her own damage. Her hair tangled around her head in a frizzy nest. She could only imagine what had become of her makeup having run through the rain and then endured all the bedroom activity that followed. Remarkably, she was not hungover at all, likely because Gabe had given her more of a workout than she'd had in years and all the alcohol had evaporated from her body like mist. Still, exhaustion clawed at her. Her body ached in the most pleasant places. She wanted to lie back down, savoring her rubber muscles and the twinge between her legs, and sleep for a hundred years.

But someone was still knocking.

She glanced sideways to see the alarm clock showing 10:05 a.m. in a slash of aggressively red digits. The last time she'd looked at the clock before the tide of sleep had pulled her under, it had been close to 6 a.m. Gauzy predawn light had already begun to glow in the room then. Now it cut in like a blade thanks to a thrown pillow having landed by the curtains and pushing them partly open.

In her sweep of the nightstand, she saw her phone and noticed three missed calls and a handful of texts from her sister.

"Shit," she muttered, hoping nothing was wrong right as she heard Piper's voice on the other side of the door.

"Emmy! Are you alive in there?" Another knock followed it.

"Shit!" Emmy hissed again, feeling like they'd been caught. They were two consenting adults with personal history sharing a hotel room, so chances were not zero they were going to sleep together, but still. The idea of Piper catching her in bed with Gabe sent a wave of panic surging through her.

She swatted at his arm. "Gabe! Wake up!"

He stirred with a grumble as Emmy thumbed her phone, scanning her texts to see what all the fuss was about.

Piper had apparently lost the ability to text words and had resorted to emojis only. A flood of dolphins, fish, and turtles filled her screen, along with popping champagne bottles, oranges, and a few boats.

"What the hell?" Emmy muttered in confusion as Gabe sat up.

"What time is it?" he said with a yawn.

She turned to see him bathed in gold like some kind of Rembrandt painting come to life. The light spilling in left him positively glowing. His stubble had magically grown into a seductive, scruffy length that hadn't existed only four hours before. And, no, his lips could not still have been that beautifully swollen from kissing.

Emmy's phone slipped out of her hand.

"You do *not* look like this when you first wake up," she muttered. *"Are you kidding me?"*

He sleepily scratched his cheek where it had been smashed into the bed, not having heard her through his yawn, and then arched into a stretch that pulled and flexed all his muscles in a way that made Emmy think she could have another orgasm just looking at him. "What's going on?" he lazily said, and rubbed a hand over his hopeless hair.

She was too stunned to speak.

"Emmy!" Piper shouted with another knock.

Gabe jerked in surprise. "Is that your sister?"

The question snapped Emmy back to reality. "Yes!" she blurted and threw herself from the bed. Their clothes from the wedding were scattered everywhere and still soggy. She ran around frantically grabbing and throwing them into a pile in the corner to hide the evidence. She didn't even think about the fact she was doing it naked until she felt the heat of Gabe watching her.

He leaned back with the sheet tangled at his waist, propped up on his arms with a hungry smile. "Well, this is quite the show."

She glared at him as she threw one of her shoes by the strap. It hit the wall with a thud and fell atop the heap of her dress and his pants and shirt. "You could help, you know."

"I think I'd rather watch." He clasped his hands behind his head and lay back against the pillows. "What's the big deal anyway?"

Piper was still knocking.

"The big deal is I don't really want Piper walking in on *all this*." She waved her hands at the slightly more kempt but still trashed in a very telltale way room. Half the bedding hung to the floor, a bra dangled from a chairback, a dress shoe stuck out from under the bed, a man too attractive for his own good sat naked in rumpled sheets with his hair looking thoroughly woman-handled. "It's very obvious what went on in here last night, and I don't want to deal with my sister's commentary right now, that's all."

He looked at her with a wicked little grin. "Then you probably shouldn't answer the door naked."

Emmy turned scarlet head to toe and ran for the closet to pull on one of the plush robes. "Can you please get dressed? Or, I don't know, hide?"

Gabe laughed. "Hide? She booked the room for us; she knows we're both in here."

"No, she doesn't," Emmy said, and turned to snatch her bra to throw it into the pile of shame. "For all she knows, we got in a fight last night, and I made you walk the plank at the pier, and you got eaten by sharks— What are you doing?" She turned around to find him standing behind her, not a stitch of clothing on, with an erection big enough to make her knees wobble.

Her eyes moved to it like magnets. Memories of last night slammed into her. Her whole body quivered.

He hooked his fingers under her chin and tilted her head up. The wicked smile had only grown. "I woke up like this," he said as if she were accusing him of something. "But it certainly didn't help to watch you run around panic cleaning naked. Either way, you get all the credit." He took her hand and placed it on the smooth, hard, hot length of himself.

Emmy's breath hitched in her throat. Every nerve twitched. She could have burst into flames and thanked him for it. "What are you doing to me right now?"

He only continued to smile. "Enjoying you."

"Torturing me."

"Enjoying torturing you."

Her heart thumped hard. Finding her voice took great strength, but she saw the familiar challenge in his eye. The glittering flicker when he was getting off on messing with her. But it was a new kind of messing. In this novel territory where they'd touched each other everywhere and panted each other's names into the dark, the old rules didn't apply.

Emmy impishly smirked at him and tightened her grip. "Dangerous game to play with your life in my hands, Olson."

He sucked a sharp breath between his teeth and slightly bounced up on his toes. "Aw, there's more to me than just a dick, Jameson. I hope you realize that."

She pulled him toward her then swung her hands around to squeeze another of her favorite body parts of his. "Yes, you're also an ass, and I don't mean this kind."

He laughed and sank his lips to her neck. He kissed and sucked and nipped at her, sending her still-waking blood dizzily looping. She melted into him, the length of him rock-hard between them.

"Emmy! Open the goddamned door or I'm calling the front desk for a key!" Piper wailed and pounded again.

Emmy snapped back from Gabe and yanked herself into focus.

"What does she want?" Gabe asked, and, thankfully, headed to the closet for the other robe.

"I have no idea. She's texting me fish emojis and champagne bottles."

Gabe frowned and pulled the robe over his shoulders. Somehow, he was even more beautiful partially dressed.

Unable to stop herself, Emmy crossed the room and looped her arms around his middle before he tied the robe shut, shoving her hands against his bare skin. He smelled divine. Rain, sweat, notes of her, diluted cologne. *Him.* She pressed a kiss into his chest. "I don't know what she wants, but can you please help me make this less awkward?"

He smoothed his hands over her wild hair and cupped her cheeks to tilt her face up. "Em, I'm not going to talk to your sister with a raging hard-on, don't worry."

She swooned at the nickname and sputtered a weak laugh.

He kissed her forehead. "I'll go in the bathroom."

"Thank you."

They parted, her heading for the front door and him to the bathroom, when Emmy stopped and spun around.

"Oh, could you maybe . . . keep the hard-on?" Her hands suddenly fidgeted in her robe's loose sleeves. She bit her lip.

He gave her another wicked grin. "It's not going anywhere without you."

She nodded, radiating desire for him in every cell down to the ends of her hair, and turned around to take a deep breath, preparing herself to pretend she wasn't about to combust so she could have a conversation with her sister.

She tightened her robe one last time and cautiously opened the door.

"Finally!" Piper greeted her with the pep of someone who'd been up for an hour and had, at minimum, three cups of coffee. "I was starting to worry. Are you—?" She cut off and leaned back to suspiciously eye her. Emmy noted she was fully dressed and looking newlywed glamorous in a flowy white dress over a bikini with wedge sandals and a wide hat. Bangles clattered on her wrist, and the new diamond band addition to her left hand set off a rainbow of sparkles even in the covered hallway. "You look like you were up all night fucking."

"Piper!"

She shrugged a casual shoulder and leaned against the doorjamb, very obviously trying to see into the room. "Whatever. I was up all night fucking too."

Emmy leaned in front of her to block her view. On close inspection, Piper had little puffed half-moons under her eyes, but that was about it. She certainly didn't look as haggard as Emmy felt. Perhaps it was due to the sunbeams of happiness shooting out of her.

"Well, sure. But it was your wedding night."

"Yes, and it was your . . . what night?" Piper leaned over and tried to peer in again.

Emmy stepped partially into the hall and pulled the door farther closed behind her. "It was my none-of-your-business night. What can I help you with? What's with all the fish emojis?"

Piper bounced up on her toes and squealed as if she'd forgotten the previous topic. She clapped her hands together. "Put on your swimsuit and grab your man. Ben's dad got us a boat for breakfast!"

Emmy blinked at her. "He— What? He bought you guys a *boat*?"

"What? *No*," Piper said, like it wasn't in the realm of possibility her new father-in-law might actually give them a yacht as a wedding gift. "As part of payback for the double-booking, Steve got the hotel to comp us a cruise. They usually use it for tours, but we get the *whole thing* to ourselves for the day. It's not as big as Gary and Cary's boat, but still good."

Emmy's eyes popped wide in excitement. "Seriously? That's awesome."

"Yep! We've got a hundred-foot catamaran stocked with mimosas and brunch buffet docked and waiting, so saddle up!" She clapped her hands again and hooked her arm in an enthusiastic *let's go* motion.

Emmy's heart stilled when the word *catamaran* fully sank in. "Oh. Um, we can't actually."

Piper's face folded into a befuddled frown. "What? Why not?"

Emmy glanced over her shoulder and noted she heard the shower running. She lowered her voice anyway because she knew he'd try to stop her from shooting down the invitation if he heard her. "Gabe gets seasick. He can't go on a boat."

Piper's frown deepened. "But he was on the boat at my party."

"Yes, and he was puking the whole time. Don't you remember?"

"I in fact do *not* remember," she said, and booped Emmy on the nose. "Which is a sign you threw one hell of a bash." Piper sighed, but it came out dreamy and content. "Well, we'll miss you, but seems like you're having plenty of fun on land anyway." She winked, and Emmy was thankful rejecting her invitation didn't prompt a tantrum.

"Have fun, Pipes. Tell your husband hi from me."

Piper squealed a delighted sound and scrunched her face. "*Husband.* I love him."

"I know you do. Marriage looks good on you."

"Thank you. Tell the first mate hi from me. And don't forget to hydrate and eat today. Gotta keep your strength up," she said with a suggestive bounce of her brows and walked backward with a bow.

"*Bye, Piper,*" Emmy called, and stepped back into her room.

Inside, she heard the shower still running. She noted the bathroom door left open with an intentional gap.

An invitation.

Her heart pumped hard, pushing heat into her face as she slipped inside. The glass stall had fogged over in the corner, but she could see Gabe's shape moving in the steam. Puffs of mist spilled over the top of the door and filled the tiled room with the sweet coconut smell of the hotel's soap.

Emmy dashed to the sink to quickly brush her teeth and saw Gabe had had the same idea from his toothbrush and toothpaste already sitting there. When she finished, she slipped off her robe and padded to the shower.

He'd been expecting her, obviously. A billow of steam poured into the room when she opened the door, and he held out a hand to help her in.

The large glass box could easily and comfortably accommodate two people, but he immediately eliminated the space between them and pulled her tightly against him.

"Hi," she said, already breathless.

"Hi."

He turned her under the waterfall spilling from overhead. As the stream washed over her, he followed it with his hands, smoothing her hair and down her shoulders to her chest, pausing the journey to circle his thumbs over her nipples. She arched into him, greedy for more. He obliged and wrapped his arms around her to pull her into a kiss. A kiss so slow and long and deep she literally gasped for air when he stopped.

"What did she want?" he asked.

"Who?" Emmy asked in a daze. Her mind was as foggy as the coconut-scented steam swirling around them.

Gabe quietly laughed. "Your sister."

"Oh. It was nothing." She rose on her toes to kiss him again. Her wet thigh slipped between his and she pushed her fingers into his hair. Her chest slid against his where he'd already soaped himself.

He gently pried her off and gazed down at her. Water clung to his long lashes and dripped off the curled ends of his hair. She'd seen him soaking wet fully clothed in the rain last night, but soaking wet naked was a whole different story. Her knees threatened to give out. "I don't think all that pounding and texting was nothing."

It took her a moment to realize he was talking about Piper and not what the two of them had spent last night and the past several weeks doing with each other. Her inability to think straight was largely due to his erection having returned full force and hotly pressing into her belly.

The need to be close to him, to drink him in and seal her body to his again, outweighed everything else in that moment, so she told him the truth to pacify his curiosity.

"Ben's dad got the hotel to comp a yacht for a brunch cruise for everyone, but I told her no thanks." She leaned in to kiss him again, but he pulled back.

"What? Why would you do that?"

"Because you get seasick."

"Well, yes, I do. But that shouldn't stop you from having fun. You should go, Emmy."

"And leave you here alone all day? No way." She shoved her way in this time and got a full two seconds of his luscious mouth before he pulled back again.

"Emmy."

"Gabe."

He sighed, sounding truly dismayed. "I'll be fine. I'll go fishing again or something. I can call Henry. Don't let me get in your way."

This time, she sighed. She gripped his shoulders and spun them around so his back faced the interior shower wall. She pushed him up against it and pinned him there. "I don't think you get it, Olson," she said in a low voice. A smile twitched her mouth at the pleasantly startled look on his face. "What happens in Mexico stays in Mexico, and we have twenty-four more hours in Mexico. I am not wasting any of them on a boat without you." She kissed him, hard, and then bit his bottom lip. "Got it?" she said with his lip still between her teeth.

He smiled as much as he could with his lip pinched. A daring spark flashed in his eyes. "Got it."

"Good." She released him and slid down his wet body, savoring the dips and grooves of his muscles under her sparking fingers and kissing a trail all the way to the flat indent of his navel.

He sucked in a sharp, hissing breath and tilted his head back against the tile. *"Twenty-four hours,"* Emmy thought she heard him mutter as she settled on her knees in front of him.

They never left the room that day. They only paused to order room service and briefly doze in each other's arms. Every second that he wasn't on top of her, beneath her, behind her, holding her up against the slick shower wall, felt like a waste of precious time. This man had lit Emmy on fire, and knowing they were going to douse the flame when they left had her desperate to keep it burning while they were together. She felt the same desperation in Gabe's touch, the hunger in his kisses, the way he promptly peeled off any stitch of her clothing as soon as she put it on.

Late on Sunday night in the dim glow of the baseball game Gabe had somehow found on TV, Emmy, exhausted in the best way possible, traced her fingers along his bare chest. She lay nestled under his left arm, the length of her body pressed up against his with nothing other than the sheet tangled around them. Sleep beckoned her with an eager hand, but she wasn't ready to surrender, not if it meant losing time with him. Gabe gently breathed with a comfortable ease Emmy felt syrupy and warm in her own veins. She was paying more attention to memorizing the contours of his chest, the hypnotic pattern of it rising and falling, than the game. She didn't even know who was playing or what country they were from.

She dipped her finger into the U-bend of his collarbone and then traced it across to the other side. The soft ridges of his scar bumped along under her fingertip. She lightly shuddered. "Were you scared?" she quietly asked, and traced her finger back over it.

His breath hitched for a second, and Emmy worried she'd crossed a line. They'd gotten very well acquainted with each other's bodies, but it might have been the most intimate thing she'd ever asked him. When Gabe shifted his weight to move, she wanted to take it back, but he turned toward her and settled with his head on the pillow inches from hers. His eyes shone even in the dim light, and she saw honesty bared back at her.

He nodded. "Yeah," he said in a soft voice, almost a whisper. "I was terrified."

Emmy reached out and pressed her palm to his cheek, wanting to take away the fear even if it was distant and faded. "What happened?"

His brow furrowed and the ghost of something dark flashed over his face. "I don't really remember the accident, but I know I caused it. I was driving home from practice one day. It had been a bad day. I was pissed off at my coach for something that in retrospect was completely irrelevant. Someone cut me off on the freeway, and it was the last straw. I sped around them intending to cut them off as payback but didn't see the slow car in the next lane." He closed his eyes and shook his head. "I swerved into the median and flipped three times."

"Jesus, Gabe." Emmy had nearly stopped breathing. She moved her hand to the back of his neck and squeezed herself against him, somehow feeling like holding him close now would erase almost losing him before she even knew him. The thought of it terrified her. The accident that had ended her brother's career and life had been slow and quiet. They'd been told he simply fell asleep and stopped breathing. Gabe's accident had been metal and broken glass, blood and snapped bones. She shook with fear at the mere thought of it.

"Hey," he said when he noticed her trembling. He looped his arm over her and pulled her close. "I'm okay, Emmy. I survived. And luckily, it was only me. No one else got hurt."

"Yes, but it could have been so bad," she said with her face pressed into the crook between his neck and shoulder.

"Well, I mean, it *was* pretty bad. I was in the hospital for a month. Honestly, the scariest part was when I woke up in traction and knew my career was over."

"Gabe, you could have *died*." As soon as she said the word, she felt him stiffen. He remained tense for a few seconds, and Emmy couldn't be sure if it was fear from a *what-if* he'd surely visited many times on his own or the realization of why the thought had her nearly rigid with angst.

He softened and pressed his lips to her temple. Then he pulled back far enough to look into her eyes. "But I didn't. I know I'm damn lucky to be alive. And I understand why this story is hard for you to hear given the parallels to your brother."

Emmy's chest felt like it expanded infinitely at the same time it splintered a crack. How was it that she was tangled up in bed with Gabe Olson already as close as they could get, and every word out of his mouth was somehow drawing her even closer? To a level beyond simply his skin touching hers. To a place that felt like they were sharing a heartbeat.

"It is hard," she said, knowing she didn't need to say any more. To justify or explain or downplay how thinking about her brother still felt like a cannonball to her chest.

He squeezed her close again. "I'm sorry," he said as if he knew it was enough. She didn't need to hear *time will heal wounds* or *he is in a better place* or any of the other standard fodder thrown her way. She just needed someone to understand and hold her while it hurt. Just like he'd let her empty out all her feelings that night on the beach, he held strong now. At once a rock and a soft place to land. It was a comfort Emmy had never known.

"Thank you for asking me," Gabe said after a few moments.

Emmy tilted her head back from the warm cocoon of his neck. "About your accident?"

He nodded. "I've never really talked to anyone about this before. Well, other than my therapist. It was the scariest thing that ever happened to me. I was happy to be alive, but I knew I'd fucked up big-time when I woke to my dad crying in the hospital." He huffed a dark laugh that sounded layers deep.

Emmy could tell by the pain in his voice that he held certain beliefs about what those tears had meant. "Gabe, I'm sure your parents were relieved you were okay."

His face pinched. "Sure, but they were also upset over the loss of the arm they'd invested my entire life in. I wrecked their dreams— and my own—and I'll never make up for it." He sadly shook his head. "That's why I feel like I have to be the best at everything. Oddly, taking me out of the game only made me more competitive."

Emmy ran her knuckles over his jaw that had grown deliciously scruffy and then traced his lips with her finger. "Well, you are much more than just an arm, but I get that. That feeling of having to make up for something. It's part of why I chase this career, to make up for what my brother will never be able to do. He was going to go far, and my parents were so proud of him."

He kissed the pad of her finger still lingering against his lips. "I'm sure they're proud of you too. In fact, I know they are. I've seen it on their faces."

"Maybe, but they don't get it. Why this career matters so much to me. It's part of who I am."

"I get that," he said with a nod. "I don't know who I am without baseball. When I lost my career on the field, I pushed everyone away. I disconnected from myself and stopped even trying to connect with other people." He softly shook his head. "Now I can't." He paused and looked so deeply into Emmy's eyes the contact felt physical. His voice came out another near whisper. "Except with you."

Those words again. The feeling that bloomed out into Emmy's chest felt dangerously big. It pushed against all her edges, her barriers and beliefs about what their relationship was supposed to be, and filled her with a heady rush of possibility.

She leaned in to kiss him. Slowly and softly at first, but then with more hunger. He rolled her onto her back and pinned her wrists up by her head while he deepened the kiss, possessively dipping his tongue into her mouth. She'd learned over the past twentysome odd hours that Gabe Olson was a little bossy in bed, and it thrilled her. She playfully bit his lip, and he smiled down at her.

Soon they were moving together in a slow rhythm so tender, his hips between hers, his hands in her hair, it made Emmy secretly hope it wasn't the last time, despite their agreement to leave things in Mexico.

They hardly made it to the farewell breakfast with everyone the next morning. Their time together slipped away too quickly, and Emmy found herself dreading having to return to real life. She didn't know how she could possibly go back to the way things were, because there would now forever be a before and an after Gabe Olson. The weekend had sharply divided her life in two.

After a round of hugs and goodbyes with her family at the hotel and then another one at the airport because most of them were on the same flights, Emmy found herself standing at the gate with Gabe and wishing she could stop time.

He stood beside her with his suitcase and wearing a backpack. He'd hooked his thumbs into the straps and looked as if he'd done it to better keep his hands to himself. They'd been in bed together just three hours before—Emmy could still see the kink in his hair from where she'd tugged on it one last time—but she could already feel the memory fading into a shimmering mirage as they moved closer and closer to leaving. Their flight had already started boarding; they were down to minutes.

"What seat are you?" Gabe asked.

"14A. You?"

"28D."

"Another aisle seat."

"I've heard they're good for the legs."

Emmy weakly smiled at his callback to the night he'd arrived. She couldn't summon the strength to laugh. They were one group away from calling her boarding group. The seconds before they took off back to reality slipped through her fingers like the stray sand still crunching in her shoes.

As the final moments dwindled, an enormous elephant stood between them. Emmy got the sense neither of them wanted to acknowledge it for fear of labeling what the weekend had meant to them, which would make it all the harder to put it behind them.

But Gabe did it anyway.

He let out a tense breath and lightly laughed. "So, this was the best weekend of my life."

"Gabe—"

"—and I know we had a deal: What happens here, stays here. But I'm wondering if maybe that doesn't have to be the case."

Emmy looked up at him with a surprising rush of hope—surprising he was suggesting it, and surprising in how sharply the idea hooked itself into her heart. "What do you mean?"

He unhooked his hand from his backpack strap and gently reached for hers. His grip was warm and strong, and Emmy knew she was already addicted to his touch. He brushed his thumb over her wristbone and gave her a soft, devastating smile. "I mean, there's no way I will be able to sit next to you every day and keep my hands to myself now that I know what you taste like."

A stuttered breath rushed out of Emmy. Her whole body quivered. Gabe felt it, and the grin on his lips grew wider.

"Do not torture me here in public," she warned.

"Even if I'm enjoying it?"

"Especially if you're enjoying it."

His face cracked into a full grin, and he laughed. He tugged her closer by the hand. She stumbled into him, awkwardly weighed down by her tote and halfway tripping over her carry-on. But none of that mattered when she felt the warmth of him and smelled the fresh, clean coconutty scent of the hotel still lingering on his skin. "What do you say? Want to give it a shot when we get home?"

She was lost in his gaze, the feel of his hand that had moved to her lower back. Reality was hard to grasp through the sensory haze, but she managed to grab hold. They worked together—not to mention, were up for the same promotion. "Gabe, how would that work? It would be too complicated."

"It doesn't have to be complicated."

Staring at the hope on his face, the memories from the weekend doing backflips in his eyes, Emmy wondered if he was right. Could they make it work? Could they officially cross a boundary back home where it mattered and not have it blow up in their faces? She knew he was right on another front—she'd never be able to share an office with him, either, now that she knew what he tasted like, the sounds he made when he came undone, if it was all behind them.

They called her boarding group, and she jerked at the harsh bite of reality.

Gabe glanced at the jetway and then cupped her cheek with his other hand. His eyes earnestly searched hers as he held her close. "Just promise me you'll think about it." He pulled her into one of his full-body kisses that left her blushing and spinning and nearly unable to walk straight as she made her way to the jetway.

She looked back at him while they scanned her ticket. He'd hooked his hands back into his backpack straps, and she knew she'd be thinking about the little grin on his swollen lips and his suggestion they give it a shot the whole way home.

Chapter 17

Emmy returned to work on Tuesday with nerves swarming in her veins. She'd spent the whole flight home and then a large chunk of Monday night, when she should have been sleeping, wondering what was going to happen when she saw Gabe again. He hadn't texted her since they returned, and she figured he was giving her time to think—which she had been doing. She'd called Beth and told her everything while she unpacked, and Beth managed to be diplomatically smug in saying *told you so* about the "favor" turning into a romantic getaway. Emmy let her have the win because she was undeniably right. She was still swooning over all of it, and she knew what she wanted now. But she needed to get her head back in the game what with decisions about the promotion on the imminent horizon. The way her pulse was leaping like a gully full of frogs as she approached their office had her worried she'd somehow slip, and all their secrets would come spilling out before they even decided if they wanted to share them.

She arrived early on purpose, both to get a head start on catching up and to increase the odds of making it to her desk unscathed. But she should have known—damn it, she should have known—Gabe would have the same idea.

She rounded the corner into their office to the sight of him already sitting at his desk. Baby blue shirt, sculpted hair, eyes focused on his computer screen. He looked like he did any of the other hundreds of times she'd shown up to work, except instead of a cool greeting, he popped out of his chair at the sight of her. He stood rigid with his jaw clenched and hands squeezed into fists at his sides. The posture might have looked angry if the swell of desire she could see him resisting wasn't swallowing her whole in the same blink.

Suddenly, she was right back in Mexico. Their clothes in a pile on the floor, nothing between them but shared air and need. In the span of one heartbeat, she knew they were in trouble.

Neither of them got the chance to speak before Pedro turned the corner with a generous morning smile. "Hey! The dynamic duo has returned. Welcome back, you two." He slapped Gabe on the back and smiled at Emmy.

When neither of them responded, too caught up in the thick tangle of tension, he stepped back.

"What'd I miss?" he said, and eyed them.

Emmy was still struggling to summon words.

Pedro frowned at her. "You don't look like you got much sun for someone who just spent five days in Mexico, Jameson."

Emmy nearly winced, caught off guard. She regretted having mentioned before she left that her sister's wedding in Mexico was her reason for being gone. "Oh, um. We were inside a lot—"

Gabe awkwardly coughed like he suddenly had a dry throat.

Pedro swiveled his gaze to him.

"I-I mean, it rained a few of the days. So we had to s-stay inside," Emmy stuttered. "And, you know, we were busy with . . . wedding stuff." She nervously tucked her hair behind her ear and wished she could hide under her desk.

"Sure," Pedro said with a skeptical arch of his brow. She thought he was going to keep digging until he unearthed the reason for her lack of tropical tan being she spent all weekend in bed with the man beside them dry-choking on nothing, but he turned and gave Gabe another slap on the back. "Get that family emergency sorted out, Olson?"

Emmy realized then she'd never asked Gabe what cover story he'd used for needing time off work on short notice.

"Uh, yes. Yeah. I did, y-yes," he stammered in response.

An awkward tension hung over them like a fishnet they were all caught in. If they were underwater, Emmy might have opted to drown.

Thankfully, Silas showed up, and right on his heels, Alice.

She clicked to a stop in the doorway and spared a second for a welcoming smile. "Welcome back, Jameson. Olson."

They both murmured hellos.

"A lot to catch up on," Alice said. "Conference room in ten." She slipped back out the doorway and continued clicking down the hall.

Grateful to be swept back up in the swing of things as distraction, Emmy walked to her desk and dropped her tote. She sat and reached for her computer glasses. Gabe loudly cleared his throat, and when she looked over at him, she saw him sitting straight as a rod and staring at his computer screen like his life depended on it. His jaw twitched. He wouldn't look at her. And she was honestly having trouble looking at him too. Every time her eyes snagged on him, a wave of want riddled with memory rolled through her. The sound of his heavy breath, the feel of his skin. His heartbeat racing against hers. She did her best to ignore it, telling herself it would wear off—it had to because otherwise how was she going to function?—but she couldn't shake it.

After only a few minutes, she couldn't take it anymore. She pushed back from her desk to head for the kitchen. As she stood, she lifted her phone to see a text from her sister and neglected to remove her computer glasses as she walked out of the room reading it.

Piper had sent her a picture of her and Ben on a colorful street in Lisbon, the first leg of their honeymoon trip. They both squinted at the camera, jet-lagged but dreamy in front of a backdrop of intricately tiled walls and painted doors.

Made it, Piper had written.

Enjoy, Emmy wrote back with a parade of hearts and the Portugal flag emoji.

She'd made it into the office kitchen where she was reaching for a coffee mug, one eye still on her phone, when she heard Gabe's voice behind her.

"Emmy," he said in a low tone. She turned to see him striding into the kitchen. He walked right up to her and was towering over her before she had a chance to put her phone down. At the sight of him so close, it took all her strength not to throw herself at him.

"What?" she asked, breathless, both thrilled and anxious to be in his presence. She glanced over his shoulder at the doorway to make sure they were still alone.

Gabe bit his lip and muttered, "Christ, those glasses . . ."

He said it in a tone that made something turn hot and melt low in her belly. He'd stepped even closer, and the need to touch him nearly overwhelmed her.

She cast him a sly little grin. "Are glasses your kink?"

"When you wear them, yes."

"Hmm, you should have told me that in Mexico."

He bit his lip again like he was remembering Mexico, and Emmy wished she could bite it for him. "So, have you thought about it?" he asked with an eager flash in his eyes.

She was nearly drunk on the smell of him standing so close. The leathery citrus was back in full force now that they were home. "Mm-hmm," she hummed, reflexively leaning toward him and sliding off her glasses.

His lips curled into a hopeful grin, and his hand found its way to her hip. She almost melted at his touch. She'd been without it for only a day, but the heat of him felt like a missing piece of her had been reattached. With a subtle flick of his wrist, he slipped his hand under the hem of her shirt and pressed his palm to her skin. His thumb skimmed the top of her jeans, dipping below for a thrilling second that almost made her knees collapse. "And what are you thinking?" he softly growled.

His mouth was an inch from hers. She could taste the mint on his breath. She wanted to inhale until she passed out.

"I'm *thiiinking* . . ." She drew the word out and watched his eyes hungrily trace her lips. ". . . you're being way too obvious. We're going to have to be more discreet if we're going to do this." She pushed his hand from her hip but smiled at him.

Gabe rocked back on his heels as if he'd been rejected but then realization dawned over his face. "You want to do this?" he asked, and put his hand right back on her hip.

"Yes," Emmy said with a laugh. "But we have to talk. We need boundaries. Rules for professional con—DUCT." The end of the word came out half squeal when he pulled her close. "Gabe, stop it," she half-heartedly protested as he buried his face in her neck. His lips hotly pressed into the vein pulsing in her throat.

"I'm sorry," he muttered. "I was hoping you'd say yes. I haven't stopped thinking about it since the airport."

"Okay, yes. I said yes. But we can't do this here." Her words were complete hypocrisy; she wanted to shove him into a utility closet and make out for the rest of the day. Somehow, knowing it would get them in trouble sent the desire flaming through her veins.

The sound of approaching voices carried in through the doorway and snapped them apart. Emmy's heart jumped. Gabe glanced over his shoulder and turned back to her with a drunken grin.

"Come over to my place tonight. We can talk. I'll cook."

Her heart was still pounding over the voices carrying closer and the rush of his mouth and hands having been on her. "Okay," she said on a quick and quiet breath. They were still standing way too close not to look suspicious to whoever was about to enter the kitchen.

"Okay," Gabe muttered. And then with the speed of a runner trying to steal second base, he leaned in and kissed her, hard, and then spun away just in time.

She stumbled back into the counter, nearly losing her footing, as he turned to the snack rack.

Pedro and Alice appeared at the doorway midconversation. Alice continued on with a nod while Pedro came inside. He pulled up short at the sight of Emmy standing rigid and stunned near the coffee station.

"You all right there, Jameson?" he asked, and cast a glance at Gabe perusing the snack rack.

"Mm-hmm," she managed, though she was anything but.

"You look a little . . . frazzled," Pedro said, and joined her.

"Oh, I'm fine," she lied once more.

Gabe grabbed a bag of rice cakes and slipped out of the room. She caught the dark grin on his lips and silently vowed there would be payback later for his little stunt.

"If you say so," Pedro said, and dug in the fridge for the oat milk.

Emmy had to gather herself before she headed for the conference room, knowing the object of all her frazzle would be there waiting for her.

When she arrived, Gabe had opened his snack and was crunching away.

"Still pretending to like rice cakes?" she said, and sank into the chair opposite his side of the table.

He turned to her and swallowed with a half grin. "I told you, I love rice cakes."

She replaced her computer glasses even though she didn't have her computer and eyed him over the tops of them. "No one likes rice cakes, Olson."

He looked like he had trouble swallowing his bite before he licked his lips. His Adam's apple bobbed again, and she felt his eyes hungrily outlining her glasses.

Payback, she mouthed as the rest of their team filed in the door.

Gabe chewed away, his grin stretching his lips as he flicked a brow at her.

They were used to challenging each other at work, but this was a new kind of competition. One Emmy knew she had the upper hand in because all she had to do was look at him. And, apparently, wear glasses.

Soon Alice stood at the front of the room going over an update on the trade prospect analysis, and Emmy should have been listening. She should have been taking mental and physical notes, but even with her body swiveled forward, her eyes would not unglue from Gabe.

The arch of his cheekbones, the curve of his jaw. The hint of oranges and amber she could smell across the room, and the way she knew how it would flood through her like an elixir if she pressed her nose below his ear and inhaled. She wanted to graze her teeth on his stubble. She wanted to peel off his shirt and trace her fingertips over his chest. She wanted to remove every layer of his clothing and—

"Jameson?" Alice's voice cut into her fantasy like a cymbal crash.

Emmy flinched. Her face burned, and she felt every eye in the room on her. Gabe's were searing hot, and he wore a victorious grin on his lips. He cleared his throat to disguise a quiet laugh.

Goddamn it. Maybe she didn't have the upper hand after all.

She took a breath and tried to focus. "Sorry, you were saying?" she asked Alice.

Alice gave her a suspicious look and paused for a few beats. "I said I want you as lead on this." She nodded at the complicated chart projected on the screen behind her.

Emmy sat up straighter and pulled her head back into the game. "Of course."

"Thank you. Now . . ." Alice continued talking, and Emmy forced herself to pay attention. Even in the moments when she could feel Gabe's gaze traveling the terrain of her body like he too was undressing her with his eyes.

When the meeting ended a half hour later, Emmy and Gabe both lingered while Pedro and Silas slipped out the door. Alice remained at the other end of the room.

"After you," Gabe said, and gestured for Emmy to go first.

She side-eyed him with a grin. "You've never waited for me to leave a room first."

"Well, I've developed a taste for the view from behind," he muttered.

Emmy's face flamed again. She stifled a laugh. "*Gabe,*" she warned right as Alice called her name.

"Jameson? Got a minute?"

Emmy froze, feeling caught.

Gabe took the cue to pretend like nothing had happened and slipped out the door.

"Of course," Emmy said to Alice and tried to keep her voice steady.

"Good. Walk with me," Alice said with a nod. She gathered her laptop and tucked it under her arm. Emmy followed her into the hallway, jittery with nerves. Alice's heels snapped off the concrete floor like little hammer strokes, each one pounding a nail in what Emmy was sure would be her career coffin. They were being way too obvious.

Once Alice deposited her laptop in her own office, she led Emmy down the hall and into an elevator that carried them up to the field level of the ballpark. All the while, Alice stayed quiet. Emmy was about to explode with anxiety when they crossed into the airy breezeway. She could see the field as a lime-green strip between the deck they stood on and the one above them. The maintenance crew milled around trimming every blade of grass and perfectly chalking the dirt.

"Thought we could use some fresh air," Alice said with an encouraging smile.

Emmy still wasn't sure what this impromptu walk-and-talk was about, so she simply smiled back.

They strolled past vendor booths being stocked for the game later that night: kegs on carts, trunks of ice, a towering trolley of hot dog buns. To their right, the empty stadium seats stretched down to the field like a sheet of shiny blue plastic.

"How was the wedding?" Alice asked in a calm, casual tone.

The tight knot in Emmy's stomach loosened. "Oh!" she said, surprised at the topic, but of all her co-workers, Alice would be the one to ask. "It was really great. Kind of perfect, actually." Her cheeks warmed as she thought back to the sand and sea, her sister's smile. The warmth morphed into a full-on heat wave when she thought of Gabe in his suit. Gabe in his bathrobe. Gabe in nothing at all. "It was actually the best weekend of my life," she quietly added.

Alice shot her a coy smile. "You're not going to run off to Mexico on me, are you?"

"No," Emmy said with a laugh.

"Good." Alice stopped walking and leaned on the rail they'd approached. Emmy joined her and gazed out at the field.

At face value, it was a diamond of dirt and some grass on which a bunch of grown men threw and hit a ball around, but it was so much more than that. It was dreams and goals and aspirations. A place where the highest level of a profession was carried out. Where legends were born, and records set. It may have been just a game, but it was also a community. A place that brought people together and gave them something to care about. Something to believe in. Something that made the rest of life a little better for the moments of delirious celebration because a collective goal was reached. Emmy's love for the sport thrummed through her as she stared out, and she knew by the look on Alice's face that she felt the same.

The significance of them standing there as two women was not lost on her.

"Emmy, the reason I brought you out here to talk . . ." Alice began, and Emmy's nerves jumped again. Alice turned to her with a serious look in her eyes. "I wanted to let you know that as of now, you are the front-runner for the senior analyst position. Olson is great, but your leadership qualities give you an edge that I would love to see continue to grow as you advance through the organization."

Emmy's breath hitched. Her heart soared. Alice's straight-to-the-point delivery almost knocked her off her feet. "Um, thank you. That's great news."

Alice nodded. "Of course. And you shouldn't be surprised. In fact, don't be. You deserve this, and you know you do, so act like it."

Emmy wiped the shock off her face and heard what she was really saying. Her discreet reference to the steel backbone of confidence they needed to make it as women in their industry. "Yes, I do deserve it. Thank you."

"You're welcome. Part of the reason I'm telling you this now is that I need you focused. You are the front-runner, and with one week left until Director Allen makes a decision, you need to bring it home. That's why I'm giving you lead on this project." She said it all with the subtext of *Don't let me down*.

Emmy heard her loud and clear. She knew Alice advocated for her where she could, and her giving Emmy a heads-up that the job was all but hers meant she'd cleared a path for her. She had to make it to the finish line. "Understood," she said with a nod.

"Great. And on that note, you seem a little distracted today. Everything all right?"

Embarrassment leapt up and gripped Emmy with two hands. Apparently, it had been obvious. She trusted Alice and had confided in her before, but she didn't feel like she could confess to her that her distraction came from the explicit fantasies about her cubicle mate playing on repeat in her mind.

"Oh, it's just some . . . relationship stuff. Sorry about that. I'll keep it in check." She knew it was a lie even as the words left her lips.

"Ah. Well. I will be the first to admit I am not a font of knowledge on that front," Alice said with a light laugh.

Emmy shot her a smile, knowing she was single and in her own words *married to her career*. Alice was someone she aspired to emulate. When she'd sworn off dating after Jacob, she'd reassured herself she'd made the right choice many times by looking to Alice as inspiration. *She's happy. She's thriving. She loves her job, and that's enough for her.* But now that her own world had been turned upside down by a fake number text, Emmy wondered if it was enough for *her.* If maybe she truly could make room for the joy that had unexpectedly filled her life for the past several weeks and make things work with Gabe.

"Alice," she said, hearing the timidity in her own voice. "Don't answer if this is too personal, but do you ever wish you'd done things differently?"

The look Alice gave her said she knew exactly what she meant, and also she didn't find the question too personal at all. "This career comes with sacrifices, but the best ones often do. Sure, sometimes I think about what it would be like to come home to a husband and kids instead of a quiet—blissfully quiet, I might add—house." She paused for a sly smile. "But then I remember why I got into this career and what I want out of it. For me, *that's* what drives me. *That's* what gets me out of bed every day. Getting to come here and be part of something big and influential, to help build a legacy—and to get to do it as one of so few women." She gave her a dazzling smile, and Emmy felt it shimmer through her body. They were so alike.

"But it doesn't have to be an either/or, Emmy," she went on. "Plenty of people find ways to make careers and families work. And you're still young." She nudged her with her elbow. "Plenty of time to figure things out. Hell, *I'm* still young. We better stop talking like I've got one foot in the grave in case we manifest it." She laughed, and Emmy joined her.

"Thanks, Alice."

"Yep. Now, let's get back to work on getting you promoted."

Chapter 18

The rest of the day took approximately ten thousand years to pass. Emmy kept her head down, spinning with happiness over both what Alice had told her about the promotion and the idea of seeing Gabe after work. The emotions were nearly too big to handle—not to mention complicated, because she wasn't sure how one would affect the other. She and Gabe definitely needed to talk.

He texted her his address when she asked for it at lunch. She had thought to suggest they ditch the rest of the day and head over right then, but she managed to behave herself. He asked her to come over around 6:30, and it took every ounce of her willpower to make it through the day.

She'd never been to his apartment before, but the North Park building looked much like hers: a boxy stone-and-glass structure lined with palms and hedges. She buzzed at the building entrance and all but ran up the stairs to his second-floor front door when he let her in.

Gabe opened his door, and Emmy had hardly crossed the threshold before he pulled her into a kiss. She immediately surrendered to it, burning to her fingertips with desire for him. He lifted her, and she wrapped her legs around him. The entryway wall was suddenly at her back and his mouth moving in a fevered desperation against hers.

"I thought I was coming over to talk," she managed to mutter.

He kept kissing her like he couldn't get enough. Like he might die if he didn't steal all the oxygen in her lungs for himself. He bit at her bottom lip and sucked on it, grazing her with his teeth and swiping his tongue. One of his arms braced under her thighs and the other hand tangled in her hair. She could feel his desire for her already rock hard pressing into the warm space between her legs. Just as desperate for him, she tilted her hips, grinding against him as much as she could. He groaned a coarse, aching sound into her mouth. "Bed, and then talk?"

"Yes," she agreed, completely ravenous.

He carried her to his room, Emmy peeling and discarding clothes along the way. She missed any view of his apartment because of the pure inability to pry her lips from his. When he laid her on his bed, she bounced and felt his hands urgently at her jeans' button. They were both nearly frantic with need.

"I've been thinking of being in your bed all day," she said, and helped him shove down her pants.

"I've been thinking of you in my bed since we met."

She briefly paused at his confession, and judging by the consumed, hungry look on his face while he removed his pants and shirt, she got the sense he wasn't aware he'd made it.

The gentle caressing and exploring they'd done in their hotel was markedly absent. Now they clawed at each other, all hands and teeth and raw ache to reunite their bodies. Gabe retrieved a condom from his nightstand and wasted no time climbing on top of her where she waited with her legs spread. Her body greedily welcomed his when he pushed inside.

The only sounds were their labored breathing and Gabe softly rasping *missed you* as he worked his way in deep, stroking at an intentional pace that both drove Emmy wild and allowed her to gradually take all of him.

Soon they were moving together as one in a rapid rhythm that had Emmy spinning all over again. She'd nearly memorized his body in Mexico, but somehow, everything felt different back here in the real world. In his bed with his home all around her, his soft sheets under her bare skin, the orangey-amber scent so close.

It was new and real, and it was perfect.

"Perfect," she murmured on a raspy exhale without even realizing it.

Gabe lifted his head at the sound of her voice. He looked down at her, pupils blown out, and darkly grinned. "Yeah. Perfect," he panted between strokes. And then he got a look on his face like he'd accepted a challenge to make it even better. "Hold on, baby," he growled.

Emmy drunkenly smiled and logged another personal fact about him. Gabe Olson: always one-upping everyone, even himself.

He swept his hand down Emmy's leg, leaving a flaming tingle in his wake, and grabbed her ankle. He hooked her foot over his shoulder and began drilling into her at a frenzied pace that had her gasping and her vision narrowing to a sparkling tunnel. She spiraled and spun. She tasted the stars. Her orgasm hit her like a line drive, and she came with a cry, the pounding pulse ripping through her and leaving her shredded.

As her legs trembled, Gabe slowed his strokes and straightened up over her, pausing to let her catch her breath and tenderly kissing her ankle. "You feel so good, Emmy. So fucking good." He squeezed her leg to his chest and gazed down at her like he'd won the greatest prize in the world.

Then he pulled out and flipped her over.

He grabbed her hips and yanked her toward him onto her knees only to sink back in and hit a spot so deep inside her that her climax gripped her all over again like it had never let go and refused to do so now. She came again in shuddering waves, nearly screaming into his pillow as he moved behind her, pushing her on and on, deeper and deeper into a blackout bliss until he joined her there, calling out her name and a flurry of swear words before he collapsed on top of her.

They lay still, hearts pounding and lungs heaving. The air crackled around them as it cooled and stilled. Gabe eventually lifted himself off her, the slick slab of his abs leaving her back damp with sweat, and rolled beside her. He turned on his back and inhaled a large breath as he pulled the sheet up over them. Emmy was boneless. Spent. A pile of limbs and untethered thoughts. He pulled her limp body halfway atop his and stroked her hair. Then he ran a hand down her arm, still somehow able to spark her exhausted nerve endings, and lifted her hand to kiss it.

"We can talk now." His voice rumbled in his chest where her ear was pressed.

"I literally don't think I'm capable."

He softly laughed and draped her lifeless arm over his chest. "Take your time."

He'd rendered her immobile. She wasn't sure she'd ever stand again. She'd spend the rest of her life liquefied in his bed—which didn't seem like a bad prospect, honestly. She let herself mentally drift into a potential future scenario as she listened to his heart calm. She'd come over after work, they'd wreck each other between the sheets, they'd have a lazy dinner together, and maybe she'd spend the night. The thought of it made her snuggle closer to him.

Her stomach loudly growled.

Gabe said, "Hungry? I promised I'd cook." He began to sit up, and Emmy reached for him.

"You promised we'd talk, too."

He looked down at her naked in his bed with an unreadable bend to his brow. He lifted her hand to kiss it. "Dinner, then talk."

As if on cue, her stomach audibly rumbled again.

"See? It's only proper to feed you after all that."

"Such a gentleman," she said with a playful grin but couldn't shake the feeling he was delaying their conversation. In fact, he might have just fucked her senseless as distraction, she realized.

Mission accomplished.

Gabe leaned in to kiss Emmy again. "Feel free to freshen up." He pointed toward the bathroom as he headed in that direction, bending over to swipe his underwear off the floor and giving her a healthy look at his muscular thighs and perfectly sculpted backside.

She swooned and luckily had a pile of pillows to catch her when she flopped backward like a damsel into a fainting chair. While he was gone, she took the opportunity to gaze around the room. It was kempt and tidy with a laptop closed on a desk beneath a window; his wallet, watch, and the notorious bottle of cologne sat on top of a tall dresser. The painting hanging above his bed depicted something abstract oiled in shades of blue and gray that could have been either a man in a field or a whale, she couldn't tell. His nightstand held a lamp, a phone charger coiled like a little sleeping snake, and a stack of five novels: the top one, a political thriller with a bookmark poking out halfway through.

Emmy heard Gabe finish in the bathroom, and aside from peeing after sex like any responsible and hygienic vagina owner, freshening up actually didn't sound like a preferable idea. The smell of him lingered on her: spicy oranges, a hint of sweat, the pure tonic of *him*, and she didn't want to risk washing any of it off. Instead, a better idea sounded like digging in his closet for something to wear since her clothes were scattered around his apartment anyway.

She slipped from the bed and padded over to the sliding closet doors. Behind them, she found a menagerie of pastel polos and smiled to herself. Instead of borrowing one of his work shirts, she opted for the old SDSU Baseball tee he'd worn to bed in Mexico. It fell to her thighs. She searched the floor for her bra and underwear, and when she didn't find them, decided with a shrug that she didn't need them. She stole into the bathroom and found herself looking properly rosy-cheeked and mussed in the mirror.

When she finished, Emmy wound her way through the hall and found Gabe in his kitchen having pulled on sweatpants and a tight T-shirt. She didn't think the man owned a loose T-shirt, save maybe the one she was wearing, and that was fine by her.

His apartment had a floor plan similar to hers with an open concept kitchen that spilled into a dining area and living room. Soft blankets buried his couch, and another stack of novels and a few statistics books were piled on his coffee table. The pale blue-and-gray decor was all rather soothing. The giant TV was turned on to the baseball game midway through the third inning.

Gabe stood with his back to her at the counter chopping something on a cutting board. A bottle of wine waited on the island behind him along with two glasses and a small tray of vegetables. When he turned to see her barefoot in his shirt, his face pulled into a warm smile. He stared at her bare legs for a hot beat. Then his eyes traveled over her chest visibly pointed through the threadbare T-shirt. He reached out to wrap an arm around her and pull her close, and in doing so, skimmed her thigh to her hip and felt that she wasn't wearing any underwear.

He froze and noticeably stopped breathing. "Are you trying to kill me, Emmy Jameson?"

With a grin, she plucked a carrot off the island and snapped it between her teeth. "Yes. This has been my long game all along to finally best you."

"Hmm." He buried his lips in her messy hair. "You win."

She pushed away from him and hopped up on the island. The icy granite through the shirt made her shiver. "What's for dinner?"

"I hope you like Bolognese. I haven't gone shopping since we got back, and it's the only thing I have all the ingredients for."

She uncorked the wine to fill two glasses. "Sounds great. Would you like a glass to toast to Hollander choking at the plate?" She nodded at the TV where the center fielder, their favorite topic of debate, was walking into the batter's box.

"Yes, but he's not going to choke."

"He's totally going to choke. With a runner on third, his batting average is one twenty-five, Gabe."

"Exactly. Right where we want him."

"Sure, if you're the other team." She handed him one of the glasses she'd filled. He clinked it against hers and sipped.

"No, if you're this team. He has a predictable pattern: troughs and peaks like anyone. He evens out."

"You did not just mansplain regression to the mean to me."

He smirked at the playful scowl on her face. "All I'm saying is he'll pull out of it. His highest highs always come after the lowest lows."

"Yeah, but we didn't pay twenty million dollars over three years for Hollander's brand of lows." She pointed at the TV right as he swung and missed on a one-one count. She threw up her arms. "Why would you swing at that? It was ten miles outside!"

She caught the grimace on Gabe's face like he agreed but didn't want to admit it as he turned back to the stove. Emmy smiled to herself and snapped another carrot between her teeth. As he continued to cook, she watched the muscles in his back move under his shirt. He reached for the cutting board and dumped its contents into the pan. Then he opened a cabinet and stretched for a measuring cup on a high shelf.

She could easily get used to watching him make dinner.

"So, if we're going to do this, what's it going to look like?" she asked.

Gabe turned and gestured at the room like it was obvious. "Like this."

"What, you cooking me dinner while I sit on the counter in your old T-shirt and tell you how you're wrong about your *feelings* about the game?" She pointed to the TV with her hand holding her wineglass.

"Yes, or you could be naked if you prefer. And I'm not wrong."

"You're *so* wrong," she said just to egg him on.

"Emmy, I'm not. When he's under two hundred at the plate, he steps it up. He picks his pitches better. His OBP is directly correlated. Because of his slump, the probability of him getting on base tonight is higher. Did you run the model I wrote for you?" Gabe let out a little huff. He walked back over to the island where she sat and picked up his wine.

She coyly smiled at him. "You're so hot when you talk about statistics. When you get passionate, this squiggly little vein pops out in your temple." She brushed her thumb over it and bit her lip.

He held her gaze for a beat, cooling off, and then smiled back. "Careful, that's my thinking vein." He leaned his head away. "So, did you? Run the model?"

"I haven't had the chance yet, no."

"Well, you should."

"Why? So you can do a victory dance about proving me wrong?" she said flatly.

"The opposite actually. I wrote it for you to level the playing field, so to speak. Since you can't be *on* the field, I figured out how to approximately quantify what I learned from that experience. Now you can have the same advantage."

Emmy stared at him, astounded. When she'd told him to write her an equation, it had mostly been a taunt because she didn't think it was possible. But he took the challenge in a direction that had her heart primed to explode. And her blood on fire.

"That might be the sexiest thing anyone has ever done for me," she said, and grabbed a fistful of his shirt to pull him toward her.

His smile grew. "So, is math your kink, then?"

"When you do it, yeah."

His mouth landed on hers when she yanked him close. She wrapped her arms around his neck and indulged in the feel of his lips moving from her mouth to her jaw and down her throat. It was far more potent than the wine. They went at it for long enough that she nearly forgot what they had been talking about.

"But really though, how's this going to work?" she asked.

"Seems to be working pretty fine right now," he mumbled to her flushed skin.

She softly moaned when he traced his tongue across her collarbone. "I mean at work. I don't want to go from being the only girl to the only girl who's also sleeping with her co-worker."

At this, Gabe unsuctioned his face from Emmy's neck. He pulled back and gave her a hard look, knowing what she meant. One that said he'd had the same thought and was frustrated on her behalf all the same. "Of course not. I don't want that either."

She could already see it, the perceptions people would have of her. Even if it wasn't true, she'd never shake the suspicion of having slept her way to advancement. All it would take was a whisper and she'd have a permanent reputation. He, on the other hand, would probably get a congratulatory slap on the back. It was wildly and infuriatingly unfair.

They held each other for a quiet moment, their breath mingling and hearts beating with the obstacle between them finally acknowledged.

"Tell me what you're thinking," Emmy said.

His lips spread into a little grin. "I am thinking many, many things, Emmy Jameson."

She grinned back. "Tell me the important ones."

"Okay. I think you look great in that shirt. I think I want you to spend the night. And I think we were idiots for ever thinking we could leave this in Mexico. What are you thinking?"

She smiled again as a flush warmed her cheeks. "I think I'm going to steal this shirt. I think I do want to spend the night, and I think I agree. Complete idiots." She looped her arms around his neck again and pulled him into another kiss. It fizzled all the way down to her toes as he held her close.

"So, what are we going to do?" Gabe asked when they stopped.

"Flee to Mexico and never come back."

He softly laughed. "I'm serious."

He was too close and too cuddly for her to answer seriously yet. "Well, judging by your inability to *keep your hands to yourself* at work." She jabbed him in the ribs with each word. "And seeing that you're a constant distraction—!"

He flinched and laughed like it tickled. "Hey, I wasn't even doing anything in that meeting today. I was just sitting there paying attention, which couldn't be said for you."

"Do not underestimate your appeal while being studious, Olson." She jabbed him in the ribs again, and he stumbled back a step.

"So, all I've got to do is talk about math and look smart, and you're a sure thing."

"I'm a simple creature."

"You—" Gabe said, and grabbed Emmy's dangling foot. He pulled her leg out straight and then used it to reel himself back in by gripping higher and higher until he got to her thigh. He hitched her knee around his hip and pulled her against him once more. "—are anything but simple, Emmy Jameson." He finished his sentence and brushed her mussed hair out of her face. He looked right in her eyes. "You're the boss. Whatever you want to do, I will follow your lead on this one."

Emmy gazed back at the open vulnerability on Gabe's face and felt her chest lift. Something her sister had said weeks ago about them jumping together flitted through her mind. Despite the challenges that might lie ahead, she *did* want to make it work. And she could see on his face he did too.

"I think we have to go to HR," she said. "Come clean. If we're going to do this, it has to be on the record. I'm already in an uphill battle as one of the only women in the department, and I don't want any rumors or assumptions."

He nodded. "Okay."

"Good. And once that's taken care of, I guess we just . . . see where this goes?" Her voice floated up with an optimistic inflection. She raised her brows and smiled at him.

He gave her a wicked grin in return and grabbed her hips. With a grunt, he scooped her off the counter and started walking toward the couch with his face buried in her neck and her legs wrapped around his back. With his hot lips working a trail down to her collarbone, she shivered in the most delicious way.

"Dinner is going to burn," she said, and leaned into him.

"We can order takeout," he muttered as he lowered onto the couch so she was straddling his lap. He slid his hands up her thighs and beneath the shirt to her hips.

Emmy tilted her head back when Gabe pressed his mouth to her neck. From the corner of her eye, she saw the game on TV, and to her shock, Hollander had made it to first base, and the runner on third had scored. "Oh, hey, look. He didn't choke."

Gabe paused his assault of her senses to look over her shoulder. His face split into a grin. "Told you I wasn't wrong."

Chapter 19

They managed to get some sleep, though Emmy had to think the reason they were walking into HR together the next morning was written all over their exhausted-in-the-best-way faces. As if he wanted to dispel any doubts, Gabe slipped his hand into hers and squeezed as they made their way to the head of HR's office.

Like the overprepared, studious nerds they were, last night they'd read their employee handbook cover to cover (of course Gabe had a printed copy of it in a binder, as did Emmy) to see what they were up against. The organization had no rules against office romances, nor did they have any requirements about disclosing a romantic relationship. Emmy couldn't say she was shocked an empire created and run by men hadn't given any thought to such regulations, but the lack of rules felt like both a blessing and a curse. Because there were no guidelines, there was no telling how HR might react.

When they'd finally decided to go to sleep, Emmy lay with her back tucked against Gabe's chest and his arm looped over her. The feel of it all, the comfort and safety of his embrace, had her at once undeniably content and terrified of losing it all before they even had a chance to get started.

"Gabe, what if they say we can't?" she'd whispered into the dark.

"They won't," he'd promised and pressed his lips to her shoulder.

She'd fallen asleep feeling his heart beat and convincing herself he was right.

Now, standing outside the HR director's office, she was second-guessing his certainty.

They knocked and entered the spacious office that boasted a window overlooking not the field but at least a street with a sliver view of the bay.

Todd Waters, a balding man in a short-sleeved button-down and tie, was turned around reaching into a filing cabinet when they entered. They'd already sat in the two chairs opposite his desk by the time he swiveled to face them. "Mr. Olson and Ms. Jameson from Research and Analytics, what can I help you with today?" he asked as he scanned the form he'd retrieved, surely something notifying him who they were. He looked up at them over the form and over the tops of his glasses with a welcoming smile. He stilled when he saw their clasped hands spanning the gap between their chairs. His smile softened at the edges. "Ah, I see. Well, okay then." He swiveled back around in his chair and reached into the filing cabinet again.

Emmy and Gabe swapped an unsure glance. Emmy decided to take the lead.

"Mr. Waters—"

"Call me Todd, please," he interrupted her.

"Todd," she started again. Emmy hadn't talked to the man other than back when she was hired and had sat in this very office brimming with excitement over her future career. "We're here because we want to formally disclose that we're seeing each other. Romantically," she awkwardly tacked on. She'd known this conversation was going to be uncomfortable, but it still had her squirming.

Gabe squeezed her hand again. "We know the organization doesn't have any rules around dating or disclosing relationships, but we want it on official record," he added. "To avoid any speculation or assumptions."

"Wise move," Todd said with a nod. "You're right the organization does not mandate that you disclose your relationship; however, now that you have, your supervisors may choose to review to determine if there are any conflicts of interest that may arise and advise accordingly."

"Like what?" Emmy asked at the same time Gabe said, "Advise?"

Todd turned to his computer and clicked around on his screen. "Yes. We want to avoid any kind of power imbalance, favoritism, unfair treatment. Things like that. And by advise, I mean should they determine any of those things exist or could occur, we will advise on recourse. Ah, I see that you are in the same department and hold the same position. Currently."

The last word rang out like a gong.

As he spoke, Emmy slipped her hand out of Gabe's and folded it with her other hand in her lap. She hadn't told Gabe what Alice had told her about being the front-runner for the promotion. The thought of the problems it might cause had swum around her mind like a predator in deep water last night. She'd tried to fight it off by snuggling herself closer to Gabe, feeling the warmth of his bare skin, listening to his heart, but she could only manage to get it to shrink, never to disappear.

Now it loomed mightily in front of them. A power imbalance was inevitable.

"It looks like you're both up for the same promotion." Todd spoke the quiet part out loud. He tapped his fingers on his desk as he briefly thought before coming to a conclusion. "I'll need to inform your supervisors of what you've shared here today, after I gather some information from you."

Emmy felt Gabe's eyes on her, perhaps wondering why she'd let go of his hand. She shot him a worried look as her nerves churned. He tried to reassure her with a shake of his head, but it didn't do much to help.

They answered Todd's brief list of questions about the duration and nature of their relationship. He then told them he'd follow up later that day after discussing the matter with their supervisors, and that was it. The whole meeting lasted under ten minutes. Emmy left the office reeling and wondering if this was what it felt like to be on the receiving end of one of the trade decisions she helped run numbers for. It was so swift and straight to the point, she felt like her budding relationship was being shipped off to another time zone before she even blinked.

The weight of it all hit her when they left the office and reentered the hallway. She paused to catch her breath and leaned on the wall.

"Are you okay?" Gabe asked, and instantly stepped to her side.

She looked up at him with a tremble in her lip and tears glossing her eyes. "Did we just ruin everything?"

He gently cupped her face to catch her tears before they fell. He shook his head. "No. Everything will be fine."

"You don't know that." Emmy's voice cracked, and Gabe wrapped her in his arms. The smell and heat of him enveloped her. Aside from that kiss he stole in the kitchen, it was the closest they'd ever been at work. She wanted to melt straight into him. At the same time, it felt forbidden to be touching so intimately.

"We're going to get in trouble," she said, and gently pushed him back with a soggy sniffle.

"No, we're not. There are no rules, remember?"

"Yeah, but there might be *recourse*."

He curved his fingers under her chin to tilt her face up. "Yes, but what's the worst they can do, force us to work together? We already can't stand each other." He softly smiled with a sparkle in his dark eyes.

A weak laugh popped from her lips. "Stop making jokes."

He caught a stray tear with his thumb. "At least you're laughing at them."

"Only because I'm sad." She fiddled with the button on his shirt and then smoothed her hand against his chest.

"Come on," he said, and pulled her away from the wall. "We better get back to the office in case anyone gets suspicious about why we're both gone. Speaking of, are we going to tell Ishida and Torres?"

Emmy snorted. "Only if we want them to never shut up about it."

"They never shut up about anything," Gabe said, slinging an arm over her shoulders. She briefly leaned into him, wishing she could stay, and then removed herself to a professional distance.

"Let's make sure we're not going to get fired before we PDA all over the place."

She was half joking, but he nodded in agreement.

They returned to their office with no fanfare. Pedro and Silas were fully occupied staring at their computers with headphones on. Emmy and Gabe sat at their desks and did their best to work. Emmy found herself jumping every time her inbox pinged, fearing an email from HR—or even Alice asking her why the hell she was throwing a wrench in her promotion plan, because surely she'd been notified by now.

But then Emmy would glance at Gabe and think about the warmth of his body wrapped around hers, the sound of his laugh. The way her frustration with him had so quickly ripened into a deeply rooted desire to be close to him, and how her heart was cartwheeling over the thought of where they might go together.

She silently prayed that there would not be a choice put before her—her job or him—because she honestly did not know what she would pick. The choice had been easy with Jacob, but with Gabe . . . The thought hollowed out her insides with fear.

At around three o'clock, her email pinged at the same second Gabe's did. The chime in stereo sent her heart beating double time; she knew what it meant. Gabe glanced over their cubicle wall at her, and she read her distress all over his face. He attempted an encouraging nod, but it fell flat. She gave him just as weak of a nod before they both turned to their screens.

An email from Todd waited at the top of her inbox.

"Always straight to the point," she muttered and clicked it.

She quickly noted both Alice and Director Allen had been cc'd.

Ms. Jameson, Mr. Olson,

Following up on our meeting this morning—after careful consideration and review, your supervisory team has determined the nature of your personal relationship is problematic to the potential for promotional advancement. Given that the senior analyst position carries seniority over your current roles as analysts, the department feels that the resulting power imbalance would be inappropriate should one of you assume the role. If either or both of you wish to continue being considered for promotion, please formally inform HR of the termination of your personal relationship by this coming Monday. If you wish to remove yourselves from consideration, no further recourse is necessary. We thank you for your cooperation.

Sincerely,

Todd Waters, Director of Human Resources

Emmy read the email twice, trying to make it sink in, but it kept bouncing off her brain as if she were throwing a rubber ball at a wall.

Problematic to the potential for promotional advancement.

Termination of your personal relationship.

This coming Monday.

The message jumbled into chaos, but those words stood out. They had five days to make a decision: the job, or their relationship.

Emmy turned to Gabe and saw an ashen look of shock on his face.

They had, indeed, just ruined everything.

She stood from her chair and headed for the door.

"Emmy, wait," he said, and followed her. She didn't slow. She beelined for the elevator at the end of the hall. He caught up in no time with his long strides. "Where are you going?"

"I need some air." She stopped at the elevator and pressed the button. Her lungs felt like they were closing off. The ceiling was lowering; the walls were closing in. Getting into a small metal box might not have been the best idea at that moment, but it was the quickest escape to aboveground oxygen she so desperately needed.

The elevator doors opened with a ding, and she stepped in. Gabe followed her. A flashback to that night in the elevator in Mexico when she'd asked him what he was thinking hit her like a truck. She could feel the heat of him, hear the velvety purr of his voice. At the same time, the memory felt like it came from another reality. One where they could be together without worry. Without compromising everything she'd worked years to achieve.

"Fuck!" she shouted once the doors had closed. The word exploded out of her in an angry rush. She mashed the heels of her hands into her eyes. She heard a loud bang and moved her hands to see Gabe shaking out his own hand like he'd punched the metal wall. She couldn't blame him; she'd have done the same if it wouldn't have hurt.

He spun around to face her. Frustration pulsed off him the same way it did her. They weren't mad at each other—or maybe they were; Emmy couldn't interpret her emotions. She was mostly mad at the situation. Mad she was falling for him and now she couldn't have him, not if she wanted her job. Part of her wanted to take it all back—the texting, the flirting, Mexico. Part of her wanted to forsake everything and rip off all his clothes right there in the elevator. The line between rage and lust was dangerously blurry. They stared at each other, silently blinking and fuming.

The elevator dinged and dumped them out onto the field level. Dim daylight cut between the concrete layers. The field below was busy with another afternoon of preparation. The food vendors had started to cook, lacing the air with the tangy bite of hot dogs and tacos as well as sugary treats.

"Are we going to talk?" Gabe asked when she stomped out of the elevator, and he followed.

"No," she snapped and kept walking. "Not right now."

He jogged to catch up and reached for her arm. "Emmy, wait. We're in this together, okay? And I—"

She whirled on him and snapped again. "I just need a minute!"

He stopped and dropped his grip, looking hurt.

"Sorry," she said with a big breath. "This is just . . . a lot." The truth spun around in her mouth: *It's going to be me; I'm going to get the job. She* was the one with something to lose here. But she couldn't bring herself to say it. With the look on his face, it would only have been salt on a freshly opened wound.

She took another breath. "I think we need some time to think."

He nodded. "Today's Wednesday, so we have five days before they want a decision." She took relief in knowing he wasn't ready to make a decision right then either.

Emmy looked up at his handsome, tormented face and wondered if she'd ever be ready to make a decision. He must have read the pain on hers because he stepped forward and smoothed his hand over her hair. "I know this is the exact scenario you're afraid of, except it's the job making you choose this time, not some insecure partner. But we'll figure this out. Together. It's going to be okay."

As much as she wanted to believe him, she couldn't see how that could be true. Not now, at least.

Emmy fought to calm her racing heart, because Gabe was right: this was her worst-case scenario come to life, again, but with bigger stakes. "Let's just get through the rest of the week, okay? We can talk this weekend."

He looked at her with a deep knit between his brows. "Okay," he said with a nod. "This weekend."

Chapter 20

Emmy threw herself into work as best she could for the rest of the week. She sought solace in numbers and equations—logical things where the world made sense, and she could find an answer to everything. She realized late on Friday night she could probably benefit from seeking solace—and advice—from another human and not just a spreadsheet. Seeing as her sister was still in Europe, and Beth had a date, and Axe Murderer was obviously out, that left her parents as the best option.

Exhausted from the week and needing sleep, she decided to pay them a visit on Saturday morning.

Her parents still lived in the house where Emmy had grown up. It was in a stereotypical Southern California neighborhood, where all the cookie-cutter houses shared identical stucco exteriors and tile roofs and sat on lots so close together the inhabitants had to think twice about walking around naked inside in case the neighbors might see.

When she pulled up outside their house midmorning after texting her mom she was coming over, the sense of home welcomed her like a pair of arms. The front lawn of her youth had been replaced by gravel and a tasteful succulent garden—much more eco-friendly and lower maintenance. Her mom's favorite wind chime gently gonged its low, soothing notes from the walkway. A wreath of rosemary and lavender hung on the door.

Emmy knocked and then entered. "Hello? Mom? Dad?"

"In here!" her dad called from the kitchen.

The short entryway spilled into a living room lined with book-shelves and photos of the Jameson children through the years. Emmy always cringed at her awkward phase of braces and untamed hair so prominently on display—especially side by side with Piper, who'd never had a bad hair day in her life. Josh's senior portrait hung among the spread, and every time she saw it, Emmy couldn't help smiling back at his big grin, even if it was only a little bit.

"Hey, bro," she murmured as she passed. Then she said, "Hi, Dad," when she turned the corner into the open kitchen. It shared space with the family room where the muted TV was playing a base-ball game happening on the East Coast.

"Hiya, sport!" her dad all but sang over his shoulder. He stood at the counter with his back to her stirring something in a pitcher. "Your mom told me you were coming over." He turned around with a tray of lemonade and acrylic glasses. He nodded at the sliding door leading out into the yard. "Get the door for me, will you?"

Emmy followed his instruction and opened the door to the crown jewel of her parents' property.

To help manage her grief when Josh died, Emmy's mother had started gardening, and she never stopped. Now the backyard oasis verged on otherworldly with all the vines and blossoms, the pots and planters, the trellises and lattices. Emmy's thumbs were the furthest things from green; she didn't even know what half of the plants were called. But her mother tended to every petal and leaf with the same care she gave her patients.

Vera stood on the yard's upper level pointing a hose at a pot of flowers the color of a construction cone. Her Crocs looked like a pair of rubber ducks on her feet. "Hi, sweetie!" she called with a wave.

"Hi, Mom." Emmy waved back and pulled out a chair at the pa-tio table. She saw her dad's e-reader sitting there with his smudged reading glasses on top of it. Reading and gardening were her parents' favorite ways to spend a Saturday morning.

Frank busied himself pouring lemonade while Vera finished spritz-
ing her plants. She eventually returned the hose to its hook and made
her way down the two short steps to the patio.

"Here you go," Frank said, and handed Emmy a glass before he
sat adjacent to her.

"How was your first week back at work?" Vera asked, and sank
into the chair opposite them. She wiped her hands on her jeans and
grabbed the glass Frank had poured for her.

Their unconditional welcome, the way they seamlessly folded her
into their day without thought, broke something loose inside Emmy.
A hard sob shook her. She clapped her hand over her suddenly wet
eyes and took a shuddering breath.

"Sorry," she sobbed.

She instantly heard the scrape of a chair and sensed her mother
move beside her. She felt her father's hand land on her arm. "Sweetheart, what's wrong?" Vera asked as she wrapped her arm around her
shoulder.

Emmy fought to keep her tears at bay but couldn't. Not with the
two people who loved her most in the world at her sides, and not
when she'd been damming it all back for so long. "I messed up," she
choked out.

Vera squeezed her tighter. "Oh, honey. Whatever it is, I'm sure
it can be fixed."

Emmy dropped her hand from her face and met her mother's concerned eyes. The ache in her own chest was reflected right back at
her. "No, I don't think it can."

"Tell us what happened, honey," her dad said, and squeezed her
arm again.

Emmy pulled in another shaky breath and did her best to speak.
She didn't really know where to start. "You know how I brought
Gabe to the wedding as a friend?"

Her parents swapped a knowing glance.

"Well, that wasn't the truth," Emmy said.

Her mother gently smoothed her hair behind her ear. "Darling, you don't have to tell us that. It was obvious you are more than friends."

"It was?" Emmy asked weepily.

"Yes," Vera said with a soft smile and a warm glow in her eyes.

"Gabe is really great," her dad chimed in. "The two of you make a great pair."

Emmy sobbed again, feeling like her heart split another crack. Her next set of words came tumbling out in a pained rush. "Well, the whole truth is, we met weeks ago, not knowing it, and now we want to be together, but we can't because we're up for the same promotion, and they're making us choose between the job and a relationship."

As she ached over everything at stake, her parents exchanged a confused look.

"What do you mean you met weeks ago not knowing it?" her mom asked. "I thought you'd been working together for years."

Realizing she was going to have to tell them everything, she took a breath and started from the beginning, from the day she got the Last night was fun text that started it all. She told them about the texting, the baseball bruise, the bachelorette party, the big reveal, a PG-13 version of what happened in Mexico, their agreement, how they didn't even make it one day when they got home before they reunited, how Alice had told her the promotion was all but hers, how they wanted to be together, and how HR had thrown a giant, heartbreaking wrench into their plan.

By the time she finished, her father was pouring them all a second round of lemonade.

"Well, that is certainly an interesting way to start a relationship," Frank said. "Who knew you could fall for someone through text."

Emmy flamed in embarrassment, but he was right. She had fallen.

"Oh, Frank, it's perfectly normal these days," Vera said. "Half of relationships start online now."

"More than half," Emmy muttered. "But the way we met is not the

problem. The problem is I have to choose between him and the job."
Another wave of tears swelled up inside her. Her voice rose in pitch
and wobbled. "And I really want that job."

Her mother rubbed away the tear that spilled down her cheek and
gazed at her with pained sympathy, knowing full well her history with
this scenario. "And you really want him too." It wasn't a question. It
was a fact, unlike with Jacob.

"Yeah," Emmy said, sobbing. She'd turned into a weepy puddle.

"Oh, sweetheart." Vera pulled her into another hug. "You've always
known what you wanted and followed your heart—that's why you
even have this job in the first place. And you've worked so hard for it."

Emmy leaned back and wiped her wet, puffy eyes. She frowned
at her mother in confusion. She was sure she would tell her to go
for the guy and ditch the job, not only because she was constantly
cheering for her to prioritize her love life but more so because she
despised baseball. But it sounded like Vera was saying the opposite.
"You think I should go for the job?" She glanced at her dad. "You
guys don't even want me to have this job."

Vera recoiled. "What? That's not true." She looked over at Frank.
"We want you to be happy, we've just never understood why you'd
want to spend time so close to the thing that—" She cut off and took
a shaky breath. Her face paled, and she looked like she was bracing
herself before continuing to speak. "The thing that took your brother
from us."

Emmy gaped in surprise, thrown. Her mother never spoke about
Josh so openly—none of them did. Except for Piper. He was usually
an enormous, gut-wrenching elephant they all avoided. But sitting in
her parents' backyard already feeling cracked open and raw, Emmy
found herself willing to broach the topic.

"Baseball didn't take Josh from us, Mom. Addiction did. And the
reason I work in baseball is because I *want* to be close to him. I love
the sport as much as he did and getting to be at the park every day
and seeing the field and the players and the fans, it makes me feel like

he's still here, even if it's just for a few seconds now and then. And I also feel like I need to—" Her voice cut off in a choke of tears. She took a breath. "I also feel like I need to make up for him being gone. So you guys have something to be proud of."

Both her parents stared at Emmy like they were seeing her for the first time. She'd never expressed her feelings to them in such certain terms before and she wasn't sure how they were going to react.

Her mother broke first.

"Emmy, we are *so* proud of you. Please don't ever think differently. You don't need to make up for anything. I've never disapproved of your job. I just couldn't understand because I could never . . ." She weepily trailed off. Frank stood and came over to wrap his arms around both of them.

"We've all done our best," he said softly.

They held one another for a long moment, and Emmy let the satisfaction of knowing she had their support flood through her.

"I love you guys," she murmured from the center of their embrace. "Sorry if I don't tell you enough."

"Oh, honey, we know. You don't have to apologize," her mother said, and pulled back to wipe her eyes. "And besides, your father and I aren't exactly exemplary models of expressing emotion." A soggy laugh popped from her mouth.

"And yet here we are having a family cry," Frank said, sniffling as he chuckled.

Emmy joined them, feeling her sore heart lift. "We should do this more."

"What, cry?" Frank said.

"No. Talk about Josh," she said, and wiped her nose with a napkin. "I miss him."

Her parents leaned on each other and laced their hands together. "We miss him too," her mom said in a thick voice.

Emmy let go of a big breath, feeling the permanent hole in her heart mend with a tiny patch. She wasn't sure she was any closer to solving her problem, but talking with her parents had soothed an ache she'd been carrying for a long, long time. "What do you think he would tell me to do?" she asked.

"Josh?" her mom asked as she got up from her chair to tuck a reaching vine into a trellis. "Oh, he'd say go for the guy. He was always a hopeless romantic."

"Got that from his mother," Frank said, and leaned over to peck Vera's cheek.

The sight warmed Emmy's heart and filled her with gratitude for inviting her brother's memory into the conversation. She'd talked about him—with Gabe, with Piper, now with her parents—more in the past few weeks than she had in years, and it felt good. There would always be pain, of course, but Josh could brighten any darkness. She just had to be brave enough to let him shine through.

"And you? What do you think?" Emmy asked her parents.

Her mother gave her a sincere look and crossed back over to her side of the table. She took her daughter's hands in hers. "Emmy, you are so smart and so driven. I know I push you to spend time focusing on other things, sometimes unfairly, but you've worked so hard to make it to where you are in your career, and you deserve to keep moving up." She paused and tucked Emmy's hair behind her ear. "But I've also never seen you as happy as you were in Mexico. He lights you up, sweetheart. And you deserve to feel that glow." She placed her warm palm on Emmy's chest and softly smiled. "We can't tell you what to do, but I know you'll follow your heart, and it'll lead you to where you're supposed to be."

Emmy wished her heart would tell her what to do, but it wasn't offering up any advice at the moment. All it was doing was beating the same confused pattern it had been for the past three days, ever since they got the ultimatum email at work. When Jacob had given Emmy an ultimatum, most of her thoughts centered on shock, and then regret for having invested in their relationship at all, but that decision came to her quickly. He was easy to let go because they weren't a good fit. But Gabe . . . Gabe fit like no one else she'd ever known, and she worried if she gave him up, it would leave an intolerable void.

"Come on," her mom said, and waved her arm. "Why don't you help me in the garden; it always helps clear my mind."

Emmy decided to take her up on the offer. The morning was already ripening into a warm day. She borrowed one of her mom's giant hats, slathered herself in sunscreen, and put on a pair of gloves. By the time they broke for a late lunch, Emmy was damp with sweat and covered in dirt. But her mind was much clearer. The simplicity of digging and pruning and working the soil under her mother's instruction helped untangle the thoughts in her head. She could see clearly, and she knew what she wanted.

She wandered over to the patio table to stand in the shade of the umbrella and gulp a bottle of water. Her phone had a new message from Axe Murderer waiting for her.

> Ready to talk?

He'd sent it a while ago, but she immediately wrote him back.

> Yes, and we should do it in person. I need to head home and shower first. I'm covered in dirt.

> I am intrigued.

> Don't be. I was gardening with my mom.

> Ah. Tell Frank and Vera hi for me.

> I will. What have you been doing?

Believe it or not, I've been with my
parents too.

Oh?

Yes. Turns out they are in fact proud of me
and don't blame me for blowing my shot all
those years ago.

Of course they are, and of course they don't.

It was nice to hear them say it. I came over to
talk to them about our situation, and a lot of
things that needed to be said came up.

Her heart swelled with warmth.

I'm happy to hear that.

So, where are we meeting?

Emmy mulled her response. She was eager too, but also nervous.
She knew enough about texting now to know things said through
screens weren't always the same as in person. Even if it seemed like
they were on the same page, she needed to see him to know where
they stood.

Beach?

Perfect. Which one?

Sunset?

> Are you asking me to meet you at sunset or at Sunset beach?

> How about both?

> This is very dramatic, Bird Girl.

> You're the Axe Murderer. I thought you'd love a dramatic moment.

> Fair. Okay. I'll see you there.

> See you.

Sunset Cliffs Natural Park stretched across the western bend of Point Loma. On a weekend in summer, it was a hot spot for locals and tourists alike. It was also less beach and more rugged coastline with rocky cliffs dropping straight into the water, but, as the name implied, offered a killer view of the sunset.

Emmy parked and walked out along the dirt path, looking for Gabe. The sun had started its final descent, melting the horizon into a hazy orange bar between blue sky and even bluer water. Waves rolled to shore and crashed off the rocks, sending a dramatic spray up every so often. The wind cut through her thin hoodie and whipped her hair around. The raw nature of it all was at once refreshing and humbling.

She spotted the familiar wave of Gabe's hair, the frame of his shoulders where he stood out near one of the cliffs. He wore Chucks and jeans and a windbreaker that seemed like a better idea than her hoodie given she'd already wrapped her arms around herself for warmth. She approached him feeling equal parts nervous and calm. She knew what she wanted, and she hoped they were on the same page.

She tapped his shoulder when she came up behind him. "Hey," she greeted.

He turned, and the sinking sun bathed him in a warm glow like that morning they woke together in Mexico. "Hey."

They stood there for a charged moment, and Emmy tried to read his face.

Instead of speaking, he reached out and pulled her mouth to meet his. The kiss was warm and soft and sent her blood looping through her body. It ached with a longing she couldn't place, either a reunion or a goodbye.

She pulled back and touched her forehead to his. "Tell me what you're thinking."

Gabe softly shook his head. "You first."

Emmy looked deeply into his eyes and saw the same nerves she felt. The uncertainty over what she would say. But one of them had to jump first. She took a breath and found her footing then let herself fly.

"I think I've never felt this way about anyone before, and I want to see where this goes."

The words were out, and with them, an enormous weight lifted. She'd thought about it all night, all morning while gardening—truly since the night they first slept together in Mexico. There was no turning back for her after that, and it felt good to finally tell him.

She waited for him to respond, feeling her heart beat in every inch of her body.

He let out a huge sigh of relief. "I thought you might pick the job, but I'm so glad to hear you say that, because I feel the same."

She nearly sagged with her own relief; she had thought he might pick the job too. "You do?"

"I do. I wanted that job, but I want you more, Emmy. I've wanted you for a long time. The truth is, I've been into you for years, but you never seemed interested, so I kept my distance. You are so smart and so . . . stubborn. And the way you look in computer glasses should be illegal." He shot her a little grin that made her blush. "You challenge me at work and make me better at what I do. And you are remarkably kind and patient; I don't know how you put up with me most of the time, but I'm thankful that you do. Honestly, I would trade anything to have a shot at being with you. I've never been able to talk to anyone the way I can talk to you. It's so effortless. And I'm profoundly thankful the connection is even stronger in person." He let out a sweet, embarrassed laugh. "When I started texting this random girl one day because of a fake number, and she turned out to be my dream girl, who then turned out to be you, when the shock wore off, I thought I'd won the fucking lottery. I want to see where this goes more than I've ever wanted anything."

Emmy laughed and only then noticed that her cheeks were wet with tears. Gabe wiped them with his thumbs and then kissed her again. This time she wrapped her arms around him, and he lifted her off the ground. It was their deepest kiss yet. Full of truth and honesty and feelings so big Emmy feared she might explode. They kissed for what might have been an indecent amount of time in public, but perhaps not given they were standing in a place famed for marriage proposals and sunset kissing selfies.

When he set her back down, she stumbled a little. She gripped his arms and shivered against the wind that felt almost icy compared to the warmth of his body. She was nearly drunk with relief, with happiness, with a bittersweet acceptance of what she was giving up for what she was gaining. She smoothed her hands over his chest and felt his heart beating inside.

"Just to be clear," she said in case her emotional brain was crossing signals, "we're giving up the job to be together, right?"

Gabe let out a big breath and nodded. "Right."

"And it's what we both want?"

"Yes. It's what I want. Is it what you want?"

She pushed up on her toes and pressed her hands to the sides of his face. "Gabe, I've never been able to talk to anyone the way I talk to you. I don't think I would have had the guts if it hadn't started with a fake phone number, but I'm so glad we're here. You understand me, and you help me feel things I was afraid of. Before all this, I had beliefs about what I could and couldn't have if I wanted certain things in life, but now I see there's a balance. You've shown me I can open myself up to try to find it. I want to do this with you."

He looked down at her with a warm smile and tucked back her hair blowing in the wind. "I want to do this with you too, Emmy." He wrapped her in his arms, and she stayed there, happily huddled against his warm chest.

"I didn't think it would be this chilly out here," she said with another shiver.

"Come here." He reached between them and unzipped his windbreaker and held it open. "Room for two."

Emmy slipped her arms around him inside his jacket. He rezipped it with her inside. "Well, now I can't see the sunset." She said it to his chest where she'd buried her nose. She inhaled her favorite scent and rubbed her cheek into his soft shirt.

"Then turn around."

She awkwardly shuffled her feet and rotated her body to face forward with her back against his chest. "Now I'm in a straitjacket."

"Yeah, but it's a warm straitjacket," he said, and kissed her head.

"Right where you always wanted me, Axe Murderer."

"You know my endgame now." He hugged her to his chest and held her tight. She leaned her head back against his shoulder and stared out at the view. The sun had inched lower, now dipping its belly into the sea and shooting a streak of shimmering gold across the water.

"This is nice," Emmy said with a contented sigh.

"It is. No wonder so many people come out here."

"Have you never been?"

"First time."

"Really? Well, I'm honored to have your Sunset Cliffs virginity."

"I'm honored to give it to you. So, what did your parents have to say about all this?" A hint of nerves hid in his voice.

"Don't worry, they are still smitten with you."

"Good." Emmy heard the smile in Gabe's voice and elbowed him. He stifled a laughing grunt. "I don't want them to think I'm getting in the way of your career and hold it against me."

"They don't. Believe it or not, they want me to make my own decision like an adult."

"Go, Frank and Vera."

"I know. We actually ended up talking about my brother too. I told them how my job helps me feel close to Josh, and they finally understood. I've spent all these years thinking they disapproved, but I'd just never explained it to them. They get it now, why I care so much."

He stayed quiet behind her for a long while. Long enough that the emotion over it all—talking about her brother, explaining her love for her job, deciding to give up the promotion—caught up with her. She tried her best to stifle the sob that shook her body.

Gabe stiffened and leaned forward to try to see her. "Hey, are you crying?"

"No," she said weepily.

"Emmy, I can hear you crying."

"It's nothing."

"Emmy."

"I'm fine."

"Tell me what's wrong, or I'm going to unzip this jacket and expose you to hypothermia."

She chortled and wove her hand up out of the neck hole to wipe her eyes. "It was going to be me," she confessed. "The job."

He stiffened again. "What?"

"Alice told me the other day, before we went to HR. They were going to give the promotion to me."

She heard him exhale and curse under his breath. She did another spin inside the jacket and felt her hoodie twist along with his shirt. "But it's okay," she promised him and wiped her eyes with a shake of her head. "I know what I want, and it's you, Gabe."

Pain creased his brow as he looked down at her.

"It's you," she repeated and pushed up to kiss his lips.

His kiss was reluctant at first, restrained, but then he leaned into it. Hard. He gripped her face in his hands and kissed her like that night in Mexico in the rain. Like he needed the air in her lungs for himself. Like he couldn't get enough. Like he was showing her she'd made the right decision by choosing him.

And she knew she had.

She did one final turn inside his jacket to face the water just in time to watch the final moments of the sun dipping the crown of its head below the surface.

"Have you ever seen the green flash?" Gabe asked.

"Of course not because it's not real."

"What? It's totally real. I've seen it, like, ten times."

"You absolutely have not. It's an urban legend."

"Incorrect. Watch, it'll happen here in a few seconds."

"It will not."

"Yes, it will." He squeezed her again and kissed her cheek.

Emmy rolled her eyes. She'd spent many a sunset staring at the horizon waiting to see what local lore promised she would: a flash of green light blaze across the line where the sea met the sky in the second after the sun fully sank. There was no scientific evidence it existed, no photographs. Just a bunch of San Diegans claiming witness. Emmy was honestly surprised Gabe fell into the believer camp.

"It's coming," he whispered in her ear.

She shook her head with a skeptical laugh as the sun crept lower and lower.

"*Right . . .*" He dramatically drew out the word while the last drops of gold melted away. "Now!"

Emmy sucked in a sharp breath and blinked.

"Did you see it?" He leaned sideways and asked her with an excited grin.

His enthusiasm was infectious, but she wouldn't give him the satisfaction.

"No."

Gabe gave her a crooked grin, seeing right through her. "Liar." And then he kissed her again.

Chapter 21

They spent Saturday night and Sunday in bed at Emmy's place, making up for lost time but also getting a feel for what it would be like to have weekends at home together. Emmy had no regrets over their decision when she woke in his arms Sunday and then spent the morning sipping coffee on the couch before they went back to bed. Gabe didn't shave on weekends, which meant his jaw became deliciously scruffy against all her most sensitive skin. As they lay in bed, she found herself tracing his lips with her fingertips and feeling lucky to have his hands on her. By the time Sunday night rolled around, she nearly had to pry herself from him like a barnacle.

"I'll see you tomorrow," he said from her doorway and planted another goodbye kiss on her swollen lips.

She dreamily leaned against the doorframe both for support for her wobbling knees and because of exhaustion. "See you."

They'd decided to spend the night separately and meet at the office before they went to HR to share their decision, agreeing it was best to have some final space in case anyone changed their mind at the last minute.

But they weren't going to change their minds. Emmy knew her mind was made up, and she could feel Gabe's certainty in every kiss, every touch, every whispered sigh.

It's you.

On Monday morning, Emmy walked into the office feeling both nervous and sure, and like she stood on the precipice of something large and thrilling. Gabe wasn't at his desk yet—no one was, actually—so she ventured down the hall to see if she might find him in the kitchen. On the way, she heard voices spilling from an open door. Familiar voices.

". . . something I've been dreaming of for a long time. I'm so thankful for the opportunity," Gabe said.

Emmy froze in her tracks. His voice leaked out from the director's office door.

"Well, I'm glad to hear it, Mr. Olson," Director Allen said. A pause passed that sent Emmy's heart racing.

Why was Gabe talking to the director?

Director Allen's voice came back a tad quieter, almost as if he was telling a secret. "And what about you and Ms. Jameson?"

Emmy stilled once more. Her breath stopped in her throat. She heard someone shuffle inside the office, and then Gabe's voice again.

"That won't be a problem."

"Excellent," the director said. "Glad to hear it. Well, we can have you in your new office by the end of the day, if you're ready for it."

"I am most certainly ready for it. Thank you, sir."

"Of course, Mr. Olson. We'll make the arrangements."

More shuffling sounds came from the room, and Emmy imagined a handshake occurring over the top of the director's busy desk.

She'd turned to stone by the time Gabe left the office. He found her standing in the middle of the hall on the verge of combustion from a deadly cocktail of shock and rage.

"Emmy!" he said, and immediately flushed.

She stared up at him while thoughts crashed together in her mind. At the same time, her heart was breaking as realization settled in.

Gabe stared back at her, cool gray polo, sculpted hair, handsome face, but all she saw was her own foolishness.

"What did you do?" she said hardly above a whisper. The earth was falling out beneath her all over again.

He didn't need to answer because it was written all over his face.

Emmy scoffed in bitter resentment and shame. She gazed around the underground hall, the stone castle ruled by men that she toiled tirelessly inside of and saw it for what it was. A trap she'd walked straight into. And the man in front of her, the orchestrator of the biggest prank to date.

"*God*, I'm so stupid," she muttered and spun on her heel.

"Emmy, wait!" Gabe said, and followed her.

But she could hardly hear him. Her own humiliation deafened her to everything except the sound of her heart pounding in her ears and her own mind screaming at her for being so naive.

"Emmy, hang on," Gabe said. He caught up and gripped her upper arm.

She whirled on him, and something inside her snapped. Something that had been about to break for a long, *long* time but that she'd kept bending because she was flexible, a team player, the Only Girl who could always take a joke.

"You couldn't stand it, could you?" she said. Her words slid out like venom. Gabe flinched, but she didn't back down. She shook her arm from his grip and poked a finger at his chest. "You couldn't live knowing I'd beaten you, could you? That *I* was chosen for something over *you*, so you went behind my back and *took it*. And of course they *gave it to you* because that's how things work around here. This goddamned *boys' club* I thought—foolishly—I'd finally become an equal in."

Emmy glanced sideways and saw Alice's office door was shut but the light was on, shining from the crack underneath. Rage roiled inside her that Gabe had skipped Alice, skipped HR, and gone straight to the director to take her job.

She smashed her hands to her face in shame. "I should have seen this coming. I should have *known* this was how it would end up." She dropped her hands and glared at him. "I can't believe I trusted you." Her voice, which had risen with all the emotions roiling inside her, cracked on the last word. The sound shot a bolt of pain across Gabe's face.

He hadn't said anything to defend himself—because what was there to say after such a betrayal?—but he suddenly looked angry.

"Emmy—"

"No." She cut him off with a raised hand. "You convinced me to agree to give up that job so you could swoop in and take it. You really are Gabe Ruthless after all. First Mikey Walker and now me. I should have known. Turns out *I've* been the obtuse one this whole time." She was fully crying now. Tears streamed down her face; her voice wobbled. A gush of heartbroken truth rushed out of her before she could do anything to stop it. "You made me fall in love with you all for a job."

Whatever retort had been poised on his tongue disappeared as if he'd swallowed it. A look somewhere between shock and tortured pain bloomed over his face. When he spoke, his words came out in a hot rush. "You're in love with me?"

Emmy didn't get the chance to respond because Alice's office door swung open. Her confused face filled the gap. "What's going on out here?"

A pang of embarrassment hit Emmy. She wiped at her weeping eyes and tried to gain her composure. Alice looked between her and Gabe in concern. "Nothing," Emmy said. "I'm not feeling well and think I need to take a sick day."

Alice eyed her like she didn't buy it, but eventually nodded in approval. "Sure. Take what you need."

"Thank you," she managed in a steady voice. She shot Gabe one last hard glare before she turned around. She half expected him to follow her, but the sound of Director Allen's voice calling him back determined his next move.

"Mr. Olson, one more thing?" the director said from his doorway.

Emmy didn't stop to see Gabe choose his new job over her because she knew without looking that that was what was happening behind her. It took all her strength not to collapse on the concrete floor. With every step forward, the fury inside her grew hotter and hotter, dampened only by the humiliation drowning her in waves. She wanted to burn the stadium down with herself inside it.

"I'm such an idiot," she muttered and gathered her bag from her desk. She needed to make it back home where she could collapse without worry of judgment. Without anyone calling her hysterical or emotional or unhinged for bringing her personal issues to work. But the line between personal and work had disappeared. They'd become one and the same, and she saw now what a mistake that was. Letting Gabe close, handing her heart over to him so he could use it as a professional stepping stone, was her own fault. She should have known better.

She'd made it all the way up the elevator and into the employee parking lot before her phone pinged.

Axe Murderer had texted her. A fresh wave of tears slammed into her at the sight of his name. Her better sense told her not to read it, not to inflict any more pain on her shattered heart, but curiosity got the best of her. Because what could he possibly have to say?

We need to talk.

Emmy realized with a swift kick of certainty she had nothing to say to Gabe. Not anymore. The absolute indignity of telling him she was in love with him burned with a flame too hot to touch. There was no way she could face him, not even through her screen. The mortification was a hundred times that of finding out his true identity that day in the park. She had to sever the tie before it strangled her.

Before she could talk herself out of it, she deleted their thread and blocked his number. She gasped like she'd been punched at such a significant move, but it had to be done. She dropped her phone into her bag and got in her car.

Later, Emmy was on the couch under a pile of blankets with cramps again and watching a *Drag Race* marathon like she really was having a sick day when her phone lit up with a notification that someone was buzzing at her door. She squinted at the screen through eyes still puffy from crying and saw a familiar wave of dark hair. Gabe leaned into the camera, chewing his lip and looking fraught.

She sat up on alert, surprised he'd come all the way to her apartment. No way was she going to let him in; she needed to maintain the barrier she'd constructed by blocking his number. He'd emailed her a few hours ago but she'd deleted it without reading. Now he was calling at her gate, and the idea of granting him entry felt traitorous to her own heart.

But he had come all this way. And he looked like hell.

Her single heartstring that remained intact vibrated like it had been plucked. In a moment of weakness, she tapped her phone screen to answer his call. She remained silent on the receiving end.

Gabe all but dove on the camera. "Emmy? Hello? Are you there?"

Again, she remained silent.

He leaned in close like he might see her through the box. "Okay, I hope you can hear me. Sorry to show up, but you're not answering my calls or texts, so I assume you blocked my number. We need to talk. About this morning—"

"I have nothing to say to you."

He jerked at the sudden sound of her voice. "Emmy, please—"

"Your actions have spoken loudly enough. All I have to say to you now is congrats, I guess. Good job on besting me in the cruelest way possible. I mean really, it was genius. It might have all started out as a mistake with the phone numbers, but once you knew it was me, you saw an opportunity, and you took it. You really are as ruthless as everyone says. Winning is all that matters to you, I can see that now. You don't care about anyone but yourself." Her words faded out bitterly. The embarrassed rage surged inside her again, and she regretted answering his call at all.

A long pause passed, filled only with the sound of her heart beating hard. Gabe blinked at the camera with a furrowed brow.

"Is that really what you think?" he eventually said.

She shrugged and then remembered he couldn't see her. "The shoe fits, Olson."

He looked down at the ground and put his hands on his hips. A sharp pain lanced Emmy's heart, but the addition to the ache already there hardly registered. He eventually nodded with a sigh. "Okay, Jameson," he said in a defeated tone and then turned away.

A gush of tears wetted Emmy's eyes. She fought to tamp them down but quickly realized it was a losing battle.

Chapter 22

On Tuesday, Emmy put on the biggest Big Girl pants she could muster and all but dragged herself to work. At least Gabe moving to his new office meant he wouldn't be sitting beside her anymore, and she wouldn't have to smell him all day.

That goddamned cologne. She had thought of tracking down the brand and requesting the company discontinue it. The odds of success didn't seem likely, so she instead decided she needed to render herself immune to its powers, starting immediately.

Thankfully, she didn't smell any trace of it when she got off the elevator, which probably only meant Gabe hadn't arrived yet because, surely, it would waft off him as he made his way down the hall to his new office. She was early again, hoping she could scoot in unnoticed and already be hard at work by the time others showed up so they'd be less likely to talk to her. By the looks of light spilling out of Alice's open door, she wasn't the first to arrive.

She was two steps past the door when Alice's voice echoed into the hall. "Jameson, a word?"

Emmy stopped in her tracks, tote still looped over her shoulder, and turned around.

Alice appeared at her doorway with an unreadable face. She wore a slate-gray skirt suit and shiny heels. "How are you feeling?"

Like I've had my heart ripped out, Emmy thought but didn't say. She forced a tight smile and remembered she'd taken a sick day yesterday and needed to act like it. "Better, thanks."

"Great. The director would like to see you."

Emmy flinched at her direct delivery, though she should have been used to it. Alice nodded her head and stepped out into the hall. Her heels began clicking, and Emmy knew to follow.

"About anything in particular?" she asked with a worried note in her voice. Hopefully she was not about to get reprimanded for allowing her personal life to affect her work.

Alice simply smiled at her over her shoulder. "Yes."

Emmy didn't have time to ask another question because the journey to the director's office was brief. They were outside his door in a matter of seconds.

Alice paused to knock twice before opening the door.

"Ah, good morning, Alice, Ms. Jameson," Director Allen said with a nod and welcomed them in. He sat at his busy desk teetering with binders—some filled with reports Emmy herself had written—a coffee mug, his computer monitor, and a handful of signed baseball memorabilia. More collector's items lined his walls: jerseys, framed photos, a glossy bat, an old catcher's mitt Emmy knew had belonged to his father. "Have a seat," he said to Emmy and nodded at the chair across from his.

Emmy nervously sank into it. She shot a glance at Alice to see her leaning against a filing cabinet with a tiny grin on her lips.

They were both in too good of a mood for the purpose of the meeting to be a reprimand.

"Sorry, what is this about?" she asked. Her voice had risen to an awkward pitch.

Director Allen smiled at her. "I just wanted to officially congratulate you on your promotion to senior analyst. Alice tells me you're more than ready to take on more responsibilities. I look forward to your continued excellent work." He stuck out his hand for Emmy to shake, but she was still three steps behind.

Her head was spinning.

"I'm sorry, what?"

The director glanced at Alice, hand still hovering in midair.

"The job is yours, Emmy," Alice said. "We wanted to catch you before you got settled at your desk because you can move into your new office today. Congrats."

Emmy felt like she'd slipped into an alternate reality—and not the type where her secret pen pal turned out to be her archnemesis. But one where the reality she'd constructed shattered.

"But Gabe took that job," she blurted, still confused.

Alice and the director swapped another look. "Mr. Olson?" the director said.

"Yes. I heard him discussing it with you yesterday morning. You said he'd be in his new office by the end of the day."

Director Allen's face pulled into a frown. He looked like his patience was wearing thin. Emmy knew his time for sit-downs was limited, so he probably expected this meeting to last no longer than a minute.

"Ms. Jameson, Mr. Olson requested a department transfer. He's been moved to the training staff. I assumed you knew that given the, um, *personal* nature of your relationship."

A wave of heat rushed up into Emmy's face. Clearly, wires had gotten crossed somewhere, but she wasn't about to make more of a fool of herself by admitting it.

"Of course," she said with a forced smile while the bricks inside her brain crumbled and fell. "Of course I knew that," she repeated. She stood and extended her hand to shake his. "Thank you for the promotion, sir. I couldn't be more thrilled."

Couldn't be more confused was more like it, but that was not a conversation to have with a man whose valuable time she'd already taken enough of.

"Excellent," he said with a nod and another grin. "I'll look forward to seeing you in the next department meeting. Best of luck in your new position."

"Thank you, sir."

Emmy was reeling when she and Alice returned to the hallway.

Alice had apparently been waiting for privacy for questions, too, be-cause she pinched Emmy's elbow and towed her into her office.

"What was that?" she asked with an arched brow.

Emmy was still finding her footing. She sat on the edge of Alice's desk as Alice shut the door. She took two deep breaths. Pieces were sliding into place but still not lining up. Snippets of the conversation she'd heard yesterday ran through her mind. *It's always been a dream of mine. Your new office. What about Ms. Jameson? That won't be a problem.*

"Sorry. I'm confused," she said to Alice. "What happened with Gabe?"

Alice gave her a skeptical look. "Do you two not talk at home?"

"Alice, please!" Emmy snapped, feeling herself spiraling with all the unknowns.

"Okay!" Alice said with a befuddled shake of her head. "He emailed me on Sunday saying he urgently needed to talk. You know me; I was working anyway, so I gave him a call. He asked what it would take to get him transferred to the training staff and, if the transfer was possible, if that would eliminate the problematic nature of your relationship because you'd no longer be in the same depart-ment. He told me— Are you okay?"

Emmy had put a hand to her chest like she might have been having a heart attack. She certainly felt something in her chest, but it wasn't pain. "Maybe," she said, somehow winded despite sitting down.

When had Alice called Gabe on Sunday? They'd spent nearly the whole day vined around each other in bed. Perhaps he'd taken the call while she was in the shower; he *had* left her waiting for a while before he joined her.

Alice cautiously eyed her as Emmy pulled her mind from a steamy memory. "Well, maybe you should fully sit down for this next part, then." She reached out and shepherded her into one of the chairs opposite her desk. Alice's office looked much like the director's: busy, organized, full of baseball memorabilia. Emmy looked straight ahead at the framed black-and-white photo of Alice's great-uncle in his uniform from the 1950s. She took another breath.

"Okay. Keep going," Emmy said. "I'm ready."

"All right. Well, he told me the two of you had decided to stay together and give up your chance at the promotion, but then when you told him the job was going to be yours, he realized there was no way he could let you give it up for him. He didn't want to stand in your way, so he requested a department transfer. That way you could stay together, and you could still get the promotion." She paused, and Emmy felt her eyes warm with moisture. "And I said, 'Well, shit. That's about the most romantic thing I've ever heard, and who am I to stand in the way of love?' So I told him I'd make some calls to see what we could do because I agreed: there was no way we could let you give up that job." She gave Emmy a stern look that was half smile and layered in warmth. Then Alice's mouth beamed into a full smile. "I swear to god, Jameson. All the doors I've opened to help you get here, and you were going to walk away over some guy." She playfully rolled her eyes, but Emmy could see the honesty shining through. She'd wondered how Alice would receive news of their decision. If she'd be disappointed in Emmy for her choices. Based on the look on her face now, maybe a little bit, but the situation was no longer relevant.

"I'm sorry, Alice," Emmy said anyway.

Alice lifted a shoulder. "Don't apologize to me; it's your life. But listen." She leaned in with a serious bend to her brow. "I know now he's not just *some guy*. He sees your potential and he wants you to succeed, Emmy. You know I'm not a relationship expert, but please listen to me when I say hold on like hell to that, okay?"

The moisture glossing Emmy's eyes washed over with a new wave. The idea she'd been wrong about what she'd heard yesterday was both welcome and terrifying because that meant Gabe hadn't betrayed her, but she'd made a terrible mistake. At the hopeful look on

Alice's face, she didn't have the heart to tell her she couldn't hold on to it because she'd already let it go.

She wiped her eyes with a sniffle as a thought occurred to her. "What about the rumors he got Mikey Walker fired?"

Alice's face flattened into a frown. "You know I'm not supposed to talk about that. But since there's obviously been some kind of miscommunication here that's got you in a state, I can tell you this: Walker was selling team secrets to scouts. Olson found out about it and reported him. Management took action off his tip. He did the right thing, and it just so happened to coincide with him getting hired. The ruthless reputation took on its own life-form, and Olson couldn't do much to stop it given the situation was confidential. Jameson, that doesn't leave this room, okay?"

Emmy slowly nodded, adding the newest addition to her list of bombshell facts redefining everything she thought she knew. Gabe hadn't gotten someone fired out of spite; it had been a morality move—and probably a difficult one to make as a young intern. *God*, she'd been so wrong.

She shook herself and tried to focus. "Thanks, Alice. I won't say anything. So, what does this mean? He's been transferred to a different department, and we're free to be together?"

"Yep. Turned out there was an opening on the pitching staff, and with his experience and the promise of taking some training courses, they were willing to give him a shot," she said with a smile. "I mean, he'll be starting at the bottom, doing the grunt work, but he was willing to do anything. We just needed sign-off from Director Allen yesterday morning. Now he'll be traveling with the team, but so will you as senior analyst. Kind of worked out perfectly, wouldn't you say?"

"Oh god, yes. Right," Emmy said, suddenly remembering her promotion came with a significant change in lifestyle. "How soon will that start?"

"For you? Next week," Alice said. "For him?" She flipped her wrist to look at her watch. "In about an hour, if they haven't already left for tonight's game in LA."

Emmy's heart hammered. So much had changed in the past twenty-four hours. She had a new job, a new office. And the things she'd said to Gabe? How would he ever forgive her? He hadn't lied to her. He'd tried to fix the problem so she could have everything she wanted.

And through it all, she still wanted him. She'd *always* wanted him.

The question now was would he still want her?

The urge to crunch into a ball and cry hit her hard, but Alice softly punched her shoulder and nodded toward the hall with a smile. "Come on. Let's get you into your new office."

Emmy followed her down the hall, awash in a complicated cocktail of emotions. She was thrilled about the job—she'd gotten everything she'd been working for. But her heart was aching over what she'd said to Gabe. She hadn't even given him the chance to explain before she jumped to the worst conclusions.

As they walked, she whipped out her phone and unblocked his number.

> I'm so sorry. I misunderstood. Can we talk?

She tapped it out in a rush, not really thinking it through, but desperate to say something to him.

His typing dots didn't appear. Nothing indicated he'd received the message. There was a good chance he'd blocked her number by now, too, she realized with a heavy heart. And she couldn't blame him.

"Here we are," Alice announced when they turned the corner to her new office. The square room was half the size of Alice's but big enough for a desk, two chairs, maybe a plant, and had the coveted internal-facing window along with a whiteboard.

A small smile lifted Emmy's lips despite her silent phone and breaking heart. "Thanks, Alice."

"Of course. IT will bring your computer over in a bit and get you all set up. We'll get you a new name plaque for the door too. Feel free to decorate however."

Emmy already knew exactly what she was going to hang on the walls; she'd had it planned for months. Her framed degrees, a championship pennant, the autographed bat she'd won in a charity raffle, and a photo of her brother from his rookie year. She smiled at the thought of Josh's photo smiling out at everyone who came to visit her. He'd hang behind her and keep an eye on the hallway while she worked.

"Congrats, Emmy," Alice said. "You deserve this." She left her alone and clicked down the hall on her shiny heels.

Emmy set her tote on the empty desk. She rounded it and sank into her new chair. She smoothed her hands over the wood and allowed herself a moment to appreciate what she'd accomplished. She looked down at her slender, feminine hands atop a surface only men had utilized before. But it was *hers* now. She'd *earned* it, and no one could say differently.

Her phone hadn't offered up any messages and as much as she wanted to forsake it all, ditch work, and go find Gabe, she forced herself to partition her personal and professional lives. She couldn't bail five minutes into her new job, nor could she be distracted with so much new responsibility.

Being an adult was unfairly distressing at times.

By the time Emmy had boxed up her old desk and Ken from IT relocated her computer for her, the morning was half gone. And she still had no messages from Axe Murderer.

"All set," Ken said, and brushed his hands together when he finished positioning her computer on her new desk.

"Thanks."

"No problem. Any questions?"

"No—actually, yes," she said with a hint of trepidation in her voice. "Is it possible to recover a deleted email?"

He nodded. "Sure. As long as you deleted it in the past thirty days, it'll be in your trash."

"Got it. Thanks."

She had in fact deleted Gabe's email yesterday in a fit of anger and wondered if she had the nerve to read it now. She sat at her new desk and entered her password. The screen shone to life, and she noted her inbox number had significantly jumped in the past hour. She had messages from HR, colleagues in different departments who'd heard about her promotion, and an intimidating number of data requests now that she held a senior position. The number pinged higher four times in the ten seconds she spent staring at it.

"Okay, guess we're doing this now . . ." she muttered and opened the first request.

The work instantly sucked her in. She was so in flow, crunching numbers, aggregating analyses, reporting out results, that she skipped lunch. She hadn't realized how late it had gotten until she had a moment to look up, and her stomach noisily growled. It was after 3 p.m.

She had thought of visiting a vending machine but the thought of hunting down Gabe's deleted email weighed heavier. She'd been working up the nerve to read it all morning but then welcomed the excuse of being too busy. Now she finally had a moment. She took a breath and navigated to her trash folder.

There amid the spam, ads, and phishing scams sat a message from Gabe Olson, sent at 11:15 a.m. yesterday. Subject line: Please read.

> My Bird Girl,
> I don't know what you heard in the hallway this morning, but I would never lie to you. I know how much you wanted the job and how much it means to you personally, and you absolutely deserve it. The truth is, you've always intimidated the hell out of me. I had my baseball career

taken away, and then when you came along and were un-stoppable at your job, I thought I was going to have this career taken away from me too. But this job was never mine to lose. I can't stand in your way. You've shown me that I don't need to win to be happy. You're better than me and you deserve the job, and I'm happy. I want you. I don't even care about the job if it means I get to be with you, and that's how I know what matters. It's you.

I wasn't sure if my plan was going to work, so I wanted to make sure I could put it in motion before we got our hopes up. I should have told you sooner. I'm sorry. I know I've done things in the past to make you question your trust in me, and I have a reputation I've never dis-pelled working against me here, so I can take some blame for your reaction, but I swear, I would never be dishonest or joke about anything that matters this much.

On that note, here's some more honesty.

That fake number is the greatest thing that ever hap-pened to me. Like I said the other day, I would trade anything to have a shot at being with you. What you said in the hallway about the way you feel, the truth is, I feel the same. I have for a long time. Because of you, I've fig-ured out how to quantify my feelings in more ways than one. I know writing messages to each other is kind of our thing, but I'd rather say how I feel to your face than here. I'm going to come over at lunch. I hope you'll let me in so we can talk.

—Your Axe Murderer

Emmy read the email twice, the second time through a flood of messy tears. Her heart was positively broken in half but somehow beating stronger than ever.

"Oh no," she said, sobbing into her hand. He'd sent the message before he'd come over, and before she'd said awful things to him. The likelihood he still felt the same seemed slim. Another hard sob burst from her throat as she ached all the way to her toes.

Quantify my feelings made her think of the equation he'd written her; the complex model that he claimed accounted for the intuitive feelings he had from being on the field. She didn't think it was possible to do such a thing, but she also didn't think it was possible to feel like her heart was beating on the outside of her chest like a battered wound.

She clicked out of his email and found the file she'd sent herself with his equation in it when she'd transferred it from the napkin. With a few more clicks and some keystrokes, she pulled it into the platform they used for analyses and called in a dataset to test it out. She found Hollander's recent game data, as Gabe instructed, and hit *run*. It spit out a series of numbers and symbols that her trained brain knew how to interpret, and she gasped. The model used on Hollander's data from the last week predicted his stats from this week, give or take a reasonable margin of error, and more accurately than if she'd used her own equation. Gabe was right. He'd figured out how to quantify a feeling.

"Holy shit," she whispered, half in awe and half in despair. He was so goddamn smart, and he'd done this for her. For *her*, to give her the same advantage he had. And she'd messed everything up. She threw her hand to her tearing eyes right as someone knocked on her open door.

"Congrat—" Pedro's voice began to singsong before it sharply cut off. "What's wrong?"

Emmy looked up to see Pedro and Silas standing at her door. Pedro held a giant cupcake bedazzled in pink frosting and golden sprinkles. It looked like something a unicorn would regurgitate, or what two men would pick out to fit the description of *congratulatory cupcake for a woman.* With a flush of embarrassment, Emmy wiped at her eyes and tried to compose herself. "Hey, guys," she said with a strained smile. Her voice came out clogged with tears.

They suspiciously eyed her and stepped inside. "Jameson, I don't know if anyone has ever told you this before, but there's no crying in baseball," Silas said.

Emmy choked out a laugh and wiped her eyes again. Good thing she wasn't wearing much makeup. "Is that for me?" She pointed at the cupcake. At the sight of it, despite being surprised they'd thought of her, her famished belly propelled her out of her chair.

"Um, yes—" Pedro hardly had the words out before she snatched it out of his hand and took an aggressive bite. It was divine. A blob of much needed pink confection. "Sooo, everything going okay with the new job?" Pedro cautiously asked. Notably, both he and Silas had leaned back toward the door.

"Going great. Why do you ask?" Emmy said around another bite.

"Well, you're in here crying and shoving a cupcake into your mouth like you're pr—"

She cut him off with a glare. "Be *very* careful about the next word that comes out of your mouth, Torres. Remember I'm your superior now."

"*Pr—obably* having a rough day," Pedro recovered with an awkward grin.

Emmy glared at him again. "I am, yes, but this cupcake is making things a lot better. Thank you."

"No problem. Ish and I wanted to drop by and say congrats. And that it's super lonely without you and Olson in the office. Never thought we'd be losing both of you at the same time."

At the sound of Gabe's name another sob punched its way out of Emmy's throat—which didn't go well considering she was midswallow on another bite of cupcake.

"Jesus!" Pedro said, and jumped back when she sputtered cupcake bits. "You sure you're okay, Jameson?"

Emmy wasn't sure what did it: her broken heart, years of suppress-ing feelings at work, the fact that her colleagues—other than Alice—were sincerely asking if she was okay, the emotional roller coaster she'd been riding all day, her overwhelming but exciting new job, or maybe the combination of it all, but something snapped.

"I messed up, you guys," she blubbered. Her face was streaked with tears and frosting. Bits of cupcake clung to her hair from the choking incident. A tide of embarrassment washed over her for cry-ing in front of her colleagues, but she couldn't stop. She expected them to bolt like frightened animals, unsure what to do with such an outpouring of emotion from the Only Girl, but to her shock, they stayed.

Silas fully stepped inside and pulled the door closed. Pedro reached out for Emmy and put a caring hand on her shoulder shaking with sobs.

"What happened?" Pedro asked.

"You guys don't care," she said with a hiccup.

They swapped a glance.

"Of course we care," Pedro said with an affronted flinch. "We're a team, Jameson."

"Yeah, maybe we're just not the best at showing it sometimes, but you're one of us," Silas said. "If you're down, we're down."

Emmy blinked away fresh tears to see them giving her the sincer-est looks she'd ever seen on their faces. Even if they couldn't fully understand what was bothering her, they were at least going to try, and if nothing else, listen. The thought warmed something in her cracked chest and made her realize that maybe the Only Girl barrier was something she'd partly constructed herself. Maybe she didn't have to keep things so bottled up at work all the time because her colleagues had her back.

She took a shuddering breath, trying to calm her tears. "Well, I don't know if you know this, but Olson and I are—*were* a thing. We went to HR the other day to make it official on paper, and they told

us we had to choose between our relationship or the promotion because they couldn't allow the power imbalance if one of us got it.
We decided to give it up and stay together, but then he secretly
transferred departments so I could have the job." She sobbed again.

"Damn," Pedro said over the sound. "That's some Prince Charming–
level shit."

"King Charming," Silas said with a nod.

A tiny laugh bubbled its way through Emmy's tears.

"So what's the problem? You got the job, and you get to stay together, right? Also—" Pedro cut off and pointed to Silas. "You owe
me twenty bucks. I totally called that they were hooking up."

Emmy burned with embarrassment. "You guys *bet* on us?"

"Oh, for sure. Like three years ago, actually. The tension between
you two could choke a horse."

"That . . . is a very strange analogy."

Pedro shrugged. "I'm still not seeing the problem here. At least
not a problem worth crying and cupcakes."

Emmy reset herself with a breath. At least their strange conversation had stopped her tears. "The problem is I misunderstood when
I heard him talking to Director Allen yesterday and I thought he'd
gone behind my back to take the promotion after we'd agreed to
both give it up. I didn't realize they were talking about his transfer,
and I said some really awful things to him." She ached anew at the
memory. "Now he won't answer my messages. I think I ruined everything when he was just trying to help."

"Oh. Yikes," Pedro said.

"Oof," Silas echoed.

She feared they'd reached their limit on understanding and advice. And they had no more cupcakes. Pedro surprised her when
he spoke.

"Then you have to make him listen," he said definitively.

"What?" Emmy asked with a frown.

Pedro clapped her on the shoulder again. "Look, we both know that guy is stubborn as hell, so don't give him a choice not to listen. Go big. Grand gesture. Put him in a position where he'll hear you no matter what, and then at least you'll know you did everything you could."

"I agree. Do something epic," Silas added.

Emmy's heart lifted a fraction at the thought of having a shot at fixing things. But how? Gabe wasn't responding to her messages. "How do I do that?"

Pedro tapped his chin like he was thinking about it. "Skywriting, radio shoutout, song dedication at a concert—"

"Realistic things, Torres," Emmy said.

He frowned at her right as Silas said, "Game in LA tonight. You could show up and find him at the stadium."

"*Ooh*, I like this idea," Pedro said. An enthusiastic grin stretched across his face. "Go out of your way to get to him. He'll have to listen if you traveled all that way just to see him."

"But it's just LA. It's not like I'm flying to London to find him," she said, and immediately wanted to take the words back based on the flat stares they were giving her. Hopping a flight to Europe would surely be more convenient than making the drive from San Diego to Los Angeles on a weekday. "You're totally right. That's a powerful statement," she said with a repentant nod.

"Damn right it is," Pedro said. "If willingly driving to LA in rush-hour traffic isn't a profession of love, I don't know what is."

Emmy flushed again, feeling the thrill of possibility. Would it work? Would showing up at the game be enough to make him listen? The thought of the pained look on his face from her building camera stabbed her in the heart. Even if she had ruined everything, she at least had to try.

She checked the time, and her heart sank. "First pitch is in three hours. I'll never make it before the game."

Pedro puffed out his chest like he'd been called in from the dugout. He clapped his hands and smiled at her. "Fear not, Jameson. I will get you to LA in three hours! Come on." He pivoted for the door, and Silas swung it open.

Emmy knew Pedro had a knack for talking his way into anything, but she was almost certain his persuasive skills didn't transfer to time travel. Getting to LA before the game started would be nothing short of a miracle. But still, she had hope.

"In rush-hour traffic?" she called into the hall as she followed him.

"In rush-hour traffic!" Pedro responded without turning around. He shot his fist into the air like a rally cheer. "Let's go!"

Chapter 23

As it turned out, Pedro's solution to getting to LA in three hours was simply driving really, really fast. Emmy half expected him to manifest a speedboat or a helicopter that would allow them to side-step the highway, but no. It was simply his black BMW she currently sat in the back seat of, making good use of the aptly named *oh shit* handle above the door.

She'd given Beth the front seat because one, she wasn't about to embark on a desperate grand gesture without her best friend there for support so of course they'd stopped to pick her up, and two, the instant connection between Pedro and Beth had been tangible enough to choke a horse, to use Pedro's words.

Emmy had reported the emergency to Beth and got her instant approval to pick her up from work on the way out of town. First, they had to clear their departure with Alice. Silas opted to stay behind since he had an obligation that night but asked to be kept in the loop. Emmy hadn't felt too bad about telling Alice she needed to leave early. Alice had said many wise things to her over the years but *hold on like hell* might have been the most important.

That's exactly what she was doing—literally gripping the handle in Pedro's car while he wove in and out of traffic, and holding on to hope she wasn't too late with Gabe.

Pedro and Beth sat in the front seat chatting like they were on a date.

When they'd pulled up outside Beth's office building and she came bouncing out in jeans and a button-down with her hair trailing behind her like a golden flag, Pedro all but leapt out of the car. He'd come around to open the door for her, and Emmy introduced them. It was the first time she'd ever seen Pedro speechless, and Beth blushed deeper than with anyone she'd ever swiped right on. Now Emmy was basically third wheeling from the back seat and listening to them flirt.

The sound made her smile.

She watched the continuous stretch of commercial development pass outside the window as they drove through Orange County. The rows of houses draped over the rolling hills like tile and stucco blankets in the distance. The mansions wedged into hillsides like crashed meteors. Sunset was approaching by the time the spires of downtown LA came into view. Despite Pedro driving like they were in the Grand Prix, they miraculously had not gotten a speeding ticket, crashed, or otherwise caused an issue on the road, save for a few horns and thrown middle fingers.

Emmy was nearly breathless as they wound the uphill road to the stadium, feeling like she'd run there in all the rushing. Cars jammed the parking lot, as expected. They'd tuned to the game on the radio and were minutes away from first pitch. Gabe's new job meant he'd most likely be in the bullpen, perhaps the dugout. Either way, he'd be more or less on the field in a place she couldn't easily get to once the game started.

They parked, and Emmy took deep breaths to calm herself. They'd left straight from their office, so she still wore jeans and a button-down. Her hair was bound back in a bun, and her ID badge hung on its lanyard around her neck. Pedro and Beth looked nearly the same, except Beth had stripped down to just her camisole, applied an impressive face of makeup from her limited emergency purse stash, and tousled her hair into beachy waves. The look had rendered Pedro speechless again, but it was all part of the plan to get into the stadium.

"Ready?" Beth asked Emmy when they climbed out of the car.

The sun had continued its descent toward the ocean, turning the evening hazy blue. The smell of fried food, hot dogs, and beer threaded through the air as the pregame entertainment poured out of the stadium: music, cheering, the uninhibited joy of sports. Emmy felt it all coursing through her veins, pounding in her heart.

"Yes," she answered Beth.

They wove their way through the parking lot along with other last-minute fans draped in team colors. Before the main gates, Pedro diverted them toward the employee entrance.

"Showtime," he said with a wink at Beth.

Beth giggled.

"You guys had better tone it down if she's supposed to be someone else's girlfriend," Emmy playfully scolded.

Pedro smoothed his hair with a flare in his cheeks. Beth scoffed and punched Emmy in the arm.

"Just calling it like I see it," Emmy said with a laugh.

Sure, they could have easily bought tickets and walked in with the masses, but they needed people to believe they were there on official business. Otherwise, Emmy had no shot at getting to Gabe. And their concocted "official business" was that she and Pedro, ID badges in hand, were escorting Beth, a player's girlfriend, to the game for the evening.

In truth, they were probably supposed to have special passes and be on an approved guest list, but they had none of that. Instead, they had Pedro Torres's silver tongue, Beth looking like an artfully tousled glambot dressed down for the ballpark, and Emmy trying not to nervously hurl over the chances of it all going to shit.

When they approached the correct entrance, someone with an earpiece intercepted them. Emmy and Pedro flashed their badges and got a nod, but the barrel-chested security guard eyed Beth.

"Who's this?" he asked in a voice lower than the bass line of the song pumping through the stadium.

Pedro tittered like the question was silly.

The security guard arched a brow.

"Sorry," Pedro said, and cleared his throat. "I'm just surprised you don't recognize her. This is Brendan Davies's girlfriend." He said the name quietly as if someone overhearing might incite a mob of fans. "We are with the visiting team. We are her escorts to the game tonight."

The security guard eyed Beth again. She tossed her hair and gave him a snooty look in return. They'd opted for *girlfriend* because surely an MLB wife would have a ring of unfathomable carats on her finger, and that was something Beth did not have stashed in her purse.

On the drive, Emmy had stalked every player's social media to find a believable candidate who wasn't already married to someone famous and/or in a recognizable relationship. Mr. Right Fielder was a perfect option.

"I'm in LA for a shoot. Do you want to see my ID?" Beth said in her best impersonation of an unimpressed influencer.

The security guard shriveled under her icy gaze and stepped aside to let them pass. "Enjoy the game."

Emmy exhaled the breath that had been lodged in her lungs. "That was amazing. And remarkably easy?" she said once they were into the hallway and out of earshot.

"You were incredible," Pedro gushed starry-eyed at Beth.

She flipped her hair with a giggle. "Thanks. So were you. I totally bought it."

"Okay, well, keep up the act because now we have to get to the field," Emmy said, and turned toward what she thought was the right direction. They'd entered a belowdecks catacomb much like the one she and Pedro worked in.

"Well, I'd hazard a guess *up* is the right move here," Pedro said, nodding toward an elevator at the hall's end. A flurry of voices came their way from around a corner. They sounded both excited and official, so they scurried into the elevator before they had to interact with anyone who might question their presence.

Soon, they were on the club level weaving in and out of fans loaded down with beers and cocktails and nachos. A few players remained on the field warming up in the final moments before the first pitch. Emmy could see the performer preparing to sing the national anthem pacing around by home plate next to a camera crew.

"Where are you, Gabe?" she murmured as she kept walking. She sidestepped a dad in a team jersey with a little boy mounted on his shoulders.

"Let's go down," Pedro said, and pointed at a staircase leading to the field level.

Emmy and Beth followed but they were quickly stopped by another security team member.

"Tickets?" the woman asked.

"Shit," Emmy quietly hissed, but Pedro wasn't fazed.

He tilted his chin at an authoritative angle and held up his badge. "We're with the team."

The woman looked at it and frowned. "You still need a valid pass to enter this section."

Beth stepped forward with another flip of her sheet of hair, ready to play the part. Emmy nervously chewed her lip and strained her eyes to see down to the field. Everyone was still too far away to make out. She scanned for Gabe's familiar wave of hair, his arms in tight sleeves, but nearly everyone down there had arms in tight sleeves and was wearing a hat.

"Don't you know who this is?" Emmy heard Pedro plead while she stepped to the side, looking for an alternative solution.

They were so close to the starting lineups announcement and the national anthem. And then first pitch, and the game would be in full swing. Emmy's chance was now. But where was Gabe?

In her desperate scan of the stands and field, she saw a small crew with a camera pointed at an in-game reporter chatting with a pair of fans midway down the seating section. The live feed was being broadcast on the outfield scoreboard forty feet high. They were in the middle of some trivia game the whole stadium was cheering on.

An idea struck Emmy at the same time her knees almost gave out. It was desperate and might get her banished from the ballpark for life, but it would get the job done.

She threw a glance at Pedro and Beth continuing the charade of being important by proxy and decided her idea had a better shot at success.

"Go big," she muttered. Before she could talk herself out of it, she shoved around them and hurried down the stairs.

"Hey!" the security member shouted after her.

"Sorry! I won't be long!" Emmy called over her shoulder. She flew down the stairs, her shoes scraping the gummy concrete, and all but threw herself at the film crew.

"Last chance to win!" the reporter singsonged at the two beaming fans in front of her.

Emmy bumped into the cameraman, jostling the shot in her attempt to get close enough, and reached for the microphone the reporter held.

"What in the—?" the reporter said, and jerked back.

"Sorry! I just need to borrow this for a second." Emmy shoved her way in front of the camera and yanked the microphone out of her grip before anyone could stop her. Everyone was too shocked to react. "Gabe!" she shouted at the camera lens. The reality of her actions didn't fully hit her until she heard her own voice echoing around the stadium like a rock show. But she couldn't stop now. Surely she had but seconds before they cut the feed.

"Gabe! I'm here. I came here to find you. I read your message, and I'm so sorry. I misunderstood what I thought I heard. I know you'd never lie to me about anything this important. And I agree: that fake number was the best thing that ever happened to me too. *You* are the best thing that ever happened to me. And what I said in the hallway the other day about how I feel—I still feel it, even more now. I've figured out how to quantify my feelings too. They are greater than. As in, greater than everything. I want to tell you to your face. So please, if you're here, I hope you are listening." Emmy hadn't realized fifty thousand people were staring at her on the scoreboard and had just heard her confession until she stopped talking. Her heart pounded and her breath rushed into the microphone. Surely she was about to be tackled by security and hauled out. Surely the cameraman was about to drop his lens, the microphone was going to cut out, and the scoreboard was going to go back to advertisements.

But none of that happened.

The whole stadium seemed to be holding its breath.

Emmy looked around in terror as everyone looked at her, either on the scoreboard or from the nearby seats. The expectant silence expanded into an eternity.

"Where's Gabe?" a man shouted from a section over. It was quiet enough that his voice rang out into the open space. Other fans started murmuring. Echoes of *Where's Gabe?* rippled around the crowd.

The reporter whose microphone Emmy had stolen pressed her fingers to her earpiece, clearly listening to instruction from the other side. Emmy expected her to snatch the mic back, but she nodded and dropped her hand. She gestured at Emmy as if to say, *The floor is yours.*

Emmy gaped at her in shock. She hadn't planned for her idea to work at all, let alone to be given permission to keep talking. She glanced back at Pedro and Beth. The security guard had given up trying to restrain them. Everyone was too invested to pay attention to anything else.

"Gabe! Come get your girl!" one of the players hollered from the field, hands cupped around his mouth. It sent a roaring cheer up from the nearby fans. Soon, a chant broke out.

"Gabe! Gabe! Gabe!"

The whole stadium was in on it.

Emmy was aflame with embarrassment and hope at the same time. She silently prayed he was listening, and she wasn't about to experience the most humiliating rejection in history. Aside from the scoreboard camera, dozens of smartphones were aimed at her, surely streaming her desperate confession online. She smiled into the camera. "I'm behind home plate, first base side," she said. She nearly had to shout over the chanting crowd. "Are you here?"

The chant carried on, everyone looking side to side for the mysterious Gabe. Emmy's heart raced until she felt like it might give out. And then it slowed when nothing happened. No one appeared. The chanting died down, and Emmy felt like she could sink into the earth. Her smile faded, and she lowered the mic. The reporter gave her a sad look like she'd been hoping for a storybook ending. The nearby fans began to murmur. Her heart somehow managed to split another crack.

And then a small cheer went up out near right field.

Emmy snapped her head up to see a familiar figure jogging across the outfield lawn, coming in from the bullpen. She knew the long strides, the swing of his arms. The feel of her heart surging in the knowledge he was near.

"Gabe!" a woman in the nearby seats shouted and pointed. "Is that him?"

"Oh my god, it's Gabe!" someone else said.

"It's him!"

Emmy nodded and felt her eyes gloss with a wash of happy tears. "It's you," she said, and handed the mic back to the reporter. The stadium had resumed chanting his name.

"Gabe! Gabe! Gabe!"

Emmy hurried down the rest of the stairs to thunderous cheers. She kept her eyes trained on Gabe jogging into the infield now. He crossed the pitcher's mound, and she could see the grin on his face.

He threw up a hand and waved at the crowd, which only prompted them to further lose their minds.

The field security crew had gathered at the short, padded wall separating the stands from the field. Emmy wasn't about to leap onto the grass and get tackled despite having fifty thousand people cheering on her side. She found her way through the safety net guarding the seats behind home plate from foul balls and stopped at the wall to wait for Gabe. He jogged the rest of the way, and instead of stopping him, the security team cleared a path for him, probably wanting the show to be over so they could keep the game on schedule. Gabe effortlessly hopped up and climbed over the small wall.

He was suddenly standing in front of Emmy giving her his signature cocky grin she knew was just for show. She knew the man behind it now, better than anyone. Every fiber of her being had missed him, and she knew without a doubt how she felt about him. The rest of the world—all fifty thousand screaming members of it—faded away as she looked for the truth in his eyes. She didn't have the microphone anymore, but their faces were still on the scoreboard; she could see them out of the corner of her eye.

"Hell of an apology, Jameson," he said.

"I considered spicy takeout but opted for larger scale."

"Had to one-up me."

"I learned from the best."

He grinned at her.

"I'm really sorry, Gabe. For what I said yesterday. I made an assumption, and with my history in the department and your reputation—"

"I deserved at least some of what you said," he said with a knowing nod. "I know my behavior hasn't always been exemplary. But those rumors about getting someone fired, it wasn't—"

"I know. Alice told me the truth. I'm sorry I assumed the worst." She shook her head in shame. "Thank you for what you did for me though. That was really selfless of you."

He gave her a small shrug. "Like I said: you deserve the job. I can't stand in your way."

She ached to touch him—and based on the noise roaring outside their bubble, everyone wanted to see it.

But she needed to know something first.

"Can you forgive me?"

He tilted his head like he might have been considering. Her heart tripped over a few beats. But then he smiled again. "Well, I mean, you *did* just make one of my dreams come true."

"Oh?"

"Yeah," he said, and gestured at the field beside them. "Never thought I'd get to hear a whole stadium chanting my name as I took the field."

Emmy hadn't even realized her plan had played right into that scenario. What a happy coincidence.

"We aim to please," she said with a casual shrug. "Any other dreams I can make come true?"

Gabe stepped forward and cupped her cheek with his palm. His eyes melted into warm pools, and he softly smiled. "You already have. My feelings are greater than everything too. I love you, Bird Girl."

The words landed both featherlight for how easy and comfortable they were to hear, and with a sudden gravity anchoring her to him in a way she'd never experienced before. She didn't even have to think before she said it back, because the feeling had been ripening inside her for ages. A seed planted years ago that had finally blossomed with the right care. The probability they'd end up together had likely always been high, but it took random chance, a fateful stroke of luck, and a ten-digit string of numbers for them to find their way.

And Emmy never wanted to turn back.

"I love you too, Axe Murderer," she told him, and then kissed him to her favorite sound on earth. A baseball stadium full of cheering fans.

Epilogue

> You know, I should have seen it coming that your endgame would be luring me to a remote location to finish me off. Well played, Axe Murderer.

> Not that kind of endgame, Bird Girl. Relax.

> I'm perfectly calm. But where am I headed?

> You didn't google the address?

> No. It wasn't one of the instructions.

Emmy smiled to herself, thinking of the scene she'd come upon in their hotel room. They were on the road with the team for a stint in Miami. After the Saturday day game had ended in a victory, Emmy headed back to their shared room, as had become routine over the past year. Gabe had been nowhere to be found, but laid out on the bed was the silky blue dress she was wearing, with a note saying *Wear me*, an overnight bag with *Bring me*, and an address written on a piece of the hotel stationery with *Meet me*. She'd followed all instructions, called a rideshare, and was now an hour into a sunset-soaked drive headed into the Florida Keys.

Well, then I guess you'll find out when you get here.

I am intrigued.

You should be.

She set her phone in her lap with a smile and leaned back against the headrest. Her driver had chatted with her for the first half hour but was now zoned out to the lo-fi music softly playing through the speakers. Emmy had slipped into a near trance too. Aside from the excited anticipation over whatever Gabe had in store bubbling inside her, she was exhausted. They were midway through a ten-game road trip. They had another night in Miami and then three games in New York before they headed back home. In truth, she would have been happy to fall asleep in front of the TV tonight with Gabe, wherever that TV happened to be, but she knew by the dress and the set of cryptic instructions he had something much more exciting planned.

She loved the life they were building together. Ever since that night at the stadium in LA—videos of which had gone viral and landed them on the local news and all over the internet—Emmy had embraced being head-over-heels. The challenge of partitioning her personal and professional lives had all but dissolved. It helped that she and Gabe no longer shared an office so the tempting physical distractions were minimal, but more than that, she realized she *could* have both. It was possible to be fulfilled in both aspects of her life without sacrificing either.

Which was good, because she had no intention of giving him up, nor he her. And they both loved what they did.

It had felt like they'd jumped off the deep end when they first started traveling with the team. So much changed so quickly but having him there to experience it with her eased the transition. They began spending the night in each other's hotel rooms frequently enough that they started having the team book just one for them to share. And when they were home, he was at her place, or she at his anyway. She was exceeding expectations as a senior analyst—she'd pushed to keep Hollander thanks to Gabe's equation, and he was having an all-star season this year—and Gabe was living out his dream getting to be so close to the field as he worked his way up on the training staff. It all clicked because they worked hard to make it click.

But being with him was as effortless as breathing.

She'd grown a little sleepy by the time her driver pulled up to a sprawling bungalow shrouded in leafy palms. The house sat down a private road and backed up to a beach. Emmy knew without seeing it that it had a killer view. Glass panels flanked the blue front door. The eaves hung low over a set of table and chairs. The sun had set, but the house glowed from within—and from the outside thanks to the clusters of flickering candles on the front porch.

"Looks like our stop," her driver said. "Have a nice night."

"Thanks," Emmy said, a little shocked by the location. Surely this place had to cost a fortune. She grabbed her overnight bag and climbed out into the humidity. The evening had cooled off thanks to a breeze curling in from the water. She'd never been to the Keys but instantly fell in love. Sweet salt hung in the thick air; the trees rustled. Waves rolled and crashed somewhere in the distance.

She made her way up to the front door, sidestepping the candles, and knocked before opening it. "Gabe?" she called as she swung it open. "I hope I'm not about to get mur—" she started to joke but her voice disappeared in her gaping mouth.

Killer view was an understatement. The back of the house was made of enough glass to look like the beach was part of the living room. Floor-to-ceiling windows framed a view of underlit palms and a deck leading to white sand and dark waves. Two rows of flickering candles lit up a small runway leading out the back doors where a dining table was set with glittering stemware and more candles.

"Um . . ." Emmy said, still shocked, as Gabe appeared from around a corner wiping his hands on a kitchen towel.

"Ah, didn't hear you pull up. Welcome," he said with a wide grin. "You look beautiful." He eyed her dress up and down. It was not something from her closet, and she had to give him credit for picking out something so flattering. The baby blue draped over her chest and fluttered around her ankles with a slit to her knees. He was barefoot in shorts and a loose button-down with rolled sleeves. His hair was tousled like maybe he'd jumped in the ocean and let it air-dry.

"Hi," Emmy said as Gabe came over and kissed her cheek. She was too stunned to kiss him back, so she kissed the empty air instead. "Um, what is this place?"

He took her bag and gestured out the open back doors. "Dinner is almost ready. I'll join you in a second."

Emmy walked in a trance toward the back doors. As she passed, she managed to note the living room to the left with comfy-looking low-profile furniture. The kitchen was off to the right; she glimpsed it from around the corner, and then saw all of it through the windows from the back deck. Gabe had a spread of food set up on an island under dangling pendant lights. The stainless-steel appliances shone from the perimeter of the room.

"Want to tell me how you got access to the Scarface mansion out here?" Emmy called, and sank into one of the cushy dining chairs. The breeze blew in off the cove and ruffled her dress. Indeed, the beach was private. A small dock stuck out into it with a pair of Jet Skis bobbing at its side.

Gabe reappeared with a bottle of champagne in one hand and two flutes in the other. "Did you forget your brother-in-law's family is filthy rich?" he said with a playful tilt of his head.

The pieces slid into place. He'd had help from Piper. Perhaps that explained the dress. She made a mental note to text her sister later. Emmy sarcastically smacked her palm to her forehead. "Silly me.

That does tend to slip my mind. Which Carmichael do I owe thanks to for this?"

"Uncle Bob," he said, and untwisted the cage on the champagne bottle.

"Thanks, Uncle Bob." Emmy toasted with the empty flute she'd picked up. "May I ask what the occasion is?" She watched the corded muscles in his forearm move under his tanned skin while he worked the cork loose with a pop.

"Well, as you might know, this weekend is the one-year anniversary of the fated fake number incident."

"Ah, yes. *Last night was fun.* Smiley face." She winked at him.

He playfully smirked back. "I thought, in honor of the event, it might be nice to spend the night here instead of in a hotel room eating takeout and running analyses and watching game footage on our laptops until you fall asleep on me."

"While you *did* just describe my ideal Saturday night, I do see your point. Good call," she said, and nodded at the white sand stretching from the back step out to the cove where water lapped and palms swayed.

"Meh, it's decent."

She held up her glass for him to fill with a smile. "It'll do for the night."

"I think it will. Cheers," he said, and clinked her glass after he'd filled his own.

"Cheers." She stood from her chair to sip and then wrapped an arm around his shoulders. She kissed him properly and let it burn all the way to her toes. "Hi. This is really beautiful. Thank you for putting it together."

"Of course. You should go feel the water. I'll bring dinner out." He pressed his lips to hers again.

She lazily swiveled from him with a happy grin, already feeling the boozy bubbles lighten her head. "Mmmm, that sounds nice. Is it warm?"

"It's perfect," he said with a smile and another peck on her lips.

"Okay," she said, and released him. She kicked off her sandals and gathered her skirt. The powdery sand had cooled in the night. It felt like a soothing balm on her feet. More flickering candles dotted the sand on either side of her as she walked the short distance down to the water. Indeed, it was warm. If they weren't about to have dinner, she might have stripped down and gotten all the way in. Surely there was no one around to see her skinny-dipping. A devilish smile bent her lips at the thought of what they might get up to later.

Emmy stood in the gentle waves and let them lap at her ankles. The tide rolled in and fizzed against the sand. The trees above rustled. She tilted her head back and gazed up at a band of stars painting a silver streak across the velvet sky. A feeling of contentment bloomed out into her every limb. She felt light and buoyant. She turned around with a smile, wanting to indulge in the feeling with Gabe.

It was then, slightly downhill from the house, that she realized the candles in the sand were not a random pattern. The dancing flames spelled out two words.

Marry me?

Her breath caught in her throat when she looked up to the house to see Gabe on the deck, hands in his pockets, softly smiling at her like he was in on a very good stunt.

She managed to smile back despite positively spinning. She started making her way back up the beach while he made his way down. They met amid the candles.

"This is impressive, Axe Murderer. Your best text to date. And I have to say, this looks pretty official what with the remote location, candles, and grand gesture."

He gave her a crooked grin, knowing she was calling back to what she'd said the day of their big reveal in Balboa Park. "It is official. And what do you want from me? You grand-gestured in front of an entire baseball stadium. I had to go big here."

She shook her head with a laugh. "Always have to one-up me."

Gabe hooked his fingers under her chin and looked deep into her eyes. "Something I look forward to doing for the rest of our lives."

Emmy almost melted at the look on his face. It was forever, staring back at her. She went weightless again. She would have floated away if he wasn't anchoring her to the earth.

He pulled a ring from his pocket. The round diamond twinkled like he'd plucked a star from the sky. "So, will you?" Gabe asked. "Marry me?"

It was the easiest question she'd ever been asked in her life.

"Absolutely," Emmy said, and she kissed him once more.

Acknowledgments

I didn't even realize I was writing a love letter until I finished this book. To baseball, to my adopted city, to all the women who know what it's like to work in Boys Town, this one is for you!

My agent, Melissa Edwards, thank you for believing in my stories and jumping on the opportunity to sell this book. Cheers to more to come.

My editor, Shannon Plackis, thank you for pushing me to dig deeper into this story to find its heart. Thank you for answering my panicky emails and always talking me off whatever cliff I invent.

The team at Avon: Kerry Rubenstein, Chloe Foster, Jeanie Lee, May Chen, Tessa Woodward, Jennifer Hart, Liate Stehlik, Samantha Larabee. Thank you for giving this book a home and getting it on readers' radars. I am excited for where we go next!

Colleen Reinhart, thank you for the perfect cover!

The authors who read an early copy of this book, thank you for taking the time, for the lovely words, for the encouragement, and for the support!

My various writers' groups: the Slack siblings, the San Diego crowd, the LA/OC gang. You are all wonderful and talented, and I'm so beyond lucky to have your support and friendship.

All the Bookstagrammers and BookTokers out there, thank you for making fabulous content and sharing your love of books.

The booksellers and indie bookstores who keep putting my books on shelves, thank you!

To all the women who came before me in male-dominated fields:

thank you for paving the way, for refusing to give up, and for teaching the next generation that there is room for everyone.

All the musical artists who provided my drafting soundtrack for this book: Taylor Swift, Manchester Orchestra, Del Water Gap, little image, the Revivalists, Nothing But Thieves, Sabrina Carpenter, Selena Gomez, Don Omar and Lucenzo, Beyoncé, Marc Anthony, Ozuna, Doja Cat, Sia, Benson Boone, Good Neighbours, Royel Otis, Carly Rae Jepsen, Van Morrison, Gracie Abrams, Myles Smith. Thank you for your words and music.

Linxiao Chen, Abby Van Wassen, and Mónica Mancillas, thank you for coming up with so many amazing bird-band puns when I asked for suggestions that I had to make it a running joke rather than a one-off like I'd planned. I'm still laughing.

My friends and family, who continue to support me on this wild publishing journey, I can't thank you enough.

My cousin Rachel Rus, thanks for giving me the behind-the-scenes scoop on working in pro sports. All mistakes and fabrications are my own! Thank you for loving books.

The 2010 San Francisco Giants, thank you for giving me one of the most deliriously memorable nights of my life by winning the World Series while I was in college at a bar with dozens of fans (and then doing it again in 2012 and 2014). Thank you for reminding me of the boundless joy found in sports.

San Diego, thank you for being so dang beautiful and full of amazing things that I had to write a book about you. To any other locals, forgive me for taking liberties with locations. (I know there is no yacht club in La Jolla!) Thank you to the Padres for being my adopted team.

My brother, Ben, and sister-in-law, Leah, thanks for that fated day when you were in college playing a pick-up softball game, and, Ben, you hit that line drive straight into Leah's thigh that ended both of your short-lived college careers. Your legacy lives on in this book.

My dad, thanks for answering all my baseball questions. All mistakes are mine!

Both my parents, thanks for taking me to all Ben's Little League games, where I was *sure* I was going to get hit by a foul ball, and for all the treks to the Bay to see the Giants. Ben, thanks for playing in all those Little League games and beyond. I've loved baseball for as long as I can remember because of our family.

My husband, I think you and I ended up on the pages of this one the most. It wasn't even on purpose! Thank you for writing equations for me, debugging code, debating the use of Bayesian vs. Frequentist methods, always listening when I rant about being the only girl in the room, for being the Emmy to my Gabe when it comes to quantifying feelings, and for being all around the hottest jock nerd I know. Also, thanks for demonstrating the mechanics of throwing a pitch over and over so I could properly describe the motion, and for making Stella think you were actually throwing a *b-a-l-l* she could chase when there was nothing there and giving us all a laugh. You are forever my MVP.

The readers, as always, thank you for joining me on another journey.

About the Author

Holly Michelle, who also writes as Holly James, is the author of adult romance and commercial fiction. She holds a PhD in psychology and has worked in both academia and the tech industry. When she's not reading or writing a book, she can be found on the beach or hiking in the woods. Born and raised in Northern California, she currently lives at the southern end of the state with her husband and their dog. Find her at hollyjamesbooks.com and on Instagram @hellohollyjames.